REBELLION

ALSO BY JAMES McGEE

Ratcatcher
Resurrectionist
Rapscallion

JAMES McGEE

Rebellion

HarperCollins*Publishers*

HarperCollins*Publishers*
77–85 Fulham Palace Road, London W6 8JB

www.harpercollins.co.uk

Published by HarperCollins*Publishers* 2011
2

A catalogue record for this book
is available from the British Library

ISBN: 978-0-00-732024-0

Set in Sabon by Palimpsest Book Production Limited,
Falkirk, Stirlingshire

Printed in Great Britain by
Clays Ltd, St Ives plc

Mixed Sources
Product group from well-managed
forests and other controlled sources
www.fsc.org Cert no. SW-COC-001806
© 1996 Forest Stewardship Council

FSC is a non-profit international organisation established to promote the
responsible management of the world's forests. Products carrying the FSC
label are independently certified to assure consumers that they come
from forests that are managed to meet the social, economic and
ecological needs of present and future generations.

Find out more about HarperCollins and the environment at
www.harpercollins.co.uk/green

PART I

1

He heard the rattle of musket fire and ducked instinctively. The horse grunted and stumbled and for one heart-faltering second he thought it had been hit; but the animal had only lost its footing on a rock loosened by the previous night's storm. Ahead of him, he saw Leon fighting to control his own mount as it scrambled for purchase on the treacherous, water-soaked terrain.

It was still raining, but the heavy downpour that had turned mountain stream into raging torrent and earthen track into quagmire had finally abated; transformed into a steady, and persistent drizzle. The easing of the weather, however, had not eliminated the risk of injury from a carelessly placed hoof. All he could do was hang on, trust in his steed, and pray that the ground remained firm beneath them.

Dawn had broken half an hour before but there was neither warmth to the day nor any evidence of sunrise, only a low ceiling of slate-tinted cloud. A gunmetal pall hung across the landscape, drenching the customary ochre-coloured hills in gloomy shades of grey.

Leon yelled a warning, indicating the crest of a ridge a quarter of a mile ahead and a row of figures outlined like stone statues on a balustrade; French infantry. At that range their blue jackets were unmistakable. A foraging party, he guessed. They were shouting and gesticulating wildly, waving their hats in the air. Some were crouched down and he assumed it was from those men that the shots had originated. Their cries carried like excited bird chatter and he realized they were yelling directions to the dragoons emerging at a gallop from the village behind them. He was immediately conscious of his own scarlet jacket and white breeches. Despite their grubbiness and the poor light, in contrast to Leon's grey coat, clay-coloured trousers and black bandana, they made a tempting target. He hunched down in his saddle, tightened his grip on the reins and drove his boots into the mare's flanks. Another fusillade sounded. It would have been a miracle if any of the musket balls had found their mark, even allowing for the downward trajectory, but it didn't stop him spurring his horse on even faster.

There was very little cover. What there was consisted of thorn bush and sharp outcrops of rock with olive trees dotted in between which, with their trunks stunted by the wind, had the look of old men bent and wizened with age.

He risked a glance over his shoulder. The dragoons were crouched low over their horses' necks; a couple had drawn sabres. They were not that far behind, and gaining ground rapidly. Beyond the knot of green-clad riders, he could see the village clinging like a limpet to the side of the hill. Idanha-a-Nova; it wasn't much of a place – a small church with a thin, square tower rising above a spiral of whitewashed houses – but it had provided a welcome respite from the storm. They had been fed and watered by their local contact and he'd slept comfortably, until rudely awakened with the news that a French patrol was searching houses at the other end of the street, which had resulted in their frantic and undignified dash for freedom.

He looked back and hope flared in his chest as his eyes settled on the sweep of wooded slopes that had appeared through the murk. He followed Leon's lead and turned his horse towards them. The trees would provide a guard against musket fire and grant them a chance to give their pursuers the slip, allowing them time to make their escape to a more permanent hiding place; providing the gods remained on their side.

The gods, however, appeared to have other plans.

His heart sank as he realized the wood was composed of

dwarf oaks which were neither tall nor dense enough to shade them completely. The trees would probably mask their flight from the dragoons but not from the soldiers on the summit who would have the advantage of height and thus a clearer view of their passage through the thickets. But they were better than no trees at all.

Sure enough, no sooner had they reached the first line of oaks than the calls from the onlookers on the high ground intensified. Even the hoof-beats couldn't mask the cries of the infantrymen as, stirred by the thrill of the chase being enacted below them, they encouraged their mounted compatriots to greater effort.

They reached the wood. By this time the enemy riders had closed the gap to less than three hundred yards. He felt an immediate wave of relief as the oaks closed in around them. Branches whipped at his face and snagged at his clothing as he steered his horse deeper into the trees. He could feel the dampness seeping through the lining of his jacket and the thighs of his breeches. He could feel his heart, too, beating like a drum.

He scanned the ridge through the overhanging limbs. The soldiers were still signalling madly. He looked away, concentrating on the path. To his consternation, the gaps between the trees were narrowing. Their progress was being hampered. The gods were definitely against them.

Without warning, Leon reined in his mount. He twisted in the saddle and spoke urgently in Spanish. "We stand a better chance on foot."

He hesitated and then decided it made sense. On foot they'd be less visible to the troops on the high ground. He nodded and they both dismounted. Pointing the animals in opposite directions, they slapped them hard on the rump to set them moving. Then they ran.

He was content to let Leon lead the way. The Spaniard was lightly built with tousled black hair curling away from the nape of his neck. A neat goatee framed his jaw. His brown eyes were bright and intelligent and set in a face scorched brown by the sun. A scar, part-hidden by the beard, ran from the corner of his chin to a centimetre below his left ear. Despite the

5

disfigurement, he was a handsome man whose looks suggested he'd be quick to smile and share a jest; though not this morning. In the sullen light, Leon's normally animated face was set in a grim mask of determination as he concentrated on the task in hand: keeping them safe.

The sword at his hip was becoming a menace, but the weapon had been a staunch ally to him over the years and he was not about to discard it like an old shoe. He unhooked the scabbard from his belt and, holding the sabre like a baton, picked up his pace. His ears caught the jangle of metal; the dragoons were in the trees. Unless it was their own mounts doubling back towards them. That would be ironic, he thought.

A small clearing came into view. They sprinted across it, keeping low. A musket ball, even from the higher elevation, would never reach that far but he still felt the hollowness in his throat knowing how exposed they both were, though he also knew the French would want to take him alive. He was more valuable to them alive. Dead meant he couldn't be exchanged for one of theirs. Dead, he wasn't worth a damned thing, except perhaps a reason for the Duke or even Marmont to raise a silent glass and for someone to carve a notch into the hilt of his sword.

They cut left. The trees thinned suddenly and they were out in the open once more. He could hear the dragoons thrashing through the foliage behind them. They would have to dismount, too, and that would give him and Leon the edge. The ground rose before them in a series of small terraced fields bordered by dry stone walls. Two enclosures away another patch of woodland beckoned: more oak trees. Up on the ridge, the infantry were running, keeping pace.

His chest was hurting now; so were his legs. He spent more time in the saddle than he did on foot and it was beginning to tell on his lungs. Leon, despite his wiry frame, also looked and sounded as if he was struggling. And the gradient wasn't helping. They came to the first wall and clambered over it. By the time they had negotiated the second one, the dragoons had emerged from the trees.

And they were still on horseback. Somehow, they had found

a way through. Realizing from the tracks that their quarry was now on foot, they had known that by remaining mounted they'd have the upper hand once they were clear of the wood. Baying like hounds, the scent of victory in their nostrils, the dragoons dug in their heels.

He tried to ignore the burning stitch in his side.

As they reached the last barrier of stone before the woods began again, a volley of shots came from their right. He heard the crack as a projectile struck the wall a few inches from his arm. There was movement to his left; more riders, approaching fast. They were close enough for him to see their scarlet-edged epaulettes and the diamond motif on their helmets. Directed by the troops on the hill, the dragoons had split their force in two, with one party having circled the wood in a bid to cut them off while the other had remained to the rear, driving them forward, like gamekeepers beating grouse before them into the trap.

God-damned Frogs! he thought, acknowledging that the French had played the game well. Then he was over the wall and clawing his way towards the shelter of the next stand of oaks.

He could hear Leon trying to suck in air. The Spaniard was labouring. His face was streaked with rain and sweat. As they hauled themselves into the trees, the dragoons were less than a hundred paces away. The drumming of hooves was as loud as thunder and he could feel the earth vibrating beneath his feet.

The Spaniard drew a pistol from his bandolier and a knife from the sash at his waist. "Run!" he urged. "Save yourself!" His features contorted.

"No, we go together!" As if a pistol and a knife would have made a difference, anyway, he thought.

They staggered on, shoulder to shoulder.

Leon was the first to go down. One moment he was in motion, the next it was as if the Spaniard's legs had turned to porridge. The transition was almost leisurely, bordering on comical; as if someone had slipped him a slow-acting sleeping draught. He managed to keep going for another dozen steps before his legs finally gave way and he collapsed on to his knees, chest heaving.

They had separated and he was ten paces in front when Leon fell. He heard the Spaniard's exclamation of defeat and turned back in time to see the first of the dragoons explode into view, followed swiftly by half a dozen more.

Leon raised his pistol. A shot sounded and he fell back clutching his shoulder, the pistol dropping from his hand.

"NO!"

Running back, he started to pull the sword from its scabbard and found himself confronted by a semi-circle of plume-helmeted horsemen, their carbines aimed unerringly at his head.

He halted and gazed back resignedly at the look of triumph on their faces. It was over. There was nowhere else to run, nowhere to hide. He slid the sword into its scabbard and waited as the dragoon lieutenant got down from his horse and held out his hand. He handed the sword over. The lieutenant took it, nodded wordlessly then walked over to Leon, who had raised himself to a sitting position. His face had lost its colour. Blood from his wound was oozing from between his fingers. He let the knife drop to the ground.

The lieutenant stared down at the Spaniard.

"Cretin!" he spat and withdrawing the sword he drove the blade down through Leon's throat. Leon's legs kicked convulsively and then stilled. The dragoon placed his boot on Leon's chest, freed the blade and wiped it on the Spaniard's jacket before returning it to its scabbard and calmly remounting his horse.

It took a second for the shock to sink in.

"You utter shit! God damn your eyes, you bastard! He was no threat to you!"

He screamed the words in English.

The dragoons made no attempt to stop him as he ran to the body. Other figures were hurrying towards them through the trees; the infantry from the ridge had arrived.

He sank to his knees, ignoring the wetness soaking into his breeches, and gripped Leon's hand in his own. He stared down at the man who had been his friend and at the blood-stained, rain-dampened moss beneath the ruined throat. He heard foot-steps approaching from behind.

A voice spoke in English, with a marked French accent.

"Get up, Major."

The rage bloomed in his chest. He started to turn.

"Get up, Major." The order was given again.

And his eyes opened.

"Time to get up, Major."

The hand was still on his shoulder as he reached for the pistol beneath the saddle he'd been using for a pillow, forgetting, not for the first time, that the weapon had been taken from him. The memory caused his face to harden. He moved his arm and felt for his sword. At least they had left him that. He traced the hilt reassuringly. The gesture did not go unnoticed by the man gazing down at him.

Dressed in the uniform of chasseur, the insignia at collar and cuff indicated he held the rank of captain. He was young, in his early twenties, with dark hair and soulful eyes. He looked concerned at having interrupted his charge's sleep.

"There's coffee by the fire. It's still hot." The captain, whose name was Fosse, gave a small, almost boyish smile. "But I apologize in advance. The taste is execrable."

Pushing the blanket aside, he watched the officer walk away and thought about the dream. It wasn't the first time it had come to him and he doubted it would be the last. He'd relived the nightmare a lot over the six weeks since his capture. During that time the anger he'd felt at Leon's death had not diminished.

They had returned his horse. It had been caught by one of the foragers on their way down from the ridge. He'd been allowed to mount up, only to have a sergeant of dragoons take the reins. Then, leaving Leon's corpse where it had fallen, they'd escorted him out of the woods. The infantry had returned to their foraging. The dragoons and their red-coated charge had retraced their path towards the village before turning north. He'd known immediately where they were taking him.

Sabugal.

Marmont's headquarters; the army commander whose

9

manoeuvres he and Leon had been tracking for the past two months. It occurred to him that Leon would have found that amusing.

The forty-mile ride along rutted, water-logged tracks, through wooded hills and valleys and across tarns swollen by rainfall, had been hard going. He'd travelled most of the way in silence, wrapped in his cloak, fighting the chill in his bones brought on by the weather, his grief at Leon's murder and an increasing awareness of the gravity of his situation.

When he arrived at Sabugal he'd discovered that word of his capture had preceded him. A small crowd had gathered; mostly officers who knew of his work and who, despite his being the enemy, had been anxious to make his acquaintance; to be able to say that they had shaken his hand.

The French were billeted in the citadel; a Moorish castle, the ramparts of which had been visible from miles away, long before he and his escort crossed the old stone bridge and entered the town. There he'd been questioned; first by Marmont's bloated, bad-tempered chief of staff, de la Martinière, and then by the marshal himself. He'd given them nothing, other than his name and rank; which they'd known anyway.

De la Martinière had wanted him shot as a spy. Marmont, an urbane man with a liking for the finer things in life and, fortunately, the antithesis of his subordinate, had asked him for his parole.

There was no doubt that both of them believed he'd been engaged in spying activities, but Marmont, unlike his foul-mouthed general and in adherence to the articles of war, had been unprepared to execute a British officer in uniform, accepting his word that he was not a spy but a field intelligence officer, a fine distinction but one which, nevertheless, reflected the accept-ance of the code that existed between the two opposing armies.

He'd given his parole willingly for the advantages it allowed. Parole meant he'd still be a prisoner, but at least he would enjoy some freedom of movement so long as he agreed not to attempt to escape, not to pass intelligence to the British army or its allies, nor to serve against the armies of France, until such time as he had been exchanged, rank for rank. The agreement didn't say anything about *gathering* intelligence during his captivity and passing it on later.

It transpired, however, that the marshal's idea of parole bore little resemblance to the accepted interpretation of the term, for he had been granted no freedom or privacy beyond that accorded to a regular prisoner. Instead, they had secured him in a room and placed a sentry on permanent duty outside his door.

Well, he'd thought, two could play at that game. If the French commander was prepared to ride roughshod over their agreement then surely that invalidated *his* pledge not to pass on intelligence. In his mind he was therefore free to relay as much information as possible back to Wellington's headquarters.

The opportunity to do that had arisen when Marmont and his staff, with their British parolee in tow, had transferred their headquarters to Salamanca. There were British agents in Salamanca, notably one Dr Patrick Curtis, Rector of the Irish College and regius professor of astronomy and natural history at Salamanca University. Curtis had been running an intelligence organization from the college for years. Stretching all the way from Gibraltar to the Pyrenees and beyond, it was composed for the most part of priests and *alcaldes*, all linked by a spider's web of runners. And it had been providing Wellington with information since the outbreak of the war.

Even the officers assigned to guard him had expressed disgust at their commander's decision to deny their captive the privileges allowed under the terms of parole, one of which was the right to receive visitors. They had viewed it as a stain on their honour and in defiance of their orders had turned a blind eye to members of the local populace who wanted to pay their respects.

Curtis and his agents had made contact two days after his arrival.

It hadn't taken Marmont long to suspect that messages *were* being passed between his prisoner and the wily old Irishman, and he'd summoned Curtis for questioning. He'd even considered placing him under arrest and imprisoning him, but he had no proof and Curtis was well respected in the city, particularly within the church's hierarchy, so Marmont had had little option but to give the priest the benefit of the doubt and let him go. But the incident had been enough to convince the marshal to take prompt remedial action against his prisoner.

"You're to be transferred," Marmont had told him. "I've two companies of infantry returning to France. They'll escort you as far as Bayonne. From there you'll be taken north, to the prison depot at Verdun, where you will be assigned a place of internment, there to await an offer of exchange."

The march across Spain through Valladolid, Burgos, Vitoria and San Sebastian had taken nearly three weeks. Now they were on the home stretch. The previous night they'd made camp outside Biriatou, a small village nestling among the Pyrenean foothills. It was their last day on the road.

The captain was right, he thought. The coffee *was* atrocious. It tasted as if it had been made from acorns. There was some bread, too; a slice of cold bacon and a wedge of gritty cheese. The captain had apologized for the quality of the food, but now that they were over the border and back in their own country, he'd been assured it would be easier to pick up supplies.

He finished the coffee and tipped the grounds on to the ashes of the fire. The troops were breaking camp around him. He rolled up his bedroll, buckled on his sword and picked up his saddle. They would be in Bayonne by nightfall.

They were two miles north of Saint-Jean-de-Luz, with the mounted troops leading the two infantry companies, when the chasseur captain broke away from the head of the column and fell in beside him. Leaning over from his saddle, the captain lowered his voice, "We have to talk, Major."

He waited for the captain to continue. It had turned into a glorious day. They were high up and the views were stunning. To his left, looking out over the green-clad hills, he could see the reflection of sun on water: the Bay of Biscay. There were ships, he saw. They were some way off the coast and it was hard to make out their flags at that distance. The French didn't have that much of a navy left. From her lines, he thought one of them might have been American.

"You look like a man with a weight on his mind, Captain," he prompted, speaking in French.

The chasseur bit his lip. "I think it would be better if we conversed in English, my friend."

An odd response, as was the use of the word "friend". He stared at the captain, trying to read the expression on the young officer's face. "As you wish."

The chasseur captain cleared his throat awkwardly. "I regret to say, Major, we've not been entirely truthful with you."

"How so?" He frowned.

"My orders, as you know, were to escort you to Bayonne."

"Indeed, and you've been splendid company. I'll miss our conversations around the fire."

"As will I, Major. Fate has declared us to be on different sides and yet I feel there is a strong bond between us and it is for that reason that I must warn you that you have been severely misled."

"By whom?"

"That whore's son, de la Martinière!" The captain spat and then recovered as he collected his thoughts, before adding just as vehemently, "And, it grieves me to say it, by Marshal Marmont also."

It was plain to see why the captain had requested they spoke in English. He hadn't wanted anyone else in the column to hear his outburst against his superiors.

"I'm not with you, Captain. In what way?"

"Upon your arrival at Bayonne, you are expecting to be met by another escort who will take you to Verdun, yes?"

"That's right."

"Not so. The marshal sent a dispatch shortly after your arrival in Salamanca. It was to Paris, for the attention of the Duke of Feltre. It was in the marshal's name, but it was composed and signed by de la Martinière. The general told me that himself."

He felt a stirring in his gut. The Duke of Feltre, he knew, was Bonaparte's Minister of War. Before he could comment, the captain's mouth twisted with disdain. "The dispatch gave details of your capture and the papers that were taken from you."

"Papers?"

"The notes you made on the composition and strength of our army, our ordnance and our troop movements."

There had been no papers. He knew better than to carry such incriminating evidence on his person. Whatever intelligence he accrued during his missions as an exploring officer was always kept in his head.

"What else?"

"Notification that you were captured in uniform and that you gave your parole but that you were not to be trusted and that you should be watched at all times . . ."

The captain's voice tapered off. He looked uncomfortable.

"And?" The unpleasant feeling that had started in his belly began to spread through him.

"And that upon our arrival in Bayonne, my orders are to take your sword and deliver you into the hands of the *Bureau Secret* – Savary's men. You're to be placed in restraints and taken to Paris for interrogation."

The secret police. His stomach knotted.

"Why are you telling me this?"

"I'm a soldier, Major, not a police lackey. I heard that the Emperor once said if he told Savary to murder his own wife and children, he knew the order would be obeyed without a moment's hesitation. I've no desire to hand you over to *his* people." The captain hesitated, then said, "And neither have my officers. We've been three weeks on the road together. Even before we swapped stories around the fire, your exploits were well known to us. We knew you to be a brave and honourable man. You're no spy, Major, despite what General de la Martinière would have us believe. Spies skulk in the shadows. You wear your scarlet uniform with pride. You've never made an attempt to disguise yourself. You make no secret of the fact that you are gathering information. It's been our misfortune, until now, that you've always had the better of us." The young officer allowed his face to lighten and he said sheepishly, "I gave chase after you once, you know. I never told you that. It was about four months back, on the road to Huerta. You led us a merry dance."

"I had a good horse."

Fosse eyed the mare speculatively. "You still have, Major." There was a catch in the chasseur's voice.

A movement in the sky overhead caught his eye. A flock of buzzards was circling the summit of a nearby hill. Something had died or was dying on the slopes, he guessed. The birds were circling for the kill. Perhaps like Savary's thugs.

"You're suggesting I break my parole and make a run for it?"

The Frenchman ran a hand over his horse's neck. His face remained neutral. "I'm merely suggesting you may wish to consider your options in the light of our conversation. Besides, I doubt an officer of your experience would be foolish enough to attempt an escape in broad daylight, in the open, flanked by two companies of armed infantry and a detachment of chasseurs. I would have little option but to order my men to hunt you down. I doubt you'd get very far. You'd be seen for miles."

The captain stood in his saddle and looked out towards the bay. "The view is quite splendid, is it not? Though not the sort of countryside I'd like to traverse at night, I venture. Which reminds me, we must press on. The likelihood is that we will not arrive in Bayonne until after sunset." The captain turned and looked at him. "You'll forgive me, Major. I must rejoin my men. Enjoy the rest of your journey."

With a brief salute, he was gone.

As he watched the captain ride off towards the head of the column, he pondered on the chasseur's words. He recalled how, back in Salamanca, in contravention of their general's orders, his guards had busied themselves with other duties whenever visitors were in the offing. Was it his imagination or had Captain Fosse just intimated that he and his men would avert their gaze at an opportune moment also? He had, he suspected, until Bayonne to decide.

It was dusk when the column finally reached the outskirts of the town. To the west, the last rays of sunset had finally given way to a dark aubergine sky. Although the coast was still three miles distant, the smell of the sea, carried inland along the river from the estuary, hung in the air like a sharp bouquet.

They entered one of the town's squares, and halted.

"My men and I will try and find somewhere for us to bed down for the night," Fosse told him as they dismounted. "I suggest you remain here while we go and look. I regret I don't know the town that well. We may be gone for some time."

The captain held his gaze for several seconds before giving a brief nod of farewell.

He watched Fosse and his men walk away. The rest of the column were paying him no heed. They had become used to his closer association with the chasseurs rather than the infantry and they were too busy attending to their own requirements. He retrieved his knapsack and the cloak from his saddle bag and slipped it on. He stroked the mare's neck and she whickered softly. They'd travelled many roads together and survived numerous adventures. If her disappearance was noted as well as his own, it was likely the alarm would be raised a lot quicker than if he alone was seen to be absent.

He knew she'd be well looked after. Fosse would see to that. He owed the young captain a debt of gratitude. Some day, he hoped he would be able to repay him. He drew his cloak around him, adjusted his hat low on his brow, slipped the knapsack over his shoulder, and without a backward glance walked purposefully into the rapidly descending twilight.

He wondered how long he had before the alarm was raised. His fate lay in the chasseur captain's hands and he knew there was a time limit on how long Fosse would wait before he started shouting. The captain might have been willing to offer him a way out, but it was unlikely he'd jeopardize his career any more than he had to. He had, he estimated, an hour, perhaps two at the most, before the alert was sounded. And then they would come after him.

It was a guaranteed certainty that when they discovered him missing, they'd assume he'd try to head south towards the mountains. They'd know he had allies within the *guerrilleros* who would be only too happy to escort him through the high passes and back into Spain. The French would search the town and then they would scour the countryside in the direction of the frontier.

But they would be looking in the wrong place, because he wasn't going south; he was heading north.

The plan had been gestating in his mind long before the chasseur captain voiced his unhappiness at his general's duplicity. The seed had been planted the day he and his escort left Salamanca.

Rumours that the Emperor was planning to invade Russia had been circulating for months. The troop movements he and Leon had observed on their sorties confirmed that the French were transferring an increasing number of men northwards, in particular contingents of the Imperial Guard. They were either being used to plug the gaps in the Empire's home defences or else they were part of an impending invasion force. But were they really destined for Russia, or somewhere else? There had even been talk that Bonaparte had resurrected his plan to invade England. Which was it? It was his duty to find out, he had decided, and to accomplish that he'd have to travel into the heart of the Empire; to the last place they would think of looking for him.

He glanced around. The streets were quite busy and there were a lot of military personnel in evidence; not that unusual, given Bayonne's proximity to the border, which made it one of the main staging posts for troop movements between France and Spain. In the poorly lit streets, however, one uniform looked much like any other. Nevertheless, he kept his cloak about him as he made his way towards the town centre.

As he drew closer to the main concourse, he spotted the entrance to a narrow alleyway and stepped into the shadows. He used the knife concealed in his boot to unpick the stitches on the inside of his jacket. It took but a few seconds to withdraw the bank notes and the two dozen guineas sewn into the lining. Then, stowing the knife and slipping the money into his pocket, he retraced his steps to the street. He kept his head bowed. All he needed was to run into Fosse and his men coming towards him from the opposite direction.

He struck lucky at his third port of call. The hotel concierge, taken in by his military cloak, weather-stained headgear and sword, was only too happy to help an officer he thought was part of the Grand Army.

In answer to his query, the concierge advised him that a public diligence was due to depart from the square outside the hotel very shortly and that one of the guests, General Souham, was booked on it. In fact, he was the only passenger.

He thanked the concierge and took a seat in the darkest corner of the lobby. General Souham! It wasn't often you were about to introduce yourself to the Divisional Commander of the Army of Portugal. He bowed his head and pretended to doze. Just another battle-weary officer seeking rest and recuperation from the war.

It was twenty minutes before the general entered the lobby, accompanied by his baggage and a weary looking aide-de-camp. Even if he hadn't been wearing his uniform, the general would have been an easy man to identify for he was very tall, well over six feet in height. Greying hair showed beneath the rim of his hat. In addition to his distinctive height, two other features marked him out: the livid scar, half visible on his temple, and the black patch that covered his left eye socket. He was also smoking a thin cheroot.

He waited until the aide had disappeared outside to supervise the loading of the general's luggage before he made his move.

The general took a draw on his cheroot, savouring the taste. He looked like a man who was relaxed and at ease with himself. But then he could afford to be. He was a general and every other soldier within sight and earshot was his subordinate.

"Forgive me, sir, General Souham?" He spoke in French, as he had with the concierge.

The general's head turned and he found himself perused through a spiral of cigar fumes. The general's right eye searched for recognition and an indication of rank. "And who might you be?"

Some senior staff might have shown irritation at being approached unexpectedly by a lower ranked officer. On this occasion there was only curiosity.

"A fellow traveller, General, if you'll permit."

A frown creased the scarred brow.

It's now or never, he thought.

"I understand from the concierge that you're about to board the diligence and I wondered if you'd allow me to share your coach. I've been on attachment to Marshal Marmont's staff and recently arrived from Salamanca, en route to Orleans. I'd be more than happy to share any expenses."

The general's right eyebrow lifted as he picked a shred of tobacco from his lip, not so much surprised by the request as intrigued.

"Your name again? I didn't catch it."

"My apologies, General. Major Hawkwood, 11th Regiment of Infantry."

The general's frown deepened. His eye moved to the patch of red jacket showing through the gap in the cloak. "Really? That's an interesting name. You'd better explain, Major."

"I'm an American, sir, as is my regiment. Assigned to the Imperial Forces by President Madison with the permission of Emperor Bonaparte. I've been serving at Marshal Marmont's headquarters in a liaison capacity. The president is most interested in the Spanish campaign."

"Ah," the general said drily, as if everything suddenly made sense. "Is he now? That's comforting. I'm sure we'll all sleep easier in our beds. And when you make your report to your President Madison, what will you tell him?"

"That the Emperor probably needs all the help he can get."

The general stared at him. "Well, your French is excellent, Major. If you hadn't told me, I'd have taken you for a native. But I'll say this: it's a damned good thing you're a soldier and not an ambassador. Diplomacy isn't your strong point."

"No, General. It's probably why I'm still a major."

The corner of the general's mouth lifted. "And how is the Marshal?"

"He's well, sir. Still complaining about the quality of the wine."

"Sounds familiar. He always did appreciate his home comforts."

The general's aide appeared at the entrance. "Your baggage is loaded, sir." The officer's glance slid sideways.

"Thank you, Lieutenant. I'll be there shortly." The general paused, then said, "You can inform the driver there'll be two of us. Major Hawkwood will be joining me. He's an American, you know; come to offer us his support."

"Very good, sir." The lieutenant nodded. "You have luggage, Major?" There was no hint of suspicion or even surprise on the aide's face, which suggested the lieutenant was well used to dealing with his general's last-minute whims and would probably have been equally unabashed had the general introduced the newcomer as the Sultan of Rangoon.

"I regret I was separated from my valise. I've made arrangements for it to be sent on. I'm carrying all I need." He indicated the knapsack.

If he asks for my papers, it's all over.

"A pity the same couldn't be said for our Marshal Marmont," Souham said as his lieutenant disappeared once more. "Do his cooks still travel with him?"

He nodded. "All twelve of them, General."

"A hell of a way to go to war." The general parked the cheroot in the corner of his mouth and shoved his hands in his coat pockets.

The aide was back again, his message delivered. "The coach is ready, sir."

Souham nodded. "Right, thank you, Lieutenant. You can relax. Go and get yourself a drink. And mind the bastards don't serve you from the bottom of the cask." He turned and removed the cheroot from his lips. "Shall we, Major?"

They left the hotel and the driver held the coach door open as he followed the general up the steps. It occurred to him, as he took his seat and the driver retracted the steps and closed the door behind him, that he hadn't bought a ticket.

As if reading his mind, Souham smiled. "You can spread yourself out, Major. We have the vehicle to ourselves. Rank, as they say, has its privileges."

He breathed a sigh of relief. It meant they weren't likely to be disturbed until they'd reached their destination. He recalled then that Souham wasn't only a general; he was also a count. He'd received the title after his victory at the battle of Vich; the same engagement that had cost him his eye.

There was a jolt as the driver released the brake and then the coach moved slowly off.

The general removed his hat and ran a hand through his thinning locks.

"So, Major, I've a cousin who served with Rochambeau during your war of independence. He tells me that America is a beautiful country."

"Indeed it is, sir."

Jesus, he thought.

He wondered how long he'd be able to maintain the charade. What he knew of America he'd gleaned only from his service in the West Indies, during conversations with American merchants in Dominica and St Christopher. He knew a little about the eastern side of the country. Everywhere else was a mystery.

"So you've never been there yourself, General?" he ventured.

Souham shook his head. "Sadly no."

Maybe the gods are back with me, he thought.

A vision of the moments before his capture came into his mind. He saw the dragoon lieutenant raise the sword – *his* sword – and drive it home. As the light died in Leon's eyes he felt the spark of anger deep within him; as if a tiny ember had burst into flame. Somehow, he would make them pay. He didn't know how. But one day he would exact his revenge for the death of his friend.

The vision faded. He realized his fists were clenched and that the general was gazing at him with a quizzical expression.

"Forgive me, sir," he heard himself say, while risking what he hoped was a rueful smile. "It occurred to me, not for the first time, that I'm a long way from home."

Souham shook his head. "No need to apologize, Major. You're not alone in that. We all are."

From outside, above the noise of the coach in motion, there came the sound of hooves on cobbles as a body of horsemen entered the square. He heard voices, someone shouting orders, but the words were indistinct. Parting the blind, he looked out into the night, to where the riders were milling. Torches flickered. He could see dark uniforms and darker-coloured shakos.

Chasseurs.

As calmly as he could, he readjusted the blind and sat back.

"Your aide had better get a move on, General, if he wants to slake his thirst. There's a unit of cavalry out there who look like they're about to drink the town dry."

The coach hit a pothole and bounced. The noise of the horsemen faded, drowned by the trundle of the coach wheels as they left the square behind. He felt his pulse begin to slow.

Across from him, General Souham's right eye glinted with amusement. "I fear you've severely underestimated Lieutenant Bellac's determination where alcohol is concerned."

Taking another pull on the last inch of cheroot, the general smiled. "So, Major," he said, settling himself back into his seat. "We've a ways to go. To pass the time, you can tell me all about America."

As he watched the light of expectation steal across the general's face, the thought struck him that this had all the beginnings of a very long night.

2

Hawkwood waited for the attack. He knew it was coming and he knew it was imminent. Timing his retaliation would be crucial.

The inscrutable expression on his opponent's face wasn't helping matters.

It seemed to Hawkwood that Chen hadn't moved a muscle for at least five minutes. It was as if the Chinaman was carved from stone. Neither did he appear to be breathing hard, which was just as disconcerting, but then in their brief association Hawkwood couldn't recall a time when Chen had ever broken sweat.

While he, on the other hand, was perspiring like a pig on a spit.

It wasn't as if the room was warm. In fact, it wasn't really a room at all. It was a cellar and it was situated beneath the Rope and Anchor public house which sat in a grubby lane a spit away from Queen Street on the border between Ratcliffe and Limehouse. Tallow candles set in metal brackets around the walls and in a wagon-wheel chandelier suspended by a rope from the centre of the ceiling were the only sources of illumination.

The rest of the walls were bare save for a row of metal hooks by the door, from which were suspended Hawkwood's coat and jacket and what looked like an array of farming implements and a selection of tools that would not have looked out of place in a blacksmith's forge.

The cellar's flagstoned floor was covered by a layer of straw-filled mattresses, thin enough so as not to hamper movement and yet of sufficient bulk to absorb the weight of the cellar's occupants and to prevent injury were they to stumble and lose their footing. They were also there to dampen sound.

Aside from Hawkwood and Chen, the cellar was empty, though anyone entering who happened to glance over their shoulder towards one of the darkened corners would have been forgiven for thinking there was someone standing in the shadows watching proceedings. A closer inspection, however, would have revealed the figure to be merely a crude wooden effigy. Though even that description would have required a degree of imagination, for the effigy was in fact nothing more ominous than an oaken pillar into which had been inserted four limb-shaped spars. It had been constructed to represent a man's body with arms extended, but to the uninitiated it looked more like a leafless tree trunk.

Chen launched his strike. He seemed to do it with a minimum of effort and without a noticeable change of expression. In fact he didn't so much move as flow. Candlelight whispered along the blade as the knife curved towards Hawkwood's belly.

Hawkwood stepped into the attack and drove the tipstaff against Chen's wrist, turning the blade away.

Both men stepped back.

"Good," Chen said softly, his face betraying no emotion. "Again."

Unlike Hawkwood, Chen was wearing neither shirt nor breeches but a wide-sleeved, indigo-coloured tunic cinched about his middle by a black sash. The tunic reached to Chen's thighs. Beneath it, he wore a pair of matching blue trousers, tucked into a pair of white leggings. His feet were shod in a pair of soft-soled, black canvas slippers.

Chen repeated his attack and once more Hawkwood countered.

"Again," Chen said patiently.

They practised the sequence a dozen times, without pause, by which time the handle of Hawkwood's tipstaff was slick with moisture from his palm. Chen, on the other hand, looked as if he'd just awakened from a refreshing afternoon nap.

Hawkwood had often wondered about Chen's age. The man's features were, like his skull, smooth and hairless. He could have been any age between thirty and sixty. It wasn't as if the city was knee-deep in Chinamen that Hawkwood could make a well-informed judgement. Lascars there were a-plenty; many of them ensconced within the East India Company barracks along the Ratcliffe Highway. But Chinamen were still something of a rarity and could probably be numbered if not on the fingers of one hand then certainly in the low rather than the high hundreds.

Hawkwood and Chen's paths had crossed three months before at, of all places, a horse fair on Bow Common.

Hawkwood had gone there with Nathaniel Jago who, to Hawkwood's astonishment, had expressed interest in buying a horse. He had a hankering, he'd told Hawkwood, to invest in a carriage so that he and Connie Fletcher could take five o'clock drives around Hyde Park with the rest of the swells.

Connie Fletcher was a former working girl turned madam who ran a high-class bagnio off Cavendish Square. Jago and Connie had been keeping company for nearly a year which, by Hawkwood's reckoning, had to be some kind of record. Hawkwood had tried to envisage Jago and Connie surrounded by the cream of London society all trying to cut a dash along the tree-lined avenues, and had failed miserably.

He suspected that the idea of riding in a carriage had been more Connie's dream than Jago's, in an attempt to garner some degree of respectability, for when they had served together in the Peninsula, his former sergeant's aversion to anything even remotely connected with equestrian pursuits had been legendary, and that included, in some instances, cheering on the cavalry. Horses were good for just one thing, Jago had told him, and that was as a supplement to rations, and only then if chickens were in short supply and the beef had turned maggoty.

Hawkwood wondered if this new-found hankering was a precursor to an attempt by Connie to persuade Jago to make an honest woman of her. Now, there was a thought to keep a man awake at night.

In the event, neither of them need have worried, for the quality of horse flesh on offer had been nothing to write home about: scrub horses and sway-backed mules for the most part. So, with Jago grumbling that he'd have to wait until the Barnet Horse Fair to continue his search, they'd turned their attentions to the peripheral entertainments, one of which had been a boxing booth. Other than its size – it was considerably larger than either of its immediate neighbours – there hadn't been much to distinguish the tent from the rest of the tawdry marquees with their fortune tellers, palm readers and freak shows, had it not been for the placard above the sagging entrance which, in florid and faded lettering, proclaimed: *Billy Boyd – The Bethnal Green Bruiser – Challenges All Comers!*

Against his better judgement Hawkwood had allowed Jago to drag him into the tent, where they'd been confronted by the reek of stale beer and even staler bodies and a roped-off square of canvas around which a couple of dozen rowdy onlookers had, over the course of the afternoon, watched a succession of rough-hewn labourers and jack-the-lads try their hand at pummelling another man senseless; their incentive being the three guineas on offer if they managed to remain upright for the duration of the three two-minute rounds, and a five-guinea purse if they succeeded in, as the booth owner put it in his sales pitch, knocking the champion on to his arse.

Not that any of them had stood a cat in hell's chance. Boyd, a stocky, broad-bellied mauler with a balding scalp, broken nose and knuckles lined with calluses, had stood there knowingly, hands on his hips, watching as, one by one, his deflated opponents were carried from the ring in varying degrees of pain and disability, very few of them having managed to land so much as one decent punch. Looking on, it had been hard to fathom why any man in his right mind would have wanted to climb over the ropes and take him on in the first place.

It had been the late end of the afternoon. The number of prospective challengers had gradually dwindled away and the

26

tout had been on the verge of calling it a day, when the slight built, strangely dressed figure stepped out of the audience and made his way to the ringside.

Someone close by had let go a snort of laughter. Hawkwood heard Jago say quietly and with some awe. "Well, now, *this* should be interestin'."

Without doubt, it was the orange coat with its high collar buttoned up to the chin that had drawn the eye; as bright as a sunburst compared to the clothing worn by the majority of men in the tent. The coat wearer's looks were just as arresting as his attire.

In the booth's dim-lit interior, his skin had seemed to be infused with an almost ethereal saffron tint. Hawkwood had also been struck by the man's uncannily symmetrical features, in particular his oval face, shaven head and deep brown, almond-shaped eyes. His demeanour had been odd, too. There had been a curious serenity in his gaze and a stillness in the way he'd held himself. He'd seemed oblivious to the reaction his arrival had caused, though he must have been aware of it.

"It's a Chink!" a gravelled voice had offered helpfully.

"Well, 'e ain't from bleedin' Chelsea!" another wit had shouted.

"Either way," Jago murmured in Hawkwood's ear, "he's a long way from home."

The tout had looked back at his man, unable to keep the grin off his face. The response had been a dismissive shrug of the shoulders, as if to say, "He's paid the entrance money, it's his funeral."

When Chen climbed into the ring, he'd done so in a hushed silence born out of the crowd's curiosity and collective assumption that the outcome was a foregone conclusion. Another challenger, who hadn't even had the sense to remove his coat, was about to receive a sharp and painful lesson in the noble science.

"Not sure I want to see this." Jago had been on the point of turning away. Hawkwood, though, stayed where he was. He wasn't sure what prompted him to remain, other than the look in the Chinaman's eyes, which had intrigued him.

At the sound of the bell, the champion had exited his corner with all the confidence of a seasoned fighter; a man prepared to give short shrift to any upstart – young or old – who had delusions of unseating him. The crowd was about to be treated not only to a contest between champion and the challenger but a pugilistic exhibition as well.

It hadn't turned out that way.

Billy Boyd liked to toy with his opponents by allowing them a few opening punches to bolster their confidence, before returning a sequence of light, irritating taps to let them know they'd probably made the wrong decision. That was usually enough to incite the challenger into firing off a salvo of haymakers that had no hope of landing but which gave the champion legitimate rein to retaliate with increasing force. Boyd was more than happy to let the challenger think he was going to last the three rounds before finally moving in and disabusing him of such a foolish notion.

Faced with the Chinaman, Boyd, for the first time in his career, had found himself flummoxed, not least because his opponent made no attempt to attack or put up a protective guard. Instead, all he did was assume a peculiar stance not unlike some kind of strange, one-legged bird. Then, holding his right hand close to his waist in an inverted fist, he raised his left arm to shoulder height, palm open towards the champion, fingers hooked as if it were some kind of claw. Settled, features immobile, as if he had all the time in the world, he waited.

By the time Boyd realized he'd been duped, it was too late. Even as he stepped forward, drawn by this most unlikely of opponents to initiate contact instead of the other way round, some sixth sense must have triggered a warning. But by then he was already committed. Even as he aimed an exploratory jab towards the challenger's torso, the Chinaman was moving.

Chen's counter-attack, a set of lightning moves that enabled him to block the punch with ease, turn the champion's arm away and drive the edge of his palm into Billy Boyd's throat, was almost sinuous in execution and so fast the crowd had barely had time to follow it from start to finish.

It occurred to Hawkwood that he might have seen scorpions strike with less speed and ferocity; estimating later that it had probably taken Chen longer to climb over the ropes than it had for him to put the champion on his back.

To a stunned silence that could have been cut with a knife.

It had been hard to tell who was the most shocked: the crowd, the booth owner, or Billy Boyd.

"Jesus!" Jago's whisper had echoed the reaction of every witness in the tent.

With Boyd still flat on the canvas, Chen had left the ring to claim his purse, only to discover that the tout was not prepared to relinquish the prize in the wake of a bout that had lasted barely ten seconds, even more so when the challenger had not even had the decency to engage in a fair contest. Especially, the tout had added, when he was a "bleedin' Chinaman" to boot. Emboldened by the belief that he had the bulk of the spectators on his side, he'd told Chen to sling his hook.

But Chen had stood his ground.

By then, factions within the crowd had begun to argue, divided between those who agreed with the tout that the Chinaman had employed unfair tactics, typical of a bloody slant-eyed little heathen, and those who thought that landing Billy Boyd on his arse had been no bad thing and worth the entrance fee on its own.

Things had been on the verge of turning ugly when, with reluctance, Hawkwood had stepped in. Having Jago at his shoulder had helped, but mostly it had been his brass-crowned Runner's baton and the magistrate's warrant contained within it that had persuaded the tout that it might be in his best interest if he reconsidered his decision. It was either that, or notice would be issued to close down the booth and both the tout and the champion could spend the night reflecting upon their decision in the nearest police cell. It'd save a lot of bother, Hawkwood promised them, if they paid the Chinaman what they owed him. Then everybody could go home.

Muttering under his breath, the booth owner had handed over the five guineas. In the interest of public order, Hawkwood and Jago had escorted Chen from the tent and, in case any of Boyd's supporters harboured thoughts of revenge, from the Common as well.

When they'd reached a safe distance, Chen had thanked them in halting English. Then he'd asked Hawkwood why he'd helped him.

There had been two reasons, Hawkwood told him. The first was because Chen had won the bout and the purse was therefore his.

The second was that Hawkwood wanted Chen to teach him to fight.

They had been using the cellar beneath the Rope and Anchor twice a week for three months. The owner, a former lighterman called Tully Robinson, owed Jago a favour. Jago had called in the debt and Tully had bequeathed one of the pub's cellars, no questions asked. It even had its own entrance, approached via a dank, shoulder-wide passage with the appropriate name of Gin Alley.

The cellar became their training room. Hawkwood had been mystified by some of the additions, the sparring tree in particular. Only when Chen had given him a demonstration, using his hands, forearms and feet to attack the bare wooden figure had it begun to make sense, as had the ridges of hardened skin along the outside edges of Chen's soles and palms. It was only after their second session together that Hawkwood noticed how compact Chen's hands were; his fingers were uniformly short and almost of the same length. As a result, his fingertips, when held rigid, were as formidable as an axe blade and just as effective as the edge of his hand.

Chen had begun by teaching Hawkwood simple sequences of blocks and strikes. Hour after hour, he would take Hawkwood through the drills until the mantra became all consuming.

"Too slow. Again."

Block, strike; block, strike.

"Too slow. Again."

The techniques that Chen employed were not entirely new to

Hawkwood. He'd served with a man during his time in Spain, a Portuguese soldier turned *guerrillero*, who'd plied his trade in the East and who'd picked up some interesting fighting skills along the way. He'd shared some of them with Hawkwood, telling him they'd originated among an order of Chinese holy men. Forbidden to carry weapons, they had devised their own form of combat using their hands and feet and whatever implements were available.

Hawkwood had remembered some of the elementary moves and indeed had used them on occasion. Watching Chen display the unexpected yet instantly familiar tactics against Billy Boyd had ignited the thought that maybe fate had presented him with an opportunity to widen his knowledge and improve upon those few basic skills he'd acquired from his Portuguese comrade-in-arms. Anything that would give him an edge over the sort of men he hunted had to be an advantage.

As the lessons progressed so did Chen's command of English. From what Hawkwood had been able to glean, Chen had no family. He came from the south of China; a province with a strange name that was almost impossible to pronounce. More intriguing was Chen's disclosure that he had indeed been a monk, a member of a religious order that had fallen foul of the authorities. A number of sacred sites had been desecrated, including Chen's own monastery. The monks had retaliated and a price had been placed on their heads. Many of them had fled the country. Chen had arrived in England on board a British merchant ship, one of hundreds of anonymous seamen recruited abroad as cheap labour by the East India Company. As a result he'd found himself marooned, an orphan in a storm, unable to return home, for fear of imprisonment or death.

He'd managed to find a bed in one of the Lascar-run Shadwell boarding houses, using the last of his pitiful wages. When they ran out he'd resorted to begging; a legacy from his time as a monk, when the only way to obtain food had been to wander the streets with a bowl and cup. But he'd soon learned there was little sympathy shown to foreign beggars – there were enough home-grown ones – and his orange robe, which would have elicited charity in his own country, counted for nothing on the streets of London. Starvation looked a likely prospect, but he'd persevered. He'd known that the best pickings were to be found wherever crowds gathered, so he had followed the fair-goers to Bow Common. There he'd seen the illustrations on the outside of the boxing booth. He had sufficient English to understand what was required in order for him to walk away with enough money to cover three months' lodgings. He'd watched Boyd through a gap in the back of the tent and even though he'd not used his fighting skills in many months, he knew he would beat him and that it would not take long.

And so it had proved.

In their training they would alternate roles and Hawkwood would take on the role of the aggressor, wielding his tipstaff or the knife in his boot or on occasion one of the tools hanging on the wall; the threshing flail, the hammer, the hand scythe or the axe. Invariably, Chen would disarm him with ease, no matter how quickly Hawkwood attacked or what weapon he favoured. Gradually, however, Hawkwood came to understand the principles Chen employed, how it was possible to defuse an attack using gravity, speed and leverage to unbalance his opponent and effect a counter strike and every now and then he found himself piercing Chen's formidable defences. But not very often.

Chen transferred his weight to his left foot and thrust the knife towards Hawkwood's throat. This time, Hawkwood was unarmed. He brought up his right hand, found Chen's wrist, rotated it and, stepping to the left, brought the heel of his left hand against Chen's braced elbow. Chen went down and Hawkwood released his grip.

Chen came off the mattress and nodded. "Better. You still slow, but better."

"Better", Hawkwood had learned, was the closest Chen ever got to awarding high praise.

They'd been in the cellar for two hours. Hawkwood's shirt was soaked. Perspiration coated his skin and his arms and legs ached. He felt a perverse pleasure, however, at seeing for the first time the thin line of perspiration that beaded Chen's temple. It meant he was probably doing something right.

In the lull, his ears picked up the faint sound of a tolling bell, signalling the change of shift at the timber yard over on Narrow Street. Chen's ears had caught it, too. He straightened, faced Hawkwood and inclined his head. Some might have looked upon it as a bow of deference but Hawkwood knew it was Chen's way of announcing that training was over for the day.

"We finish now," Chen said.

Hawkwood hoped the relief wasn't showing on his face; or the pain, for that matter. It had occurred to him during the sessions in the cellar that over the years he'd suffered enough hurt in the service of king and country and latterly as a police officer, without it seeming necessary to risk further injury to life and limb trying to master some obscure fighting technique. But then, it had also struck him that, had he mastered the techniques before he'd taken up soldiering and policing he might well have avoided some of the injuries in the first place. Life, he thought, as he wiped his face and neck with a drying cloth, probably wasn't meant to be that complicated.

Though he couldn't deny the exhilaration he felt every time he staunched one of Chen's attacks, which more than made up for any discomfort suffered in the acquisition of bruised bones, scraped knuckles and the occasional bloody nose.

His thoughts were jolted by a hesitant knock on the cellar door; an unusual occurrence. Tully, true to his agreement with Jago, had rarely encroached upon his and Chen's privacy before. Even Chen, a master of stoicism, turned his head at the interruption. He looked at Hawkwood for direction. Hawkwood nodded and reached for his coat. Chen opened the door.

Tully Robinson stood on the threshold. He was a heavily built man, with thinning hair and a hangdog look.

"Beggin' your pardon, Captain. Told to give you this." He threw Chen a wary glance and held out a folded note.

Hawkwood took the paper, broke the seal and read the contents.

"Who delivered it?"

"Didn't catch the name. Small fella; bow legs and spectacles; wore a wig, dressed like a pox doctor's clerk."

Hawkwood didn't react. "How long ago?"

"'Bout 'alf an hour. I knows you likes your privacy, so I waited. Then I got to figuring it might be important after all. You know 'im?"

Hawkwood nodded. "For my sins."

Tully regarded Hawkwood's tall frame with some apprehension, taking in the dark hair tied off at the nape of the neck, the scarred features and the blue-grey eyes. Tully had worked on the river most of his life and had known hard men, but this one, even if he hadn't been a friend of Jago's, was a man he knew he wouldn't want to cross. He'd called him "Captain" because that's how Jago had addressed him, but as to Hawkwood's profession, he wasn't prepared to hazard a guess. The small, bespectacled messenger had provided no clue. He'd simply described Hawkwood and asked that the message be passed on.

Tully stared at the Chinaman. He still couldn't put his finger on what the two of them got up to in the cellar. The walls and door were thick enough to deaden most of the noise from within. All he'd ever heard in passing were dull thumps and grunts and clunks that might have been wood striking metal. He'd never plucked up the nerve to ask either Jago or his friend the captain what they used the room for; indeed, that was part of the arrangement. It hadn't stopped him wondering, though. And as for the presence of a Chinaman, God alone knew what *he* was doing there. Tully didn't like to think. Message delivered, he departed, no wiser than he'd been before he knocked on the door.

Hawkwood considered the note, imagining the look on Twigg's face had he heard Tully's description of him. He did not wonder how Ezra Twigg had tracked him down but accepted the fact with weary resignation. Twigg's resources were both extensive and bordering on the mystical. Speculation would have been a waste of time.

Chen collected a hessian sack from a hook on the wall and slipped it over his shoulder. He did so in silence, his movements controlled and precise. Hawkwood suspected that Chen had

34

very few possessions; a leftover, he assumed, from Chen's former vocation as a monk, where a vow of poverty would have been a prerequisite. He had a feeling Chen also travelled without baggage for another reason; a man on the run, even so far from home, would not want to be weighed down by unnecessary encumbrances.

They let themselves out of the cellar. At the end of the alley, Chen bowed again and without pausing turned and walked away; a small, slight and innocuous figure among the grime of his surroundings. Hawkwood watched him go. Chen did not look back. He never did. Hawkwood guessed he'd be heading for the East India Company mission on Fore Street, which catered for Lascar and Chinese seafarers who found themselves in extremis. In exchange for a roof and a bed, Chen carried out odd jobs, most of them menial, such as cleaning and preparing meals. In all likelihood, given his history, he probably provided spiritual guidance as well. As foreigners on a foreign shore, the Asian seamen had learned early on that there was safety in numbers. Hawkwood wondered if Chen taught them how to defend themselves, as well. Still wondering, he turned. Leaving Queen Street behind, he strode west, towards Sun Tavern Fields and on to the city. If Tully Robinson's laconic observation was accurate, he had an appointment with a pox doctor.

And it wouldn't do to be late.

Arriving at Bow Street, Hawkwood made his way to the first floor. Halfway up the stairs, his ears picked up the harsh scratch of nib on paper. In the ante-room, Ezra Twigg was bent low over his desk, his small mouth pursed in concentration. A tatty grey wig hung on a stand behind him. From a distance it looked like some kind of dead animal. It wasn't often the wig was discarded. Hawkwood could count on the fingers of one hand the number of times he'd seen the clerk without it. Hanging alongside the wig was a black tricorne hat that had also seen better days.

"Why, Mr Twigg!" Hawkwood said breezily. "And how are we this fine morning? Enjoy your constitutional?"

Ezra Twigg did not look up, though the pen in his hand may have paused momentarily. "Most efficacious, Officer Hawkwood. Thank you for asking." Light from the window behind the desk reflected off Twigg's spectacles. He looked like a diminutive, slightly disgruntled owl awoken upon his nest.

The pen resumed its pedantic scroll across the document. The little man's flaking scalp showed palely through his receding hair. The hunched shoulders of his coat were liberally sprinkled with flecks of fine grey powder. As well as the wig, the clerk had also forsaken his ink guards. The cuffs of his shirt were edged with dark, uneven stains.

"Should have waited for me, Ezra," Hawkwood continued cheerfully. "It's a nice day. We could have strolled back together."

The clerk muttered under his breath.

Hawkwood cupped an ear. "Sorry, Ezra; didn't catch that. Did you say something?"

Twigg sniffed. "Only that some of us have work to do." Again, the clerk did not bother to look up, but added dolefully, "He said you were to go straight in."

Hawkwood grinned and crossed the room. He took off his riding coat, draped it over a chair back and tapped on the door. Behind him, Twigg gave the coat a pained look and shook his head in resignation.

"Enter." The order came crisply from within.

Hawkwood pushed the door open.

Chief Magistrate James Read looked up from his desk.

"Ah, there you are." Read put down his pen. His eyes moved towards the longcase clock that stood like a sentinel in the corner of the dark-panelled room. If he was irritated by the time it had taken Hawkwood to respond to the summons, he chose not to show it, but got up from his desk and made his way to the fireplace where bright flames danced behind a large mesh guard. Standing with his back to the hearth, he raised his coat-tails. Dressed in coordinating shades of grey, he was a slim, fastidious-looking man, with silver hair combed neatly back from a strong, aquiline face.

Hawkwood stepped into the room and closed the door. And immediately found himself perused.

"So, Hawkwood, how are you? I keep meaning to enquire. On the mend after the Morgan affair?"

"Every breath is a victory, sir," Hawkwood said.

Read accepted Hawkwood's response with a flinty stare. "Wounds no longer troubling you?"

"I'm well, sir, thank you." Hawkwood tried to keep the wariness from his voice. The Chief Magistrate wasn't usually this concerned for his health; at least not to his face.

"Splendid. Plenty of exercise, I trust? My physician tells me that a diet of regular physical activity can be a great aid to recovery, providing one doesn't indulge in over exertion, of course."

The Chief Magistrate fixed Hawkwood with another penetrating look. If he'd been wearing spectacles like his clerk, he would have been regarding Hawkwood over the rims, as if daring him to contradict.

"An excellent idea, sir. I'll bear that in mind the next time I'm stabbed or shot."

The corner of Read's mouth lifted. Lowering his coat-tails, the Chief Magistrate gazed towards the window to where the sounds of the city rose stridently from the street below, as a bewildering variety of vendors and costermongers attempted, without much success, to drown out the incessant cacophony of cart wheels and clattering hooves.

Hawkwood waited expectantly.

James Read turned back. "I've a job for you." The Chief Magistrate paused and then said, "I'm placing you on secondment."

Not something Hawkwood was expecting. The word carried a distinct sense of foreboding, though he wasn't sure why.

"Secondment?" He tried to keep his voice calm. "With whom?"

"Superintendent Brooke."

Hawkwood wondered if the name was supposed to mean something. It didn't.

"Never heard of him. Who is he?"

Read's eyebrows rose momentarily at the less than reverential tone in Hawkwood's voice and then he sighed.

"I'd be surprised if you *had* heard of him, frankly. Superintendent Brooke prefers to keep to the – how shall I put it? – less well-lit side of the street. In fact, I doubt there's a dozen people who *have* heard of him. Even within his own department," Read added cryptically.

Which sounds even more bloody ominous, Hawkwood thought.

Warmed through, Read stepped away from the hearth and walked to the window. "The superintendent's responsibilities fall within the remit of the Home Office."

Was that supposed to mean something? Hawkwood wondered.

"So, what are my duties to be . . . sir?"

Read hesitated, looked thoughtful, and then said, "It's best if I leave it to Superintendent Brooke to brief you." The magistrate glanced towards the clock dial. "Talking of whom; you are to present yourself without delay. Number 20 Crown Street."

Read stepped across to his desk and retook his seat. "Caleb's waiting downstairs. He has instruction to convey you to the address." Read picked up his pen and reached for some papers. "That is all. You may relay my respects to Superintendent Brooke."

Dismissed, Hawkwood headed for the door. He was on the threshold and about to close it behind him when he thought he heard Read's voice. He paused and looked round. "Sir?"

The Chief Magistrate, he saw, had his head down and was engrossed in a document. There was no outward sign that he'd spoken. He did not look up.

Must have been my imagination, Hawkwood thought, though he could have sworn he'd heard the Chief Magistrate whisper the words, "*Bon chance.*"

As he let himself out, he wondered why he found that idea disquieting.

3

Whitehall was as busy as Smithfield on market day.

But then Whitehall was always busy. Every time he'd travelled down it, whether by carriage or on foot, Hawkwood had never known an occasion when it wasn't. Though that was to be expected, he supposed, given the nature of the business conducted in the grand buildings sited along its broad expanse. That and the fact that the nation was at war; for a nation at war was always on the move. The decisions reached in the offices of state concealed behind the impressive façades affected the lives of every man, woman and child in the land. As a soldier in the service of the king, Hawkwood had been subject to the whims and vain posturings of statesmen more than most. As a police officer, too. It was a depressing fact that there didn't seem to be any escape from officialdom, no matter who, where, or what you were. And this place was at the centre of it all; the heartbeat.

The road was thronged with carriages; most of them in motion, though a good few were parked, either awaiting the return of their passengers or else competing for fares. Pedestrians hugged the verges in a vain bid to avoid the mud, dust and dung that coated the road. Those who were bold enough to attempt a crossing did so at their peril for the oncoming traffic invariably showed no inclination to cede its right of way.

Carriages weren't the only means of transport in view. There were plenty of people on horseback, too, a great many of them in uniform, including a phalanx of cavalry heading for the exercise ground. The troopers drew applause as they trotted past.

In the wide forecourt of the Admiralty building, anxious blue-coated naval officers scurried around the high porticoed entrance like ants. It was the same with the Horse Guards. The only difference lay in the cut and the colour of the uniforms. From this imposing building had been issued the orders dispatching Hawkwood and thousands like him to Spain, Portugal and South America and a score of other outposts scattered across the furthest reaches of the globe. He gazed up past the sentry boxes and wondered what new strategies were being hatched on the other side of the high windows.

The cab skirted the front of the Treasury and the defile that was the entrance to Downing Street. Crown Street lay a few yards further on, between Fludyer Street and Charles Street, tucked away from the noise and bustle of the main avenues. Here, the low-hanging sun was partially obscured by inconvenient rooftops, so corners of the narrow street still lay in chilly shadow, giving it a disquieting air of gloom. There were a few strollers about, but Caleb's was the only carriage. The horses' hooves echoed on the road like stones in a hollow log.

The cab halted. Hawkwood alighted and told Caleb there was no need to wait. Caleb touched two fingers to his cap and drove off.

From the outside, Number 20 looked to be as unremarkable as its neighbours, save for the small, unobtrusive brass plate that was positioned to the right of the door. On it were inscribed the words: ALIEN OFFICE.

Hawkwood stared down at the plate.

So that was why Magistrate Read had been so evasive.

A middle-aged, lank-haired clerk with pockmarked skin and a lugubrious cast to his features answered Hawkwood's summons on the bell and, after fixing him with a baleful stare and taking his name, instructed him to wait. When the clerk returned he was accompanied by a formally dressed and much younger man, who looked Hawkwood up and down with ill-disguised con-descension. Unlike his colleague, his hair looked freshly barbered. Hawkwood's nostrils detected the faint whiff of pomade.

"Officer Hawkwood? My name is Flint. This way, if you please." He crooked a finger. Hawkwood resisted the urge to snap it off.

Moving primly, Flint led the way upstairs. Apart from the sound of their footsteps, the building seemed eerily quiet. If it hadn't been for the nameless functionary on the ground floor, they might well have been the only two in the place. Leading Hawkwood to a door at the top of the stairs, Flint knocked twice, opened the door and stood aside.

Hawkwood found himself in a spacious, high-ceilinged room that resembled a library more than it did an office. Books were displayed on every wall. The areas of panelling that did not contain bookshelves supported an impressive gallery of maps; the majority of which appeared to cover Europe – France and the Peninsula mostly – though India and Egypt, Hawkwood noticed, were also represented. The autumn sunlight was admitted into the room through a pair of large windows, in front of which sat a hefty mahogany desk, containing more books and piles of documents secured in red and black ribbons. Leaning back against the desk, arms folded in repose, was a tall, sombre-looking man dressed in black.

"Officer Hawkwood?" The man straightened, unfolded his arms but did not extend his hand. "Henry Brooke. Welcome to the Alien Office." He nodded towards Flint, hovering by the door. "Thank you, Stormont. You may leave us. I'll ring if I have need of you. Oh, and perhaps you'd be kind enough to take Officer Hawkwood's coat for him, there's a good fellow."

Hawkwood removed his coat and handed it over. Flint looked none too happy at being relegated to footman. He didn't quite turn his nose up, but it was a close-run thing. He left the room with the coat held at arm's length and the door closed softly behind him.

Brooke continued to regard the door, as though expecting it to spring back open. Eventually satisfied that wasn't about to happen, he pushed himself away from the desk and regarded Hawkwood with calm appraisal.

"You've come direct from Magistrate Read? How is he? In sound health, I trust?"

"He asked me to convey his compliments," Hawkwood said.

"How kind of him." Unhurriedly, Brooke stalked around the desk and took his seat. The superintendent's jacket and breeches were beautifully tailored. Hawkwood could see stripes of very fine gold thread running through them.

Hawkwood glanced towards the fireplace. The hearth was empty and despite the azure sky visible through the windows, the room was by no means warm. James Read's office was a positive furnace in comparison. Perhaps Brooke had spent all his money on his wardrobe and had nothing left over for kindling. Hawkwood wondered if surrendering his coat had been a wise decision.

"So, Officer Hawkwood," Brooke said, somewhat regally. "What has Magistrate Read told you? Anything?"

Hawkwood shook his head. "He told me he'd leave that to you, sir."

There was no invitation to sit down, though there were two empty chairs in the room. Hawkwood had no doubt it was a deliberate ploy rather than an oversight. By keeping him standing, Brooke was effortlessly and effectively emphasizing his authority.

Brooke smiled indulgently. "Did he now? How convenient." Leaning forward, he stared down at a sheaf of papers on his desk. His eyes roved across the page. "You were a soldier. The 95th Regiment of Foot, I see."

Brooke looked up. The expression on his face was reassuringly benign. Interpreting the remark as a comment rather than a question, Hawkwood kept quiet. He assumed Brooke would continue, which he did.

"A fine regiment." Brooke did not expand upon the statement but lowered his eyes and continued to read. Without looking up, he said, "From my conversations with him, I know that Magistrate Read holds you in extremely high regard. You should be flattered. He's not one to award praise lightly." There was a pause. "Though he also advises me you have what he calls an ambivalent attitude towards authority." Casually, Brooke lifted his gaze. "I imagine that's a polite way of saying you've a tendency to disregard it. I'd also hazard a guess it did not serve you well in your army career; would I be right in that?"

Hawkwood considered his response and decided it would probably be more prudent if he remained silent, though it didn't prevent him wondering what was coming next.

"I suspect that rather answers my question," the man at the desk said, looking and sounding mildly amused. "Though the Rifle Corps, from all I hear, does allow its men a degree more latitude than most." The smile evaporated. "Tell me about Talavera and Major Delancey."

Hawkwood felt his stomach muscles contract. *What the hell was this?*

Brooke moved the document aside as though it was no longer of consequence. He leant forward, steepled his fingers and rested his elbows on the desk. The dark gaze was unwavering. "You may speak freely."

It struck Hawkwood that Brooke had exceptionally long fingers. It was impossible not to compare them with Chen's stubby digits. The silence stretched, while Brooke, seemingly content to prolong the moment, remained resolutely mute. He looked, Hawkwood thought, not unlike a praying mantis about to pounce upon a moth.

"Major Delancey was a Guards officer," Hawkwood said, "with a misguided opinion of his own abilities. He wanted to make a name for himself. He gave a bad order and a lot of good men died because of it. I told him it would have been no great loss if he'd been counted among them. He took exception and called me out. That was his second mistake." He stared down at the man behind the desk. "But you already knew that, sir. Didn't you?"

The seated man raised his eyebrows. "You don't think a man's entitled to make a mistake?"

Hawkwood shook his head. "Not at all. The trouble with Delancey was that he abused the privilege. Most men have the

43

capacity for regret. They learn from the errors they've committed. Delancey didn't have the wits for that."

Brooke's face hardened. "It's war. Men die. Isn't that the way of it?"

"Yes, it is," Hawkwood said. "But they shouldn't have to die because some tomfool officer is hell-bent on glory."

There was silence, then Brooke said sternly, "*You* were an officer. A captain, no less. How many men died under *your* command?"

"Too damned many," Hawkwood responded coldly. "But unlike Delancey, I valued the lives of my men, I could name every bloody one of them. Would you care to tell me why I'm here . . . *sir.*"

A flash of irritation showed on the superintendent's face but it disappeared in the blink of an eye, to be replaced by a thin smile. He lowered his hands on to the desk. "Well, Magistrate Read warned me you were direct; and I must say you don't disappoint. As for the reason you're here; we'll come to that shortly. The Delancey affair cost you, though, didn't it? You lost your commission."

There didn't seem much point in either denying the fact or elaborating upon it.

"Yes."

"You were cashiered." Brooke pulled his notes towards him and glanced down at them. "Which should have seen you reduced to the ranks or sent home. Yet, instead, you took to the mountains and joined the *guerrilleros*. Most intriguing. Of your own volition, or was it really with the blessing of your commander?"

Brooke was undoubtedly referring to Wellington. Hawkwood suspected that, once again, the superintendent already knew the answer to his question. Brooke clearly had his military record to hand and seemed keen on letting him know it. Hawkwood decided there and then not to grant the man any further concessions. If Brooke wanted additional information he'd have to bloody well work for it.

"Your time in the Peninsula served you well," Brooke went on. "You speak Spanish, yes?"

He appeared undeterred by Hawkwood's reluctance to respond to the previous enquiry.

This time, Hawkwood nodded. Brooke seemed intent on changing course every five minutes. Sooner rather than later, Hawkwood supposed, the superintendent would get to the point.

"In fact," Brooke continued, "you've quite a flair for languages. You're fluent in French, as well, I hear?"

"I've been fighting the bastards for twenty years. There was a general once; he said you should know your enemy." Hawkwood shrugged. "Learning the language seemed as good a place to start as any."

Brooke's eyebrows lifted. He looked genuinely startled by Hawkwood's reply. "You're a student of Sun Tzu?"

"Sun what?" Hawkwood said. He had no idea what Brooke was talking about.

Brooke sat back in his chair. "Not what; it's a name. Sun Tzu – T, Z, U. He's your general. He was Chinese. He lived over two thousand years ago. He wrote a book on military strategy known as *The Art of War*. It's been used by military leaders down through the ages. He wrote: 'If you know the enemy and know yourself, you need not fear the result of a hundred battles.' They do say Bonaparte's a devotee," Brooke added, with what might have been a hint of admiration. Then, intrigued by the expression on Hawkwood's face, his brow furrowed. "What is it?"

Hawkwood was thinking of Chen, recalling how the Chinaman had scrutinized Bruiser Billy Boyd disporting himself with his previous opponents, then swiftly defeated him. Hawkwood wondered if Chen had heard of this Sun Tzu. He'd have to ask him. He had the strong feeling that the answer would be in the affirmative. He shook his head. "I wasn't aware of his name."

"Then it appears we've both learnt something today," Brooke said serenely. He studied his notes. "I see you fought alongside Colquhoun Grant."

Another name; this one known, however. Although it was from the more recent past, it was not one that Hawkwood had been expecting to hear.

45

"Not exactly."

"What?" Something approaching alarm showed in the superintendent's eyes. "Are you saying I've been misinformed?"

"I was in the mountains when Captain Grant joined Wellington's staff. I reported to him when I delivered information back to the general's headquarters. It was after I left Spain that the captain became Lord Wellington's chief exploring officer. He inherited my informers and he was able to make use of the *guerrilleros* I'd been working with."

"Ah, in other words, he was your successor," Brooke said, sounding relieved.

Hawkwood nodded. "That would be a more accurate description, yes."

"Well, you clearly made a favourable impression, whichever way it was. He provided the references that enabled you to join Bow Street, no?" Brooke threw Hawkwood another questioning stare.

"Captain Grant had friends in high places," Hawkwood said.

"Had?" The reply came sharply.

"He was captured," Hawkwood said heavily. "Six months ago. The French finally managed to track him down and Bonaparte ordered him hanged as a spy. Another thing that Corsican bastard has to answer for. Now, forgive me, sir, but would you mind telling me what I'm doing here?"

Brooke leant back in his chair, his face severe. He remained silent, as if pondering his decision. Finally, he gave a curt nod. "Very well. What do you know of this department?"

"According to Magistrate Read, you're part of the Home Office."

"Anything else?"

"Yes," Hawkwood said. "You hunt subversives."

Brooke looked slightly taken aback by Hawkwood's forthright response. Then he frowned. "Subversives? I do declare that's a word I've not come across before. Though I must say it's a good one, and remarkably apposite. From the French, possibly?" He regarded Hawkwood with renewed respect. "Is that all?"

Hawkwood hesitated.

When he'd seen the brass plaque to the side of the front door, the name "Alien Office" had triggered a faint memory that went deeper than his confessed store of knowledge. He wasn't sure what it was a memory of, exactly, other than the vague remembrance of whispered conversations and rumours voiced in dark corridors about even darker deeds. It was probably best to claim ignorance. That way, at least, any information he did receive would be straight from the horse's mouth.

"Perhaps you ought to tell me, sir."

From the look in Brooke's eye it was clear the superintendent suspected that Hawkwood was being deliberately obtuse.

The moment passed. Brooke nodded. "As you wish. Well, Magistrate Read was quite correct. We do indeed fall under the aegis of the Home Office, though we operate independently from it."

"And what do you operate *on*, exactly?"

"Oh, all manner of things," Brooke replied, showing his teeth. The effect was not so much jocular as disarmingly menacing. "You know it was your Chinese general who said that a hundred ounces of silver spent on intelligence can save a thousand spent on war. You might say it's my duty to try and prove him right."

"And how do you do that?"

"By spreading confusion among our enemies."

Brooke pushed himself away from his desk and stood up. He shot his cuffs and began to pace the room, his hands clasped behind his back.

He looked over his shoulder. "As a police officer you are, no doubt, familiar with the workings of the Alien Act?"

Hawkwood nodded.

The act had been inaugurated in '93, long before his arrival at Bow Street. It required all foreigners to register with the customs officials at the port where they landed or at a police office. Despite the latter stipulation, to Hawkwood's knowledge there had been no direct impact from the legislation on his own duties as a Runner. Up until now, that was.

"I'm relieved to hear it," Brooke said. Eyes front, he continued to pace. "However, what you may not know is that the Act was

47

actually prepared in response to advice from the *émigrés* themselves. That was how this office came into being. The Prime Minister was becoming increasingly concerned by the number of refugees arriving on our shores, having fled the Terror. There was no knowing who we were letting through, no guarantee that some of them weren't agents who'd smuggled themselves in to spread dissent among the populace."

The superintendent performed an about turn. "The last thing this country needed was for the seeds of republicanism to start germinating on this side of the Channel. God forbid there should be a mob laying siege to the Tower! So, subversives, revolution-aries, agitators, spies – call them what you will – it was and is the Office's task to root out the bad apples. And I'm happy to report that we have enjoyed considerable success in that regard."

Brooke stopped pacing. He was standing before a map of Europe. He stared up at it, his eyes narrowing. "Then came the war." The words were spoken softly, almost wistfully. It was as though Brooke was thinking aloud.

Collecting himself, he continued, "It was my predecessor, Wickham, who took the initiative. He decided it was time to give the French a taste of their own medicine. He proposed that we set up a web of correspondents throughout Europe, using our embassy in Berne as the collecting house for information."

Brooke reached out and ran the flat of his hand over the map's surface. "The intention was not only to gather intelligence about the revolutionaries on their own soil but also to find ways of discrediting them. The best way to do that, he believed, was to initiate contact with royalist sympathizers who'd infiltrated republican organizations in the hope of disabling the régime and restoring the Bourbon monarchy. We were already in league with the royalist government in exile over here, so it made sense for us to continue taking advantage of their expertise. It also helped that Wickham had been appointed our ambassador in Switzerland." The superintendent tapped the map with the end of his forefinger.

"Dangerous work," Hawkwood said, still wondering where all this was leading.

Brooke nodded. "You're not wrong there. Needless to say, the damned Frogs kept putting pressure on the Swiss, with that worm Fouché pulling the strings. In the end, Wickham was forced to resign his post. He did uncommonly well though; managed to last right through until Amiens. He came home when the peace was signed."

Brooke turned. "Nobody believed for a moment that was the end of it, of course. But we went through the motions. Our foreign correspondents were told to stand down, laid to rest if you like, and the office reverted to its domestic role. Wickham's tenure ended and I received my appointment." A thin smile split the aristocratic features. "I dare say some would regard it as the poisoned chalice"

Brooke returned his attention to the map on the wall. "As I was saying: we never for a moment thought it was all over. We knew as soon as Bonaparte appointed himself Consul for life he'd be looking for ways of expanding his damned empire. We heard from our royalist friends that he was already making plans, building up his forces, even as we were putting pen to the treaty. It didn't take a genius to know that we'd be in his sights again. Only one thing for it; we had to rouse our correspondents from their slumbers and put them back into service. While our little corporal plotted to increase his military might, we chose to pursue a more surreptitious approach. You recall what I said about your Chinese general and the hundred ounces of silver?"

"Guile not guns?"

"You have it." Brooke looked pleased that Hawkwood had remembered. "By the time war was re-declared, our correspondents were back in place and in stronger positions than before. They've been active ever since, burrowing their way into the heart of the Empire, like moles in a garden; keeping us abreast of events and Bonaparte's intentions."

Brooke's face grew more serious. "Which brings us to the reason you're here."

Here comes the rub, Hawkwood thought.

"A situation has arisen," Brooke said slowly. "We've received a communication from one of our correspondents which we feel merits serious and immediate attention. It concerns a proposal – I'll call it no more than that – which, if acted upon, could well pave the way towards a cessation of hostilities. Magistrate Read and I have held various discussions on how we should proceed and your name was put forward. You have – how shall I say? – a number of talents that we believe could be relevant to the task."

"Talents?" Hawkwood repeated cautiously. He'd no intention of querying why Brooke should have been consulting with James Read in the first place. Hawkwood was well aware that the Chief Magistrate's responsibilities extended far beyond the confines of a small, dark-panelled office at 4 Bow Street. He'd long since ceased to be surprised at the influence James Read wielded within the serried ranks of the high and mighty.

Though that didn't prevent another warning bell chiming inside his ear. A similar blandishment had been voiced prior to his last assignment, and he hadn't long recovered from that bloody enterprise. James Read's enquiry into his well-being suddenly started to make sense.

"Magistrate Read was kind enough to furnish me with some details of your previous undertakings, in particular the infiltration of the French community on the prison ship *Rapacious*. Most impressive. You posed as an American officer attached to a French infantry regiment."

The job which James Read had termed the *Morgan Affair*. Hawkwood had been sent to investigate the fate of two Royal Navy officers who'd disappeared while trying to infiltrate a British smuggling ring specializing in helping French prisoners of war get back to France. Though there had been a satisfactory conclusion to the assignment, a not inconsiderate amount of blood had been spilt along the way.

Hawkwood said nothing.

Brooke pursed his lips. "Could you not have passed yourself off as a French officer?"

Hawkwood's response was immediate. "No."

Brooke's head came up quickly, indicating it wasn't the answer he'd been seeking. "Why not?"

"Because I'd've had to pretend I couldn't speak English and that would have been impractical."

"How so? I don't follow."

"The alternative would have meant trying to speak English with a French accent, and that would have been stupid and damned near impossible. They'd have been on to me the moment I opened my mouth. It made more sense to pass myself off as an American who could speak French."

"Ah, yes, indeed. I see. Fair point." There was a pause, then Brooke said, "What if there was no *requirement* to speak English? Could you pass yourself off as a French officer, then, do you think?"

"You mean to other Frenchmen?"

"Yes."

"Why?" Hawkwood asked, warily.

"Just humour me," Brooke said. "Yes or no?" Caught in the light from the windows, the superintendent's face was unnaturally still. His raptor eyes were bright. Tiny dust motes tumbled and spiralled above his head.

The small distinct voice buried deep inside Hawkwood's brain came to life again and hissed urgently, *Say no, you damned fool! Say no!*

"Probably," Hawkwood said.

As soon as the word was out of his mouth, he felt the atmosphere in the room change. A nerve trembled along the superintendent's jaw. The reflex was followed by what might have been a sigh. Though, like the last words he thought he had heard pass from James Read's mouth, Hawkwood could well have been mistaken.

"I assume you're about to tell me why that's important," Hawkwood said.

Brooke hesitated and then said, "We require someone to liaise with our correspondent to verify the feasibility of the proposal and, if it is at all viable, to assist in its implementation."

"And that would be me?" Hawkwood said.

"That's why you're here."

"You don't have your own men?" Hawkwood asked.

"Oh, indeed I do, and very capable they are, too, but none of them have quite the qualifications that we're looking for."

"Which would be?"

"Let us say there are certain parameters attached to the enterprise which would require the involvement of someone with a military background. You clearly have proven expertise in that field. You are also fluent in French and you are no stranger to taking on an assumed identity. In short, you are uniquely qualified for this particular . . . assignment."

"You want me to go to France and pass myself off as a French officer?" Hawkwood said.

"As a French citizen, certainly. As to the exact identity you would have to adopt, that has yet to be determined. It would depend on the prevailing circumstances. I'm afraid I cannot be more precise than that. Would you be willing to undertake such a task?"

"You're giving me the option?" Hawkwood asked, surprised.

"Your attachment to this office is at my request but at Magistrate Read's discretion. On that basis, he advised me that, given what befell you the last time you placed yourself in jeopardy, it would be unconscionable of me not to draw attention to the hazards and allow you the opportunity to make up your own mind as to whether you accept the undertaking, or return to your law-enforcement duties. In short, Officer Hawkwood; it will be your decision."

"Based on what?" Hawkwood said.

"I'm sorry?"

"You've hardly told me anything," Hawkwood pointed out. "You've given me no specifics."

Brooke shook his head. "Regrettably, at this juncture, nor can I. There's the grave and overwhelming matter of secrecy. The essence of the assignment is such that it would not be wise to furnish you with all the details in case you're apprehended by the French authorities. Were they to suspect you to be in league with this department, they would not be averse to employing coercion in order to extract information from you. There's always the danger that, no matter how resistant to persuasion you believe

52

yourself to be, you would still reveal our intentions. We cannot afford to take that risk.

"You'll be provided with identity papers and travel documentation and a point of rendezvous from where you'll be taken to meet with our correspondent, who will then familiarize you with the salient details of our . . . deception. All I can tell you at this stage is that this could be of paramount importance with regards to the course of the war. If the plan *is* successful, there is no question that a great number of lives will be saved. Naturally, there is a proviso."

"There is?" Hawkwood said. "Who'd have thought it?"

Brooke ignored the remark. "If you were to be apprehended, this department would deny all knowledge of your existence. You would be on your own and left to your own resources. You comprehend me?"

"I'd say you've made that part of it perfectly clear," Hawkwood said. "How long do I have?"

"How long?" Brooke echoed, puzzled. "I'm sorry, I don't follow."

"To decide."

"Ah, perhaps I didn't make that clear, either. Forgive me. I'd be obliged if you could let me know your decision before you leave this room."

There was an uncomfortable silence before Hawkwood said, "That long? And there I was thinking you'd want to know this very second."

Hawkwood turned and looked at the map.

"So, where is this correspondent of yours? That's another thing you've neglected to tell me."

Brooke followed his gaze. "Is it? That was remiss of me. He's here –" Brooke reached out and stabbed the map with his finger.

And waited.

"Well, there's a coincidence," Hawkwood said softly. "I've always wanted to see Paris."

4

"Well, you were right," Brooke said, raising the coffee cup to his lips. "He's certainly a recalcitrant devil."

"That's been said before," James Read responded wryly.

Brooke took a drink and set his cup down.

"He achieves results," Read said. He took a slow sip from his own cup. "That's the main thing."

"Set a fox to catch a rat, eh?"

"Indeed."

The two men were seated at a table in the first-floor coffee room in White's. They were by the end front window, through which they had an uninterrupted view over the narrow balcony down on to the northern end of St James's Street. There were other club members around them but the tables on either side were unoccupied so both men were able to converse freely without the likelihood of being overheard.

"Y'know it was Sidmouth who first brought me here," Brooke murmured absently as he gazed down the long room. "Just as well he's a Tory. If he'd been a Whig I'd have ended up in that other place, which would have been rather amusing. Mind you, it would probably have guaranteed a decent table for supper." Read acknowledged the remark with a polite smile. He didn't have to look to know that the building being referred to sat almost diagonally across from them on the opposite side of the street. The premises housed a similar retreat called Brooks's.

James Read was a private man and not, as a rule, a patron of gentlemen's establishments. He found them somewhat claustrophobic, though he acknowledged that they did provide a convenient forum in which to conduct business, especially business of a clandestine nature. The staff was uniformly efficient and discreet which, given both Brooke's and Read's professions, was a decided advantage and, despite his cynicism, the dining room could usually be called upon to produce an acceptable bottle of claret and a competent lamb chop at relatively short notice.

"An interesting fellow, though," Brooke said, still musing. "What's his full story? What was he doing before he took the king's shilling? Do you know?"

"I'm not sure I'd consider that relevant," Read said.

"But . . .?" Brooke pressed.

"You know, I was thinking that I may well stay on for luncheon," James Read said, looking off towards the door to the dining room. "I hear the new chef serves a rather fine truffle sauce with the turbot." He dabbed a napkin along his lips.

The superintendent, who was well aware of Read's antipathy towards the surroundings, sighed. "All right, point taken."

Brooke studied Read over the rim of his cup. "You knew he'd accept, though, didn't you?"

"He responds to a challenge," Read said. "It's what drives him."

"There's no family, I take it?"

Read shook his head. "No."

"Mmm, probably just as well, in the circumstances. Not many friends either, I suspect."

"They're few in number, but impressively loyal."

"And demons? I'd hazard a guess he has his fair share."

"Show me a man with twenty years of soldiering who hasn't," Read said.

"And I'll wager those scars could tell a few stories," Brooke said.

Read, refusing to rise to the bait, made no reply.

Brooke smiled, finally accepting defeat.

Both men took another sip of coffee.

"How much did you tell him?" Read asked.

"What we agreed. That we'd provide him with all documentation and a meeting point. After that he . . . they . . . are on their own."

"Can I assume you did not reveal the correspondent's identity?"

"You can. That omission was covered by the need for secrecy."

Read reached for the coffee pot, drew it towards him and proceeded to refill his cup.

"You look . . . worried," Brooke said.

Read put the pot down. "Merely pondering upon their chances of success."

"It sounds as if you've a soft spot for the fellow."

"He's a good officer. He's *my* officer. I don't relish placing any of my men in harm's way if I can help it."

"Well, he's mine now, or at least for the duration. And the opportunity's too good to pass up. We'd be fools if we didn't try to take advantage."

Read tried to quell the feeling of disquiet prompted by Brooke's crass proprietorial comment. "I believe that's what was said the last time this was attempted."

"Ah, but the bugger was in Spain, remember. This time, he's in Russia; not so close to home. It's an entirely different kettle of fish."

"Then let us hope it is to our advantage," Read said. "Have you informed the Prime Minister, by the way?"

Brooke shook his head and used his fingertips to smooth a non-existent bump in the table cloth. "Not as yet."

"Is it your intention to do so?"

"I'm of a mind to keep it between ourselves for the time being," Brooke said. "Given that we're still in the preparatory stages." He favoured Read with an oblique glance. "Unless you have any objections?"

Read shook his head. "Whatever you think is appropriate."

"I think it's for the best," Brooke said. "Besides, there's no requirement for him to be privy to *everything* we do."

"And our *émigré* friends?" Read asked.

Brooke shook his head again.

"Not even the *Comité*? Their collaboration's proved of great benefit to us in the past."

"Indeed it has, and my department is exceedingly grateful, but you can't be too careful. We live in dangerous times. We must exercise caution, even where our so-called allies are concerned."

Composed of *émigrés* drawn from the ranks of former government ministers, senior clergymen and a coterie of aristocrats all loyal to the French crown, the *Comité Français* was effectively the royalist government-in-exile. Its goal was the restoration of the Bourbon monarchy.

"Besides, they've been rather peppery of late," Brooke added.

Brooke was referring to the rift between the heirs to the French throne: the Comte d'Artois and his brother Louis Stanislas. Having fled France in the wake of the Revolution, both were now resident in England. Although Louis was the next in line following the execution of his brother and the death of his nephew while detained in the *Temple* prison, it was the Comte d'Artois to whom the majority of the *émigrés* looked for guidance, a state of affairs that had led to deep mistrust between the two siblings.

"You'd have thought sharing a common foe would have put paid to the damned bickering," Brooke said. "It makes you wonder why we continue to support them. It's costing us a fortune. It'll only take one slip for Parliament to get wind of our special donations and they'll be at our throats. They've been looking for excuses to reduce our funding. If that happens, we're all out of a damned job."

"In that case, we must pray that Hawkwood and . . ." Read paused ". . . your correspondent . . . are successful in their endeavours."

"Indeed," Brooke said. He smiled silkily and raised his cup. "Here's to good fortune."

"When does he embark?" Read asked.

"Tonight," Brooke said. "A private coach is transporting him to Dover. There's a vessel waiting. If the weather's kind to us, he'll sail on the evening tide."

"Then we should pray for calm seas, as well," Read said.

Brooke kept his cup raised.

"Amen to that," he said.

Maddie Teague watched silently from the open doorway as Hawkwood rolled the spare shirts and breeches he had removed from his army chest and laid them on the bed next to a battered valise. The lid of the chest remained propped open. Inside it, a curved sabre lay sheathed atop a dark green tunic. Even though it was folded, it was obvious that the uniform jacket had survived many campaigns and had been repaired innumerable times. Next to the tunic was a pair of grey cavalry breeches and a waist sash the colour of dried ox blood. Below the tunic and breeches lay an officer's greatcoat and under that, partly hidden, was a long bundle wrapped in oilcloth. One end of the oilcloth had worked loose, revealing the polished walnut butt and brass patch-box cover of an army rifle.

"Matthew?" Maddie said softly.

Hawkwood turned.

Maddie lifted her gaze from the contents of the chest. Her eyes held his. "Should I keep the room?"

Hawkwood found himself transfixed by her look.

"It was a jest," she said, though her emerald eyes did not hold much humour.

Maddie was tall and slender. Her auburn hair, pale colouring and high cheekbones hinted at her Celtic roots, while her strength of character could usually be measured by the depth and force of her gaze. On this occasion, however, there was only concern on her face.

She continued to stare at him. "What are you thinking?"

Hawkwood shook his head. "Nothing."

Maddie stepped forward and placed her right hand on his chest. "You're a poor liar, Matthew Hawkwood."

Hawkwood smiled. "I was thinking yes, you should definitely keep the room for me."

Her face softened. She tapped his waistcoat with her closed fist.

"It's my job, Maddie. It's what I do," Hawkwood said.

"I know."

She rested her palm against his cheek. Her hand was cool to the touch.

He thought back to the first time they'd met. It was not long after his return to England from Spain. He'd been in search of a roof over his head and Maddie was the landlady of the Blackbird Inn, with two empty rooms in need of an occupant. The financial arrangement had suited both of them; Maddie in particular. Her husband had been a sea captain and he'd bought the inn to provide an additional source of revenue when he retired. But Captain Teague had perished when his ship had fallen prey to the storm tossed waters of the Andaman Sea, leaving his widow with a string of unpaid bills and a lengthening queue of creditors. Hawkwood's timely arrival had kept the wolves from the door and given Maddie the time she'd needed to turn the Blackbird from a debt-ridden back-alley hostelry into the respectable establishment it had become.

It had taken some months before their business partnership developed into something more; for the trust between landlady and lodger to grow into a bond of friendship, and it had still been a good while after that when Maddie Teague had first visited Hawkwood's bed. Neither of them had ventured to translate feelings into words and yet it had become clear over time that what existed between them had long since transcended the need for mere physical gratification. There had been dalliances along the way, on both sides, and yet the affection and the closeness had endured.

"If you don't hear from me and you need help, go to Nathaniel," Hawkwood said. "You know how to get a message to him?"

She removed her hand and nodded. "Yes."

There was a silence, mirrored by the look in her eyes. "How long should I wait for news?"

"You'll know," Hawkwood said.

She absorbed that. "Does Nathaniel know where you're going?"

"I'm not even sure I do," Hawkwood said.

She lifted her hand again and ran a fingertip along the line of his cheek, below his eye, tracing the scars. "Your wounds have barely healed."

"No rest for the wicked, Maddie," Hawkwood said. "You should know that by now."

Her green eyes flashed. "That's what you said the last time." She stepped back and folded her arms about her, as if warding off a sudden chill. "Just don't expect me to cry myself to sleep. That's all."

Hawkwood had always suspected Maddie Teague was too strong a woman for that, though in truth her comment made him wonder; was she still jesting, or not?

"Curious," Hawkwood said. "That's what I was going to say."

She gave a wan smile and waited as he placed the shirts and breeches in the valise. Sensing her eyes on him, he turned.

"Take care, Matthew," she whispered.

He nodded. "Always."

Maddie lowered her arms and smoothed down her dress. "I'll have Hettie find something in the kitchen for your journey. We don't want you going hungry."

"Perish the thought," Hawkwood said.

She frowned. "Now you're making fun of me."

He shook his head. "I'd never do that."

She gazed at him intently and took a deep breath. Then, without speaking, she leaned forward and kissed him fiercely before turning on her heel and exiting the room.

Leaving Hawkwood to his packing, alone with his thoughts.

There was something eerily familiar about her lines, even by moonlight, and as he drew closer Hawkwood saw why. She was a cutter. The long horizontal bowsprit, the sharply tapering stern and the preposterous size of her rig in proportion to her length and beam were unmistakable. The last time he'd boarded a similar vessel it had been at sea, in the company of Jago and the French privateer, Lasseur, and he'd been fully armed with a pistol and a tomahawk and screaming like a banshee. This time, his arrival was a lot less frenetic.

The journey from London had taken four changes of horses and the best part of the day, so it was late evening when the coach finally made its bone-rattling descent into the town; by which time Hawkwood's throat was dry with dust, while his spine felt as if it had been dislocated by the constant jolting.

Even if it hadn't been for the silhouette of the castle ramparts high above him and the lights clustered at the foot of the dark chalk cliffs, it would have been possible to gauge his proximity to the port purely by the miasma of odours arising from it; the most prominent being smoke, cooking fires and sewage, the unavoidable detritus of closely packed human habitation.

Dover was home to both an ordnance depot and a victualling yard, and keeping the navy armed, watered and fed was clearly a twenty-four-hour operation, if the number of people on the streets – both in uniform and civilian dress – was any indication. The town looked to be wide awake. The public houses in particular, to judge by the knots of men and women weaving unsteadily between them, were still enjoying a brisk trade.

The coachman, clearly adhering to prior instruction, steered the vehicle away from the main part of the town and into a maze of unlit cobbled alleyways leading down towards the outer harbour. After numerous twists and turns, the coach finally drew to a halt and Hawkwood, easing cramped muscles, stepped out on to a darkened quay.

The cutter had the dockside to herself, her tall, tapering mainmast and canvas-furled yards reaching for the moon like winter-stripped branches. Lantern lights were showing above the closed gun ports and Hawkwood spotted shadows moving around the deck. He turned his coat collar up.

The concoction of smells was even stronger here and he guessed they were within spitting distance of the navy supply stores, for the combined aromas of unrendered animal fats, stale fish, offal, baking bread and fermenting hops hung heavily in the night air alongside the more familiar dockyard scents of grease, cordage, tarred rigging and mildewed timbers. Though, he supposed, looking around, it could all have been just an exaggeration of Dover's natural reek.

Noise always seemed magnified at night and the thudding of hammers and rasping of saws floated across the ink-black water from the surrounding jetties. At the same time, from the opposite direction, a stiff breeze was coming off the Channel, carrying with it a soulful requiem of creaking spars and clinking chains from craft moored along the outer harbour walls. To add to the lament, a watch bell clanged mournfully in the darkness.

Behind him, the coachman, satisfied that his passenger had been delivered safely, clicked his tongue and the coach trundled off into the night.

As Hawkwood neared the ship, he noted that the vessel wasn't displaying a man-of-war's standard colour scheme. Instead of the customary buff-painted hull, he saw that all the external timbers, from bowsprit to counter, were as black as coal. As his mind deciphered the significance, a slim, uniformed figure stepped nimbly from the cutter's gangplank.

"Mr . . . Smith?" The speaker touched the brim of his hat. "I'm Lieutenant Stuart. Welcome aboard *Griffin*."

He hadn't taken Brooke all that seriously when the superintendent had given him his boarding instructions. Brooke's explanation for the false name, when he'd seen the sceptical expression unfold across Hawkwood's face, had been that it simplified the process and avoided prevarication. Hawkwood had been tempted to ask Brooke what the procedure was if there was more than one passenger per voyage and then had decided against it. Brooke, he'd suspected, wouldn't have found the enquiry amusing.

As he took in Hawkwood's appearance, the lieutenant's head lifted, revealing more of his features. He looked, Hawkwood thought, disturbingly young to be in charge of his own ship; though as vessels went, Stuart's command was unlikely to see an admiral's pennant fluttering from her masthead any time soon. She was too small and too far down the lists for that.

Nevertheless, from the serious expression on his boyish face it was plain her captain thought no less of her for that.

The lieutenant led the way on board. A second officer, and the only other man Hawkwood could see dressed in uniform, was waiting by the rail.

"Lieutenant Weekes," Stuart said. "My second-in-command."

There wasn't that much difference in their ages, Hawkwood thought. Weekes may have been a year or two older, but that was all. Though it might have been his deep-set eyes and serious expression that made him appear so.

"Sir." Weekes favoured Hawkwood with a brief nod before looking expectantly at his captain.

Stuart obliged. "Prepare for departure, Simon, while I take our passenger below."

"Very good, sir."

As his first officer turned away, Stuart turned to Hawkwood. "Just as well you arrived when you did. The tide's already on the ebb. Another half an hour and we'd need deeper water beneath our keel. We'd've had to anchor her outside the walls and ferry you out in the jolly boat. I don't think you'd have cared much for that." The lieutenant threw Hawkwood an unexpected and surprisingly roguish grin. "I'll show you to your quarters. I apologize in advance; there aren't too many home comforts."

The lieutenant took off his hat to reveal a mop of unruly dark hair, and led the way past the tied-down carronades towards the cutter's stern and an open hatchway. Hawkwood noticed that none of the crew were paying much attention to his arrival. As he followed the lieutenant across the deck, he wondered if that meant they'd become used to passengers embarking in the dead of night.

The lieutenant drew Hawkwood's attention to the top of the ladder. "Watch your step."

Hawkwood, reminded of the last time he'd been below decks, nodded dutifully before following Stuart down the near vertical companionway.

Stuart said over his shoulder, "As you see, it can get a mite cosy at times. We're not rigged to carry passengers. Though we've had our fair share," he added conspiratorially. "Mind your head."

It's still not as bad as a prison hulk, Hawkwood thought, as he ducked below the beam, but he didn't tell Stuart that.

Stuart opened the door to the cabin and stood aside to allow Hawkwood to enter, which he did, shoulders lowered.

"You'll forgive me if I leave you to get settled," Stuart said, remaining by the companionway. "I must return to my station."

Without waiting for an answer the lieutenant, with another hesitant smile, turned and made his way topside. Hawkwood surveyed his quarters.

The lantern-lit space was just about large enough to accommodate the single narrow cot, table and locker. If he'd been of a mind to assume the crucifix position in the middle of the cabin, Hawkwood was quietly confident his palms would have touched the opposing bulkheads. Not that there was much space to stand upright, save for the square of deck immediately beneath the closed skylight. The thought struck him that if there was a cat on board, there'd be precious little room to swing it. The air smelled vaguely of bilge water, candle grease, tobacco and sweat.

Footfalls sounded throughout the ship as the crew made last-minute haste, stowing and making fast all items not required in getting the vessel underway. From somewhere – Hawkwood presumed it was the galley – there came the ringing clatter of a pot falling to the deck, followed by a sharp, one-word obscenity, quickly hushed.

A low call sounded from above and Hawkwood caught the order: "Let go forrard!"

The deck moved beneath him and the light in the cabin dipped as the lantern swung. As he held on to the side of the cot for support, he was reminded, not for the first time, why sea voyages failed to excite him.

And we haven't even left the bloody harbour yet, he thought dismally.

A drawn-out groan came from close by and the hairs on the back of his neck prickled before he realized it was only the rudder turning below the transom on the other side of the bulk-head. Slowly, *Griffin*'s bow began to come around.

Another directive sounded from on high: "Let go aft!"

There were no stern windows in the cutter and thus no means of fixing upon either the horizon or an aligned point in order to counteract the movement of the ship, save for the deckhead lantern which continued to swing gently on its hook as though it had a mind of its own. Hawkwood had the sudden over-whelming desire to feel cool air against his cheek. Leaving his unopened valise on the cot, he left the cabin, closed the door behind him and made his way back up the companionway and on to the deck, in time to see one of the hands hauling in the last few feet of stern line.

Reliant on the momentum of the tide and the helmsman's control of the tiller bar, the cutter continued her gradual revolution. The quayside, Hawkwood noted, looking over the rail, remained dark and empty, unlike the rest of the dockyard where random lights flickered like tiny glow worms. Hawkwood supposed that was why the *Griffin* had had the isolated mooring to herself. So that their departure would go unnoticed.

His gaze travelled beyond the quay, up over the congested, smoke-stained rooftops and on towards the Western Heights, the near vertical rock face that rose behind the port like the encircling tiers of a vast and moonlit amphitheatre.

"Found your sea legs, Mr Smith?" The enquiry came from Lieutenant Stuart, who was standing by his shoulder. "Chances are you'll need them before the night's out."

"You're expecting rough weather?" Hawkwood asked, his heart sinking at the prospect.

Stuart laughed. "It's the English Channel and it's October. What else would I be expecting?"

Hawkwood knew his expression must have reflected what was in his mind for Stuart said immediately, "Don't worry, *Griffin* might not be the youngest or the largest cutter in the fleet, but she'll get us there." Stuart patted the high bulwark affectionately and looked over his shoulder. "You may ready the mains'l, Mr Welland."

"Aye, sir." The acknowledgement came from a burly man with long side whiskers and dark jowls, dressed in a pea jacket and dun-coloured breeches. The ship's bo'sun, Hawkwood guessed. He looked older than his commanding officer, by at least ten years.

"All right, you idle buggers. You heard the lieutenant – stand by. That includes you, Haskins, if you're not *too* busy."

Hawkwood saw the corner of the lieutenant's mouth twitch as the order was relayed.

There had been no raising of the voice, Hawkwood noted, as the crewmen readied themselves, and no tongue lashings. The order – even the aside to seaman Haskins – had been spoken rather than shouted and yet every word had carried the same quiet authority. The tone had been more reminiscent of a schoolmaster coaxing his pupils to open their text books than a hardened warrant officer demanding unconditional obedience. Hawkwood knew that only a man with many years of experience under his belt could draw that amount of respect. It also said a lot for the quality of the cutter's crew that they were anticipating the commands before they were given and were reacting accordingly: with speed and efficiency and in relative silence. There was little doubt that they'd been well drilled.

"Volunteers?" Hawkwood said, taking a guess.

If Stuart thought the question surprising or impertinent he didn't let on. Instead he looked faintly pleased and nodded. "Not a pressed man among them and locals mostly, save for the master. They know these English coastal waters like the backs of their hands. That's not to say there aren't a few former scallywags, but I've no interest in what mischief they might have got up to in their past lives. It's how they conduct themselves on board that matters and, right now, I wouldn't trade a single one of them."

"Including Haskins?"

The lieutenant grinned. "Including Haskins. Not that I'd trust him with my sister, mind you." The grin was replaced by a soft chuckle. "Or my mother, come to that."

Stuart's reply took Hawkwood back to his army days. He'd

commanded soldiers with similar reputations; practitioners of every vice, from gamblers and horse traders to poachers, rustlers, bigamists and thieves, and some blackguards whose exploits would have made a tinker blush, but in a fight, for the honour of the regiment, there were no better men to have at your back. Stuart's comment was proof that the maxim applied to the Royal Navy as well.

Welland's voice cut into his reminiscences. "Hoist mains'l!"

A squeal came from the blocks as the huge four-cornered sail rose from the boom, followed by a sharp crackle of spreading canvas as *Griffin* completed her turn. He looked over the cutter's long running bowsprit towards the entrance to the narrow passage that ran down between the port's north and south piers and linked the inner basin to the harbour mouth.

Stuart turned towards his helmsman. "Steady as you go, Hodges."

Hawkwood felt spray patter against his face. The breeze, forced along the funnel created by the converging pier walls, had found its teeth. The bite was not strong enough to impede the cutter's progress, however. With infinite slowness, *Griffin* continued on towards the twin signal lights that marked each side of the gap in the harbour wall; through which Hawkwood could see only a funereal darkness.

He stared back over the taffrail. There was something strangely comforting in the huddled shapes of the lantern-lit buildings they were leaving behind. He wondered when, or even if, he would see them again.

The cutter's bow lifted; the swell increasing the closer they got to the harbour entrance.

"Stand by fores'l halliard!" Welland's voice again, encouraging, not strident.

Stuart addressed his helmsman once more. "All right, Hodges. Easy on the helm."

"Hoist fores'l!"

Griffin's crew sprang into action.

"Smartly does it, boys! Secure that halliard! Stand by braces!"

Gripping a stanchion to steady himself, Hawkwood watched

the triangular sail unfurl like a great leaf, snap briefly and then continue to draw taut. A tremor ran through the hull. For a brief second the cutter hung suspended upon the uproll and then, like a hound loosened from the slips, she swept forward, out from the harbour mouth and on into the jet black waters of the English Channel.

Bound for France.

5

"There," Stuart said, sounding almost eager and jabbing the chart with the end of his forefinger.

They were in the cramped cabin. The chart was laid across the table, held down by a brace of glass paperweights, a set of dividers and two half-full mugs of scalding coffee, courtesy of *Griffin*'s cook.

Stuart continued. "That's our destination. We'll lay off shore and ferry you in using the jolly boat. There's a small hamlet – Wimereux – not much more than a couple of dozen houses in all, but we've an agent there so you'll be met. We'll be landing to the north of the *ville*. There's a cove, protected by cliffs, and a small headland called La Pointe aux Oies. It's a place we've used before."

Hawkwood stared down at the whorled lines and symbols that looked as though they'd been drawn by a battalion of inebriated spiders. It occurred to him that he was entirely in Lieutenant Stuart's hands and in an environment that was as foreign to him as the far side of the moon, or even the coastline of France, come to think of it; a place he'd only ever seen as a dark smudge on a distant horizon.

"When we're close, we'll hoist French colours," Stuart continued. "We've the advantage in that the Frogs have cutters too, so if they see us it's likely it'll take a while before we're challenged. With luck, we'll be in and out so fast that even if they do have doubts about the cut of our jib, you'll be on your way and we'll be homeward bound before they can do anything."

"What about French ships?" Hawkwood said.

Stuart shook his head. "They're unlikely to give us trouble. The Frogs don't tend to patrol their Channel coast as we do. Their heavy vessels are either based further north, in Flushing, or to the west in their main dockyards at Brest and Rochefort, which give them access to the Atlantic or southwards and the Cape. That's not to say there aren't small fry darting about. The nearest danger will probably be the privateer base at Dunkerque. The others are Saint-Malo and Morlaix. But they're irritants, nothing more. I doubt we'll be bothered. We might spy a free trader or two trying to slip in under cover of darkness, but chances are they'll be more interested in avoiding us than coming closer. The likelihood is they'd take us for a Revenue cutter and steer clear." Stuart sighed. "Not that we haven't had our run-ins with the beggars, mind you. When we're not transporting you fellows to la belle France we lend assistance to the Waterguard. It's what you might call the legitimate part of our business."

Hawkwood wondered what Lasseur would have thought about being described as an irritant.

Stuart hadn't finished. "As you were probably informed, from Wimereux you'll be taken to Boulogne to board the diligence which will convey you to Paris. It'll take you a few days –French coaches ain't the speediest in the world, but they're comfortable enough . . . or so I'm told."

Hawkwood looked at him.

The young lieutenant smiled. "We run passengers both ways."

"Are they called Smith, too?"

"Not all of them," Stuart replied, the corner of his mouth lifting. "We do get the occasional Jones and Brown. Not to mention the odd Jacques and Pierre, when the need arises."

Which, Hawkwood supposed, went some way to answering his question.

"Are you familiar with this part of the coast?" Stuart asked.

Hawkwood shook his head, bracing himself against the cot as the cutter drove down through a trough. "No."

His mind went back four months, to the last time he'd set sail across the Channel, on board Lasseur's ship *Scorpion* in an attempt to intercept the smuggling cutter, *Sea Witch*. The privateer's speed had won the day. *Sea Witch* had been overtaken and boarded fifteen miles from the French port of Gravelines. Fifteen miles; it might as well have been five hundred for all the intelligence it had afforded him.

"By your answer, am I to assume that this is your first, er . . . intervention?" Stuart enquired, somewhat cautiously.

"Intervention?" Hawkwood said. "That's what they're calling it?"

Stuart smiled. "I confess you don't look much like a Smith or a Jones."

"Is that so? And what do *they* look like?"

"Actuaries and lawyers, for the most part."

"And Pierre and Jacques?"

"Frog actuaries and lawyers."

Hawkwood laughed. He couldn't help himself.

"And if I may say so," Stuart said, eyeing the scars on Hawkwood's cheek, "you don't look much like an actuary." No sooner were the words out of his mouth than a look of mortification flooded the lieutenant's face. "My apologies. That was impertinent of me. It is of course no business of mine what your profession might be. I spoke out of turn. I meant no offence."

"None taken," Hawkwood said. "From what I know of actuaries, I should probably be flattered. And you, if I may say so, look too damned young to be the captain of this ship."

Stuart drew himself up. When he spoke the pride was back in his voice. "*Griffin*'s my first command."

"How long?"

"Seven months. I was First Lieutenant on the *Aurora*. I had thought that my next promotion would be to a fourth rater, a third if I was lucky. I did not think I would be given my own ship and that she would be engaged upon special duties."

"Someone once told me that those who seek advancement should be careful what they wish for," Hawkwood said.

Stuart smiled. "I'm familiar with the saying, but I have no

regrets. Indeed, I consider myself most fortunate. I've a sound ship, an able crew and a purpose to my endeavours. What more *could* I wish for?"

Before Hawkwood could respond there was another muted groan from the timbers and the deck listed once again. Both men made a grab for their drinks with one hand and the overhead beam with the other. The attempt was not entirely successful. Recovering his balance, and using his sleeve as a mop, Stuart wiped the chart where liquid had slopped over the rim of his mug.

"I'd settle for fair weather," Hawkwood said. He risked a sip from his own salvaged drink. The liquid was strong and bitter and he could taste coarse coffee grounds at the back of his tongue.

"Ah." Stuart looked almost apologetic. "I'm afraid in that regard, we must place our trust in the Almighty." An expression of sufferance moved across the lieutenant's face. "Though if you want my opinion, I'm not sure the English Channel pays deference to anyone, be they mortal *or* celestial."

Hawkwood tried to ignore the queasy feeling that was beginning to worm its way through his insides. It had been a bad idea to take that last sip of coffee. He wasn't sure eating the plate of cold beef provided by the galley had been a wise move either. He stared again at the chart. Wimereux lay in the Pas de Calais, on France's northern coast. As the crow flew, it didn't look much more than thirty or so miles from Dover, but Hawkwood knew that ships very rarely, if ever, travelled in straight lines. What *Griffin*'s eventual track might be was anyone's guess.

"How long is this likely to take us?"

Stuart hesitated then said, "The Channel's a fickle mistress at the best of times, particularly at night. The wind and tide are her henchmen and we're at their mercy. They can be notoriously cruel . . ."

"So you're telling me there's no way of knowing?" Hawkwood said flatly.

The lieutenant pursed his lips, though he looked for the most

74

part unflustered by Hawkwood's less than ecstatic rejoinder. "The glass is dropping, the wind is increasing and there will be heavy rain before the night's out. Our passage is unlikely to be a smooth one."

"Not good then?" Hawkwood said.

"Nothing we haven't met before," Stuart responded.

Hawkwood wondered if the lieutenant was as confident as he made out. "You expect me to be reassured by that?"

Stuart drained his mug. "Admiralty orders. It's my job to get you there, come Hell *or* high water." He nodded towards the cot. "If I were you, I'd try and get some sleep. There may not be a chance later, if the weather worsens." Swaying in rhythm with the ship, the lieutenant rolled up the chart and headed for the door.

"*If?*" Hawkwood said.

Stuart paused on the threshold and grinned at Hawkwood's jaded expression. "There you go, Mr . . . Smith. I do declare we'll make a seaman of you yet."

A loud crash brought Hawkwood awake. For a brief second, he had no idea where he was and then the cabin tipped to one side and he heard the familiar grinding sound from the rudder behind his ear, and he remembered, and groaned.

He was still on the bloody ship. He'd been awakened by waves pounding against the outside of the hull.

He sat up quickly and held on to the edge of the cot as the deck pitched violently once more. His stomach churned and then steadied. Looking up at the skylight, he watched as spray sluiced across the glass. It was still dark – with little moon from what he could see – which told him that dawn had not yet broken. He could also hear a strange keening sound, which confused him for a moment until he realized it was the wind searching for a path through the ship's rigging.

How long had he slept? He'd no recollection of dozing, no memory of any last-minute tossings and turnings before sleep had overtaken him. It was a measure, he supposed, of how tired he'd been following the journey down from London.

He'd been introduced to more of Stuart's senior officers at the wardroom table; the acting-master, George Tredstow, a stout, ruddy-cheeked Cornishman; Lucas Mendham, *Griffin*'s quarter-master, a broad shouldered, former gunnery captain with a shock of sandy-coloured hair, and the purser, Miles Venner, a fair-skinned, donnish-looking man with startling blue eyes, who looked almost as young as his commander and who doubled as the ship's clerk.

When he'd been introduced as Smith, the pronouncement had drawn subdued nods of welcome as well as, somewhat inevitably, the raising of more than one cynical eyebrow. The conversation had been polite and uninvolving and Hawkwood, accepting that he was the interloper, had expected nothing less. In that regard, *Griffin*'s wardroom was no different to an army mess. The rules of military and naval etiquette dictated that visitors were made welcome, but they would never be regarded as family.

Following dinner and armed with their coffee mugs, Hawkwood and the lieutenant had moved from the wardroom to the cabin, where Stuart had produced the chart and outlined his plan of campaign.

A small stub of candle was still burning. Hawkwood pulled on his boots in the lantern's sickly light. Standing, he reached for his coat. The temperature in the cabin was bearable but he knew it would be a lot colder on deck. As he shrugged the coat on, a large drip from the corner of the skylight splashed on to his sleeve, warning him it was going to be considerably wetter out there, too.

The deck corkscrewed and he swore under his breath. Previous voyages he'd been forced to undertake on military transports came to mind, prominent among them being the passages to South America and Portugal; not one of which could have been described as pleasant. And judging from the creaks and moans coming from within the hull it sounded as if *Griffin* was voicing her own dissent at having to run the gauntlet of a worsening wind and tide.

The clang of a bell sounded from the forecastle. Hawkwood knew it was an indication of the time, but what hour the single note represented he had no idea. He wondered if it signified a change of watch as well. He tried to remember from his limited maritime experience what it might mean. Given that he'd probably managed at least a couple of hours' sleep, it obviously heralded *some* god-forsaken early hour of the morning.

Mindful of his footing, he groped his way from cabin to companionway and emerged on to the cutter's heavily slanted deck, where he was immediately struck by a barrage of cold spray as *Griffin* punched her way into an oncoming roller. Blinking water out of his eyes, he looked aft to where the cutter's young commander was standing, legs apart, steadying himself against the binnacle as he watched *Griffin*'s bowsprit pierce the darkness ahead of them.

Hawkwood glanced heavenwards. There were no stars from what he could see and the moon, hidden behind clouds, was visible only as a wraith-like glimmer high in the ink-black sky.

He lowered his gaze. *Griffin* was running close hauled on a port tack. Her main and foresail were set fore and aft, her long boom braced tight so as to gather as much speed under her keel as the wind would allow. On either side, there was nothing to see except dark, roiling waves tipped with a frenzy of whitecaps that tumbled along the breaking crests like small avalanches. There were no lights visible that might have suggested the existence of other vessels; nor was there any sight of land.

There were perhaps a dozen or so crewmen in evidence, among them Lieutenant Weekes and the bo'sun, Welland. Most, like their commander, were clad in tarpaulin jackets and all looked wet through, some more bedraggled than others. As when he'd first come on board, none of them paid Hawkwood any notice, save for the bo'sun, who rewarded him with a brief nod of recognition.

Hawkwood slithered as the cutter lurched and then recoiled as a huge wave rose high above the starboard bulwark and cascaded in torrents along the steeply canted deck. With the ship leaning hard over he looked towards the lee scuppers and saw that the water was even forcing its way through the gaps around the edges of the sealed gunports.

As *Griffin* rose and then plunged down into yet another watery trench, her commander acknowledged Hawkwood's arrival with a thin-lipped smile. "The glass is dropping fast. There's a storm moving in."

"Can we outrun it?" Hawkwood asked, and saw by the expression on Stuart's face what the answer to that was.

"How far have we come?" Hawkwood asked, trying to steady himself and not let his apprehension show.

"Not far enough. By my reckoning Cap Gris Nez should be about two leagues off our port beam." Stuart swayed and pointed. "Perhaps a little less."

Hawkwood tried to picture the chart in his mind. If *Griffin*'s commander was correct in his calculations they were still some distance from their destination. Though he knew the gesture was useless he looked to where the lieutenant had indicated. All he could see were endless herds of white horses galloping away into the Stygian darkness.

"There's nowhere we can run to?"

The lieutenant shook his head. His face serious, he looked up towards the great spread of canvas suspended above them like a vast Damoclean blade.

A bulky figure materialized from behind the upturned hull of the jolly boat that had been stowed amidships. It was Tredstow, the acting-master.

Rolling with the ship, the Cornishman made his way aft. "Time we came about, Captain."

Stuart nodded. "Very good, Mr Tredstow." The lieutenant, his dark hair ruffling, looked Hawkwood's way. His voice rose in a warning. "Hold on and keep your head low, else you'll lose it to the boom."

Hawkwood looked to the side and saw that a second crew member had joined the man at the tiller bar. Neither of them was the previous incumbent, Hodges, indicating that there had indeed been a change of watch since Hawkwood was last on deck.

Stuart called to his helmsmen. "Bring her up two points!"

"Two points it is, sir!"

The lieutenant turned to his bo'sun. "Mr Welland!"

"Standing by, sir!"

Stuart's hand swept down. "Helm-a-lee!"

Welland yelled, "Let go and haul!"

The helmsmen heaved the tiller over. The cutter's bow lifted. The deck was a confusion of bodies, or so it seemed to Hawkwood as he watched *Griffin*'s crew fight to turn her through the eye of the wind. For a few chaotic seconds the ship yawed as the bow swept round, causing the mainsail to flap like a broken wing, then the whole world tilted in the opposite direction as the boom, braces slackened, catapulted across the deck. Hawkwood ducked instinctively and although the boom was set some way above his head he was shocked at the speed of the manoeuvre. He saw he wasn't the only one taken unawares. Caught off guard, two crewmen also lost their footing. Soaked, jackets and breeches plastered to their bodies and looking faintly embarrassed, they clambered to their feet from the scuppers where they had fallen, still holding on to their ropes.

The ship slewed violently.

Stuart yelled at his helmsmen: "Hold her! Hold her!"

Hawkwood hung on grimly. As the bow came up and the mainsail was sheeted home, he straightened, bit back the sour taste that had surfaced at the back of his throat, and found he was sweating profusely beneath the coating of spindrift.

"How was that, Mr Smith?" The lieutenant, one hand thrust into his jacket pocket, the other still attached to the binnacle, gave one of his trademark grins, though Hawkwood thought it might have been a little forced. "Bracing enough for you?"

At that instant a white-hot bolt of lightning shot across the cutter's starboard bow. In the space of a heartbeat night became day, followed a split second later by a colossal thunderclap that sounded as if the entire sky had split asunder.

Several of the cutter's crew flinched; some ducked as though expecting an enemy broadside.

"Lord save us!" Tredstow exclaimed loudly. He stared heavenwards.

Hawkwood wasn't certain if it was the reflection from the

lightning that had turned the lieutenant's face pale or if the blood had drained away of its own accord.

Griffin's commander found his voice. His jaw tightened as he said hollowly, "It would seem the storm's a lot closer than I'd thought."

A profanity hovered at the tip of Hawkwood's tongue. He swallowed it back quickly and let out his breath.

"Which places us in a dilemma . . ." Stuart continued. "We've still a fair distance to cover. In clement weather I'd raise more canvas, but with the storm upon us, I can't risk it. I've no option but to reduce sail. We'll do our best but it could be that our only option is to try and ride it out."

The words had barely been uttered when the rain began to lance down.

It shouldn't have come as a shock. Its arrival had been prophesied only a few hours before, but the sheer force of it took every man by surprise.

God really does have a sense of humour, Hawkwood reflected bleakly, as icy needles rattled against his face and shoulders with the force of grape shot.

"At least it'll keep the Frogs at bay," Stuart said, grimacing at the sudden inundation. "If they've any sense, they'll still be a-bed."

Which is where I should bloody well be, Hawkwood thought. *On dry land, if possible.*

"Perhaps you'd rather go below?" Stuart offered.

Hawkwood suspected that the lieutenant had made the suggestion not so much to keep him out of harm's way as to prevent his one and only passenger from getting under everyone's feet and jeopardizing the safety of the ship.

The prospect of returning to the cabin's claustrophobic interior held little appeal. The combination of the ship's gyrations and the odours below deck would more than likely result in him spewing his guts out the minute he lay down. Retreat, he decided, was not an option.

He shook his head. "If it's all right with you, Captain, I think I'd prefer to remain upright."

At first, Hawkwood thought the lieutenant was about to deny

him the choice, but his feelings must have been evident in his expression for *Griffin*'s commander merely nodded. "Very well. In that case, I'd be obliged if you'd keep your movement about the deck to a minimum. We don't want any accidents." The lieutenant's gaze shifted. "Stand by to reduce sail, Mr Welland, if you please!"

"Aye, sir!" Welland raised a hand in acknowledgement. From the speed of the response, it was clear the bo'sun had been waiting for such a signal. He yelled across the deck: "Stand by fores'l!" He turned and eyed his lieutenant expectantly.

Stuart nodded. "Now, Mr Welland!"

The bo'sun's face streamed with spray. He turned back towards the men waiting by the ropes. "Take in fores'l!"

Blocks squealed like stuck pigs as the jib and bowsprit were hauled in. Hawkwood marvelled at the men's skill. He stared up at the mast and yards and the huge mainsail and the spider's web of rigging and pulleys radiating from them. It was a miracle, he thought, how anyone could tell one rope from another. Nautical jargon had never failed to confuse him, nor, if he were honest, had it held much allure. It was a language as foreign as any he'd encountered during his long army service.

And yet, he wondered, would it be any different for a sailor who found himself marooned on a battlefield? Was army slang any more intelligible to the uninitiated? Probably not, he decided. And, be he sailor or sapper, so long as every man knew what he was doing, what did it matter?

Hawkwood became aware that someone was leaning towards him. It was Tredstow. Water coursed in shiny rivulets down the seaman's grizzled cheeks. He put his lips close to Hawkwood's ear, while a hand gripped Hawkwood's arm like a steel claw. "I were you, I'd hang on tight. This 'un's going to be a right cow!"

Hawkwood had once been told that on clear days, depending on the location, it was possible to stand on an English clifftop and view the other side of the Channel. Sometimes, it was said, France looked close enough to touch.

Had he first heard that from one of *Griffin*'s crew, he'd have considered the man at worst a liar, at best an imbecile. Cloaked in darkness and dwarfed on every side by waves almost as high as the cutter's main yard, the prospect of an imminent landfall looked an unlikely prospect. For all the headway she was making, *Griffin* might as well have been not two leagues from France but two hundred. But she was trying her best to get there.

Cutters, Hawkwood knew, were built for speed. It made them ideal for patrols and the carrying of dispatches. He did not know, however, how many men it took to crew one. If pushed, he'd have hazarded a guess and estimated about forty. From what he could see, every man jack of them appeared to be topside, including, he supposed, Purser Venner, though it wasn't easy to make out features in the tumult and the darkness. Either way, every spare inch of decking looked to be occupied, with the men at their stations, ready to defend the ship against the elements; which they were doing, heroically.

From the moment of its opening salvo the storm had raged without let-up, increasing in strength with each passing minute. Under the relentless assault from wind, rain and waves the deck had become as treacherous as an ice sheet. All hatches had been battened down and it would have been a foolish man who tried to make his way from bow to stern unaided, so safety lines had been rigged, running fore and aft. With a dark and angry sea only too eager to ensnare its first victim, the men of the *Griffin* were clinging on for dear life.

Hawkwood knew that in the running of the ship he was no more than excess cargo. The knowledge didn't sit well. He'd never been comfortable with the role of spectator. It was one thing to relinquish all responsibility for transporting him to his destination to the lieutenant, but to entrust his safety to another party made him distinctly uneasy. He needed to be doing *something*.

So he'd put his proposal directly to *Griffin*'s commander.

"I'm a spare body, Captain. Put me to work."

The lieutenant had been about to dismiss Hawkwood's offer out of hand but then, as before, the look on his passenger's face had made him pause. After an exchange of meaningful looks with his second-in-command, he'd nodded, turning quickly to his two helmsmen.

"Fitch! You've a new volunteer! Bates, you're relieved! Report to Mr Welland for new duties! Before you do, find Mr Smith a tarpaulin jacket." To Hawkwood, he said, "It'll be less cumbersome than that riding coat you're wearing." Adding, "Please do exactly as Fitch tells you. No more, no less. Is that clear? Anything happens to you, they'll have my innards for garters!"

"He yells *pull*, I pull," Hawkwood said.

Stuart nodded. "You have it. Tell me, Mr Smith, do you know your opera?"

Hawkwood stared at him.

"'Heart of oak are our ships . . .?' It's something my father used to sing to me. I suspect we're about to discover if the words hold true. Bates! Hurry up with that damned coat!"

The moment the helmsman, Fitch, moved along, allowing him room to grasp the tiller bar, Hawkwood discovered why it was a two-man job. Above him, *Griffin*'s mainsail still stretched between gaff and boom but under the lieutenant's orders the sail had been reefed in tight, leaving just enough canvas aloft to enable the helmsmen to preserve some semblance of authority. Trying to maintain steerage-way, however, was like wrestling a bucking mule. It felt to Hawkwood as if his arms were being torn from their sockets. There was only one course of action: hang on, obey Fitch's directions as best he could, and trust to salvation.

In times of adversity he'd often wondered whether death might not be some sort of merciful release. Inevitably, the feeling had always dissipated, but every now and then a new situation would arise when the notion reared its ugly head. This night was fast turning into one of them.

Fighting in the Spanish mountains, he'd known cold and rain, but nothing like this. The wind force hadn't lessened either. If anything, it had escalated substantially, causing them to tack more times than Hawkwood could remember, with the inevitable drenching results. Despite the tarpaulin jacket, he'd never been so wretchedly wet in his entire life. Spray or rain, it made no difference. His hands were numb; he could hardly feel the ends of his fingers. He'd also lost all sense of time. The passing of the hours had become irrelevant. All that mattered was survival.

The sense of dread rose in his chest as, yet again, the cutter's bow disappeared beneath another enormous wave. As the mass of water exploded over the forecastle it looked for one terrible moment as though the end of the shortened bowsprit had been sheared away. But then, ponderously, *Griffin* began to rise. At first, it was as though the sea was refusing to relinquish its grip until, with a supreme effort, she broke free, thrusting herself into the air like a breaching whale, the water running in gleaming cataracts from her forward rigging. Her bow continued to climb until it seemed she would fall back upon herself, such was the steep angle of her ascent. Finally reaching the vertex, *Griffin* hovered, but only for a moment before gravity took hold once more, drawing her back down into the seething well below.

The hull shuddered under the impact. A vivid streak of lightning zig-zagged across the sky. It was followed by another massive rumble directly overhead. As the echoes died away, it struck Hawkwood that if there was such a thing as the voice of God, it would probably sound a lot like that last roll of thunder.

And if thunder was a vocal manifestation of the Almighty's wrath then the howling of the wind had to represent the grief of ten thousand souls trapped in purgatory. Which was why Hawkwood missed the warning shout. The first he knew something untoward had happened was when he saw a knot of seamen break apart as if a grenade had been tossed into their midst.

He heard Fitch bellow, "Keep hold, God damn it!" and as he hung on to the tiller he watched helplessly as the carronade broke free from its cradle and 10 cwt of cast-iron ordnance careered towards the lee bulwark, shedding slivers of twisted eyebolt from the damaged carriage in its wake, along with threads of pared cordage that were left whipping to and fro across the deck like decapitated sea serpents.

Gathering momentum, the carronade headed for the port

scuppers, trailing mayhem as the more quick thinking among *Griffin*'s crewmen tried to grab on to the pieces of rope still attached to the metal barrel. The slippery conditions proved too much for them, however, and they found themselves dragged along by the weight, while others scrambled aside, slipping and sliding on the water-soaked planking, some falling full length as they tried to get out of the way. The sound of the carronade hitting the bulwark was loud enough to be heard over the storm. As was the scream.

The bulwark absorbed the brunt of the collision, the remainder was borne by the one crew member who'd been unable to scramble clear in time. Sent sprawling, he'd only been able to watch, paralysed with fright, as the heavy metal cylinder hurtled towards him. As the carronade hit the raised side of the ship it tipped, trapping the seaman beneath it, crushing his chest and shoulders and shattering his ribs and pelvis into matchwood.

It took eight men under the guidance of Lieutenant Weekes to pull the wreckage free and drag the body to one side, but by then it was too late. The crewman was beyond help. Even as they strove to gather up the corpse the rain and seawater were already rinsing the blood from the scuppers.

As the debris was cleared away and the dead man was carried below, Fitch turned and glared at Hawkwood over his shoulder. Despite the water teeming down the coarse face, there was no hiding the anger in the helmsman's eyes. "By Christ, I hope you're worth the bloody trouble!"

Hawkwood kept silent. There was nothing to be gained by responding to Fitch's outburst. Had he been in the helmsman's position he'd probably have come close to voicing the same sentiment and if he hadn't put it into words, he'd likely have thought it. Seafaring men, much more than soldiers, were prone to superstition. Any break with routine that resulted in catastrophe was likely to be deemed portentous by the less rational members of a close-knit crew. He suspected the men of the *Griffin* were no different in that regard. They'd now lost one of their own and despite the death occurring while the ship was effectively on a war footing, it wasn't beyond the bounds of possibility that given the absence of both women and albatrosses, they'd place the blame for the freak accident squarely on the presence of a stranger. Which, Hawkwood supposed, was true, indirectly, though he'd had no personal hand in the man's death. But suspicious minds had a habit of creating their own twisted brand of logic. The diplomatic thing to do, therefore, was remain silent, let Fitch vent his spleen and pray they didn't lose anybody else.

For the storm showed no signs of weakening; unlike the cutter's crew who, bruised and battered by the ordeal, were growing ever more weary.

Hawkwood wasn't a religious man. Had he been, he might well have regarded the struggle being waged about him as some sort of fitting parable in which a gallant David was battling the storm's fearsome Goliath. But *Griffin* was no David. There was no sling and no stone. Here, Goliath was in the ascendancy.

The wind had forestalled all efforts to gain headway. For *Griffin*'s crew, there was only one priority: to try and stay afloat. So far they were succeeding, but only just.

Then another spectacular streak of lightning stabbed across the sky, ripping the heavens in two and revealing, in that moment of incandescence, a dark shadowy mass, rising like a behemoth from the waters, less than a cable's length off *Griffin*'s larboard beam.

Griffin's commander turned with a stricken look on his face. "PORT HELM!"

Fitch gasped. Eyes wide with shock, his voice rose in a scream. "Pull! For the love of God, pull!"

The sighting had been so sudden and so fleeting that Hawkwood wondered if his eyes had deceived him, but the lieutenant's warning, allied to Fitch's frantic cry and the expressions on the faces of the men about him, confirmed that it was not some mythical sea beast that he'd seen rising half hidden behind the moving curtain of rain but the dark unbroken line of a sheer cliff face and waves exploding on to a rock-strewn foreshore beneath it.

There was no time to think; no time to reflect on the power

of the storm or how it had managed to drive *Griffin* so close to land; no time for recriminations against an error of navigation, if such was the case. There was only raw panic.

Fitch threw himself against the helm like a man possessed, leaving Hawkwood no option but to dig his heels into the deck and follow suit. As spray burst over *Griffin*'s weather side and stampeded in glistening shards along the deck, Hawkwood knew that even with their combined strength bearing down, it was unlikely the two of them would be able to hold the ship steady. The pressure of the sea against hull and rudder was just too strong.

He was suddenly aware of a tarpaulin-jacketed figure clawing his way towards them. It was the quartermaster, Mendham. Thrusting himself between Hawkwood and Fitch, he clamped his hands around the helm.

Feet scrabbling, the three men hauled back on the tiller. Hawkwood glanced up towards the mast. It was vibrating like a bow stave and looked ready to snap.

But slowly and sluggishly, *Griffin* began to come round.

Only for her prow to rise, swept up by the sheer power of the water beneath her hull.

"Pull, y'buggers!" Mendham yelled. "Pu—!"

And almost as quickly, she was falling away again. The quartermaster's voice was drowned out as *Griffin* plummeted once more into the abyss. As the sea smashed over the drift rail, the lee scuppers vanished under a rampaging tide of foam and swirling black water that raced along the deck, sweeping all before it. Hawkwood's boots began to slide. He saw that a good number of the crew had been left floundering as their legs were taken from beneath them. Most were struggling to their feet. Others had found a stanchion or a stay to cling to, while a few fortunate ones were grabbed by their shipmates and pulled to safety.

But, momentarily, resistance against the rudder eased.

The other two felt it at the same time.

"Now!" Fitch yelled hoarsely. "Put your backs into it!"

Led by Fitch, Hawkwood and the quartermaster redoubled their efforts. Gradually, the starboard bulwark began to drop.

Griffin was answering! Hawkwood sensed the cutter was returning to an even keel. Relief surged through him.

And then he looked out beyond the bow and a fist closed around his heart.

Mendham followed his gaze. The quartermaster's face sagged. "Oh, sweet Jesus."

Hawkwood's first thought was that some callous twist of fate had inadvertently caused them to turn the ship completely about, and that it was the same stretch of cliff he could see, lying in wait at the edge of the darkness. Disconcerting enough in itself, until he saw that the top of the cliff was in motion and growing in height and width and he realized to his horror that it was a wave, a huge black wave, far larger than anything that had gone before, and that it was bearing down upon them and gathering speed at an astonishing rate. He felt his insides contract.

For *Griffin* was still partially beam on and there was no time to turn her into the approaching threat. Fitch yelled again. Hawkwood didn't catch the words; they were borne away by the shriek of the wind. He saw *Griffin*'s commander staring over the rail, head lifting as he took in the full significance of what he was seeing. The lieutenant spun round.

It was too late for a warning.

There was an awful inevitability in the way the mountainous wall of water was racing towards them; devouring everything in its path, like some ancient malevolence, risen from the deep to spread chaos upon the world. As Hawkwood watched, a skein of frothing whitecaps appeared, like pale riders cresting the brow of a hill; tentatively at first but then, as if gaining in confidence, they began to spread out across the wave's rapidly swelling summit. It was, Hawkwood thought, like staring into a boiling cauldron. With her weather side exposed to the full might of the converging sea, *Griffin* stood no chance.

The wave broke across her with devastating force. The starboard bulwark vanished, swamped beneath the deluge which splintered the topsail yard like a twig, tore the gaff from its mountings, the forward hatch cover from its runners and more than a dozen crewmen from their stations. Their cries were cut short as the remains of the mainsail collapsed around them, sweeping them over the port bulwark and into the sea in a welter of spiralling limbs, broken spars and flayed canvas.

The force of the water wrenched the tiller from Hawkwood's hands. He tried to grab on to it but there was nothing beneath his feet to give him purchase and it sprang out of his grasp as if on a coiled spring. The world became a maelstrom of sound and fury. He sensed rather than saw Fitch and Mendham being flung aside and then everything went dark. Bracing himself, he felt a stunning blow as his spine collided with the corner of the binnacle. Pain shot through him.

The backwash had barely receded before the sea crashed over them once more. The crewmen who'd survived the initial cataclysmic onslaught were given no chance to recover. All had tried to wrap themselves around what they had hoped were secure fixtures. The stronger ones hung on grimly only to see their more exhausted companions plucked from safety and into oblivion like sodden rag dolls.

Hawkwood, still dazed and smarting from his encounter with the compass box, was unprepared for the impact. Sent careening across the deck like an empty keg trapped in a mill race, he was finally brought up short at the base of the mast. Spluttering and coughing, tangled within a cat's cradle of torn rigging and waterlogged canvas, he felt something grab his arm – a disembodied hand – and saw, through a blur of agony, that it was the helmsman, Fitch. The look in the seaman's eyes as the reflux bore him away was one of abject terror.

The ship gave another violent lurch. A terrible rending sound came from deep within the hull as *Griffin* was slammed on to her larboard beam and Hawkwood, still coughing, found himself dislodged and adrift once more. He grabbed for the main hatchway grating and missed, then saw a strand of rope – one of the safety lines – and made a desperate lunge towards it, just as the port bulwark submerged. A strained voice yelled frantically from close by, "She's going!" and before Hawkwood could advance his hold, the line jackknifed from his clutches. His link with the ship severed and with the cutter's deck at a near vertical incline and still rotating, there was nothing he could do, except fall.

He was wet already, but the coldness of the water drove the rest of the air from his lungs as effectively as a mule kick. As the weight of his tarpaulin jacket dragged him beneath the waves, his last comfortless thought was that he hadn't expected it to end like *this*.

6

Cannon fire; no doubt about it.

Howitzers, from the sound of them, or maybe six-pounders. Whatever they were, they were clearly raining hell down on some poor devils. Though he could tell they were a fair distance away; a couple of miles at least, perhaps more.

He lifted his head slowly and opened his eyes.

And wasn't sure whether to be disappointed or relieved when he saw that it wasn't cannon fire that he'd heard. No six-pounders or howitzers; in fact there was no artillery of any description. There was only the surf crashing on to the beach behind him, loud enough to wake if not the dead then certainly any half-drowned, shipwrecked soul who happened to be within earshot.

He remained prone, taking stock while his head cleared. There was daylight, and he was alive. For the moment, that was all he needed to know. Cautiously, he tried flexing his arms and legs. To his relief, all four limbs appeared to be in full working order, which had to be another kind of miracle, though there was enough residual pain in the small of his back to make him wince and think twice about making any sudden movements. There was blood, too, he saw, where his skin had been scraped down the inside of his forearms, which struck him as odd. The side of his skull was sore to the touch, as well. He flinched when his fingertips hit a tender spot beneath his hairline.

He continued the examination of his other aches and pains.

Further probing confirmed he had no major injuries. Finally confident that he could get to his feet without falling over, he took a deep breath and pushed himself up. It still took a while. The involuntary coughing fit was a hindrance, though it did help to clear his lungs, as did the retching. When there was nothing left to expel, he straightened and looked about him.

A narrow, rock-strewn foreshore rose gently towards the foot of a sandy-coloured and heavily eroded cliff face. The beach wasn't long, no more than a couple of hundred paces in length. A jumble of boulders littered the edge of the water at either end. He could see dunes and clumps of tussock grass in the distance where the cliffs flattened out. There were no signs of human habitation.

He spat out another clod of mucus and turned. The sea was a uniform grey and still rough, with high waves and strong swells, but the heart of the storm had moved eastwards leaving behind a grainy sky filled with dark, scudding clouds. There was no sign of the ship; an observation which afforded him neither surprise nor comfort. He shivered, not so much from his damp clothing but from a memory of the cutter's final death throes.

An object lying a few yards away drew his attention. It was *Griffin*'s forward hatch cover. Hawkwood stared down at it. Proof, he thought, that saviours, whether by accident or divine intervention, came in all shapes and sizes. He realized the contusions along his arms had to be the result of his skin chafing against the wooden battens.

His mind went back to the panic that had gripped him as he fell and the terror that had turned his bowels to gruel when he entered the water, knowing without a shadow of a doubt that the next few minutes were to be his last.

It was the coldness of the water that had shocked him the most; the bone-numbing, blood-freezing chill that had him gasping for breath within seconds. Though there had been enough cohesive thought filtering through his brain for him to know that he had to rid himself of the tarpaulin coat. It's weight had been pulling him down and shedding the thing hadn't been easy, with the mast, shorn of its main yard and looming over him like an uprooted tree and the hull about to capsize at any second, not to mention he'd ingested enough sea water to float a frigate. But, somehow, he'd managed it, summoning a reserve of strength he hadn't known he possessed, only to find himself at a distance from the ship that made retrieval impossible.

With every feeble thrash of his arms widening the gap between hope and despair, he'd almost been on the point of surrendering to the inevitable when the hatch grating that had been ripped away by the first rogue wave struck him a heavy blow on his right shoulder and he'd reached for it, knowing it was the only chance he had of remaining afloat. It was after he'd pulled himself on to it that things had become hazy.

Fortune, he'd heard, favoured the bold. It seemed it favoured the lucky, too. The circumstances that had almost driven the cutter on to the rocks, causing the crew to take evasive and disastrous action, had, in the end, been the saving of him. Had *Griffin* been struck further from land, Hawkwood knew he wouldn't have been carried ashore; he'd be dead.

Though where he'd ended up was anyone's guess. He looked towards the south. The land sloped more quickly in that direction. Knowing his first priority was to get off the beach, he set off, stumbling on the uneven surface, ignoring the hurt, shaking and windmilling his arms in an attempt to generate warmth. It occurred to him that anyone looking on from afar would probably take him for a complete half-wit; in other words, someone worth avoiding. He windmilled harder.

He'd travelled less than a hundred paces when he came upon the first body. It lay face down in a shallow tidal pool, at the base of one of the large boulders he'd seen earlier. He splashed his way towards it, causing small crabs to scuttle for cover.

Squatting, Hawkwood turned the body over. It wasn't easy. The dead were never cooperative and his fingers were cold and when he saw the state of the face he wished he hadn't bothered. The waves and the rocks had inflicted a lot of damage and sea creatures had already taken full advantage of a free meal. Hawkwood doubted the man's own mother would have known him. Though she might have recognized the tattoos on the left forearm; a Union Jack and an anchor, under which was inscribed the word: *Dido*. The name of a ship, Hawkwood presumed, rather than a wife or sweetheart.

Despite the discrepancy, it was safe to assume this had to have been one of *Griffin*'s crew. He thought about the forty or so men that had made up the ship's complement and looked to where the sea was pounding relentlessly against the edge of the rocks. Rising to his feet, still shivering, he scanned the broken shoreline.

The second body lay about fifty paces from the first, though he nearly missed seeing it. The black tarpaulin coat merged closely with the surroundings and, even as he drew near, Hawkwood thought it looked more like a dead seal than a man. It, too, rested face down. He hesitated before raising the head and was relieved to see that this one hadn't taken as much of a battering as the first, though the lips and eyes showed clear evidence of nibbling from teeth and claw. There were enough of the features left to aid recognition but as Hawkwood hadn't been introduced to the cutter's entire crew, despite there being something vaguely familiar about the face, he wasn't able to put a name to it.

With some difficulty he removed the coat. He felt no guilt at doing so. The dead man had no use for it and, though it had received a soaking it would help provide extra insulation on top of his shirt and waistcoat.

He was about to get up when he saw the remains of the boat. A stempost and four feet of splintered bow lay several feet away, wedged among the seaweed-encrusted rocks like shattered pieces of discarded bone. There were no markings to suggest what ship they might have come from. He looked around for more wreckage but couldn't see anything and he knew it was probably pointless to continue the search. In any case, it was time to move on. Still finding his feet, he made his way back to the beach.

He looked up at the cliff face. The worn parts of it looked soft and crumbly. There had been recent slippage, he saw, which suggested that a good many of the boulders he was skirting were the results of landslides. Emerging from the debris, he placed that thought firmly at the back of his mind and headed for the dunes.

A distant, low-hanging smudge drew his gaze. Drifting wood smoke; which meant a dwelling of some sort, but the contours obscured his view so whether it was evidence of a village or town or a single isolated abode, it was too far away to tell. By-passing the place and proceeding on his way was one of the options open to him, but when he thought about it, that idea didn't make much sense. Where was he proceeding to? Far better to find out where he was and then determine his next move. And the only way to accomplish that was either look for a convenient signpost, or ask somebody.

That was when he heard the groan.

He stopped dead and listened, his skin prickling. The noise came again, from close by; a low exhalation, as if someone was in pain. He turned towards the source and saw movement; a dark shape slinking behind a bank of grass close to the entrance of what looked to be a narrow gulley running between two dunes. There was something else, too, leading away from the gulley back towards the sea; shallow and uneven depressions in the sand; scuff marks, as if an animal had dragged its way ashore.

God's blood! Hawkwood thought.

He moved swiftly and silently, keeping low, knowing it was still a risk, but driven by a feeling of expectation that was impossible to ignore. The hairs rose along the back of his neck when he saw the black jacket and the hunched shoulders of the figure that was trying desperately to burrow itself into concealment.

Sensing imminent discovery the figure stopped moving, but only for a second and not before Hawkwood had seen that it was favouring its left arm. As fear overcame caution, the prone man suddenly tried to rise and run, but the effort proved too much and he stumbled and fell to his knees, chest heaving. Hawkwood stepped forward. The man turned and looked up over his shoulder, resignation on his pale, pain-streaked face, which expanded into shock when Hawkwood said evenly, "Going somewhere, Lieutenant?"

He knelt quickly, just in time to allow *Griffin*'s commander to collapse into his arms.

There were livid bruises and abrasions on Stuart's cheeks and forehead. His clothes were damp and encrusted with sand. He stared up at Hawkwood as if he couldn't believe what he was seeing. "Good God, you're alive!" he breathed hoarsely.

"I could say the same to you," Hawkwood said, cradling the lieutenant's shoulders. "Can you sit up?"

Stuart nodded. With his back propped against a stout tuft of grass, he swallowed and coughed. When he'd recovered, he stared at Hawkwood. "I still don't believe it! We launched the boat but when we couldn't find you, we thought you'd perished." He cleared his throat again and with an expression of distaste wiped a loop of spittle from his chin.

Hawkwood looked at the lieutenant in amazement. "The bloody ship was turning turtle! How in God's name were you able to launch the boat?"

To Hawkwood's further astonishment, Stuart shook his head, wincing as he did so. "She didn't sink." And from somewhere, a wry smile appeared. "I told you she was a sound ship. It'd take more than last night's blow to break her. *Griffin* lives to fight again." Suddenly, the smile fell away, replaced by an expression of acute sorrow. "Though the cost was far greater than I would have imagined."

"How many did you lose?" Hawkwood asked, thinking about the difficulties the crew must have endured just trying to get the boat into the water, let alone conducting a search in waves as high as a three-storeyed house.

The lieutenant hesitated and then said with despair in his voice, "Fifteen, including Marlow and Sheldrake."

"The men in the jolly boat?"

Stuart looked at him, his brow furrowing. "How . . .?"

"I found their bodies," Hawkwood explained.

The sadness remained etched on Stuart's bruised face. His jaw tightened. "They were good men. When I asked for volunteers they were the first to step forward. But the waves proved too much for us. They carried us ashore but the boat foundered on the rocks. We were cast into the water and separated."

Another of the Almighty's cruel japes, Hawkwood thought bitterly. It had been the jolly boat, built for purpose, that had fallen victim to the fierce and unforgiving sea while he'd been transported to safety on what had amounted to little more than a piece of driftwood. He recalled Fitch and the wrath in the helmsman's face when he'd voided his anger in the midst of the storm. Hawkwood hadn't even reached his destination and already the mission had cost the lives of fifteen men.

Stuart emitted a grunt of discomfort as he shifted position. He continued holding his left arm close to his chest.

"Let me take a look at that," Hawkwood offered.

It didn't take a moment to confirm the arm wasn't broken but the lieutenant's wrist was badly sprained.

"We should get off the beach and find shelter," Hawkwood said.

Stuart nodded and Hawkwood helped him to his feet. When they were both standing, he found that Stuart was gazing at him. Sorrow had been replaced by a kind of weary amusement. "What is it?"

"I was thinking it's true: the Lord *does* work in mysterious ways."

"How so?"

"We're alive when we've no right to be."

"You sound disappointed."

"On the contrary, I'm exceedingly grateful. I'll make a point of telling Him so when we do finally meet."

Hawkwood smiled. "Paradise over purgatory? You're that certain you'll be going up, not down?"

Stuart returned the smile with a tentative one of his own. "Well, if I wasn't sure of it before, I am now. Why else would He have chosen to save a poor sinner?"

"You've a theory, I take it?" Hawkwood said drily.

The lieutenant tilted his head and threw Hawkwood a speculative look. "Perhaps we've been delivered for a reason. Did it ever occur to you that you may have been put on this earth to serve a higher purpose?"

"Every God-damned day," Hawkwood said, wondering if Stuart had expected him to give the enquiry serious consideration. "But I've learned to live with it. Now let's get off this bloody beach, shall we?"

The lieutenant nodded firmly. "An excellent suggestion."

"By the way," Hawkwood said, tugging on the coat he'd taken from the dead seaman. "Where's the ship? You never said."

"I instructed Lieutenant Weekes to ride out the storm as best he could and if possible lay three miles off the point, out of sight and range of the shore battery."

"Shore battery?" Hawkwood paused, the coat half-on and half-off his shoulder.

"Fort Mahon." Stuart nodded towards the northern end of the line of cliffs. "At Ambleteuse, the next town up the coast. The fort guards the town and the mouth of the Selaque River. It was due to be one of Boney's embarkation depots when he was planning his invasion back in '05. Turned out that wasn't such a good idea. There's too much silt. It makes navigation a bugger. The winds along this coast don't help either, as we found out. The garrison's been reduced since then; reassigned to other districts. Now it's us who're doing the invading. There's a kind of justice there, don't you think?"

Hawkwood didn't respond to that. The history of the place didn't interest him. It wasn't as if he was taking the Grand Tour. However, the proximity of a fort *and* a shore battery, irrespective of troop numbers, was relevant only in as much as it called for one thing: a rapid departure. He pulled the rest of the coat on and secured it. It was heavy and damp and a dry coat would have been far preferable, but the tarpaulin was still a welcome protection against the snappy sea breeze.

"*Griffin* will rendezvous later this evening and pick me up," Stuart added.

Hawkwood gave him a sceptical look. "Your jolly boat's wrecked. How do you propose to get out to her? Swim? I wouldn't recommend it."

Stuart shook his head. "Our agents will provide the necessary assistance. As fortune would have it, we've landed remarkably close to our intended destination. Wimereux's not much more than a mile or so yonder." Stuart indicated in the direction of the smoke, still visible beneath the overcast sky. "We should make our way there with all dispatch. The Frogs might not be too conscientious when it comes to maintaining seaborne surveillance of their coastline but they've an annoying tendency to send out shore patrols, so it doesn't pay to be too conspicuous." The lieutenant slid the wrist of his injured arm between two of the fastened buttons on his coat to form an improvised sling.

Amen to that, Hawkwood thought, though he wondered if the French would seriously expect anyone to have come ashore during the furore of the previous night's storm and then felt infinitely foolish when it struck him that's exactly what had happened, albeit at nature's behest.

As if reading his mind, Stuart added, "The sooner we make contact with our friends, the better. There's likely to be concern for our safety. They'll be expecting word and in any case we need to send you on your way."

The colour was gradually returning to the lieutenant's face and there was a renewed confidence in his tone. Ten minutes ago, he'd been a shipwrecked mariner, alone and injured on a hostile coast with a third of his crew missing, presumed drowned. Now, his spirits lifted by the unexpected arrival of an ally, he appeared anxious to get back into the fray.

They left the beach behind. The dunes began to give way to an area of grassy hummocks freckled with clumps of wind-blown gorse. Further inland, the gorse merged into thickets of prickly, waist-high scrub. Beyond the scrub, Hawkwood could see pine trees. The smell of resin hung heavy in the damp morning air. Sandy, needle-strewn pathways weaved through the gaps between the thickets. They were criss-crossed with enough tracks to suggest it was an area well visited by humans and animals – mostly of a domestic kind, to judge by the amount of sheep and goat droppings that lay scattered about like fallen berries – which explained the shorn state of the turf, Hawkwood reasoned.

He glanced over his shoulder. The reward was a limited view over a choppy sea corrugated with heaving swells. He looked towards the horizon, but visibility was poor and there was no sign of land and then Hawkwood remembered that north lay on his right-hand side and he was, in fact, looking *down* the Channel towards its far western approaches. He felt an unexpected knot form in the pit of his stomach and wondered why that should be. God knows, he'd served his country and fought the king's enemies in more foreign climes than most men could dream about and only rarely had he felt the tug of England's green and pleasant pastures, and yet here he was, striving for a glimpse of a coastline not thirty miles distant and feeling bereft at his inability to catch so much as a whiff of familiar headland.

There was no sign of the ship, either, but as it was hard to tell where the sea ended and the sky began, it would have been difficult to spot any vessel more than a mile or two from shore. In any case, Stuart had told him that *Griffin* was lying off the point and the curve of the coastline still hampered his view. And there was no telling if she had even survived the night.

Hawkwood looked towards where Stuart had told him the fort was located but the cliffs and vegetation blocked his line of sight that way as well. He turned back, in time to see Stuart tense and say suddenly and softly, "We have company!"

Hawkwood followed the lieutenant's gaze and his pulse quickened as a blue-uniformed rider trotted his mount out from the edge of the trees. Half a dozen similar-hued infantry men materialized in a ragged line behind him. All the foot soldiers carried muskets.

It was too late to hide. The troops would have had to be blind not to have seen them.

Stuart swallowed drily. "Any suggestions?" There was a new-found fear in his voice.

"Don't run's the first one that comes to mind."

Act like a fugitive and you'll be treated like one, Hawkwood thought.

The soldiers – fusiliers from their dress – were perhaps two hundred paces away. A musket ball would be ineffective at that range but Hawkwood had yet to see a man outrun a horse; not that there was anywhere to run to. He wondered if his and Stuart's appearance had come as a surprise to the patrol or whether they'd been under observation for a while. Best to assume the latter, he thought.

"How's your French, Lieutenant?" Hawkwood asked.

"I've a fair understanding," Stuart murmured. "But I ain't fluent enough, if that's what you were hoping."

It was, but Hawkwood didn't say so.

"Are you wearing anything likely to identify you as a British naval officer?" Hawkwood asked Stuart quickly, assessing the lieutenant's garb. He was acutely conscious that both he and Stuart bore all the damp and bloodied evidence of their traumatic arrival, on their faces and in the condition of their clothing.

There was a pause. "No." Then, his composure slipping, the lieutenant hissed feverishly, "We've no bloody papers. They'll shoot us as spies!"

It was on the tip of Hawkwood's tongue to point out that if their identities were discovered they were liable to be shot as spies anyway, whether they had papers or not.

"You men! Halt! Stay where you are!"

The command came from one of the foot soldiers, a corporal; Hawkwood could make out the chevrons on the sleeve.

Too late to take evasive action, anyway, Hawkwood thought. *They've seen the state of us.*

Led by the mounted officer, the patrol drew near, fanning out in a semi-circle, muskets levelled. Close to, Hawkwood could see that their uniforms – those of the foot soldiers at least – were not in the best of condition but rather well worn and with a grubby cast. The way they were hefting their weapons was also telling. Hawkwood had the distinct impression these were far from frontline troops and he recalled Stuart's remark about the bulk of the garrison – presumably the more seasoned of the fort's contingent – having been transferred. The way these men carried themselves seemed to bear that out for, despite the uniforms, the squad had all the deportment of a militia force rather than a detachment of regulars.

"Not a word," Hawkwood said. "Let me do the talking."

"I was hoping you'd say that," Stuart murmured.

"One more thing," Hawkwood said.

"What's that?"

"Fall down."

"Eh?" Stuart flashed him a look of alarm.

Hawkwood said. "You're injured. Your ship's foundered and you've just crawled ashore. You're exhausted. Fall down. Do it now."

Stuart's collapse was rather more theatrical than Hawkwood would have liked and probably wouldn't have looked out of place in a Drury Lane pageant, but anything that gave the patrol pause for thought and less reason to fix bayonets was all he was looking for.

With Stuart slumped on the ground, Hawkwood raised his hand and called out in French, "Help! Over here!" He gestured frantically and then knelt, as if he was trying to help a stricken comrade regain his sea legs.

"Not a word, Lieutenant," Hawkwood said again, though he knew the warning was superfluous. He looked towards the oncoming troops, adopted what he hoped was an urgent expression, and called out once more: "We need help here!"

The officer reined in his horse. He was a gaunt individual with pale, sullen features. A thin moustache that looked as if it had been pasted on as an afterthought traced the line of his upper lip; a futile attempt to add character to an uncharismatic face. Late thirties, Hawkwood guessed, and rather old for his rank; suggesting a career path less distinguished than a man his age might have expected, or hoped for. Which could account for him being put in charge of a shore patrol, Hawkwood thought as he stood up, leaving Stuart screwing his face in agony and clutching his arm, giving a credible impression that his injury was worse than it actually was.

The lieutenant's eyes took in Hawkwood's matted hair, the torn clothing, the scars, the cuts and the stains and the man at Hawkwood's feet.

"What's going on here? Who are you men?"

"Lieutenant!" Hawkwood hoped he wasn't over playing the relief in his voice. "By God, you're a welcome sight!"

The lieutenant gestured his men to close in. "Identify yourselves."

Hawkwood drew himself up. "Captain Vallon, 93rd Regiment of Infantry. And you are?"

The lieutenant's eyebrows rose.

Hawkwood had dragged the name out of the air and awarded himself the promotion to circumvent the man on the horse from pulling rank. The ploy worked. Taken aback and not sure whether he should offer salutations to a senior officer whose dishevelled appearance was, to say the least, questionable, the lieutenant's eyes moved back to the still wincing Stuart.

"I am Lieutenant Gaston Malbreau of the Mahon garrison. Where are you billeted, Captain? I wasn't aware the 93rd was deployed in this district." The lieutenant's gaze lifted.

"It isn't," Hawkwood said, deflecting the question and uttering a silent prayer as he did so. *Another snippet of information to be stored away.*

The lieutenant frowned. "Then where *have* you come from?"

Hawkwood jerked his thumb seawards. "There."

The lieutenant followed Hawkwood's gesture and stared out towards the Channel's murky horizon. His features twisted in puzzlement. He turned back. "I'm not with you, Captain. What are you telling me?"

"That I'm here by the grace of God and the efforts of this brave fellow," Hawkwood said, indicating Stuart. "And I'd appreciate a couple of blankets and a canteen, Corporal. Sharpish, if you please. We're thirsty and we're bloody freezing." Hawkwood held out his hand impatiently, indicating that the corporal didn't have a choice in the matter.

The corporal blinked and looked to his lieutenant for authorization.

The lieutenant hesitated and then nodded curtly as if annoyed at having his chain of command usurped. As the corporal directed two of his men to hand over their bedrolls and a canteen, he addressed Hawkwood once again. "I'm still not following you, Captain. Are you telling me you've just come ashore?"

"That's one way of putting it."

Hawkwood's enigmatic response drew an immediate frown. "I see no signs of a vessel."

"No," Hawkwood said drily. "You wouldn't. She was lost in last night's storm. We're the only ones who made it. The rest of the crew went down with her. Between you and me, Lieutenant, I wasn't so foolish as to expect a garland of flowers and a kiss on the cheek from the Emperor, but this wasn't the way I wanted to return to the motherland, not after two years in a God-damned British prison ship."

The lieutenant's chin came up sharply. "*Prison* ship?"

A murmur ran through the rest of the patrol. Hawkwood draped one of the blankets around Stuart's shoulders and held the canteen to the lieutenant's lips. Stuart took the canteen with his good hand and gulped greedily. This time there was no fakery in his actions.

Hawkwood took back the canteen and raised it to his own mouth. The water was warm and brackish but it tasted like nectar after the amount of salt water he'd ingested. He wiped his mouth on his sleeve. "Eight hundred of us; kept like animals and fed on swill you wouldn't feed to a goat. You ever tasted salted herring and turnips, Lieutenant? You wouldn't like it, trust me. Two years was more than enough."

"You escaped?"

Hawkwood nodded wearily. He handed the canteen back to the corporal and made a play of wrapping the remaining blanket around himself. The material was threadbare and in keeping with the rough state of the patrol's uniforms. As a result there wasn't a great deal of comfort or warmth in it, but beggars, Hawkwood reflected, couldn't be choosers. "Damned right, I did."

The patrol's musket barrels, he saw, were beginning to droop.

Malbreau nodded towards Stuart, his face set. "And this man? He was also a prisoner?"

Hawkwood shook his head and placed his hand on Stuart's shoulder. "No, he's a British sea captain and if it weren't for him I wouldn't be talking with you now."

The members of the patrol exchanged startled glances. The lieutenant stiffened. His eyes narrowed. "How so?"

"He's a smuggler; what the English call a free trader. It was Captain Stuart's ship that I took passage on. Cost me a fortune; four thousand francs, if you can believe it. Not what *I'd* call free trade. Not by a long shot! But I'll say this for them: they're damned well organized. Arranged my escape from the hulk, accommodation *and* all my transportation."

Hawkwood gave Stuart a reassuring pat on the shoulder and wondered how much of the conversation *Griffin*'s commander had managed to follow. "So I want him taken care of until we can arrange his return home. His arm needs looking at. You've a medical officer back at the garrison, I take it?"

"Surgeon Manseraux." It was the corporal who replied, to a tart look from the lieutenant, Hawkwood noted.

"Competent?" Hawkwood asked.

"He's a bloody butcher." The soldier grinned, showing teeth as yellow as parchment.

Hawkwood returned the grin. "Excellent. What's your name, Corporal?"

Hawkwood had no interest whatsoever in the corporal's name but he was following one of the first principles of military prudence: cultivate the non-commissioned men. Get them on your side and you could win wars.

The corporal straightened. "Despard, sir."

"Then I thank you for your advice, Corporal Despard." He turned to the man on the horse. "I regret I'm not too familiar with this part of the country, Lieutenant. How far are we from this garrison of yours? Mahon, did you say?" Hawkwood forged an expression that suggested he was trying to search his memory. "Wait, that would be . . . Ambleteuse, am I right?"

The lieutenant twisted in his saddle and jerked his chin towards a point over his shoulder. "Two miles up the coast beyond the dunes."

Still very formal, though, Hawkwood noted. A warning bell began to tinkle.

"Good. Then we should proceed there without delay. The

sooner I'm reunited with my regiment the better. Now that I'm home, I'm anxious to get back to the fight. But then, who wouldn't be, eh?"

The lieutenant turned and drew himself up. "Quite so, Captain. Permit me to congratulate you on your safe return." The lieutenant paused and his face took on a new severity. "My men and I will of course accompany you to the fort, though I regret we are required to escort you under arms."

Malbreau flicked his hand at the corporal and his men, who responded with a look of surprise before taking a renewed grip on their muskets. "As you've been away for some time, you may not be aware that the Empire is still under considerable threat from Bourbon sympathizers. There have been a growing number of incursions by royalist agents disembarking from British vessels along our northern coasts and we've been warned to remain vigilant, so you'll forgive me for taking precautions."

In that one moment, the expression on Malbreau's face told Hawkwood all he needed to know. He'd sensed his comment about wanting to return to the fight had hit a raw nerve. The lieutenant's response confirmed it. At some time in his past, Malbreau's army career had obviously been blighted, probably due to an indiscretion or a poorly judged command. As a result, despite the Emperor's dire need for able troops to reinforce his eastern divisions, the lieutenant had been consigned to the doldrums: a small, once significant but now poorly manned coastal garrison miles from anywhere. Mahon was going to be the pinnacle of Malbreau's army career, and he knew it and the inevitability of it consumed him.

And as with all such men, the lieutenant clearly placed the blame for his misfortune squarely on everybody's shoulders but his own. The bitterness was engrained in every frown, shrug and thrust of his jawline. It oozed from his pores like sweat on a toad. As far as Lieutenant Malbreau was concerned, he was still a cut above everyone else, be they a general, a corporal or, more specifically, anyone holding the rank immediately above him, which on this occasion, turned out to be one Captain

Vallon of the 93rd Regiment of Infantry: frontline officer, escaped prisoner of war and, therefore, in the hearts and minds of the Republic, a returning hero. In Malbreau's eyes, targets of resentment probably didn't come any bigger.

Hawkwood forced himself to nod in acquiescence and keep his voice calm. "Absolutely, Lieutenant. Quite right, too. For all you and your men know, we could well be subversives, come ashore to wreak havoc about the Empire. It wouldn't do a lot for your career if you let someone like that slip through your hands without adequate investigation, now, would it?" Hawkwood added blithely.

A nerve moved along the lieutenant's pale cheek. Hawkwood looked sideways and caught the corporal regarding him with what appeared to be a degree of embarrassment. In response, Hawkwood offered Despard what he hoped was a wry shrug. A corner of the corporal's mouth lifted; silent affirmation that Lieutenant Gaston Malbreau wasn't much liked by his own men either and that it was a friction that appeared to transcend the boundaries of rank. Possibly something worth exploiting, Hawkwood mused, should the need arise. He stored that thought away.

His authority sealed, at least in his own mind, Malbreau gripped the reins of his horse. "When we reach Mahon I've no doubt the garrison commander will be able to verify your particulars and arrange for your onward journey. Though it may take a while. The same goes for your . . . companion. Does he speak French, by the way?"

Hawkwood shook his head "A few words only and I'm no linguist, alas, so I can't tell you much about him, other than his name. We were introduced at the beginning of our voyage. Since then, I'm afraid our exchanges have consisted mostly of pointing and waving our arms about. You know how it is."

"I see." Malbreau nodded. There was no warmth in his voice. He stared hard at *Griffin*'s commander and, in passable though heavily accented English, said. "You are Captain . . . Stuart? Is that correct?"

Christ! Hawkwood thought. *If Stuart contradicts the story we're dead men.* He held his breath.

Stuart lifted his head. Slowly he got to his feet. Cradling his

107

injured arm, he nodded. "Captain Jonathan Stuart at your service, Lieutenant."

"What is the name of your ship?"

For a tiny second, Stuart hesitated. Then he frowned, as if deciphering the lieutenant's pronunciation, and said, "The lugger *Pandora*, out of Rye. Or at least she was until the storm ripped her to pieces. I'd like to know who's going to bloody pay for her."

The lieutenant's brow creased. "What do you mean?"

"What the hell do you think I mean?" Stuart replied hotly. "You think I was on my own time? I was working for you lot when she went down. Delivering the captain here to the bosom of his family. It wasn't only my ship. I lost my living and my crewmates in that bloody storm. Like brothers to me, they were; with wives and children. *They're* going to need recompense for a start. You going to arrange for me to speak to somebody about that?" Stuart glared hard at the lieutenant before throwing Hawkwood an equally accusatory look.

Hawkwood was struck by the emotion in the English captain's voice. Stuart's outburst had not been a piece of theatre; it had been genuine. Angry and distraught at the loss of the crewmen from the *Griffin*, he was letting anyone within earshot know it, Hawkwood included. Stuart was also, Hawkwood knew, sending him another message: that he'd understood the gist of his exchange with Malbreau.

Feigning incomprehension and bemusement at Stuart's tirade, Hawkwood turned to the French officer. "What did he say?"

Malbreau gave a derisive snort. "The scoundrel's only demanding compensation for the loss of his boat."

"Is he indeed?" Hawkwood appeared to give the matter some thought. "Well, you can't deny the fellow has a point. Seems only fair after the risks he's taken. I've no doubt something can be arranged. Tell him, I'll do my best to see he's suitably reimbursed."

Malbreau stared at Hawkwood askance.

Hawkwood raised an eyebrow. "What? You doubt the fellow's claim? You do realize that without friends like the captain here,

108

a lot of good Frenchmen are likely to be spending the rest of the war and possibly the rest of their days in British prisons. What do you think'll happen if Captain Stuart returns home to tell the rest of his smuggling brethren that we didn't see right by him? I'll tell you, Lieutenant: there'll be no one to give aid to our brave comrades; no one to provide them with shelter or arrange their safe passage across the Sleeve. From what I've heard, the war hasn't been going at all well. France needs every able body. You wouldn't want to deny experienced men the chance of returning home and answering the Emperor's call, would you?"

Malbreau flushed. "No, of course not."

"Damned glad to hear it," Hawkwood said, turning the screw. "Then tell him what I said."

Malbreau, after hesitating with his teeth clenched, did as Hawkwood instructed. Stuart listened to the grudging translation then turned to Hawkwood and, after fixing him with a calculating stare, gave a brief nod as though acknowledging the offer of restitution. Hawkwood nodded back. For Malbreau's benefit, Hawkwood hoped, honour had been satisfied.

"So." Hawkwood stroked the mare's smoothly muscled neck. "That's settled then." He looked up. "Well, lead on, Lieutenant. The sooner we report to this garrison of yours, the sooner we can arrange Captain Stuart's repatriation. That way, he's out of our hair and ready to bring more of our men back. And if either of us drops by the roadside I'm sure Corporal Despard and his men will be only too happy to manufacture stretchers for the two of us."

Unseen by Malbreau and the other members of the patrol, Hawkwood and Stuart exchanged another quick glance. It wasn't hard to interpret the desperate query in Stuart's eyes. Hawkwood didn't have to be a mind reader to know that Stuart was asking him what the hell they'd got themselves into. And, more to the point, how the hell were they going to get themselves out?

As Lieutenant Malbreau wheeled his horse about, Hawkwood was asking himself the very same thing.

7

They headed north.

Malbreau had told them it was only two miles to the fort. Two miles in which to come up with a plan of escape. Not far enough, Hawkwood calculated bleakly. To make matters worse, he was being herded further away from his destination: Wimereux and the diligence that was to transport him to Paris. So far, the mission was turning into an unmitigated disaster.

He thought about the consequences of their being taken to Mahon. There was a slim chance the subterfuge might work. Ultimately, their fate lay in the hands of the garrison commander, but if the latter was cut from the same cloth as his subordinate, they were in trouble. Hawkwood revised that thought. *Deeper* trouble. Just how deep remained to be seen.

The path wound its way through the pine trees, rising steadily before finally emerging on to a narrow road bordered to the east by scrubby heathland and to the west and north by a rolling landscape of grass-topped sand dunes which, Hawkwood presumed, sloped all the way back down to the sea. The path was heavily indented with cart tracks and hoof prints, many cloven, indicating it was a well-worn route for cattle as well as horses and probably a main drover road, linking settlements up and down the coast.

As if taking Hawkwood's direction literally, Malbreau had chosen to ride ahead of them, guiding his horse along the ruts, maintaining point in haughty silence. Hawkwood wasn't sure about the horse. He couldn't recall if it was a requirement for a French officer of fusiliers to be mounted or whether it was a personal affectation. He suspected the latter. Either way, it was another facet of Malbreau's style of command that distanced him from his men, which made Hawkwood wonder if that was why Malbreau had chosen it. Perhaps, Hawkwood thought cynically, the lieutenant considered it more convenient than having his men carry him around in a sedan chair.

Though, in truth, he was thankful for Malbreau's lack of civility. Had the lieutenant been the garrulous type, anxious to discuss the course of the war or exchange tales of hearth and home, Hawkwood knew the journey to the fort would require constant vigilance on his part to ensure he didn't say the wrong thing and inadvertently let something slip which would lay open his and Stuart's deception. Malbreau's unwillingness to engage in conversation had granted Hawkwood a useful respite in which to think. Or at least, that's what Hawkwood had supposed when they'd set off.

Blankets over their shoulders, Hawkwood and Stuart made no attempt to communicate with each other, for obvious reasons. In that regard, Hawkwood had drawn the short straw for, as none of the patrol other than Malbreau understood English, Stuart had been left guarding his own thoughts. Unfortunately, this had left Hawkwood, not to his own devices, as he'd first hoped, but prey to interrogation by his new-found friend, Corporal Despard who, in the absence of supervision by his lieutenant, was most interested, almost to the point of sycophancy, in Hawkwood's fictitious capture and flight from the bastard British and their infamous prison hulks.

It might have been wiser, Hawkwood knew, to have pulled rank and kept the corporal in his place from the outset, in keeping with his masquerade as a French officer. But with Malbreau having removed himself from conversational range, Hawkwood had revised his original thinking and reasoned that, if his disguise was to be believed, a prisoner of war newly restored to his own country would probably want to converse with a fellow soldier – irrespective of rank – if only to avoid marching in a strained silence, which would have made the journey to the fort smack even more of prisoners being transferred under escort. Which might have satisfied Lieutenant Malbreau, Hawkwood reflected, but it wouldn't have been conducive to either his or Stuart's sense of well-being. So, remaining alert, he'd given in to the corporal's enquiries.

Fortunately, Hawkwood had been able to draw on his own experiences to satisfy Despard's curiosity. The events that had taken place on the hulk, *Rapacious*, and his association with Lasseur were still vivid in his mind and the physical scars he bore added credence to his story. There had been no need to manufacture detail or events.

Also, as it turned out, the information had flowed both ways. By the time they crested the final rise to find the estuary and the coastline spread out before them, Hawkwood's store of newly acquired knowledge included the troop numbers and disposition of the Mahon garrison, the calibre of the shore battery's seven cannon, the proclivities of the garrison commander's mistress and the name of the best inn and brothel in Ambleteuse. Admittedly not all the intelligence was strictly relevant, but as Hawkwood had learned over the years, one never knew when accumulated facts *might* prove useful.

The first thing that struck Hawkwood was that there wasn't a great deal of town to see. What there was of it – a cluster of unexceptional buildings huddled behind a low sea wall on the estuary's northern shore – lay a little under a mile distant and it didn't look as if the place could support more than two or three hundred souls at the most. It was even doubtful whether Ambleteuse qualified as a town. Hawkwood thought back to what the corporal had told him. The place had likely been a quiet spot before the army arrived. Despard's brothel probably hadn't existed either until the soldiers decided they wanted another form of entertainment to complement their alcohol intake. In that regard the place was undoubtedly no different to any garrison town in England, or anywhere else for that matter. It was the same with soldiers the world over. When they weren't marching to war they were either fighting among themselves, or whoring or drinking. The only difference lay in the languages they spoke and the colours they fought under.

The fort drew the eye immediately, though it wasn't nearly as formidable as Hawkwood had been expecting. Neither was it situated in a commanding position on the high ground as so many garrison fortresses were. Instead, the squat, semi-circular construction was perched in lonely isolation on a rocky shelf at the mouth of the river. It looked not unlike a large wide-brimmed hat that had been washed up by the tide and deposited at the edge of the sand. The fort's curved side butted into the Channel, its thick crenulated battlements forming a defensive barrier against the wind and waves. An oblong, grey-roofed blockhouse dominated the top of the keep. Smoke rose from the single chimney stack and a flag, buffeted by the breeze coming off the sea, flew stiffly above it. The fort was tethered to the shore by a concrete causeway and Hawkwood could see that, come high tide, the garrison would be completely cut off, leaving the troops stranded on their stone island. It didn't look like anywhere he'd want to be posted in a hurry; which went a long way, he thought, to explaining Lieutenant Malbreau's churlish disposition.

His gaze shifted to the mouth of the estuary and the jagged bend in the river directly behind it. His eyes moved upstream towards a low stone bridge. There were people in view; early risen townsfolk going about their business, some driving or pushing carts, a few herding livestock, either to market or fresh grazing land, Hawkwood presumed. He could see milking cows, a dozen or so sheep and a small flock of geese. It was a tranquil scene. What he couldn't see were other fording places, which suggested the bridge was probably one of the district's main crossing points.

"There she is," Despard announced without noticeable affection and nodded towards the fort as if it had just materialized out of thin air.

Malbreau neither paused nor bothered to follow his corporal's gaze but continued on towards the river with all the aloofness of the local squire returning home after a morning's hack.

The indifference, Hawkwood noticed, as they followed Malbreau down the track, appeared to be mutual. If any of the locals were curious at the sight of two civilians flanked by a patrol bearing weapons at shoulder arms, they gave no outward sign. The garrison had been there long enough to ensure that troop movements had become a daily normality; either that or familiarity really did breed contempt.

Approaching the bridge, Hawkwood glanced towards the sea and the fortress outlined against the low-hanging sky. Differing in size but with the same shade of tiles covering its summit, it bore a vague resemblance to the bastion that had guarded the entrance to the Medway and the Sheerness dockyard that had been the mooring place of *Rapacious*. As omens went, Hawkwood thought, it left a good deal to be desired.

A cry from the direction of the bridge cut into his thoughts. Following the sound, he saw that a cart had come to a skewed halt at the far end, with one of its wheels dislodged. A mule waited patiently between the cart's shafts as the carter tried to untangle its harness. Half the cart's produce had been spilled. Several empty wicker cages lay strewn across the road and a dozen squawking hens were making a valiant bid for freedom. Hawkwood wished them luck, though he didn't think they'd get very far.

And then he saw that another catastrophe was about to ensue. A couple of drovers approaching from the opposite direction had failed to notice the damaged cart. Their half dozen or so head of cattle had obviously been blocking their view and they'd allowed them to get too far in front. With exquisite timing, the beasts had also decided it was time to pick up speed and a minor stampede was under way. On the bridge, the cart driver was too intent on rescuing his goods to have noticed the new threat bearing down upon him.

By the time Malbreau got there the bridge was milling with livestock and a heated altercation had broken out between cart owner and drovers. *So much for tranquillity*, Hawkwood thought.

Unflustered by the contretemps, however, Malbreau, shoulders erect, manoeuvred his mount slowly and surely through the small jostling herd and past the arguing trio without so much as a sideways glance. Neither did he try to avoid the carpet of fruit and vegetables lying squashed beneath his horse's hooves. Not that there was much of anything edible left to salvage. The cattle had taken care of that.

By the time Hawkwood and the others arrived, Malbreau was some twenty horse lengths ahead of them and the row was still in full flow, raising grins from the corporal and his men, who wasted no opportunity in grabbing up several fruit that had survived the collision. They did not try to conceal the theft and laughed as they slapped the now docile cattle out of the way and tossed the purloined apples back and forth between them.

As the patrol passed by the spilled cart and the raised voices, Hawkwood saw Stuart's eyes flicker to one side and widen. He followed the English captain's look and was surprised to see that one of the drovers was a young woman, and an attractive one at that. Hawkwood found his attention drawn to a pair of cornflower blue eyes set above a pert nose, framed in an oval face. The auburn hair poking out from beneath the hat emphasized her pale complexion. One thing was certain: she bore little resemblance to the drovers he was used to seeing around any of the Smithfield pens. He was still thinking that when she broke off from berating the carter, drew a pistol from beneath her coat and with calm precision shot Corporal Despard through his right eye.

And all hell broke loose.

In the time it took the ball to exit the back of the corporal's skull, Hawkwood was already moving, throwing the blanket aside and scooping up Despard's musket before it hit the ground. As Despard's corpse was flung against the parapet, Hawkwood swung the weapon up and smashed the butt into the shocked face of the next fusilier in line. From the corner of his eye he saw the girl turn and the second drover step back, sweep aside a basket of vegetables and snatch up the pistol that had been hidden beneath.

The pistol flashed, another loud report sounded and a third

fusilier spun away, his chest blossoming red. A body thrust past Hawkwood and he saw it was Stuart, making a grab for one of the other discarded muskets.

The remaining fusiliers, caught between the decision to return fire or make a run for it, were left floundering; their dilemma made worse by the cattle who, already unnerved by their aimless rush to the bridge, were immediately driven into fresh and increased panic by the gunshots. The scene suddenly became a mêlée of terrified soldiers and bellowing livestock all trying to choose the safest direction in which to flee.

Hawkwood heard the girl call out and saw her point. He looked immediately for Malbreau and caught sight of him across the backs of the scattering herd. The lieutenant had wheeled his horse about. It occurred to Hawkwood, as he watched Malbreau draw his sabre, that what the man lacked in humility he made up for in grit.

There was a loud crack from close by and Hawkwood felt the wind of a musket ball as it flicked past his cheek. One of Despard's surviving companions had decided to make a stand, but in the fusilier's excitement he'd fired too soon. An ear-splitting clamour filled the air as the ball struck one of the milk cows. The animal went down as if poleaxed. Hawkwood had never heard a cow scream before. It was a terrible sound. A spinal shot, he thought instinctively as the beast continued to writhe in agony, legs thrashing in the dust.

He saw Stuart raise the musket he'd recovered from the dead fusilier. Somehow, with his good hand, the lieutenant had managed to haul back the musket's hammer. Jamming the muzzle into the midriff of the soldier who'd loosed off the last shot, Stuart pulled the trigger. There was a vivid flash and a loud crack and Stuart's features disappeared behind a cloud of smoke from the ignited powder. The fusilier fell back with a shriek, arms spread wide as he went over the side of the bridge into the water below.

Hawkwood didn't wait for the splash but raised Despard's musket to his shoulder, ignoring the yell as the less nimble of the two fusiliers who'd taken to their heels lost his footing and slipped beneath a frenzy of trampling hooves.

Another pistol shot rang out and Hawkwood saw the remaining fusilier throw up his hands and pitch forward on to his face.

Then he was concentrating.

It had been a while since he'd hefted a musket. Compared to the Baker rifle, the weight and balance were all out of kilter. The damned thing was over a foot longer, for one thing. As for the weapon's accuracy; that didn't bear thinking about. The Charleville was supposed to be the best musket in the world. From Hawkwood's point of view, as a rifleman, it was about as much use as a pair of sugar tongs.

He drew back the hammer.

Malbreau was seventy yards away and coming in fast when Hawkwood fired.

He doubted it was a killing shot the instant he squeezed the trigger and thought he might even have missed the target, for as the musket slammed back into his shoulder he saw Malbreau's horse stumble. The ball, however, struck Malbreau high on his right breast, plucking him backwards as if by an invisible hand. The sabre dropped from his grasp and he pitched sideways out of the saddle. As the weight on its back shifted, the horse veered sharply, the sudden movement causing Malbreau's boot to catch in his stirrup, trapping him by the ankle and spinning him over. Frightened anew by the now unfamiliar object attached to it, the horse turned upon its tracks once more. As Malbreau's body hit the ground, his shako came loose and fell away, tumbling like a drum across the dirt. The horse began to pick up speed and with Malbreau's body flopping and twisting behind it like a blood-stained scarecrow it headed towards the fort.

With the echo of the shot ringing in his ears, Hawkwood lowered the gun and surveyed the carnage.

All the cattle had bolted, save the one that had been struck and which now lay still, leaving the bridge wreathed in a choking mixture of dissipating dust, cow shit and powder smoke. Despard's body lay where it had fallen. The stones beneath it were blackening with blood. Another body lay on its side close by, jacket front and crossbelts stained crimson. Hawkwood looked for the fusilier who had been shot by Stuart and then remembered that the man had gone over the side of the bridge. There didn't seem any point in looking for him. The soldier that had taken the musket butt to the face was also dead. The crushed cheekbones and the sightless eyes told their own story.

A fifth one lay on his back, groaning, his chest rising and falling slowly, while his left leg lay folded beneath him at an unnatural angle. Hawkwood assumed he was the one who'd slipped beneath the cattle hooves.

The last man had had nowhere to run to. The pistol ball had taken him between the shoulder blades. Still alive, he was trying to drag himself along the ground.

Beyond him, the townsfolk who had taken cover in the dirt were rising cautiously to their feet. Others were still running.

Hawkwood turned to find Stuart and the girl facing each other. The girl still had the pistol in her right hand. She was holding the flat of her left hand alongside Stuart's cheek. Stuart dropped the musket, reached up and pressed the girl's palm to his skin. Her features were drawn with concern. Beyond her, the second drover and the cart driver were busying themselves, collecting the fusiliers' uncharged weapons and checking pouches for powder and ammunition. The soldier whose leg had been broken cried out in pain as his kit was rifled. Hawkwood watched as the carter, still kneeling, drew a knife from his belt and cut the wounded man's throat. The dispatching was as swift as it was brutal. As the carter walked purposefully towards the fusilier who had been shot in the back, his knife held low, Hawkwood turned away and found himself face to face with the girl.

Stuart said, "Allow me to present Mademoiselle Nymphe Roussel de Préville."

"Mademoiselle," Hawkwood said. He took in the startling blue eyes and wondered if she lived up to her name. *If there was any justice*, he thought.

A new sound reached his ears: the clanging of a distant bell.

The alarm was being raised at the fort. The shots had alerted the garrison and spotters on the ramparts had witnessed the fight on the bridge. They'd also have seen Malbreau's horse dragging its wounded – probably dead – owner home to barracks.

119

Hearing the bell, the girl did not smile but merely nodded at Hawkwood's response. When she spoke, she did so in English, her accented voice as soft as her complexion. "We must hurry. They will be coming."

"How did you know we were here?" Hawkwood asked.

Her eyes flashed. "After the storm, we were worried about the landing and came to look for you. We saw you stopped and taken by the patrol. We guessed they'd want to take you to Mahon. Fortunately, they brought you by the slower route along the main road. We know the back ways and so were able to get here first. The cattle and the cart were the only way we could think of hiding our intentions and weapons. If they hadn't been available . . ." The girl's voice trailed off and she shrugged.

The ambush, Hawkwood knew, had been both audacious and reckless and had succeeded more through chance than sound strategy. But it had proved the courage of Stuart's agents. He stared at the girl.

"Not what you expected, eh?" Stuart said.

"No," Hawkwood said truthfully.

"There's a few who've made that mistake."

Corporal Despard, for one, Hawkwood thought.

The ringing of the bell had become very insistent. Witnesses to the ambush were making themselves scarce, hurrying towards the town, back to their homes and anonymity.

Stuart looked towards the sound and his face fell. "Damn it." He addressed the girl. "You have to get him out of here, now." He turned to Hawkwood. "Reinforcements."

Hawkwood looked to where a line of blue-clad soldiers was splashing across the partially submerged causeway. Galloping towards them was a single rider-less horse, its stirrups empty. Somewhere along the way, the lieutenant's body was lying in the dust, gathering flies.

Quickly the girl turned and called out, "Alain! Raoul!" She beckoned urgently.

Her two companions hurried forward, carrying the captured ordnance. They weren't as young as the girl but their sharp, dark-eyed, saturnine features framed by black curly hair were close enough alike to suggest they might be related; brothers or perhaps cousins.

One of them, slightly older and taller than the other, greeted Stuart with a wry, almost vulpine smile. Then, acknowledging Hawkwood with a brief nod, he turned to the girl and raised a questioning eyebrow. Hawkwood realized he was the one who had used his knife on the wounded soldiers.

The girl nodded towards the other man. "Alain will take him while we hold the bridge."

"What the hell do you mean, you'll hold the bridge?" Hawkwood said. "And take me where?"

The girl turned, unsurprised by Hawkwood addressing her in fluent French. Her eyes flashed as she replied in the same language. "Wimereux. We've no time to explain. You must go." Reaching into the pouch that was slung around her shoulder she drew out a powder flask and began to reload the pistol; her movements were calm and unhurried.

"And Lieutenant Stuart?" Hawkwood stared at her.

Stuart smiled. "I was tasked to deliver you in one piece. My job's done."

Hawkwood swung round. "The hell with that! You can't stay here. None of us can. What about them?" Hawkwood nodded towards the approaching blue jackets. "We've just slaughtered seven of their men. What do you think they'll do to you? Invite you for supper?"

"We have weapons. We'll slow them down and give you and Alain the time you need." Stuart held out his hand and the girl passed him the newly charged pistol. Stuart indicated his injured arm and grinned. "Easier to handle than a damned musket."

"This is bloody madness!" Hawkwood said.

The girl's companions had laid the captured muskets aside and were releasing the mule from between the cart's shafts. Slapping the mule on the rump, the eldest man tapped his companion on the shoulder and together, as the animal cantered away, they put their combined weight against the cart and tipped it over on to its side.

"Maybe," Stuart said, "but not as mad as you staying as well.

My job was to get you here. *Your* job is to get to Paris. If you die here then the deaths of my men will have counted for naught. That wasn't part of the bargain. My mission's been completed. Yours ain't even halfway through."

"You must go now!" the girl urged.

Hawkwood stared at them both in exasperation.

"Don't worry. I don't plan for them to take me," Stuart said, indicating the troops, who were about twenty in number and, to Hawkwood's eyes, getting dangerously close. Another hundred yards and they'd be within musket range. "We'll keep them busy until you're over the other side of the hill and then we'll make a run for it. Nymphe and Raoul here know all the hiding places. I'll burrow myself away until tonight and then rejoin *Griffin*."

He looked towards the fort. The soldiers were slowing and showing understandable caution at having to approach the bridge over open ground. Hawkwood suspected they were also taking time to catch their breath after their initial rush from barracks.

"We must go," Alain said, tugging Hawkwood's sleeve.

Hawkwood looked across to where the carter, Raoul, was loading the discharged muskets. His face was set in concentration.

Hawkwood knew Stuart was right. But that didn't make things any easier. The chances of the three of them holding off a score of soldiers with such a pathetic array of weaponry even for a short time were, Hawkwood knew, minimal at best. Though, if the advancing fusiliers were of the same calibre as Despard and his men, all things were possible. He realized that Stuart was throwing him one of his maddeningly boyish grins. "Don't look so downhearted, Mr Smith. Remember your history? Horatius and two stout companions defended the Pons Sublicus against fifty thousand Etruscans, saved Rome and lived to fight another day."

"The Etruscans", Hawkwood said, "didn't have bloody muskets."

"Ah, but Horatius' heart was true and he had right on his side."

Hawkwood stared at him and then sighed. "Hell or high water?"

122

Stuart smiled. "There's the spirit, Mr Smith."

"They're coming," Raoul said, cocking the hammer on his purloined musket. He had propped the rest of the loaded weapons against the now vertical cart.

"Come," Alain said to Hawkwood.

Hawkwood nodded. He looked at Stuart. "It's not Smith, by the way."

"No," Stuart grinned. "I didn't think it was." He held Hawkwood's gaze for a couple of seconds and then turned away.

"Bon chance." For the first time, the girl favoured Hawkwood with a smile.

"You too," Hawkwood said.

He turned abruptly and followed Alain up the track.

A minute later there came the sound of a musket shot.

Hawkwood did not look back.

PART II

8

The old man had to be eighty if he was a day. Venerable was the word that sprang to Hawkwood's mind when he looked up and saw the white hair and the serene, bespectacled face gazing down at him.

"Forgive me, monsieur, but I couldn't help noticing you've space at your table. Would you mind if I joined you?" The old man pointed with his cane.

"Not at all," Hawkwood said. He put his coffee cup down, lowered his newspaper and glanced around the mirrored room. His wasn't the only table with an empty chair beside it.

The old man sat down with a small nod and a smile of gratitude and rested his hat on the seat next to him and his walking cane against his knee. As they were at a corner table which had only three chairs in total he had effectively staked his and Hawkwood's claim on their privacy. It had been neatly done, Hawkwood thought.

The old man beckoned with a liver-spotted hand and as the waiter approached, he addressed Hawkwood. "I've never cared much for drinking alone. You'll join me in a glass, perhaps?"

Hawkwood placed the newspaper aside. "I rarely refuse the offer of a good vintage."

"Splendid. It's settled then." The old man gave the waiter his order and then nodded towards the newspaper. "I see you were reading the *Journal*. What news from the war?"

"They're saying we lost fifteen thousand at Borodino," Hawkwood said. "And that it was a magnificent example of brave men sacrificing their lives for the motherland."

The old man raised an eyebrow. "And they're calling it a victory?"

"If they're reporting fifteen," Hawkwood said, "it probably means at least thirty."

"Thirty thousand men? In one battle?" The old man looked horrified.

"That's not counting the Russians," Hawkwood said. "They'd have lost even more."

The old man shook his head. "So many; one wonders when the madness will end."

Hawkwood saw that the waiter was on his way back. The old man reached for one of the three empty upturned glasses that were on the table and, with a firm hand, turned it over. Hawkwood waited and then did the same with one of the two that were left. As soon as he had done so the old man frowned and picked up Hawkwood's glass.

"Don't use that one; it has dirt on it, see?"

The glass was without blemish.

Hawkwood turned the third glass over. "How's this one?"

"Much better," the old man said.

The waiter arrived and the wine was poured. The old man took a swallow, sat back and sighed with pleasure.

Hawkwood raised his glass and took a sip. The wine was rich in colour and full bodied with a warm, almost spicy, after-taste. "A fine choice."

His table companion smiled and lifted his glass in acknowledgement. "From the Languedoc; the oldest vineyards in France. They were planted by the Greeks, you know, though some say it was the Romans. Hot baths *and* fine wine. One does wonder how they lost an empire."

"They bit off more than they could chew," Hawkwood said. "Like all the others."

The old man smiled and toyed with the stem of his glass. "You may be right." He looked around the room. "Oldest

128

café in the city, you know; been coming here for years. It's one of the few places where you can still get a decent drink." He nodded towards Hawkwood's cup. "You were lucky this week. The damned blockade's created a shortage in everything: coffee, rum, sugar. I heard they've hung lumps of sugar from the ceiling in the de Caveau. You're permitted one dip in your cup and then you have to move on." The old man took a sip of wine. "I'll wager that never happened to Voltaire. Fellow used to drink forty cups of coffee a day. I used to compliment him on his bladder. Two glasses of this . . ." the old man raised his drink ". . . and I'm up half the night. All the great thinkers have walked through that door: Rousseau, Diderot; Franklin, too, when he was Commissioner." The old man took another swallow. "Now, he *was* splendid company. All you had to do was pick a subject: literature, philosophy, electrical science, you name it. Talk the hind leg off a donkey, if you let him."

The old man chuckled, then his expression changed and he leaned across the table. "Seen its share of villains as well; Robespierre, for one." The old man's hand tightened on the glass stem. Hawkwood saw the whitening of knuckles and had a brief vision of the glass shattering. "If ever a man got what he deserved it was that bastard."

The old man had spoken as if he'd expected the last name to have meant something. Hawkwood thought back and was rewarded with a misty recollection that Robespierre had been one of the guiding lights of the Revolution and the mastermind behind the Terror, the sequence of purges and mass executions carried out against the enemy within, namely anyone who opposed the newly installed government and its bloodthirsty arm of justice, the contradictorily named Committee of Public Safety.

The old man fell silent, took a drink and then sat back. After several seconds, he said, "Bonaparte was a patron, of course, though he was only a junior officer at the time. Used to leave his hat as security while he went off to find the money to pay his bill. Mind you, they say that about half the other cafés around here, too. I suspect he left a lot of hats in a lot of places and ran up a lot of bills. I'll wager most of them have remained unsettled."

"I wouldn't be too hard on him," Hawkwood said. "He's had a lot on his mind of late."

129

The old man grinned delightedly and a light danced in his eyes once more. "Ha! Hasn't he just? So, tell me, is this your first visit? I don't believe I've seen you in here before."

"No," Hawkwood said. "You wouldn't have."

"Ah, new to the city? And what brings you here, if you don't mind me asking?"

"Passing through," Hawkwood said. "Though I'm also looking for a good watchmaker. I don't suppose you know of anyone?"

The old man's eyebrows rose. "A watchmaker, you say? Well, bless my soul. It just so happens I know the very fellow!"

"You do?" Hawkwood said. "Well, that's a rare piece of luck. Where can I find him?"

The old man grinned again and raised his glass. "Modesty forbids, but you're looking at him."

"Really?" Hawkwood said, wondering if the pantomime had outlived its usefulness. The rigmarole involving the turning of the glasses had been bad enough.

"It's true; I assure you. It just so happens that I'm a jeweller by trade and I've a small establishment only a short walk from here. Perhaps you'd like to accompany me there? You never know; I may be able to help with whatever it is you're looking for. What do you say?"

"I'm in your hands," Hawkwood said. "When do we leave?"

"As soon as I've finished my glass. I'll ask the waiter to find a cork and we can take the bottle with us. Shame to waste the rest, eh? Don't worry, they know me here. They're used to it. By the way, we haven't been introduced, have we?" The old man extended his hand. "The name's McPherson, James McPherson."

Hawkwood hid his surprise. Like the man's age, it was the last thing he'd been expecting. The old man's French was faultless. Not that the name meant anything in itself. The Scots had been fighting alongside the French in one form or another for centuries. One of Bonaparte's generals, MacDonald, was of Scottish descent and he was a Marshal of France to boot.

"Dumas," Hawkwood said. "Paul Dumas."

130

The old man frowned. "Dumas? You don't say? I knew a Dumas once; a while ago. Family came from Wimereux. You wouldn't happen to be a relation, would you?

"Probably a distant cousin," Hawkwood said.

The old man's grip was firm. "Well, I'm delighted to make your acquaintance, Monsieur Dumas." He drained his glass and, after catching the waiter's eye, lifted the half-empty bottle and mimed tapping a cork into it. He picked up his hat, sat it on his head and retrieved his cane. The waiter took the bottle and returned with it re-corked and wrapped in a napkin. McPherson dropped a coin into the waiter's hand and looked at Hawkwood. "Shall we?"

They left the café and entered the street.

"We'll walk," McPherson said, holding the wine to his chest. "Can't trust the cabs. They may be cheap but they're filthy and you never know when the driver's listening in. Police spies almost outnumber the rats here, and there are a powerful number of rats so it's hard to tell them apart. Best if we stick to the language, too. Besides, it's been that long I can barely recall the Gàidhlig, never mind your heathen tongue. You'll have heard about walls having ears. As far as this place is concerned, you can take that for granted."

The old man cast an oblique eye over the knapsack slung across Hawkwood's shoulder. "You've no luggage?"

"I'm travelling light," Hawkwood said.

McPherson, picking up the dryness of the response, nodded. "So I see. In that case, I won't ask if you had a comfortable journey."

The diligence had delivered Hawkwood to the dépôt on the rue Notre-Dame des Victoires at a little after eight o'clock, after an early departure following the last change of horses at Chambly. He was dressed in his own clothes and he was uncomfortably aware that it probably looked as though he'd slept in them for most of the journey, which wasn't that far from the truth. He'd left the tarpaulin coat behind, thinking it might draw unwelcome attention. Though he now realized he needn't have worried. The knapsack contained the change of

131

attire he'd been given by Alain, along with a razor and few toiletries also bequeathed prior to his boarding the coach. At the time, his own clothing hadn't fully recovered from its soaking and he'd had to wait until the first overnight stop at the inn at Abbeville to dry everything by the fire in his room. The journey, via Amiens and Beauvais, had taken three days and both he and his wardrobe were in need of restoration.

"You're fortunate," McPherson said, almost gleefully. "There was a time when it used to take a week. These days, you're here before you know it."

Hawkwood presumed from his tone that the old man was still joking.

"This way." McPherson indicated the direction with his cane.

Hawkwood's first impression of Paris had been that it wasn't that much different to London. It would certainly have given the latter a run for its money as far as the smell was concerned. It was the first thing that had hit him even before he'd stepped down from the coach. London was rank, especially on market days when blood and offal clogged the gutters, and Dover hadn't exactly been a bed of roses, but Paris had a reek to it that seemed to encompass the most foetid elements of both, with perhaps a shade more emphasis on the displacement of night soil than even Hawkwood was used to.

Negotiating the muddy, excreta-stained streets on foot had held no allure and as he didn't know the city anyway he'd trusted to luck. Armed with the name of the eating house where he'd been told one of Brooke's correspondents would make himself known, he'd travelled from the diligence dépôt to the café in one of McPherson's despised *fiacres*, the city's main form of public transport. Hawkwood had discovered that McPherson's dislike of them was well founded. True to the old man's description it had been a toss up which had been the dirtier: the coach's piss-stained floor or the streets through which he had been driven.

The journey had been a short one – no more than a mile at the most – but it had been long enough for Hawkwood to observe that, away from the main boulevards, the narrow streets and the buildings that lined them were just as dark and dilapidated as any Thames-side tenement. Glancing into the alleyways he could see their similarity to the squalid rat runs that led off the Haymarket, Leicester Square and Covent Garden. The noise was much the same, too. The clatter of hooves and the rattle of wooden and iron-wheeled carriages created an abrasive and common backdrop, as did the cries of the street traders. From colliers and cake sellers to water carriers, bill stickers and knife grinders, the drawn faces and ragged clothing of people trying to eke out a living in desperate times told an all too familiar story. The language may have differed but filth and poverty were universal.

And yet, despite the obvious signs of deprivation, there was also evidence of greater wealth in the grander avenues and squares, where the broad buildings with their colonnades and high windows were a match for any of those that lined Parliament Street and Whitehall.

And the building work, from what he'd seen on his brief journey through the city, was still ongoing; or at least if not the work itself then some semblance of it. Several of the main boulevards that he'd travelled along had been piled high with rubble, though there hadn't been more than a handful of men with shovels in sight.

But McPherson was leading him away from all that. In no time at all, they had left the busier streets behind and entered a neighbourhood of dingy lanes and dank passages where the pavements were too narrow to walk upon and where the buildings loomed over them like broken tombstones. As he followed McPherson further into the warren, the sound of their footsteps rebounded hollowly from the drab, damp walls.

Moving from one street into an even more crooked alleyway, Hawkwood looked up to where a dull metal sign revealed they were about to enter the rue Serpente.

Perhaps it was the name, but following McPherson beneath the rusted iron balconies and louvred shutters, with the plaster peeling away like rotting scales, it wasn't hard to imagine the surrounding houses coiling around them in reptilian folds and squeezing out their life's blood through cracks in the dark, pitted stonework.

McPherson turned under a low archway and led the way across a small, secluded courtyard towards the corner of a building and a stout wooden door. Inside the entrance, a winding staircase disappeared towards the roof. The building had obviously been well appointed at some time in the past, but now it had the feel of a place that had long since fallen on hard times, like an elderly dowager reduced to penury while still trying to maintain a dignified state of grace.

McPherson led the way upstairs and stopped outside a door on the fourth floor. Breathing heavily from the climb, he handed the bottle to Hawkwood while he fumbled for a key.

Before he placed the key in the lock, he lifted the knocker and rapped it on the door in what was clearly a pre-arranged signal; twice in quick succession, followed by a gap and then the same pattern repeated.

Before a reply could be given, McPherson unlocked the door and stepped inside.

"In you come," he wheezed.

As Hawkwood entered, the old man locked the door behind them then took the bottle and led the way down the hallway.

"He's here," McPherson said, pushing open a door at the end of the passage.

For a second Hawkwood thought he was the one being addressed until he followed McPherson into the main room.

As the old man stepped aside, a solitary figure appeared, framed by the window.

"Captain Hawkwood!" The figure spoke in English but there was no disguising the faint Highland burr. "Good morning to you. It's been a while."

"God Almighty!" Hawkwood said. His eyes dropped to the pistol held in the figure's left hand. Its muzzle was pointed towards the floor.

"Not quite." The speaker smiled and stepped forward, his right hand extended. "Only a poor sinner who's delighted to greet an old friend." He turned to McPherson. "A wee dram for our guest, Jamie. Smartly now! He looks as though he's seen a ghost!"

Hawkwood had to concede that, for a man who was supposed to be dead, Captain Colquhoun Grant of his Britannic Majesty's 11th Regiment of Foot was looking in remarkably fine health.

"So, laddie," Grant said, still pumping Hawkwood's hand, "how've you been?"

The smile on Grant's face was irresistible. It had been nearly three years since their last encounter, at Wellington's headquarters in Badajoz when, as one of his last duties before returning to England, Hawkwood had come in from the field to brief Grant on French troop movements and *guerrillero* activity along the eastern reaches of the Guardiana River.

"How have *I* been?" Hawkwood said, as he watched the Scot place the pistol on a side table. "You've got a bloody nerve."

Grant looked as hale as when Hawkwood had last seen him. The Scot had always tended towards leanness and as an exploring officer who spent a lot of time in the saddle, spying on the enemy and living off the land, he'd always been a lithe and fit man. It was odd, Hawkwood thought, how similar some of Grant's features were to those of Wellington. Both men wore their hair short and un-powdered. They shared the same long face. They even shared the same long nose; though whereas Wellington's was famously hooked, Grant's was straight and even. The difference was in their eyes. The intelligence and the strength of character were there for all to see. Wellington, however, was known for keeping his emotions under control. With Grant, there always seemed to be a hint of amusement in his clear, forthright gaze. The humour was there now, as McPherson passed round the glasses.

Grant grinned. "It's not the Glen Garioch, regrettably, but you can't deny the Frogs make uncommonly fine brandy." Grant raised his glass. "*Slàinte mhath!*"

"*Slàinte mhor!*" McPherson gave the reply and the three of them drank.

"So," Grant said, clapping Hawkwood on the shoulder. "Welcome to Paris."

"To hell with that," Hawkwood said. "They said you'd been

taken prisoner. They said you were hanged. You're supposed to be lying in an unmarked grave in some God-forsaken Frog cemetery."

"Excellent!" Grant said enthusiastically. "Then we should drink to that, as well."

"We should?" Hawkwood said warily.

"It means we've fooled the buggers into thinking I'm dead, too."

"And why have we done that?"

"To spread confusion among the enemy, Captain Hawkwood, why else?"

Which was exactly what Brooke had said, Hawkwood recalled.

"It's not just the enemy who's confused," Hawkwood said.

"Aye, well, if you'll sit yourself down, I'll explain everything."

"Are you telling me you weren't captured?" Hawkwood asked when they were seated. "They didn't take you prisoner?"

Grant shook his head. "Och, no, they caught me all right. That part's true enough. April sixteenth; in the hills outside Idanha-a-Nova. I remember it as if it were yesterday." He took a sip of brandy and his face darkened. "You know the place?"

Hawkwood shook his head. The name had a vaguely familiar ring, but he suspected that was because it sounded like every other mountaintop village in the Peninsula. He couldn't remember if he'd been told it when he'd learned that Grant had been captured. He took a stab. "Portugal?"

Grant nodded. "About fifteen miles from the border. There was a bad storm the evening before and we had to spend the night there."

"We?"

"Leon was with me."

Hawkwood remembered Leon, Grant's Spanish guide; a staunch companion and a good man to have at your shoulder. Like Nathaniel Jago, he thought immediately.

Grant paused as if collecting himself and then said, "We were

136

surprised by a patrol and tried to make a run for it." Grant's jaw tightened. "They chased us down. They killed Leon."

Hawkwood said nothing. There was nothing he could say. He knew how close the two men had been.

"They butchered him, Matthew. Killed him in cold blood. The bastard ran him through with my sword. My own bloody sword!"

Grant fell silent. He looked, Hawkwood thought, bereft.

"I'm sorry, Col," Hawkwood said eventually. "He was a brave man."

Grant looked at him, his mouth still set. He remained that way for several seconds and then nodded. "Aye he was that." Slowly, he raised his glass. "To Leon, my good friend."

Hawkwood and McPherson raised their glasses. "To Leon."

They drank and the room fell silent. Finally, Grant lowered his glass and took a deep breath. "They took me to Sabugal where, I have to say, Marshal Marmont was a most attentive host. Then Salamanca. After that it got a wee bit tricky."

"In what way?"

"You were there with Moore. Did you ever have any dealings with the good Doctor Curtis?"

"At the university?" Hawkwood shook his head. "Not personally. I knew *alcaldes* who had dealings with him, but we never met."

"But you'll remember the old rascal has more ears on the ground than olive pits."

Hawkwood nodded.

"He came to visit me while I was there. Marmont thought I was passing him information. He wasn't best pleased."

"And were you?"

"Passing information? Damned right I was! It was Marmont and de la Martinière – that's his bloody Chief of Staff by the way, odious little turd – who broke the terms of my parole, not me. As far as I was concerned, I was only evening the score."

Grant took a sip of brandy. "Anyway, Marmont decided I'd become too much of a threat; told me he was sending me north, to Verdun. I even had my own escort; two infantry companies and a troop of chasseurs."

"Nice to know he cared," Hawkwood said drily.

"Well, they weren't *just* for me. They were being re-deployed anyway. I was what you might call a last-minute appendage. But as luck would have it, the chasseur captain and I got along famously. Fosse, his name was. It was he who told me that I wasn't being taken to Verdun; his orders were to hand me over to the police for questioning. He didn't like that idea. Went against his code of honour. Mine, too, frankly. Anyway the upshot was that Fosse told me that he and his men were prepared to look the other way when we got to Bayonne. Unlike the marshal, he was true to his word. While he went off to secure accommodation for the night, I made my departure."

"And you came to Paris?" Hawkwood couldn't hide his doubt at the wisdom of Grant's decision.

"The last place they'd look. I knew when they found me gone they'd think I'd try to get back to Spain. Besides, Curtis and I had been hearing rumours that Boney was drawing up an invasion plan. Word was that he had Russia in his sights, but I thought if he was intending to invade England like the last time I might be able to gather information and either send it to London or back to Wellington. Turned out, of course, that it wasn't England he had his eyes on; it really was Russia."

"How did you get out of Bayonne?"

Grant grinned. "By posing as an American infantry officer."

Hawkwood stared at him.

"Thought that'd amuse you. Great minds think alike, eh?" Grant's grin widened. "What, you think I wouldn't know about your last escapade? Eyes and ears, Captain Hawkwood; eyes and ears. And you want to know the best part?"

"I've a feeling you're going to tell me anyway," Hawkwood said.

"I travelled as the guest of General Joseph Souham, Divisional Commander of the Army of Portugal."

"And how, in the name of all that's holy, did you manage that?"

"I introduced myself as Major Matthew Hawkwood of the 11th Regiment of Infantry. Told the general I was the personal envoy of President Madison of the United States of America. What do you think of that?"

"I repeat what I said last time," Hawkwood said. "That you've got the devil's own bloody nerve." He looked at McPherson. "I note you're not saying much, Mr McPherson."

McPherson waved a hand dismissively. His eyes blinked behind his spectacle lenses. "Och, I've heard it all before. Though I have to say it's an honour to meet you, Captain. Major Grant's been most complimentary."

It was the first time McPherson had reverted to English. Despite his pronouncement earlier that his use of the language was rusty, it was obvious the opposite was true. His English speaking voice was quite soft and lilting, more so than Grant's.

"*Major?*" Hawkwood said, turning. "Is there anything else you'd care to tell me?"

Grant gave a self-deprecating shrug. "Och, brevet rank only. I'm still on a captain's wages. Nothing to write home about, if that's what you mean. Look what good it did me." Grant smiled. "Stuck in a Frog garret with a damned Jacobite."

Hawkwood cocked an eyebrow.

McPherson sighed and shook his head despairingly. "It's plain to see the young man has no manners, Captain. It'll be the Sassenach influence, I'm thinking, that'll have caused such a deterioration in the respect for his elders."

"He's been telling me that since I turned up on his doorstep," Grant said, smiling.

"Monsieur Ouvrard has much to answer for," McPherson murmured, though without any real malice.

"Curtis's man in Orleans," Grant explained, smiling. "Our good doctor has a long reach. I thought it prudent if I didn't travel *all* the way to Paris with the general, even though he was excellent company. A very interesting fellow all round, in fact. Generous with the cigars, too. Anyway, I gave him the impression that I'd business elsewhere by concocting a rendezvous in

Chartres. He seemed to take me at my word. Told me to look him up if I was ever in Paris."

"Decent of him," Hawkwood said. "I'm assuming you haven't done so."

"Too late now, alas. He's back in Spain, as Wellington's finding out to his cost; though just as well for me, as it happens. Were we to bump into one another, I'm not sure I could keep up the pretence. Now, where was I? Oh, yes, it was Ouvrard who passed me on to James, here. I have to say, when I heard the name, I was expecting the *descendant* of a Highlander, not the real thing."

Grant threw McPherson a sly look.

McPherson caught the gesture and shook his head wearily. He looked at Hawkwood and his eyes took on a steely glint. "In case you were wondering, I am James Lachlan McPherson, kinsman to Ewen MacPherson of Cluny, Chief of Clan Chattan and I was with Charles Edward Stewart when he took passage to France on the frigate *L'Heureux* in the year 1746."

Hawkwood stared at the old man in wonder, calculating that he'd not been that far out in his estimation of McPherson's advanced years. He wondered if *his* eyes would shine as brightly or if his limbs would support him with such vigour at that age, were he to live that long. He couldn't think of many, if any, octogenarians he'd met who were so fit and, it had to be said, quite so fly with it.

"Ever been back?" Hawkwood asked.

"To Scotland?"

Hawkwood nodded.

McPherson thought about it. "No, though I did go to England once. I accompanied the Prince when he went back to try and raise another army. Can't say I was taken with the place. I realized, too late, that it was naught but a dream, anyway. The Prince was not the man he once was. He'd become a little too fond of the bottle; the ladies as well, it had to be said. The shine was wearing off, if you catch my drift. And I had a new life here by then, and a wife. I had other . . . obligations."

"You've lived here ever since?"

"I have indeed."

"Your family . . .?"

"My wife's been in her grave these past fifteen years."

"I'm sorry," Hawkwood said.

"We had a good marriage. It was her time."

"Children?"

McPherson shook his head. "Only my work."

"Are you really a jeweller?"

Amusement shone in the old man's eyes. "The devil makes work for idle hands, Captain. I needed something to occupy my time. It was either that or wandering the streets. And you've seen the state of the streets. I've a wee room set aside here and I also have a small shop, though not as close as I told you, on the other side of the river. I think it would be fair to say that business has been . . ." the old man gave a rueful smile ". . . rather sporadic of late, but I'm able to keep busy with the odd commission here and there."

"*And* you're working for the English?" Hawkwood said. "That seems strange. What is it you call us? The auld enemy?"

The old man put his head on one side. There was no sign that he'd taken offence. "'The enemy of my enemy is my friend'; isn't that what they say?"

"You now see *France* as your enemy?"

"Not France, Captain," McPherson said quietly, almost as if he was afraid of being overheard. "Bonaparte."

"Some say Bonaparte *is* France," Hawkwood pointed out.

"Aye, that they do; but his extravagances and this latest enterprise against Alexander are costing him dear. His star's waning."

"You don't believe the reports about his victories?"

The old man waved a hand dismissively. "Och, I've no doubt he's been victorious, but the newspapers are slaves to the state. They're told what to write. You said it yourself: he may have won the battle but they will have undoubtedly understated the number of casualties. If the army had been defeated, I doubt we'd even know about it."

"'Among the calamities of war may be jointly numbered the

diminution of the love of truth, by the falsehoods which interest dictates and credulity encourages,'" Grant intoned.

Hawkwood and McPherson looked at him. McPherson raised an eyebrow. Grant shrugged. "I believe it was said by Johnson."

"Johnson?" Hawkwood said.

"Doctor Johnson, the noted lexicographer. He also penned a book called *A Journey to the Western Isles of Scotland*. I found it uncommonly good reading."

"I thought it was a trifle dry myself," McPherson said, pursing his lips. "Though I believe he also said that a peace will equally leave the warrior and relater of wars destitute of employment. So perhaps he's more perceptive than I give him credit for."

Grant chuckled. He turned to Hawkwood. "Would you listen to the man! There's nothing like a Scot moaning about life to remind you of home. It's like being back in a Kingussie bothy on a Saturday night."

Hawkwood had no idea what a Kingussie bothy was. He suspected it was probably the Scottish equivalent of a Deptford drinking den. If so, he had some idea of what Grant had meant.

Grant drained his glass. "I'm assuming you had no problems with your documents?"

"No," Hawkwood said. "There was nothing wrong with the documents."

Grant's head came up, his eyes hardened perceptively. "Something else, though."

Hawkwood nodded. "I should have told you sooner. We had trouble at the landing point. You've received no word?"

"No," Grant said, instantly alert. "What kind of trouble?"

Hawkwood told him.

"God damn," Grant swore. He exchanged looks with McPherson.

Hawkwood said, "I need to know that Stuart and the others made it to safety. Can you find out?"

"James?" Grant said.

McPherson nodded. "I'll see what I can do."

Grant looked at Hawkwood. His face was serious. "Neither

Captain Stuart nor the young lady know anything about the purpose of your journey here, correct?"

"Damn it, Col! *I* don't even know why I'm here," Hawkwood said. "Superintendent Brooke wasn't disposed to discuss the finer details with me. He left that to you. He told me it was safer that way."

"Aye, well, he was quite right." Grant sat back, still looking thoughtful. He remained silent for several seconds and then said, "With the patrol and their officer dead, I think it's safe to assume that your presence on French soil has gone unnoticed by the authorities. That's something in our favour, at least." He held Hawkwood's eye. "The patrol couldn't be allowed to alert the garrison to the landing of one of our agents from a British warship. Mademoiselle and her accomplices did the right thing in intercepting you at the bridge."

"I know that. I just need to know if they all got away. How long will it take you to find out?"

"James has good people working with him, but the lines of communication are somewhat fluid, so it may take a wee while. But we'll make enquiries, I promise you."

It wasn't the answer he'd been hoping for, but it would have to do. Hawkwood nodded. "I'm obliged."

Grant said, "At least we can be thankful your arrival *here* has gone un-remarked. A citizen of recruiting age travelling on his own when the country needs all eligible men for war service can sometimes lead to awkward questioning."

"I'll take that as a compliment," Hawkwood said. "As it so happens, I'm an officer on personal leave returning to join my regiment and I've the papers to prove it."

"*Personal* leave?"

"Wounded in the course of my duties and visiting a sick father."

"Ah, indeed," Grant said, nodding sagely. "My commiserations. So, definitely no trouble in that regard, then?"

"No . . ." Hawkwood assured him.

Which wasn't to say there hadn't been that moment of concern when he'd shown his papers to the slovenly dressed official at

143

the Paris Customs Barrier; this despite Stormont Flint having told him that the blank documents he'd been given in London were the genuine article. They'd been obtained, Flint had assured him, through the royalist underground and smuggled to London by special courier. All they'd needed to make them valid had been the addition of Hawkwood's alias and the forged signatures of a municipal administrator and a representative of the Parisian Central Bureau, both of which Flint had provided with a flourish of his pen.

Hawkwood had secured the documents inside an oilskin pouch sewn into the lining of his waistcoat; a precaution which he later came to realize had been a miracle of foresight, for the papers had survived the drenched landing completely intact. And so far they'd done their job. Flint's confidence had been well placed. Though it hadn't stopped Hawkwood from holding his breath as he'd handed them over for inspection.

He'd felt a similar apprehension when he'd identified himself as the fictitious Captain Vallon to Lieutenant Malbreau, though for a different reason. That deception had been made on the spur of the moment based on his and Stuart's then circumstances. Had they arrived at Mahon and been thoroughly searched and the passport discovered in another man's name . . . well, that was something Hawkwood preferred not to dwell upon. Thinking about Stuart, he knew the sooner he discovered the fate of *Griffin*'s captain and the girl, the sooner his mind would be set at rest.

He found Grant was staring at him.

"What?"

Grant's face softened. "I was thinking you've gained a few more scars since I saw you last. Looks to me as if you've survived as many skirmishes back home as you did in Spain. The criminal element would appear to be growing more brazen. Am I right?"

"Could be I'm just getting slower in my old age," Hawkwood said.

"I doubt that," Grant responded with a smile. "Oh, and I almost forgot; how's that reprobate Jago? I take it *he's* not retired yet?"

"He's thinking of buying a horse and carriage," Hawkwood said.

"Good God!" Grant looked genuinely shocked at the thought.

"Besides, Nathaniel's too young to retire," Hawkwood added. "At least, that's what he keeps telling me." He eyed Grant speculatively. "But I suspect you probably knew that already, didn't you?"

Grant laughed. "Ha! Still no flies on you, eh, Captain? Aye, well, it's true I've been keeping a weather eye on your . . . exploits. You've made quite a reputation for yourself in certain quarters. And may I say how relieved I am to hear that your unconventional approach to policing appears to be just as cavalier as your disregard for the finer points of military discipline."

Hawkwood looked at him. "What the hell am I doing here, Col?"

Grant chuckled. "All in good time, I promise you." He slapped his knee enthusiastically. "Tell me, have you eaten? Are you hungry?"

"I'd prefer to wash the dust off first," Hawkwood said.

"Splendid!" Grant grinned and stood up. "I know the very place!"

As he got to his feet, Hawkwood wondered where a man everyone thought was dead was about to lead him.

9

It was an odd feeling, accompanying Grant; for two main reasons. The first was because they were conversing in French – an obvious and sensible requirement they'd both agreed to uphold whenever they left the apartment – and the second was that Grant, in a bizarre juxtaposition, was clad not in civilian clothes but his British army uniform.

"Might seem risky, I know," Grant said, as they descended into the courtyard. "But wearing the scarlet helps me blend in. Here, I'm just another soldier. I've removed some of my insignia in case anyone's been tempted to look too closely, but so far they haven't. As far as the world's concerned, I'm Major Connor Grey of the American 11th Regiment of Infantry."

"*Grey?*" Hawkwood said. "What happened to Major Hawkwood?"

"I thought it best to discontinue with the name when I parted company from General Souham; just in case he had a hankering to make enquiries. I chose Connor to keep my own initials. It's close enough to my own name, too; which means I'm less likely to be caught unawares if I'm addressed by it."

"Just as well," Hawkwood said. "I'd find it bloody strange talking to myself."

"Probably wouldn't be the first time though, eh?" Grant quipped. He clapped Hawkwood on the shoulder and grinned infectiously. "Fortunately, the American regiment was only created earlier this year, so I'm unlikely to be unmasked; as far as the uniform's concerned, anyway. And, like you, I have papers. James provided me with the necessary documents shortly after my arrival."

"He produced them himself?"

Grant chuckled. "Who's to know? He did assure me he's not averse to a little counterfeisance when the need demands."

"A man of many talents," Hawkwood said, as they crossed the courtyard and walked under the archway into the street.

They had left McPherson upstairs. The old man had a commission from a favoured customer to complete and the time spent in his workshop, he told them, would give him the opportunity to decide how best to address Hawkwood's request for information on the fate of Stuart and Mademoiselle de Préville and her knife-wielding associate, Raoul.

Grant nodded. "That he is, and all of them serve *our* purposes admirably. Thanks to him, I've been accepted as an American major on secondment. I've been strolling the boulevards ever since, keeping my eyes open and my ears to the ground, visiting the places frequented by army officers and members of the government: coffee houses, theatres, reading rooms; that sort of thing; even those new galleries at the Musée. It's proved damned useful. Just goes to show: if you look the part and act with confidence, no one gives you a second glance."

Grant looked around, but apart from a couple of feral cats and a scrawny dog and an old woman swathed in black who emerged from a narrow doorway to tip a bowl of dirty water on to the cobbles, the street was empty. The crone gave them a cursory inspection as she closed her door but offered no sign of greeting. Her face was as creased as a walnut shell.

Reaching the end of the street, they left the rue Serpente behind and with Grant leading the way they began to retrace the route Hawkwood had taken earlier that morning.

As they made their way towards the more crowded thoroughfares, Hawkwood, in absorbing the sights and smells around him, saw that Grant was right; it was impossible not to be aware of the number of uniforms on view.

He'd noticed a similar preponderance during the coach journey from Boulogne when the diligence had passed several army units marching along the roads or in some cases bivouacking beside them. It was clear that troops were being re-deployed in substantial numbers. What had been equally apparent had been their direction of travel: inland, away from the coast. It suggested Bonaparte was still rounding up men to bolster his armies in the east. And the vast majority of them had all been either alarmingly young or very old. Looking around, it wasn't dissimilar to the military on display in Paris.

Hawkwood shared his observations with Grant, who nodded in agreement. "You're right. It was the first thing that struck me when I arrived here in June. I thought it had all the markings of a nation falling back upon its last resources. Turns out I wasn't far wrong."

"What have you found out?" Hawkwood asked, as they turned right on to a narrow and busy shop-lined street. They were heading north, he knew, towards the river.

"Oh, the Empire's in dire straits, no doubt about it. The rot started a while ago, mind. It's not recent. The bugger was in trouble even before his army crossed the Nieman."

"How so?"

Grant was walking with his hands clasped behind his back. He might have been out for a Sunday stroll through Hyde Park had it not been for his eyes, which were constantly on the move. Evidently sharing McPherson's distrust of public transport, he'd suggested they proceed on foot to their destination as walking the city would give Hawkwood a better feel for his surroundings. Hawkwood had readily agreed.

The rattle of carriages and the cries of shopkeepers accompanied them along the street. Less strident but just as insistent were the voices of the beggars, who seemed to occupy the entrance to every alcove and alleyway. Many were children, their faces pinched with hunger. There were a lot of cripples, too, with a large proportion of them missing an arm or leg, sometimes both. Hawkwood couldn't help noticing that the majority of the amputees were wearing the remnants of military uniforms.

"He had to delay the invasion, for one thing," Grant continued. "It had been his plan to go in April, but he didn't have enough men. He was forced to order Clarke to increase conscription." Grant shook his head in what might have been despair. "When you've an army that's going to be fighting on two fronts, you know you're in trouble; or you would if you had any damned sense."

Henri Clarke was Bonaparte's Minister of War; of Irish descent, his role in thwarting the British invasion of Walcheren three years before had led to the Emperor creating him Duke of Feltre. Yet another Celt fighting for a foreign crown, Hawkwood mused.

Grant pursed his lips. "Clarke's been recruiting heavily and transferring men ever since. He's had to pull them in from all over the damned place: Rochelle, Naples, even Spain. That's why Fosse and his chasseurs and those infantry companies were given their marching orders. Clarke was told to find as many bodies as he could and send them to Germany to join the Grand Armée."

Grant paused in his narration to negotiate yet another basin-sized pothole, one of scores that pockmarked the streets like shell craters. As Hawkwood side-stepped the other way it struck him, remembering the amount of earth that he'd seen piled along the edges of the larger boulevards, that a good deal of the debris could have been put to good use mending the road surfaces. He was forced to dodge again as a *fiacre* swerved violently to avoid a deep, rain-filled rut; a manoeuvre which caused several other pedestrians to leap aside to avoid being run down and splattered with mud and manure. A stream of invective followed the carriage as it continued to veer its way up the street.

The hazard avoided, Grant picked up the conversation once more.

"You were saying the soldiers at Mahon didn't look up to much; my guess is they were probably National Guardsmen drafted in. The uniform's not that dissimilar, as you'll see, and it was all part of Clarke's brief. He was tasked to reorganize the Guard units and use them to replace regular garrisons."

150

Grant looked up to get his bearings and then added, "He was also told to scour sick battalions to weed out malingerers."

"Things must have been bad," Hawkwood said.

"And from what I've been able to glean, they ain't improved much. Just before I got here he was forced to round up most of the Army of Italy. It did the trick in the short run. He was able to send some of the surplus cohorts to Germany to augment the reserves. Boney had damned near four hundred and fifty thousand men under his command by the time the offensive began, and that's not counting the Austrians and Prussians."

"Half a million!?" Hawkwood couldn't hide his astonishment at the figure. It was a colossal army by anyone's measure. "My God, how can he fail?"

"Ah, but it ain't the number of men; you know that. It's their mettle that counts. The question is: do they have the stomach to fight?"

Hawkwood guessed the question was rhetorical so he remained silent. Grant said heavily, "If you ask me, I doubt it'll be the size or courage of his army that'll determine the outcome of his campaign. It'll be the weather."

"The weather?"

Grant nodded. "There's more than one person I've spoken to who's told me that the plans to prepare the army for a winter campaign have been insufficient. No heavy clothing's been issued. There's been no provision for horse care; no winter stockpiles and no transportation has been made available, even if supplies *were* ready to go. It'll be a bloody disaster. His troops are going to die in their thousands. Take my word on it."

The remark made Hawkwood think about Malbreau and the men who'd perished in the ambush. If the alternative to a posting with the Mahon garrison was a transfer to the Russian front, perhaps in the long run it was they who had been the fortunate ones.

Grant halted. They had run out of street. Directly in front of them was the river, with an uninterrupted view to the opposite shore across a wide and imposing stone bridge.

"They call this side the Left Bank," Grant said. "We're standing

151

on the Quai des Grands-Augustins." Giving a small smile, he added, "You'll find they do have a tendency to name a lot of their streets after their saints and holy orders."

The stench from the river rose to greet them. It was worse than the Thames, a lot worse. Hawkwood wouldn't have thought that was possible, though given the state of the streets he knew he shouldn't have been that surprised.

Grant, catching the expression on his face, said, "The Seine's only tidal as far as Rouen. There's nothing to wash away the shit this far upstream. It's not like London."

The river may not have had the rise and fall of the tide to cleanse its banks or permit large vessels to navigate its upper reaches – and in any case its distance from the sea, not to mention all the bridges, precluded it from being a major port – but Hawkwood could see that there was still a high volume of traffic.

Grant nodded towards the large island that occupied the middle of the river and the jumble of rooftops, gables, windows, cupolas and chimney pots that dominated the centre of it. "The Île de la Cité."

Hawkwood found his eye drawn to the right; the eastern end of the island, where another large edifice with dual towers was outlined against the gloomy sky: the city's magnificent cathedral.

The bridge – Grant identified it as the Pont Neuf – grazed the Île's westernmost tip and as the two men reached the juncture and looked east through a gap in the buildings towards the centre of the island, Hawkwood found it hard not to liken it to cutting across the prow of a huge ship.

Through the gap, he could see a wedge of tree-lined square and beyond that, partially concealed by the autumnal foliage, the vague shape of a building; probably one of those he'd seen previously from the quayside. Flanked by tall, red-brick houses, the street leading down towards the square looked narrow and uninviting, like the entrance to a hidden canyon.

Reaching the north shore – referred to by Grant, somewhat inevitably, as the Right Bank – Hawkwood found his eyes drawn back to the island and a long, sinister-looking building several hundred yards down from the bridge. Built close to the bank, its huge bulk rose out of the water like the side of a cliff. Set into the walls were four large towers, three circular and one square. Each of the rounded towers was surmounted by a steep conical roof with the middle two towers set either side of what might have been an ancient sallyport. With the river flowing alongside it like a defensive moat, the building's curious and distinctive architecture gave it the look of an impregnable medieval fortress.

Grant followed Hawkwood's gaze and his face grew still. "The Conciergerie. They call it the antechamber."

"To what?"

"The guillotine. It's a prison. You see the towers there? They all have names. They call that one the 'blabbing tower'. It's where the poor bastards were tortured to loosen their tongues. Not that it did them any good. Most died anyway."

Grant turned away and said, almost matter of factly, "James told me it was the most bestial place he'd ever seen. That was his word for it: bestial."

With Hawkwood staring at him, Grant said, "He was held there during the Terror. He was accused of plotting against the Republic and circulating counter-revolutionary literature."

"Tortured?"

Grant shook his head. "I don't know that for certain. He doesn't talk about it. Fortunately for him, his accuser fell foul of the Tribunal before any sentence was carried out. When Robespierre and his cronies were executed, he was set free."

"*Robespierre* was his accuser?"

It explained the old man's vehemence at the café and why his allegiance had changed.

Grant nodded. "One of them. They say Robespierre was the only man to be guillotined face up; so that he could see death approaching. Have to say, I'd rather look a firing squad in the eye than watch a damned guillotine blade falling towards me." Grant shuddered at the thought.

Hawkwood looked again at the prison and tried to imagine what it must have been like, knowing the tumbrils and the

153

screaming crowds and the blade were waiting for you. You'd probably be able to hear the baying of the mob from inside your cell. He thought about McPherson. Less than twenty years had passed since the height of the killings, when the streets had run crimson with blood. McPherson would have been in his sixties, Hawkwood estimated; no spring chicken. There was obviously a lot more to the elderly Scot than first met the eye.

Hawkwood diverted his gaze and looked out over the balustrade down on to the river to where two squat and scabby barges were moored in a line along the bank. They were draped with washing lines; each one festooned with drying towels.

"Bathing boats," Grant said. "Contrary to what you might have heard, the Frogs do like their ablutions."

"*That's* where you're taking me?"

"Good Lord, man, don't be daft!" Grant shook his head in disbelief and tut-tutted, appalled that Hawkwood should even have considered such a calumny. "Can you not see the state of the water? No, I've something much more salubrious in mind, don't you fear!"

Leaving the river behind, they continued on their way, with Grant pointing out more street names and landmarks.

"You'll see that Boney does covet his monuments," Grant chuckled. "Especially when they're to commemorate his own victories. Though to be fair he does like to honour his own heroes, too."

As if to illustrate the point a large statue appeared before them, a towering and very well-endowed bronze figure holding a sword, nude save for a scabbard belt draped over the right shoulder. "Meet General Desaix," Grant said. "Just as well he died at Marengo so he couldn't see what they've done to him. You can imagine the comments."

As he considered Desaix's splendidly cast torso, Hawkwood pondered on the chances of viewing a nude statue of Wellington in St James's Square. All things considered, it didn't seem a very likely prospect.

He was still trying to erase that disturbing vision from his mind when, a few streets later, Grant proclaimed with a flourish,

"We're here!" and Hawkwood found himself confronted by one of the most gaudily offensive structures he'd seen since his last visit to the Vauxhall Pleasure Gardens.

It was the salmon pink façade that first drew the eye, followed by the water dragons, fish-shaped weather vanes, paper lanterns and bright golden pennants that adorned the blue-tinted, pagoda roof. At ground level, two massive boulders flanked the entrance to the front courtyard. Adorning the summit of each was a cross-legged figure holding an open parasol. While above the entrance, framed by carvings of birds and winged serpents, was a small plaque upon which was engraved the word: BAINS.

Collecting their tickets from the payment booth, they entered the building.

The first person Hawkwood saw as he walked through the door was Chen.

Grant opened one eye. "So, how does it feel?"

It felt, Hawkwood had to admit, bloody wonderful. He looked down. There wasn't a part of him, he suspected, that wasn't glowing, including, quite possibly, his earlobes. He glanced to his left, where Grant was leaning back in the adjacent tub, eyes closed, savouring the moment. Wisps of steam rose like tendrils from the water around them.

Grant grinned. "Not sampled the pleasure before?"

"Nothing like this."

"You never paid a visit to the *Baños Árabes* in Badajoz?"

"No. If you remember, I was otherwise engaged."

With the guerrilleros in the mountains, trying to stay warm and one step ahead of the French scouting parties, Hawkwood thought, though without resentment because he knew that Grant, as an exploring officer, would have experienced the very same thing.

"Ah, well then you missed a rare treat. Splendid establishment; a legacy of the Moors. I had the occasion to be taken there by one of our Spanish allies, Don Diego Ruiz; aide to General Ballesteros. Did you ever meet the general?"

"Can't say I did," Hawkwood said.

"Well, frankly, I doubt you'd have forgotten him if you had. Never risked a fight that he could avoid. Ruiz, on the other hand; ah, now there was a natural fighter. Very attractive daughter, too." Grant winked. "Anyway, that's where I first dipped *my* elbow in the waters. Couldn't believe my luck when I discovered this place. The locals call it the Chinese Baths. Lot of nonsense, of course. Doubt there's a bathhouse within a thousand miles of China that looks anything like this one, but who's to know? It's one of those fashions the French seem to have taken a fancy to. They can blame his supreme majesty for that. The man's like a magpie; always latching on to something. First it was Egyptian obelisks, now it's everything oriental. Including bloody elephants."

"Elephants?" Hawkwood said. "What on earth have elephants got to do with anything? Are there even elephants *in* China?"

"Buggered if I know. The Emperor seems to think so. He's having one built."

"An elephant?"

"Where the Bastille stood, before they tore it down. It's going to be forty feet high and they're going to forge it from British cannon captured in Spain."

"An *elephant*?" Hawkwood said again, in case he hadn't heard it right the first time. "He's dragging British cannon over the mountains and all the way to Paris to build an elephant?"

"So they say. My own feeling is that it's more likely to look like a bloody big stove with a bent chimney. Still, you never know. It might take attention away from old Desaix for a while. Though, on second thoughts, as we appear to be winning in Spain, he could end up a mite short of materials."

The world, Hawkwood thought, had gone stark staring mad. As Grant fell silent alongside him, he watched a bath attendant walk past with a collection of warm towels over his arm. With the same compact stature, almond-shaped eyes and shorn scalp, the attendant's similarity to Chen was uncanny.

He wondered if any of the facilities in the baths would be familiar to his sparring partner and whether there was a similar establishment in London. Maybe he'd ask Chen if and when he returned home. It was definitely something he could grow used to, now that he knew what it entailed.

When they'd entered the baths, Hawkwood had been content to let Grant take the lead. They'd been directed to a row of cubicles, where they'd placed their clothing in a locker and received in exchange a towel and a numbered wrist chain.

Wrapped in their towels, they were escorted into large tiled washroom. Slatted wooden benches were arranged on the floor, with drainage holes beneath. As they took their seats, pails of water and bars of soap wrapped in soft cloth were placed beside them. Hawkwood looked around. They were not alone. There were a dozen or so men scattered around the room. Some wore towels; others were naked. The atmosphere was relaxed and convivial.

Hawkwood had no qualms about communal bathing. You couldn't be a soldier in the company of other soldiers without foregoing all inhibitions when it came to attending to personal hygiene. So, when Grant removed his towel and began to wash himself energetically from head to toe with the items provided, while still seated, Hawkwood followed suit. Though he did begin to wonder about the level of Grant's enthusiasm for what appeared to be no more than a wooden bucket and a brisk lather with a soapy rag, in water that could best be described as just the right side of tepid.

Grant, catching his doubtful expression had laughed. "Don't worry, it'll all become clear."

And so it had.

When they were fully soaped, pails of clean water had been brought to them to rinse the suds and grime from their bodies. Fully cleansed, with the dirty water gurgling into the drainage vents, they moved on to the next part of the ritual, the soaking room.

When he stepped into the tub and lowered himself gingerly into the clear, clean water, Hawkwood knew immediately what a fresh-plucked guinea fowl being dropped into a stew felt like. But then, within a few moments, the initial intensity of the water temperature gradually dissipated and, as his body had grown used to the heat, he'd felt his muscles begin to relax.

"Blessed clever, these Orientals," Grant said, grinning. "People say it in jest but, by God, you've got to admit it's a damned civilized way to spend an hour or two. Ought to be compulsory for all officers in the field, though I can't see Horse Guards including it in King's Regulations, can you?"

The heat was intoxicating. Hawkwood's scars showed white against the rest of his reddening skin. Struck by a vision in which he was attempting to introduce Nathaniel Jago to the therapeutic delights of hot tubs, he had the sudden urge to grin. Now, that *was* something he'd pay good money to see.

The decor was astonishing. The gilded mirrors, lacquered screens and frescoes of strange-looking men in flowing robes surrounded by all manner of fabled creatures looked suitably exotic but as to whether they were authentic, Hawkwood was inclined to support Grant's theory that any decorations would have sufficed, providing they weren't French. He was also inclined to think the same maxim probably applied to some of the attendants.

There were several Orientals working in the baths and Grant had laughed when he'd seen Hawkwood's reaction to their presence and heard his explanation as to why he'd been so taken aback.

"I doubt any of them have been further east than Marseilles," Grant had told him. "Not like *your* fellow. I'll wager they're here only because they look mysterious and the proprietor thinks it's good for business. My guess is he'd be just as likely to employ dancing girls and bare-arsed boys in togas if he thought there was a demand for it. But you can visit the Cabaret over in the Courtille for that sort of thing, if you've a mind. The clientele here tends towards the nobs rather than the ne'er-do-wells."

"And yet they've let *us* in," Hawkwood countered. "Times must be hard."

Grant made a face. "I did hear the place is running at a loss. In case you hadn't noticed when we arrived, this is a very expensive stretch of boulevard. The Chaussée-d'Antin's just around the corner. They say it's the finest street in Paris. Mind you, you still wouldn't want to walk around there at night. In fact, you wouldn't want to walk anywhere at night, if you can help it. This city's got more pickpockets than it has fleas. Not that we need worry about them here, though, eh?"

"Fleas or pickpockets?"

"Ha! Well, fleas certainly. As for the other; speaking for myself it ain't their pockets I'm interested in picking, it's what they have up here that's far more valuable." Grant reached up and tapped the side of his skull with a puckered forefinger. "Information, old friend. Information. It's a well-known fact that when a gentleman drops his trousers, he's liable to lower his guard at the same time. You recall I told you I'd been visiting various haunts and watering places? Well, this is one of them. Take a look around; I'll wager half the arses on display belong in military breeches."

"And the other half?"

"Toffs and swells. What you and I might call the gentry; people of means and influence."

"I thought they'd got rid of them during the Revolution," Hawkwood said. "Wasn't that the point of the bloody thing?"

Grant snorted. "Don't you believe a word of it. They might not saunter around in their frills and their finery, but they're here. A lot of the old-style aristos lost their heads to the blade, but new ones have sprung up in their place. Egalité's all very well for the masses, but the man proclaimed himself Emperor, for God's sake. Ever since his coronation he's been conferring titles on his cronies, creating his own aristocracy. What? You didn't think it was going to be just him and the peasantry did you? He needs someone to talk to. And if you think any of them would be seen shedding their drawers on a common bathing boat, you've got another think coming.

"With the types they get in here, I've picked up quite a few snippets in between the soapings and the soaks. There's no limit to how unguarded the undressed can become, especially when they think they're conversing with a fellow officer and a gentleman. No one to check my uniform and credentials here, eh? You're not likely to find any of Savary's people with their arses out, either, I can tell you that. Leaves them too exposed! Ha!"

Grant fell silent. Hawkwood waited. The Scot pursed his lips. "It occurs to me that we've digressed from our earlier discussion. As I recall, I was telling you about Clarke and the trouble he's been having."

Hawkwood knew Grant well enough from their previous liaisons to know that the Scot was not a man to be rushed and he respected him for that. Grant was setting the scene at his own pace and Hawkwood was content to let him do so.

"You said he was still trying to recruit men. With half a million on the march, I'm surprised there's anyone left."

"There isn't. That's why Bonaparte's sent word that he wanted hospitals and sick battalions cleared out as well."

"He's emptying *hospitals*?" Hawkwood said disbelievingly.

"He's going for anyone he can get; doesn't matter if they're sick or lame. It'll be the lunatics and the blind next. I think we can safely say he's not far off the bottom of the barrel."

Listening to Grant's tale of woe, it sounded, Hawkwood thought, as if the Empire was falling apart at the seams. But the Scot hadn't finished.

"Actually, that's not strictly true. I heard a rumour a couple of days ago that the Emperor might even be going after men who've already served their time and been mustered out."

"Retired veterans?" Hawkwood considered the implications. He stared hard at Grant. "How have you managed to find all this out?"

"It's as I told you; I've been using my eyes and ears."

"And you've passed all this on to London?"

"To London *and* to Wellington. Every last snippet of intelligence I've been able to gather. You now know what they know."

"Except why I'm here," Hawkwood said pointedly.

"Ah, yes." Grant smiled. "That."

"I'm assuming it has something to do with what you've been telling me?"

"It has *everything* to do with what I've been telling you."

Grant's eyes suddenly took on a new gleam. "Let me ask you this: on your journey here and during our walk this morning, what did you see?"

This time, Hawkwood knew, the question was not rhetorical. His mind went back to his first impressions of the city and what his eyes and ears had told him in the intervening hours since his arrival and he sensed immediately the answer he was expected to give. It was the one he would have voiced anyway.

"I saw a country that's losing a war."

"Anything else strike you?" Grant regarded him keenly.

"It knows it's losing, and it's tired of it."

And Grant smiled.

"And when something gets tired," Hawkwood said, thinking aloud, "it gets careless."

"And fractious, and we all know what happens then."

"It turns on itself," Hawkwood said, and saw in Grant's steady gaze confirmation that he'd passed the test. "You think that's what's happening?"

"I don't think it; I *know* it. You heard what McPherson said: Bonaparte's star is no longer in the ascendance. When he first arrived the people saw him as their salvation from the chaos of the mobs. Not any more. They see him for what he is, a usurper whose actions have become more extreme with each passing proclamation. Any gains that were made by the Revolution were swept away the moment they voted the bugger Consul for Life. Anyone foolish enough to give a man unlimited power finds out soon enough what he's going to do with it. You only have to look at his latest flight of fancy to know that. He's let his obsession with Alexander get the better of him and in doing so he's left the country to fend for itself. He's draining France of its lifeblood. Walk down any street and you can see the effects!

"This city's littered with abandoned projects: buildings and monuments to his glory started and left half finished, either because he's underestimated the cost or else he's had to use the money to fund his war chest. And while he's financing his war, people are starving to death. And it's not *just* because of the blockade. The harvests were so bad last year the country almost ran out of flour. Flour, for Christ's sake!

"Smuggling's become a way of life and half the beggars are old soldiers. You saw that in what's left of the rags they're wearing. He promised them pensions and nursing homes, and he's provided neither. Not that they'd have need of them anyway because he doesn't want them to enjoy what's left of their old age. If they can walk, he wants them to pick up a bloody musket and march off to war.

"But even the able-bodied are ignoring the call now. It's deserters who are responsible for most of the crime. And you know how to spot the villains? They'll be the ones missing their trigger fingers and teeth. That way they can't get called up. No fingers, no teeth – means they can't open the musket cartridges. Clever, eh?"

Grant held up his hands and waggled his fingers to emphasize his point. "Oh, and did I tell you that the country's nearly run out of money? That's because the banks have over-extended themselves trying to offer better discounts than their rivals, which has left the weaker houses with nowhere to go for help. Businesses are failing because they can't secure a line of credit. So, not only do the citizens have a potential famine to deal with, there's a financial shortfall as well. The deficit was that bad last year, they had to cancel the back pay owed to the widows and families of soldiers who'd died in the line of duty. You can imagine what that did for morale." Grant's jaw tightened. "And how does his nibs deal with the crisis? He invades Russia!"

The Scot shook his head in exasperation. "Even the army's turning against him. I sensed rumblings during my conversations with Captain Fosse. Clarke's recruiting methods haven't gone down well with the senior staff; they see the redeployment as diluting the quality of their frontline troops. And I'm not just talking about Spain – the commanders in Italy and Germany feel the same way. If he can't rely on *their* support, *who* can he turn to?"

The Scot added grimly, "They say that when they were conscripting men for Spain, one in ten was deserting the ranks. God only knows what the number is now. The man's spread himself too thin. Alexander the Great made that mistake. So did the great khans and, if you recall your history, you'll remember what happened to the Caesars. It wasn't only the barbarians at the gate that led to the demise of the Republic; it was the enemy eating away from within. That's what we have here. The people have had enough. Oh, they won't dare say so out loud, for fear of being overheard by police informers and carted off to that hellhole we passed this morning, but believe me, it's true."

Grant fell silent, marshalling his thoughts. Eventually, he said, "Everything I've learned during my time here tells me we cannot let an opportunity like this slip through our fingers. We'd be fools if we did. The chance may never come again. *That's* why I put my proposal to London. *That's* why I had them recruit you."

"You *asked* for me?" Hawkwood said.

Brooke had implied that the suggestion had come from James Read, following consultations between Bow Street and the Alien Office.

Another reason why it didn't pay to trust politicians, Hawkwood thought. *Not to mention their devious civil bloody servants.*

"Damned right, Captain. You were the first one I thought of. I wanted someone by my side who I'd worked with before, someone I could depend on."

"To help you do what, exactly?"

Superintendent Brooke's words came to mind: *We require someone to liaise with our correspondent to verify the feasibility of the proposal and, if it is at all viable, to assist in its implementation.*"

Grant's eyes shone with excitement. He glanced around and then leaned close.

"Seize an empire!"

10

"Just the two of us," Hawkwood said. "You and me; *we* are going to depose an Emperor . . ."

"Well, not *just* us," Grant said. "We'll have *some* assistance."

Hawkwood waited.

Grant reached for his towel, smiled mischievously and whispered quietly, in English, in his soft Highland brogue, "Come on, bonny lad. Let's go to war!"

Grant turned away from the window. "It was General Souham who gave me the notion."

"Souham?" Hawkwood repeated, cautiously.

They were in McPherson's apartment. The view over Grant's shoulders was a sprawling panorama of slate rooftops and soot-blackened chimneys. Washing lines drooped between buildings. Laundry hung from them in listless rows, like signalling flags, smoke stained and faded with wear.

Grant moved towards the table and the remaining empty chair. He sat down and said, "Well, it didn't come from the general's own lips. It was later. Turns out Jamie here knows a good deal about my travelling companion. The more he told me, the more it got me thinking. Did you know Souham joined the army as a private, worked his way up through the ranks? There aren't many as can lay claim to that. Served with Jourdan in Flanders; Pichegru in Holland *and* with Moreau on the

Danube. It's Spain that's been the making of him, though. He gave Wellington a right bloody nose at Aldea da Ponte, even though he lost more men. Brave bugger, no doubt about that."

Hawkwood said nothing. He knew Grant had to be leading up to something.

Finally, Grant said, "But the most interesting fact is that our brave general wasn't always the hero." He turned to McPherson. "Why don't *you* tell him, Jamie?"

McPherson was sucking on a short-stemmed pipe and in his black coat and breeches he looked not unlike a local vicar come to partake of an afternoon's cake and conversation. A half-full glass of wine and the bottle he'd liberated from the café that morning stood by his elbow. The remains of a meal lay scattered across empty platters resting on the table between them.

McPherson removed the pipe stem from his mouth and fixed Hawkwood with an inquisitive eye. "Tell me, Captain, what do you know of the attempts to assassinate Bonaparte?"

Not a question Hawkwood had been expecting. He knew puzzlement must have shown on his face. "Only rumours. Anyway, the bastard's still alive, isn't he? Shows you how successful we've been."

McPherson smiled thinly. "I wasn't referring to the British, Captain. I was thinking more of his own countrymen."

"Corsicans?" Hawkwood ventured warily.

McPherson shook his head. "The French, as it happens, though I sense from your response that you weren't aware that any such attempts had taken place."

Hawkwood was about to confirm his ignorance when a vague memory raised its head. "No, wait – they tried to blow the bugger up. When was that? Ten years ago? They put some kind of bomb in a wagon."

McPherson nodded. "That was one of the more extreme efforts. The Emperor was on his way to the opera. An explosive device was attached to a barrel of gunpowder concealed beneath a cart. It was timed to explode as the royal entourage passed down the rue Saint-Nicaise. The bomb went off and several bystanders were killed. A couple of dozen were injured. His

Majesty's evening was not entirely ruined, however," McPherson added drily. "He was still able to attend the second act."

The elderly Scot drew on his pipe and expelled smoke. "The plot was funded by your government, but the main conspirators were Chouans. Their leader was a man called Cadoudal."

"Chouans?" Hawkwood said, noting the *your government*.

It was Grant who answered.

"Rebels against Bonaparte. They were the first to rise up against the revolutionary government back in the nineties. Well organized, too, in the beginning; stirred up a revolt – they called it the Chouannerie – from the Channel all the way down to the Mediterranean. Exacted a fair amount of damage, too. Bonaparte was concerned enough to offer them a truce if they laid down their arms. Quite a few did, but a small core, including Cadoudal, carried on fighting. He ended up with a price on his head and fled to London. Formed an alliance with the Comte d'Artois; worked with him in trying to restore the Bourbons to the throne."

Grant offered McPherson a contrite look. "Forgive me, James. Didn't mean to interrupt. You were saying . . ."

McPherson waved away the apology and tapped the bowl of his pipe against his palm to loosen the ash. "The plot failed, obviously, and the bomb makers were executed. Cadoudal got away, though. He managed to get back to England; lived to fight another day."

"I remember the name now," Hawkwood said, nodding. "He ran *émigré* training camps on the coast near Folkestone. They employed British troops to teach them how to use weapons. One of my chosen men told me he'd been at Shorncliffe at the same time."

Grant nodded. "That's the fellow. A Breton by birth. Hated Bonaparte with a vengeance. The two of 'em met once, when they tried to arrange the truce. If he'd killed the bugger then, it would have saved us a good deal of grief."

"You said he *hated* Bonaparte. That either means he's dead or he changed his allegiance."

Grant turned to McPherson. "Jamie?"

McPherson had been in the process of taking a sip of wine.

He put down the glass. "The plotters tried again four years later. It was the same as before; initiated by the Comte d'Artois, with Cadoudal's help and financed by the British. It was better planned this time. They also had the support of two senior army officers, generals Pichegru and Jean-Victor Moreau. You recall Major Grant referred to them earlier."

Hawkwood nodded and then, struck by a thought, said, "But why would Bonaparte's own generals want him dead?"

McPherson reached for his glass. "Pichegru was a staunch royalist. Back when he was Commander of the Northern Army, he supported a plan to bring Louis Stanislas back from exile, but the plot was discovered. He resigned his commission and became leader of the royalist faction in the revolutionary government."

"They didn't execute him?"

"Too popular with the rank and file. Probably felt it was better keeping an eye on the devil they knew rather than disposing of him and having to worry about who might be rising in the shadows. But in '97 he fell foul of the régime again, and that time he didn't fare so lucky. They shipped him off to Guiana."

"Arse-end of nowhere," Grant said, grimacing. "The Frogs maintain prisons on some of the smaller islands. They call the place the dry guillotine. The Alien Office managed to get him out, though; it made arrangements with a local *émigré* who bribed the prison guards. A Royal Navy frigate picked up Pichegru, along with a handful of fellow escapers, and brought them to England. That's where he joined d'Artois and met up with Cadoudal."

"And Moreau . . .?" Hawkwood said.

"Pichegru's second-in-command. Fought alongside him in Flanders. Awarded the Army of the Rhine for his services. When Pichegru fell from grace, Moreau was tarred with the same brush and made to stand down on half pay, even though he wasn't involved specifically. He was reinstated soon after, though, when they realized they needed someone to stem Suvorov's advance through Italy. He was back in Paris by the time Bonaparte returned from Egypt. Neither of them liked the way the Republic was leaning and Moreau provided support when Bonaparte overthrew the Directory. As a reward, Bonaparte restored his command."

"He defeated the Austrians at Hohenlinden," Hawkwood said.

Grant nodded. "That he did. Forced them to sue for peace."

"And Bonaparte always resented him for it," McPherson interjected softly. "He felt that Moreau had taken away his glory."

"And the general's been a thorn in his side ever since," Grant said.

"He's a republican," McPherson cut in. "Not a royalist like Pichegru." Adding wryly, "A Breton, too, so maybe there's something in the blood that turns a man bitter."

"And the two of them combined forces?" Hawkwood said.

McPherson nodded. "They'd already been corresponding by letter, using British agents as couriers. The idea was that Cadoudal's men would kill Bonaparte during a military parade. They'd then set up an interim government with Moreau installed as temporary head until the legitimate heir was able to return home and take the throne."

"But that didn't happen," Hawkwood said.

McPherson nodded. "Savary's predecessor, Fouché, got wind of the plot. Pichegru, Moreau and Cadoudal were arrested. All the authorities had to do then was haul in the nets. They caught about three hundred, all told."

"Including a Royal Navy crew," Grant said heavily. He threw Hawkwood a meaningful look.

"How in God's name did they manage that?"

"As soon as London got word of Moreau's arrest, the Admiralty gave orders for a British cutter to stand off the French coast in case any of the others were able to escape. By the time the ship arrived, the French were waiting."

"What happened to the crew – or shouldn't I ask?"

"The commander, fellow name of Wright, was sent to the Temple, along with Moreau and the ring leaders. The rest were dispatched to the French hulks." Grant paused and then said, "Wright never made it home."

Hawkwood waited. He suspected it was going to be bad.

"He was found in his cell with his throat cut and a razor in his hand."

A picture of Lieutenant Stuart appeared in Hawkwood's mind and a knot formed in his stomach. "Suicide?"

Grant shrugged. "The Frogs said so. Though there were rumours the razor was closed when the body was discovered, so who's to know? They said that Pichegru took his own life as well, though how a man can strangle himself using a stick twisted inside a scarf is also beyond me."

"And the others?"

"Cadoudal went to the guillotine. Some went to the blade with him or died under torture; the rest were locked away."

"But Moreau survived."

McPherson took a long draw on his pipe and shrugged. "Bonaparte didn't dare kill him. The man was too popular; like Pichegru had been before, only more so. During the trial, you couldn't move for people lining the streets. Even the troops who were supposed to control the crowds shouted out his name and saluted when he was taken past. It got to the stage where Bonaparte feared for his own life. He knew if Moreau was executed he was likely to be next and after Pichegru's suspicious death there was no way he could allow Moreau to be found dead, so his only way out was to show mercy. He agreed to Moreau going into exile in the United States."

"Even though he had evidence against him?"

"A moot point. Moreau's guilt was based partly on the testimony of his secretary. It turned out that he was one of Fouché's people. Fouché obviously didn't want that to come out, so he had a word in the royal ear and by some means he persuaded Bonaparte to let the secretary go, which obviously weakened the State's position. Added to that, what people didn't know was that Fouché had been playing both ends against the middle. He knew that if Moreau was executed, the Emperor wouldn't be the only one looking over his shoulder. So the sly dog approached British agents for funds to bribe the judges on the Tribunal into sparing Moreau's life. Which they did.

"As you can imagine, this placed Bonaparte in something of a quandary. He couldn't kill the man and if he kept him in prison there was always a chance that Moreau's supporters would try to free him. Banishment was the only option."

"God Almighty!" Hawkwood said.

"A tangled web indeed," Grant murmured softly.

"And General Souham was implicated because of his connections with Pichegru and Moreau."

"You have it. He was arrested and sent to the Temple with the rest of them. He wasn't the only officer implicated, either. There was a whole host, including MacDonald and Masséna."

"MacDonald?" Hawkwood said, shocked at the revelation.

"Fortunately for them *and* for Souham," McPherson continued, "there was no definitive proof of their involvement and they were able to convince the tribunal of their loyalty. It took Souham three years to get his good name back, though. That was when he joined Saint-Cyr in Spain. The rest you know."

Hawkwood sat back, turning over in his mind what he'd just heard. He looked at Grant. "Forgive me, Col, this is all very interesting, but –"

"Patience, bonny lad," Grant cut in. "I know what you're thinking: what has this got to do with anything? Don't worry, it'll all become clear. It was my learning about Souham and his connection to Moreau that ignited the flame."

He turned to McPherson. "Why don't you tell the captain how His Majesty took his revenge and reaped the whirlwind?" Grant leaned across the table and helped himself to a glass of wine.

Hawkwood looked at McPherson and waited.

McPherson said, "Bonaparte knew the British and the Bourbons were behind the conspiracy and he wanted them both to pay. He went after one of the princes first. Unfortunately, he picked the wrong one. Instead of going after d'Artois or Louis Stanislas, he went for the Duke of Enghien, son of the Prince of Condé. He was closer to home – just the other side of the Rhine, in Ettenheim – so Bonaparte sent a squadron of dragoons across the river at night to bring him back over the border. The lad was hauled before a military commission, found guilty of sedition and shot."

Grant put down his glass. "It was the worst thing Bonaparte could have done. You don't go around kidnapping and murdering innocent princes of the blood without making a lot of enemies among the other crowned heads, especially those he'd been trying to entice to his side of the table. Didn't gain him many friends at home, either. Bonaparte lost his integrity when he sanctioned the prince's murder. Everyone – the army included – knew then that the revolution was over; all they'd succeeded in doing was to exchange one absolute bloody monarch for another one. They began wondering whether maybe, just maybe, they'd be better off if he wasn't around."

"Which was why the generals tried again in '08," McPherson said.

Hawkwood frowned. "Bonaparte would've been in Spain by then."

"What better time to strike?" Grant said. "Why waste time trying to kill the bastard when it'd be easier to dethrone him from a distance? Forget the bombs and the knives and the damned bullets, do it by document and decree instead!"

McPherson interjected: "There are no signalling telegraphs between the Pyrenees and Paris, so word of a coup would have to be delivered by rider. Even with a change of fresh horses, that's a two-day journey, which meant there would be at least four days before any countermanding orders came back from the Emperor's headquarters. The plotters knew if they could hold out that long, they had a chance. It'd take longer, of course, for the Emperor to muster troops and march on Paris to regain personal control."

"How close did they get?" Hawkwood asked.

"Damned close. They had everything prepared: weapons, passes, senatorial ordinances, proclamations for the troops – they were all set."

"Who was in charge?"

"General Joseph Servan de Gerbey, Minister of War to the Girondist government; one of Henri Clarke's predecessors, ironically."

172

"What about support?"

"A damned sight more than there was before, that's for sure. Around forty generals, by then, still including MacDonald and Masséna. Along with a swarm of doctors and lawyers and senators, including Sieyès, the former President of the Senate. They even had members of the clergy. Moreau was to be the figurehead as before. They thought his appointment would inspire confidence in Tsar Alexander and others and that he'd be able to act as intermediary and start peace negotiations once the provisional government was installed."

"There's one thing I don't understand," Hawkwood said. "You're telling me the reason for all this was to return a Bourbon prince to the throne. But if they've already butchered one king and they don't want Bonaparte as Emperor because there'd be no getting rid of him, why would they want to replace him with more bloody royalty? Wouldn't that take them back to where they'd started?"

"The ones that want to see a restoration ain't after some glorious potentate. That's why they've become sick of Bonaparte. Under his rule they can see the country returning to the old régime, and that's the last thing they want. They've no objections to a king, as long as his power's limited. They want a king and an elected parliament ruling under a constitution."

Hawkwood said, "So what went wrong?"

"Servan died before the plan could be put into action."

"Murdered?"

Grant shook his head. "Mischance, as far as anyone could tell. Some form of illness. I don't know the full details. He wasn't a young man."

"And the rest of them?"

"A complete bugger's muddle. When Servan died all his papers came to light. Also someone had overheard a couple of the conspirators and reported them to the police. With that and what was found in Servan's documents, the whole lot folded like a house of cards."

"Reprisals?"

"There weren't any."

"What!?"

"Well, no executions, at any rate. Rumour was that Fouché knew about the conspiracy and secretly supported it. In fact some say he was still involved in clandestine correspondence with London, so when the plot collapsed, he diverted attention away from himself by telling Bonaparte that the police had over-reacted and there'd been no attempted coup and it was all nothing more than the rumblings of harmless malcontents. The conspirators weren't deemed worth the bother of execution, so some were thrown into military prison, others were exiled from Paris to the provinces and a couple were sent abroad. Compared to the last lot, they got off lightly."

"But they failed," Hawkwood said. "That's the nub of it. Bonaparte's still here."

"Well, yes and no, bonny lad." Grant threw McPherson a sideways glance.

"He's only here in spirit, Captain," McPherson said, blinking. "The rest of him is with his Grand Army in Russia –"

"Two thousand miles away." Grant's eyebrows lifted suggestively.

"Which is a lot further than Spain," McPherson continued. "Even for an experienced messenger that's two *weeks*' hard riding, at least. A month there and back."

"Might as well be on the other side of the moon," Grant finished.

The two men fell silent. Gazing at Hawkwood, they waited.

The seconds ticked by; stretching, or so it seemed, into a long and rather nerve-wracking minute. Random thoughts hurtled their way through Hawkwood's brain.

"It's bloody mad," Hawkwood said eventually. "You really think it's possible?"

Grant smiled. "Why not?"

"I told you," Hawkwood said. "Because it's bloody mad."

"Don't mean it can't be done. It'll be the last thing anyone will expect."

"You certainly have that right."

"It won't be anything like before."

"That's probably what Servan said," Hawkwood responded drily. "What makes you think you – we – can succeed when others have failed?"

"Because we'll be better prepared and because there won't be so many loose tongues. That's what did for the others."

Hawkwood knew his scepticism was still showing.

Undismayed, Grant leaned forward, his face animated. "Think on it, Matthew. The bastard's in the depths of Russia. No one knows where, exactly. And he's taken just about every able-bodied man with him. There's hardly anyone left to defend the country, save for the gendarmerie, a few under staffed-regimental depots and what's left of some National Guard units; and they're made up of men who've been rejected for active service. There'll be no resistance. You've seen it with your own eyes. The whole damned country's weary of war. My guess is they'll welcome a new government with open arms. It's what they've been waiting for."

"And you've a plan, I take it?"

"Aye, as it happens, I do have a few ideas, but they're not strictly mine. You could say I've borrowed them, temporarily."

"From whom?"

"General Claude-François Malet."

Another bloody general?

Hawkwood thought he might be losing his mind. He took a deep breath and shook his head in bewilderment.

"Who the *hell* is General Claude-François Malet?"

"Servan's successor. When Servan died, his followers picked Malet as their new leader."

Grant paused to let the information sink in and then said, "He's a soldier, born and bred. Comes from an old aristo family. Started out as a king's musketeer; a lieutenant in the Royal Household Troops. Served as a Head of Brigade in the Rhineland, Adjutant-General of the 6th Division at Besançon and Chief of Staff to the Army of the Alps in Italy – he received honourable citations for defending the Little St Bernard Pass in '99. He's a Commander of the Legion of Honour and he was with Masséna in '05, so he knows the right people. I can also tell you he hates Bonaparte with a vengeance and he's a diehard republican."

"Yet he's a son of the nobility? How does that square?"

"As far as his family's concerned, it doesn't. His father disowned him. His conversion began while he was a musketeer. He saw enough of the excesses at Versailles to convince him there was need for a change. Then, when he was in Germany, he fell in with a cadre of republican officers who introduced him to the writings of Rousseau. Given his military skills, his ability to command authority and delegate men in the field, and the fact that he's conversant with all the aggravation that goes with civilian bureaucracy, it's plain that he's the only logical choice."

"For what?"

"It's going to take someone of stature to lead the charge. Seeing as he was the one who inherited Servan's baton, it'd be a damned shame not to offer him another chance to carry it through to the end, don't you think?"

A small voice in Hawkwood's brain told him that Grant was holding something back.

"So, where is he?"

"Ah," Grant said, casting a quick look towards the silent McPherson. "I was coming to that. There is just one . . . minor inconvenience."

Just the one? Hawkwood thought.

"And what might that be?"

"Unfortunately, General Malet was among the conspirators who were rounded up after the last coup attempt. He's still being held under lock and key."

And there it was . . .

"He's in *prison?*" Hawkwood had a sudden vision of the dark and brooding Conciergerie, its thick-walled dungeons stifling the cries of desperate men.

Grant shook his head. "Fortunately, no. Well, not exactly. He's in a private clinic."

Hawkwood stared at Grant in mounting disbelief. A vision of Bedlam's dripping walls floated into view. "A clinic? You can't be serious? The last thing I need is another lunatic!"

"It's not an asylum; it's a clinic. There's a difference. In fact it's closer to a nursing home. The establishment does cater for those of an indelicate disposition but, from what we know, a good proportion of the gentlemen living under its roof are prisoners, sent there as punishment, rather than patients. In fact, I'd say the facilities are more gentlemen's establishment than anything else."

"Maybe I should apply for membership," Hawkwood said. "They might have hot baths."

Grant gave him a look.

"All right," Hawkwood conceded, "so you're telling me he's neither mad nor enfeebled."

"Far from it. As far as we're aware, he's in excellent health and waiting for the call to arms. Which is where you come in."

Hawkwood sighed. "I had a feeling you were going to say that."

"Well, you didn't think I brought you here just so's you could sample the bloody waters did you, laddie?" Grant said, a wide grin on his face. "You'll be the bugger sounding reveille."

11

"We've an ally inside the clinic," Grant continued. "Though he doesn't know it. He's been keeping the general company for the past three months, cultivating him, as it were, preparing the ground. All that's needed is a little added incentive."

"And that would be me," Hawkwood said.

"That would be you, yes."

"This . . . ally," Hawkwood said. "One of the staff?"

"No, he's one of the residents."

God save us, Hawkwood thought, though he noted Grant's use of the word *resident* rather than *patient.*

"His name's Lafon; Abbé Jean-Baptiste Hyacinthe Lafon."

A name exotic enough to rival that of Nymphe Roussel de Préville.

Hawkwood groaned inwardly. "A *priest*?"

"You've something against padres?" Grant looked amused.

"Not a damned thing, provided they're not trying to kill or convert me. What's this one's story?"

"Apart from detesting Bonaparte almost as much as the general, you mean?"

"That doesn't sound very Christian," Hawkwood said. "Whatever happened to love thine enemy?"

"If you recall, the Church ain't too well disposed towards Bonaparte at the moment, nor he to it, on account of he's had the Pope locked away in Fontainebleau for the past four months. I'm assuming you were aware?" Grant added.

Hawkwood nodded.

Hostilities between Bonaparte and the Vatican had been simmering away for years. Events had finally come to a head when Bonaparte sent his armies in to force the Pope to close his ports to English shipping. The Pope's response had been to issue an excommunication order, whereupon Bonaparte exiled the pontiff, first to the Gulf of Genoa and then, fearing a rescue attempt by the British Navy, to Paris. There had been reports of the relocation in the English news sheets back in June.

Grant made a face. "There are a few churchmen who've capitulated, but most of the clergy want Bonaparte out of the way as much as we do. They've not seen eye to eye with the bugger since his coronation; all that business about lowering the crown on to his own head rather than appear subservient to the Pope, and carrying on as if the Church existed solely to glorify Napoleon I, Emperor of the French. They want Pius freed and back in Rome where he belongs – and they've been prepared to sup with the devil to make that happen."

"The devil being . . .?" Hawkwood said.

"The British," McPherson said, rising to his feet and moving towards the window as if trying to keep the blood circulating after remaining too long in one place. On reaching the glass, he turned.

"Several years ago a group of priests hostile to the Republic got together to promote counter-revolution by uniting all those within the royalist resistance who wished to practise their religion in freedom and restore the monarchy. They christened themselves the Congrégation de la Foi. London, recognizing an ally in its war against Bonaparte, put up the money. It wasn't long before the Congrégation's tentacles spread from the Midi to Normandy and the Pas de Calais. It was the main guiding force behind the Chouan revolt. Members are referred to as *chevaliers.*

"Three years ago, when the Pope was confined, they switched from trying to restore the monarchy by force to a campaign of

180

subterfuge, circulating pamphlets and counter-imperialist literature.

"They're still careful, though. To avoid detection, each chevalier knows only two other people, and then only by assumed names. Messages are committed to paper strictly as a last resort. Mostly, they're carried verbally, by emissaries known as *voyagers*. Masonic lodges are used as meeting places. There are special passwords and signs of recognition. Like the one we used at the café this morning."

"The wine glasses," Hawkwood said.

Still pacing the room, McPherson nodded and tapped his pocket. When he realized he'd left his pipe on the table, he clicked his tongue in annoyance.

"Abbé Lafon's a courier for the chevaliers," Grant said.

"Does Malet know that?" Hawkwood asked.

"The chevaliers tend to keep their allegiances to themselves," McPherson said, moving back to the table and his pipe. "He probably has his suspicions. He undoubtedly knows Lafon's one of a number of clergy who were deemed potential agitators and rounded up after the Pope and his cardinals were moved to Fontainebleau. Lafon's been able to get close to the general because they share a common history. Although their arrests were some years apart, prior to their arrival at the clinic they were both inmates of La Force prison. The experience has created a special bond between them."

"Which we can exploit," Grant said firmly.

The Scot placed a palm on the table and studied the veins on the back of his hand. He looked up. "Due to its financial involvement, London's always maintained a close liaison with the Congrégation's hierarchy and Jamie has several informers within its ranks. It came to our notice that throughout his confinement in both La Force and the clinic, Lafon's been in regular contact with the chevaliers. We've become privy to their communications. It's been most illuminating." Grant turned to his fellow Scot. "Jamie . . .?"

McPherson picked up his tobacco pouch. "From Lafon's conversations with the general it appears that Malet's years in

181

confinement have not weakened his resolve. He's continued to harbour great misgivings about the state of the Empire. His one regret is that he wasn't granted the opportunity to put General Servan's plan into operation."

"In other words," Grant said, "he's as committed as ever to the overthrow of the régime. He's realized you wouldn't have to destroy the Empire in order to return to the principles of the Revolution. In fact, he doesn't see the Empire as something concrete but more of a mystical ideal, based on one man's delusions of grandeur. The only realities are the layers of officialdom: proclamations, decrees, and reams of documentation; that sort of thing. If you add ambition, greed and superstition to the mix you've something that's no more solid than a grass house built on sand. There's only one thing that's keeping it all together."

"Bonaparte," Hawkwood said.

Grant nodded. "Malet believes that if he's removed, all that would be needed to maintain order would be a new set of decrees; ones that would keep intact the ideals of the revolution and restore France to the glory she deserves. They'd have a government based on the will of the people, not on the whim of some despot more interested in conquering the world."

"I thought Malet had no love for the monarchy," Hawkwood said. "And you told me Lafon's a staunch royalist. That would make them strange bedfellows."

McPherson shook his head. "No more so than Pichegru and Moreau. The difference has become immaterial. What's important is their common aim: the overthrow of Napoleon. According to Lafon's dispatches, they've never really discussed what sort of government would follow Bonaparte's demise. The priority's the removal of the man. In that regard, Lafon's hinted that the general may be becoming less rigid in his stance. He's suggested that Malet would probably concede that even a constitutional monarch is preferable to what they have at the moment: a leader who rules not because of his popularity or even his strength of personality but by the intrigues of his secret police."

Grant clenched his fist. "We must seize the day, Matthew! Malet's convinced that Servan's plan can be resurrected. He's convinced it'd be possible to carry out the coup now that the Emperor's even further from the capital than he was the last time. I think so, too. With Bonaparte in Russia, I reckon we can steal his bloody Empire from him, and there's not a God-damned thing the bastard can do to stop us!"

A nerve twitched along Grant's jawbone. His eyes were aflame with infinite possibilities.

Hawkwood looked at McPherson. "What about you, Mr McPherson? What do you say?"

McPherson looked up from tamping tobacco leaf into his pipe bowl. "I'm an old man, Captain; old enough to remember the first king across the water – James Francis Edward Stuart. I followed his son when he crossed the Channel to try and raise an army. We failed. France took me in when I had no home. She gave me a roof over my head, a loving wife and a good living. It's true that I became a supporter of the Revolution, though not with its appetite for blood and revenge. I had nothing personal against the Bourbons, but as far as d'Artois and Louis Stanislas are concerned, I do know what it means to be an exile from your own land. So perhaps it's time I gave something back." McPherson lit a taper from the candle and touched it to his pipe. "Besides, what do we have to lose?"

"Our bloody heads, for one thing," Hawkwood said. "I don't know about you, but I'm quite partial to mine."

"Then we'll have to make sure we hang on to them, won't we?" Grant said.

Hawkwood stared at Grant and suddenly a light dawned.

"I know that look, you bugger. It doesn't matter what I bloody think, you're going to do it anyway, aren't you?"

Grant smiled. "Would you care to be inside the tent pissing out, or outside the tent pissing in?"

"Nice to know I'm being given a choice."

"It's the least I could do, laddie, seeing as you've come all this way."

Hawkwood glanced towards McPherson. Maddeningly, the old man seemed more interested in enjoying his smoke than contributing to the conversation. He was sitting back in his chair puffing contentedly, as though waiting for Hawkwood to speak.

Hawkwood sighed. "How much do we know about Servan's original plan?"

Grant smiled again. Hawkwood couldn't help likening it to the expression on the face of a gamekeeper who'd just nabbed a poacher. Or, perhaps more aptly, a spider that had caught a fly in its web. It probably had a lot to do with his use of the word *we*, he realized. Grant had laid the bait too well.

"Only the rudiments; to take control while the Emperor was out of the country. However, Lafon's communiqués suggest that General Malet has devised a way not only to achieve that goal but also to make the enterprise appear legal."

"Legal? How?"

"'Cut off the head and the body will fall.'"

"*Kill* Bonaparte? That's impossible. The man's two thousand miles away. And I thought you said there was no need for that, anyway."

"There isn't. I didn't mean it literally and it's not what Malet had in mind. He believes it'll be enough merely to *convince* the people that the Emperor's dead; the rest will follow."

Hawkwood looked at him.

"The greater the lie, the more people will believe," Grant said.

"Because they wouldn't think anyone'd be mad enough to make such a thing up?"

"Correct. It'll depend on the credibility of the person spreading the lie, of course. But if the integrity of the messenger's beyond question, why would anybody not accept the message as truth?"

There was a kind of tortuous logic to Grant's words, Hawkwood supposed.

"And if the people do swallow the falsehood," Grant added, "it follows they'll be looking to someone to deliver them from the crisis and restore morale."

"And that would be General Malet," Hawkwood said.

"Armed with authority from the Senate allowing him to take possession of the city and install a provisional government."

"You do know Brooke said it was up to me to decide if your proposal was feasible?" Hawkwood said. "That was the word he used: *feasible*."

"A grave responsibility," Grant agreed solemnly.

"So it'd probably be remiss of me if I didn't at least give it some serious consideration," Hawkwood said.

"Most remiss. Seeing as you're here, anyway."

Hawkwood's head was starting to spin. The ramifications, if they went ahead with Grant's astonishing proposal, were almost beyond measure. He pushed his chair back, stood up, and tried to marshal his thoughts. Grant had described Bonaparte's Russian campaign as a flight of fancy. How could any sane person not view Grant's intention in the same light? The idea went beyond audacious. It almost went beyond comprehension. And yet . . .

He found himself turning to face them.

"This . . . clinic – my apologies, this nursing home – I'm assuming it permits visitors?"

"Of course. In fact the director, Doctor Dubuisson, actively encourages it."

"So, you can get me in there to meet with Lafon and our tame general?"

"All things are possible," Grant said slowly, a brightness showing in his eyes. "I'm sure that could be . . . arranged."

Hawkwood regarded Grant with renewed suspicion. "You're not saying he's expecting me?"

"He has no idea that you or I exist. Or James, for that matter. Neither has Lafon."

"So they've no knowledge of the Alien Office's . . . involvement?"

"And what involvement would that be?" Grant raised his eyebrows.

Hawkwood's mind went back to his conversation with Brooke. What was it the superintendent had told him?

If you were to be apprehended, this department would deny all knowledge of your existence.

He saw that Grant was still regarding him closely.

"My apologies," Hawkwood said. "It would appear I was misinformed."

Grant smiled.

"So, how do I gain access? Any suggestions, other than ringing the bell and telling them I'm there to see General Malet with regards to his overthrowing the Empire?"

"Well, that would certainly be one way of announcing yourself. I think, however, a less flamboyant introduction might be more appropriate."

"And you, of course, have one already prepared," Hawkwood said.

"Och, you know me too well, bonny lad."

"I'm listening."

Grant smiled. "Let's just say: God will provide."

A chill wind was coming off the river as Lavisse turned up his jacket collar and padded quickly and purposefully, shoulders hunched, away from the darkened wharf and across the Quai Bonaparte towards the entrance to the rue du Bac. A second man kept pace beside him, also bracing himself against the cold. Their footsteps made little sound on the cobblestones.

There were no street lamps and some of the narrower lanes were as black as pitch. Of the people who were on the streets, the innocent ones scurried on their way like nervous trespassers, anxious to return to their homes or to their places of refuge before the predators emerged in force. The not so innocent ones turned their faces away from the light, as cautious as cats in the darkness, biding their time.

Lavisse took the initiative, leading the way beneath overhanging balconies, skirting the gutters where rats slithered through the filth, sleek fur glistening like quicksilver. He was a tall man, well built, with dark eyes and a hard, intimidating face. His companion, Favier, was shorter, with broad shoulders, a bullet-shaped head and large, thick-wristed hands. A woollen cap was pulled down low over a Simian brow.

Decent pickings, Lavisse had decided, were looking more and more unlikely; an increasingly common occurrence as

186

unemployment and food shortages continued to squeeze a population already wearied by decades of revolution and war. In times of adversity there were always those prepared to profit from the misfortunes of others, either through influence or intimidation, and Parisians, aware of the ever present nocturnal dangers, were becoming much more careful about wandering around after dusk, unless it was absolutely necessary.

"We don't find anything soon," Favier muttered gloomily, "we're going to be out on the street."

"Sablon'll be wanting his rent," Lavisse spat, thinking that they were already out on the bloody street, or hadn't Favier noticed? "We don't have a choice. Keep your eyes peeled."

Sablon was the overseer of a vermin-infested retired coal barge moored below the Pont Royal which served as a dosshouse for itinerants and the dispossessed who didn't mind bunking up four to a mattress. How the man had the nerve to even think of charging for accommodation in such a stinking, dilapidated wreck, Lavisse had never been able to fathom, but as Sablon had informed him just before he and Favier had set out, demand far exceeded supply and if the pair of them didn't come up with the wherewithal by midnight at the latest, they'd be back in the catacombs, competing for floor space with the rest of the beggars.

The one advantage of having Sablon as their landlord – a term which allowed for a certain degree of flexibility – was that the man didn't mind in what form the rent was paid. Money, jewellery, consumables; it made no difference. Barter was the currency of choice, particularly among the denizens of the water-front. There was a market and an exchange rate for everything, provided you knew where to look.

Lavisse and Favier were on the lookout for the unwary. The trouble was that most of the people out after dark in this neigh-bourhood were, in all likelihood, also on the prowl and as such very much alert to the possibility of being set upon. So sorties to separate an owner from his or her valuables had become something of a cat-and-mouse game among the thieves that roamed the streets and alleyways of the 10th Arrondissement. And no one crossed the boundary into the next district, because that would mean encroaching on someone else's territory and there were strict, albeit unwritten, rules about that, and severe consequences if those rules weren't followed.

So Lavisse and Favier had set off to scout the familiar hunting grounds on the off chance that some fresh, unsuspecting body might even now be heading their way, oblivious to the perils lying in wait in the dark recesses of the night.

But so far: nothing.

Crossing the rue de Lille, they continued on their way, senses tuned to the world around them. Though the streets were still, the night was far from quiet. Dogs barked, cats howled, infants squalled and drunken men argued loudly with foul-mouthed whores and tearful wives behind windows made opaque by dirt and grime. Vehicles were few and far between. A cabby took his life in his hands if he ventured too far after sundown. As a result, there were no jangling harnesses or hoof-beats to be heard. Apart from plaintive animal cries and the strident voices of humans engaged in heated exchange, only the occasional hollow scrape of metal-shod boot heels and hurrying footsteps broke the silence.

Lavisse's belly suddenly emitted a low gaseous rumble. It had been a couple of days since he and Favier had eaten anything approaching a decent meal. Another reason for persevering with the hunt.

I'd have been better off back in the army. At least I might have been housed and fed, even in bloody Russia, Lavisse thought bitterly, before remembering why that particular career path was no longer viable. Often, when he looked down at the remains of his right forefinger, sheared just above the first knuckle, he would swear he could feel it flexing as solidly as his other digits. Sometimes, maddeningly, it even developed an itch . . .

"Which way?" Favier's rasping voice broke into his thoughts.

Lavisse nodded to the right. The sign above them indicated they were entering the rue de l'Université, a long, tapering street lined with shabby rooming houses, run-down shops and narrow apartment buildings. There were a few dimly lit windows and doorways showing but they were in the minority. As a consequence, much of the street was swathed in shadow, creating plenty of opportunities for concealment. Ducking into a narrow alleyway, Lavisse and Favier gathered close to the wall and prepared for the arrival of their first victim.

When choosing potential prey, there were some categories best left alone; anyone who looked as though they might fight back, for instance. Which generally eliminated groups of two or more, as well as anyone in uniform – they might well be armed, and therefore dangerous. That still left plenty of scope, however. The easiest to subdue were the old and the infirm. Lavisse and Favier weren't above going after both. The only problem being that, traditionally, such targets rarely provided a lucrative source of income. But you never knew. Sometimes they could surprise you. It was always best, Lavisse had found, to keep an open mind.

Several pedestrians had made their way past the alley since Lavisse and Favier had taken up their positions, but they'd been allowed to proceed unscathed. A few had been in groups and from their rolling gait had clearly partaken of the grape, but drunks, while not in full command of their faculties, had a tendency to be unpredictable, especially in a gang, so it was best to let them stagger by. Some folk had been on their own but Lavisse and Favier had stayed their hands as there had been other people too close in proximity at the time and the last thing Lavisse needed was a witness or, God forbid, somebody who was looking to be a hero. The remainder had been children, scabby street urchins; but children were generally lucky if they had one belt and a shoe buckle between them and thus were not worth the effort.

So far, so bad. The catacombs were beckoning.

Until Favier, whose turn it was to act as point man, gave Lavisse a nudge in his ribs and said softly, "Eyes right."

Lavisse peered around the corner.

A little over one hundred paces away, a lone figure was making its way along the street; slightly built, with a carriage and walk that were undeniably female.

Lavisse felt a ripple of excitement. Women were definitely fair game; up there with cripples and the elderly in terms of access. You didn't get too many out on their own, however. Even whores, who knew the streets better than most, never strayed far from their home patch if they could help it. Whores, however, often carried cash, even after their pimp – if they had one – had taken his or her cut. Sometimes they had trinkets. So this one, Lavisse decided, as he watched her approach, was definitely worth considering. He glanced up and down the street. There were still a few people in sight but they were some distance away and unlikely to count as an immediate threat. And Lavisse and Favier were used to working in relative silence. They'd be able to take care of business and be away before help could be summoned, and in any case the darkness would hide the deed.

Ducking back into the alley, Lavisse drew his knife while Favier slipped a small cudgel into his hand.

The woman drew closer. Her features were partially obscured by a dark, hooded cloak but Lavisse, sticking his head carefully around the side of the wall, could tell from her posture that she wasn't old; which meant she was most likely a working girl on her way to or from a customer. The woman passed through a dense patch of shadow and disappeared momentarily as her cloak melted into the darkened doorway behind. When she re-emerged from the gloom she had halved the distance between herself and the men lying in wait.

A small sliver of moonlight suddenly appeared before her and as she stepped through it, she reached up with her left hand and drew the hood of her cloak closer about her. In that one fleeting moment, Lavisse caught the gleam of gold on her finger and a metallic reflection at her throat and he felt a shiver of excitement as he realized what he'd seen: a wedding band and a locket chain. He turned to Favier and nodded.

The woman was twenty paces away when Favier strolled unthreateningly out of the alleyway and, without giving any sign that he was aware of her presence, set off in front of her, walking nonchalantly in the same direction.

From his concealed position, Lavisse saw the woman start but then, just as quickly, her nerves recovered, she continued on her way, although at a slightly slower pace so as to allow the man in front to widen the gap between them. Lavisse waited five seconds before stepping out silently in her wake.

Fifty paces further on, without altering stride, Favier turned abruptly off the street and ducked under an archway. Lavisse quickened his pace. He'd almost caught up with her when she became conscious that there was someone following along behind. Still walking, she turned her head and glanced back.

For a stout man, Favier was very quick on his feet. Even before the woman had a chance to cry out, Favier's hand was around her mouth and as his right hand encircled her waist, trapping her arms inside her cloak, Lavisse was there, helping to sweep her up and bundle her protesting form through the archway and into the passageway beyond.

As she fought against their grip the hood of her cloak fell away, revealing a pale face framed by a halo of black hair. She was older than Lavisse had expected, but still in possession of her looks. A pair of dark eyes widened in panic at the sight of the knife. Her struggles intensified.

Lifting her almost off her feet, Favier pulled her further into the alley. Quickly, Lavisse pressed the point of his knife against her throat. She stopped fighting and shrank from him, releasing a low moan into Favier's cupped hand. Her eyes reflected her fear as her body pushed back against him, breasts rising and falling in her effort to break free. Favier felt himself harden.

"Scream," Lavisse hissed, "and I'll rip your throat out."

Favier kept his hand over her mouth.

"You hear me?" Lavisse asked.

She nodded mutely, eyes pleading.

This was going to be a particular pleasure, Lavisse thought. He kept the blade at her throat and moved it down towards the hem of her bodice, sliding the edges of the cloak aside. Using the point of the knife, he lifted the locket from her pale neck. Favier moved his hand aside and she let out a small gasp as Lavisse reached forward and, with a swift jerk, ripped the chain from her throat. Pocketing the plundered items, Lavisse reached down inside the woman's cloak and gripped her left wrist.

"The ring," he said.

The woman shook her head and tried, despite Favier's hold on her, to pull her arm away. A desperate plea broke from her lips.

"*Don't, I beg you . . .*"

"Hold her," Lavisse instructed Favier. Grabbing the woman's wrist with his left hand, he pulled her arm straight and tried to insert the knife point between the ring and her finger.

Terrified, with Favier's hand clamped once more over her mouth, the woman tried to pull her hand away. With a snarl of annoyance, Lavisse let go of her arm, removed the knife, and drew back his fist.

"No," a voice said from behind them. "I wouldn't do that."

Lavisse saw the shock expand across Favier's face. He spun around.

The last thing he expected to see was a priest.

Lavisse stared at the black cassock, the broad-brimmed hat and the pale band of white at the priest's throat. Moonlight filtered through a gap in the buildings above them, but with the hat brim worn low, the priest's countenance remained in shadow.

"Let her go." The command was spoken calmly and precisely.

Lavisse threw Favier a sideways look. Favier's expression was still one of disbelief. A man of the cloth was the last person either of them had expected to see. Lavisse turned back. "I think you've taken the wrong turning, Father. If you're looking for the seminary, it's back the other way." Lavisse jerked his head. "And I believe you'll find it's closed. Best run along."

"Perhaps you didn't hear me," the priest said. "I told you to take your hands off her."

Lavisse frowned and took a step forward. "And I told *you*, Father; you've come to the wrong place. Priests hold no sway in this city. Haven't you heard? Besides, this is a private matter."

"It was." The priest's head lifted. "But not any more."

Lavisse frowned.

Despite his garb, the stranger didn't sound like a priest. And when he raised his head and removed his hat to reveal his face, he didn't look much like one either. There was no fear in his expression; no hesitancy at being confronted by a man with a knife. Lavisse experienced the first flicker of uncertainty.

"Last chance, Corporal," the priest said evenly. His blue-grey eyes moved over Lavisse's scruffy tunic, with its patches and its frayed cuffs and collar and the faded marks on the sleeve where his stripes had been affixed all those years ago.

Hearing himself addressed by his old rank, Lavisse blinked. Then, although he wasn't sure why he did so, he looked down. His glance alighted on the unbuttoned gap at the bottom of the priest's cassock and on the boots the priest was wearing. They were, he noticed, even in the darkness of the alley, very fine boots; officer's boots, if he wasn't mistaken. He thought about what he was looking at. His head came up sharply.

"You're no priest!" he spat, and lunged forward, the knife blade sweeping up and round.

Hawkwood flicked the hat towards Lavisse's eyes with his left hand. Instinctively, Lavisse jerked his head aside and immediately his centre of gravity shifted. Hawkwood moved in, gripped Lavisse's wrist and, as Lavisse grunted with surprise, rotated the arm, locking it rigid. As the knife fell to the ground with a clatter, Hawkwood drove his right fist into Lavisse's exposed throat. It was a killing blow, fast and brutal, with Lavisse's larynx taking the full force of the strike. In the time it took his body to hit the ground Lavisse's tenuous lease on life was already beyond salvage.

Favier, caught between hanging on to the woman and going to Lavisse's aid, gasped as his associate went down. The speed with which the priest – if that's what he was – had retaliated had been frightening. Finally, his decision made, Favier hurled the woman aside and, with a growl of rage, launched himself at the black-clad figure.

Hawkwood saw the attack and turned. Scooping up Lavisse's discarded knife he pivoted, slamming his boot against the side of Favier's knee. As Favier staggered, Hawkwood reversed his grip on the knife and rammed it back-handedly towards the side of Favier's throat. The blade went in to the hilt and Favier died with the look of astonishment still affixed to his face, the weapon protruding from his jugular. Black blood began to bubble over the hilt on to the cobbles beneath.

Hawkwood straightened and stepped away cautiously. The three months spent training with Chen in the Rope and Anchor's cellar had paid off, he thought, staring down at the bodies. In fact, it had been almost too easy. From the moment the taller one had shown his colours, every movement had seemed natural. There had been no thought of quarter, either. There had been only the knowledge, born of instinct, warning him that one inadvertent move would mean the difference between life and death. Kill or be killed. There had been no contest, in any sense of the word.

He turned to look for the woman and saw that she was slumped against the wall. He crossed to her quickly. She was conscious but a small abrasion above her right brow showed where her forehead had come into contact with the brickwork. As Hawkwood bent down, she shied away and raised her hands to fend him off and Hawkwood realized she thought he was one of her attackers returning to finish what they'd started. Presumably, she'd been too dazed to have seen the outcome of the fight.

"It's all right, madame," Hawkwood said. "You're safe."

It took several seconds for the words to register. Then, as their meaning sank in, she lifted her head and stared at him and then she frowned.

"Father?"

That'll be the day, Hawkwood thought.

He helped her to her feet. She held on to his arm until she had regained her balance and then her hand went immediately to her throat. She gave a sharp intake of breath and looked around, a desperate expression in her eyes.

"Wait," Hawkwood said.

He went to Lavisse's body, knelt, and rifled through the dead man's pockets, ignoring the combination of ripe smells rising from the corpse. When he returned to the woman, he held out his hand. "Here."

She took the locket and chain from him without speaking

and clasped them to her breast. Still close to tears, she stared at him. "Thank you," she whispered.

"We should leave," Hawkwood said. "Now."

She tightened her grip on the locket as if afraid she might let it fall and nodded. Her eyes moved to the bodies. "They're dead?"

"Yes."

She frowned then. "They were soldiers?"

"One of them was." Hawkwood looked down at Lavisse's corpse, at the threadbare tunic and the mutilated finger. "Unless he stole the jacket. The other one, too, most likely. They were probably comrades. Their kind usually stick together."

He looked for the other man's hand but it was folded over and he couldn't see if the forefinger had been shortened. Not that it mattered, anyway. It was a strange subject for small talk, he thought.

"You're going to leave them there?" she said.

"The Empire can pay for their burial," Hawkwood said. "If they *were* soldiers it probably owes them that much."

She gave him a strange look and he wondered if she was expecting him to perform some sort of eulogy. If so, she was going to be sorely disappointed.

"They'll be stripped bare before then, as likely as not. Nights are getting colder. There's many who could find a use for coats and breeches, even if they have been worn."

"Maybe that's how *they* came by them." She said the words quietly, as if she was speaking to herself.

It was odd, Hawkwood thought, that she appeared to be neither horrified nor particularly distressed at the sight of two dead bodies, one of which had a knife sticking out of his throat. Perhaps bloodied corpses were more common in the back streets of Paris than he'd thought. Or perhaps she was considering that they had only received their just deserts for attacking her. Even so, her apparent equanimity in the face of such a gruesome tableau was intriguing. Still, better that, Hawkwood reflected, than him having to deal with an hysterical female bent on screaming the house down.

"Maybe," he said, looking again at the half finger. He took her arm. "We need to get away from here."

This time she did not draw back but accompanied him through the archway. When they emerged on to the street, Hawkwood swore under his breath and said, "Wait here."

He returned to where he'd left the bodies and picked up the priest's hat. Dusting it down, the incongruity of the moment hit him. He'd give Grant a severe talking to the next time he saw him, he thought. He turned and saw that the woman was watching him intently. She had drawn the hood over her head and her face seemed even paler against the dark material. He walked back to her and looked up and down the street. There were even less people in view than there had been before and nothing to indicate that anyone had been alerted by the ruction in the alleyway. There also appeared to be less moonlight. Hawkwood wondered if the clouding over was a sign of more rain.

"Do you have far to go?" Hawkwood asked.

She shook her head. "I'm almost home."

"I'll escort you," Hawkwood said.

"That's not necessary, Father."

"I think it probably is." Hawkwood looked back into the alleyway. Shadows hid the scene. If no one ventured beneath the archway, the bodies were unlikely to be discovered before daybreak, by which time their clothing would almost certainly have been removed; the knife and cudgel, too. In the event some right-minded citizen found them instead and called the authorities, the deaths would probably be put down to a drunken altercation. Not much of an epitaph, either way, Hawkwood thought. He saw that she was following his gaze. Her face was very still.

"Come on," Hawkwood said, putting the hat on and angling it so that the brim was low. "We've been here too long."

She took his arm and they walked away, not in undue haste but calmly and quickly, as though they were a couple caught out after dark whose only intent was to reach their destination without mishap or delay.

They'd gone less than twenty paces when, without turning her head, she said softly, "I'm not a whore, Father."

196

"I know that," Hawkwood said.

"A woman out after dark, on her own; people – men – sometimes get the wrong impression. I wouldn't blame you if that's what you were thinking."

"It wasn't."

She considered that. After a pause, she said, "So, what *is* a priest doing, wandering the streets in this neighbourhood at night? Looking for lost souls?"

"I'm the one who's lost," Hawkwood said. "I was on my way to visit someone and I think I must have taken the wrong turning. I'm new to the city. I'm still finding my way around."

"It can be confusing at night."

"And dangerous," Hawkwood said.

"That, too, but I have a feeling you're not a man who's afraid of the dark." She turned her head and looked at him perceptively.

"I trust in the Lord to light my way," Hawkwood said, straight-faced.

"I doubt that," she said, a half-smile forming. "And you shouldn't take His name in vain."

"No," Hawkwood agreed. "I probably shouldn't. Old habits die hard." He winced inwardly. "So, why are *you* here?"

"I was visiting someone as well, but no cab will deliver to this area after nightfall, so I had to walk." She seemed not to have noticed the unintentional play on words, or if she had, she had chosen, wisely, to ignore it.

"Could your husband not have accompanied you?"

"No," she said. "He couldn't."

A subdued silence followed. Hawkwood made no attempt to engage her in further conversation. She would talk when she was ready, he presumed. He wondered if she was thinking of the men he'd killed. Perhaps now the realization of what had happened had finally sunk in. One hundred yards further on, she stopped.

"We're here," she said.

She pointed across the street towards a lantern-lit doorway, one of the few that were visible. Above the door was a sign.

The paint was so faded the letters were barely legible. Hawkwood could make out only the first word: HOTEL; and even then, it took an effort.

"It aspires to be a hotel," she said. "It's really only a rooming house. But it's all we can afford."

As they drew nearer to the entrance, Hawkwood saw the second word above the door take shape.

"Is something wrong?" she asked.

He realized the shock must have shown on his face.

"You live *here*?"

"Yes; I told you." She frowned. "Why?"

"This is the address I was looking for," Hawkwood said. "The Hotel Patrice."

"You were visiting someone in *this* hotel?"

"If this is the *only* Hotel Patrice," Hawkwood said. "Then, yes."

"How remarkable. Who is it you were coming to see? Perhaps I can help. It's possible I may know them."

Hawkwood hesitated and then said, "I was hoping to call on Madame Malet."

A strange look stole over her face. Surprise, curiosity, a touch of caution, perhaps? The name obviously meant something to her.

"Madam Malet does not receive many visitors," she said.

"I've come a long way," Hawkwood said. "It's a private matter of some urgency."

Hawkwood saw that she was still clasping the locket. She'd carried it in her hand all the way from the scene of the attack.

Her gaze remained fixed upon him. "May I ask you a question?"

"I've a feeling you'll probably ask anyway," Hawkwood said.

"You're not really a priest, are you?"

Hawkwood hesitated then shook his head. "No. My name's Dumas, Paul Dumas."

She absorbed the information. Her eyes moved across him, taking in the dark attire before settling, finally, on his face. She stared at his scars. He could see there were many more questions in

198

her eyes. Finally, as if coming to a decision, she sighed.

"It would appear your footsteps were guided here after all," she said softly.

"How so?" Hawkwood asked.

"I am Denise Malet," she said.

12

Hawkwood had assumed she'd be a good deal older. General Malet was in his late fifties, according to Grant. His wife was considerably younger than that. Despite the tiny but noticeable creases at the corners of her dark, expressive eyes and the more obvious worry lines etched into her face – caused no doubt by her husband's confinement and her own reduced circumstances – Hawkwood guessed that Madame Malet was probably around forty years of age and, as he couldn't help observing, a very handsome woman.

Another reason, he thought, for having a quiet word with Grant, who could at least have had the courtesy to warn him beforehand. Doubtless, another of the Scot's little amusements.

The interior of the hotel was just as depressing as the exterior. If the establishment had once enjoyed more prosperous times, there were, from what Hawkwood could make out, scant signs of them in the dim-lit lobby. He waited to one side as Denise Malet retrieved her room key from the clerk, seated in sullen repose behind the reception desk, most of which lay in shadow. Hawkwood wondered if the paucity of illumination meant there was a candle as well as a sugar shortage in the city or if the hotel proprietor was just being obsessively frugal. Though, looking around, it was probably just as well the place was in semi-darkness. Spying a raiding party of cockroaches scuttling along the edge of the floorboard by his right boot, he wondered

201

what other delights might be lurking beyond the range of the candle glow.

On the positive side, the gloom did help to conceal his features. He kept his head deliberately low and at an angle as the clerk handed the key over, though he knew that had the woman not identified herself he would have had to present himself at the desk anyway, but in circumstances like these, you took full advantage of the situation whenever possible.

From beneath his hat brim, Hawkwood watched the clerk's eyes as they followed Madame Malet across the lobby. As the man shifted his gaze towards him, Hawkwood, without making the movement too obvious, turned his face from view.

"This way, Father," Denise Malet said, taking down her hood and speaking just loudly enough for the clerk to hear. Hawkwood followed. He could feel the man's eyes upon them as they made their way towards the staircase.

"You're not worried that your reputation will be compromised?" he asked her as soon as they were out of sight of the desk. "A married woman taking a man who is not her husband up to her room?"

In the poorly lit stairwell, his question drew a wintry smile.

"Your concern is touching, Monsieur Dumas, but I'm afraid any positive reputation I may once have enjoyed frittered away a long time ago. And if you think the concierge cares two figs for such things you're sadly mistaken. His only interest in me is whether my account is paid on time. Besides, he takes you for a priest; for all he knows, you could be accompanying me upstairs to hear my confession."

Which was ironic, given one of Grant's reasons for presenting Hawkwood with the cassock.

"People will notice you," Grant had told him, "but they won't *see* you. And while Bonaparte may not have a high regard for the Black Robes, the general populace still hold the church in some esteem. Just don't go presenting any sermons. That happens and you won't last five minutes. If the concierge at the hotel does enquire as to your business, you can tell him you've been summoned to render spiritual comfort to the lady in her time of need."

The stairs seemed to get steeper and grimier the higher they climbed. Damp patches covered the walls. By the time they halted, Hawkwood suspected they were almost at the top of the building.

"Welcome to my world, Monsieur Dumas," she said as she unlocked the door and led him into the apartment. "As you'll notice, fears for my propriety are the least of my woes." She turned from him, removed her cloak and hung it on a stand behind her.

The accommodation, from what Hawkwood could see as she went round lighting candle stubs, consisted of one large room, divided in two by a low archway strung with a length of curtain behind which, Hawkwood guessed, lay the bedchamber. Stout ceiling beams confirmed his earlier suspicion that they were close to the eaves and that in a previous incarnation the room had formed part of the attic. The stains running along the length of the coving suggested that the damp was severe and widespread. Clearly, the deterioration in the hotel's fortunes extended to all areas of the building.

"If you will excuse me for a moment," she said. Picking up a lighted candle, she drew aside the curtain, disappeared from view and closed the material behind her. A moment later there came the sound of water being poured into a basin.

Hawkwood took off his hat and looked about him at the worn furniture. He'd seen campaign trunks that had suffered less wear and tear. The atmosphere, as with all cheap hotels and rooming houses, was one of drab transience, though a few personal touches had been added to try and make the space more habitable: some books, a selection of china ornaments, a vase of dried flowers and on the stand behind the door, hanging alongside the cloak, a folded parasol, a long coat and two ribboned bonnets. A two-day-old newspaper lay on one of the two weathered chairs that sat in front of the empty fireplace. Three small, framed portraits stood in line abreast atop the mantelpiece. He was about to go over to them when the curtain was pulled back and Denise Malet re-emerged.

"May I offer you a glass of wine?" she enquired formally, smoothing down her dress.

"Thank you," Hawkwood said.

She went to a cabinet on which were stood a decanter and goblets. The graze on her forehead was still there but the smudges of dirt on her face that she'd picked up from her encounter with the wall had gone, and some loosened strands of hair had also been secured. From the self-conscious gesture as she patted the last errant wisp into place Hawkwood knew he was seeing a woman who was determined to retain some semblance of dignity despite the tawdriness of her living conditions.

As she reached for the decanter one of the objects on a nearby table caught Hawkwood's eye; a wooden box containing half a dozen lead soldiers. He picked one up. It was an Imperial Guardsman. The paint was chipped and faded but the Grumbler's moustache and side whiskers were still recognizable. He put it back and lifted out another figure; this time a mounted warrior on a grey horse. Bonaparte, on his charger, Marengo.

"They belong to my son, Aristide," Denise Malet said. She held out a glass. Her fingers were well formed and slender. "He's fourteen and he insists he's too old to play with toy soldiers, but I couldn't bring myself to throw them away."

Hawkwood took the proffered drink. With the exception of the toy box there was no other evidence that a child was living there.

"He's staying with friends in the north," she said, reading his mind. "The general and I thought it best if he went to live outside Paris, away from all . . . this."

Hawkwood placed Bonaparte back in the box and wondered if that small action was symbolic of his and Grant's planned, and possibly ludicrous, endeavour.

"The family he's living with has stables. He wrote telling me he rides every day and that he wants to join the cavalry." Her face softened.

"When was the last time you saw him?" Hawkwood asked.

She played with the stem of her glass. "Not long, a few weeks. He may be far away but he is still close to my heart."

Her left hand lifted to her throat and Hawkwood saw that she'd made a small knot in the broken chain and replaced it around her neck. He wondered what memento the locket contained; a likeness or a lock of the boy's hair?

"This and my wedding band are worth more to me than all the rest of the gold in the world, Monsieur Dumas. If you had not been there, they would have been taken from me. I owe you a debt of gratitude beyond price."

Her eyes moved to the portraits above the hearth. Hawkwood followed her gaze. Two of the likenesses were of a slim man in military uniform at different ages; one was of a small, serious-looking boy.

"My husband and my son," Denise Malet said. "In happier times." She smiled. "As you can see, he takes after his father."

Hawkwood thought the likenesses too small to make an adequate comparison – a mother's indulgence – but he nodded dutifully. "He's a fine-looking lad."

Denise Malet regarded the portraits with affection before turning her gaze away.

"You said you were visiting someone," Hawkwood said. "May I ask if it was the general?"

She nodded. "You may, and it was. Doctor Dubuisson's clinic is on the other side of the city. It's a long walk. I'm rarely home before dark."

She laid the journal aside and sat down. Despite having freshened herself in the other room, Denise Malet looked, Hawkwood thought, suddenly beset by weariness. It was as though a mask had slipped. Gone was the indomitable general's lady; in her place was a vulnerable wife and mother who'd been forced to carry the weight of the world upon her shoulders; most notably the imprisonment of her husband and the absence of her only child. As he looked on, she stroked her forehead absently and Hawkwood saw the despondency creep into her eyes.

But then, as if aware of Hawkwood's study, she glanced up. At once, her posture altered. She straightened and drew back her shoulders.

"So, Monsieur Dumas, you were telling me there was a matter of some urgency you wished to discuss. I wonder what could be *so* urgent that you chose to present yourself under cover of darkness. And please, do be seated. There's no need to stand on ceremony, not after our dramatic introduction."

Taking a sip of wine, she waited expectantly.

Hawkwood placed his hat on a side table and took a seat. There was, he knew, no other way to begin, except carefully.

"I regret I may have been slightly economical with the truth, madame."

"Really?" Her eyebrows rose, the glass poised halfway to her lips. "How so?"

"It is not you that my business concerns, but your husband."

"I see." Only two little words, and already her voice had lost some of its warmth. She put her glass aside and placed her hands in her lap.

"I came bearing a message for the general and I was hoping you would be able to assist me with its delivery," Hawkwood said.

"And who is this message from?" she asked guardedly.

"General Jean-Victor Moreau."

She frowned. "I understood General Moreau to be in America."

"That is what General Moreau would like people to think." Her eyebrows rose again.

"I regret I'm not at liberty to say more," Hawkwood said.

She regarded him closely. "You are aware that General Malet *is* permitted to receive visitors? Subterfuge is not a requirement."

"Yes, madame, but I did not want to present myself without solicitation or to draw unnecessary attention. It was my hope that I might persuade you to approach General Malet on my behalf."

"You wish me to arrange an introduction?"

Hawkwood nodded. "If that's possible, yes."

The way to the general is not to visit him unannounced, Grant had told him. *If we want to get to Malet we should go through the one person he trusts implicitly: his wife. She's stuck with him through thick and thin. It was her efforts, petitioning people in power, that eventually gained the general his transfer from La Force to the Dubuisson house. If anyone can subvert Malet to our cause, mark my words, it'll be Madame.*

She stared at him, uncompromising in her directness.

"May I assume from your guise that the message you wish to impart is of a covert nature? Answer truthfully, Monsieur Dumas, if you please."

There was steel in her voice. Immediately, Hawkwood knew why she hadn't baulked at the sight of the bodies in the alleyway. They'd held no revulsion for her. She was the wife of a general and thus, in her own way, she'd probably become as resilient as any battle-hardened veteran.

"You may, madame."

"And am *I* permitted to know the contents of this . . . message?" she asked coolly.

It was a question he'd been anticipating.

Hawkwood feigned hesitation and then said, "You'll appreciate, madame, it would be indiscreet of me and indeed a grave dereliction of duty if I were to furnish you with specific details. What I can tell you is that it is General Moreau's understanding that certain . . . contingency measures . . . have been drawn up; to be implemented in the event of the Emperor meeting his death during his current eastern campaign.

"I'm here to convey Jean-Victor's respects to General Malet and to advise the general that were such an event to occur and if the general's circumstances were to change as a result, he – that is General Moreau – would be honoured to serve the motherland in any capacity."

Denise Malet remained silent for several seconds. Finally, she nodded. "I see. Well, that is most generous of General Moreau, and just the sentiment one has come to expect from such a distinguished hero of the Republic."

"Indeed," Hawkwood said piously.

Denise Malet pursed her lips. "Though I suspect there are those who might, just as equally, regard General Moreau's words as bordering on further treason, were one to employ them in an inappropriate context."

"People do say there's a thin line drawn twixt treason and patriotism," Hawkwood said.

"I suspect that rather depends on which side of the line you happen to be standing," Denise Malet said. "Does it not?"

"Yes," Hawkwood agreed. "I suppose it does."

Intelligent and perceptive, too, he thought.

She sat back and unclasped her hands. Reaching for her glass, she regarded him levelly.

"Forgive me, Monsieur Dumas, but it occurs to me – given the nature of your visit – that even at this late stage I should ask you for some form of identification. You have papers, I take it?"

"Yes, madame." Hawkwood reached into his pocket.

Not that it would prove anything, he thought, as he handed her the passport. He suspected she was aware of that and wondered if she was going through the motions purely to gain more time in which to consider his petition.

He watched as she ran her gaze down the document.

It doesn't matter how genuine she considers it to be. Either she trusts me or she doesn't; because that's all that matters in the end.

Finally, she looked up, held his gaze, and handed the passport back.

"Very well. It is my intention to visit General Malet tomorrow. I will convey your request to him."

"Thank you, madame," Hawkwood said. "I'm most grateful."

As she raised the glass, he saw a faint smile touch her lips. "Did you think I'd neglect to mention tonight's incident to my husband, Monsieur Dumas, or your timely intervention?"

Hawkwood cursed silently. *Idiot! Of course she'd bloody mention it.*

"I think the general would be rather interested in meeting the gentleman who came to the aid of his wife in her time of peril, wouldn't you agree?" Taking pity on him, she added, "There is a small café just off the rue Saint Jacques called Le Moineau. A message will be left for you there. Ask for Fabien. He served with my husband back in Italy and has remained a staunch ally. There are not too many of those left," she added with a wry smile.

Placing her glass down again, she rose to her feet. "Now, if you will excuse me, it's been a long day and it grows late and I should like to retire."

"Of course," Hawkwood stood.

"Besides, we wouldn't want the concierge to gather the wrong impression over the severity of my sins, would we?"

"No indeed," Hawkwood said.

She walked with him to the door. "I thank you again, monsieur, for your assistance."

"My pleasure, madame," Hawkwood said.

"And for your candour," she added, opening the door. "I've found that to be a rare commodity of late."

Ignoring the sharp prick of conscience in his chest, Hawkwood nodded and turned to go.

"Monsieur Dumas."

Hawkwood turned back. He saw she was holding something out to him.

"Don't forget your hat," she said.

"Well, by God!" Grant said, grinning. "I knew your roguish charm'd do the trick!"

"That and two dead bodies," Hawkwood said. "I could have done without those."

Grant made a face. "Aye, well, that's true. I'll not deny I didn't expect you to go around dispatching footpads at the drop of a hat, but *carpe diem*, bonny lad. Didn't I tell you that?"

"Yes, you did," Hawkwood said, slightly irritated by Grant's ebullience. "But I didn't seize anything. What's the Latin for 'I just happened to be passing'?"

"Buggered if I know," Grant said. "And I could care even less. We have our introduction and that's all that matters. By God, it couldn't have worked out better if we'd hired the black-guards to attack the lady just so's you could ride to her rescue!" He paused and threw Hawkwood a speculative look. "You didn't . . .?"

"No," Hawkwood said. "I bloody didn't. How could I? I didn't know what she looked like. And *you* didn't tell me she's a lot younger than her husband, either," Hawkwood added pointedly.

"Did I not? Must have slipped my mind. Well, in any case,

I'm not sure it's strictly relevant. Did you think it'd have made a difference if I had told you? This way, it made your surprise at meeting her all the more bona fide."

Which, Hawkwood couldn't help admitting with some annoyance, was undoubtedly true.

As he watched Grant spread his palms towards the fire, it occurred to him that the contrast between McPherson's ageing though moderately comfortable apartment and Denise Malet's depressing hotel room couldn't have been greater. And then another voice within his brain reminded him that this was an enemy he was dealing with. It didn't matter that she was a general's wife down on her luck and trying to eke out a living the best she could. She was a conduit; a means to an end, nothing more. But then, looking back to another age, that's what he'd first thought about the privateer, Lasseur. And look how that escapade had ended.

The Scot turned his back on the hearth. This time his face was serious. "With regards to our villains, you're certain there's nothing to link you to their deaths?"

"Only Madame," Hawkwood said. "And she's not going to say anything."

"You're sure?"

"Why would she?"

"I confess I can't think of a single reason," Grant agreed. The light re-entered his eyes. He slapped Hawkwood on the shoulder. The devil-may-care attitude was back. "You did well! Damned well! How about a wee dram to celebrate?"

Maybe the warmth of the fire had something to do with it, but Hawkwood was too weary to resist. It had been a long day. It didn't seem possible that he'd only arrived in the city that morning. So much had happened in the intervening hours. He tried to remember when he'd last enjoyed a decent night's rest. Sleep during the trip from Boulogne had been an intermittent luxury and any respite he had accrued had been swiftly negated by the rigours of each succeeding stage of the journey which, without exception, had involved long stretches of spine-jarring discomfort interspersed with inadequate transit stops, which had allowed the driver to change horses but the handful of passengers barely enough time to stretch their aching limbs or visit the privy before re-boarding.

It was late by the time he'd returned to the rue Serpente. Thankfully, his journey back from the hotel had passed without incident, though that wasn't to say that he hadn't been aware of the sense of menace pervading the less frequented lanes and passageways.

Denise Malet had been correct when she'd suggested that the dark held no fear for him, but that didn't mean he wasn't alert to the dangers that stalked the night.

During his time as a Runner he'd grown used to treading the fine line between light and shadow. Be it London or Paris, it made no difference. Twenty years of soldiering and killing had given him that confidence and he was a better law officer because of it. His duties as a police officer had seen him venture many times into London's violent slums. Rookeries like St Giles, Saffron Hill or Rosemary Lane were the natural haunt of transgressors who'd committed just about every horrific deed known to man, and then some. It was a poor officer of the law who, in the pursuit of miscreants, allowed himself to be frightened or even discouraged from entering those territories. Although it was true there were some who shied away from confrontation with the more vicious members of the criminal fraternity, Hawkwood wasn't one of them.

Though, as his profession held no sway on the streets of the French capital, he suspected it had been his priestly attire that had been the deterrent to any would-be assailant and in that, despite his initial reservations, he'd had to agree that Grant's recommendation had been the correct one.

However, it had been his own idea to travel alone; against Grant's better judgement, it had to be said, but Hawkwood's argument had been that he needed to be able to find his own way across the city, day or night, and the sooner he learnt to do that, the better.

Besides, he had a tongue in his head. He could always stop someone and ask the way and who would deny such a request from a priest? In the end, Grant had relented and had provided him with directions to the rue de l'Université and the Hotel Patrice. It had been a relatively easy walk anyway, with few turnings. Only in the last few hundred yards, prior to his confront-ation in the alleyway, had he needed to backtrack, a detour which, as it turned out, had paid unexpected and opportune dividends.

Hawkwood took the glass from Grant and let the brandy slide to the back of his throat. As he did so, there came two sharp knocks on the apartment door.

Grant was already turning towards the table and reaching for the loaded pistol when the second part of the signal sounded, followed by McPherson's soft voice coming to them from the hallway. "Stand down, gentlemen. It's only me."

Grant rolled his eyes, put the pistol down and poured out a third measure. "Jamie! Excellent timing!" he cried cheerfully as McPherson entered the room. "The captain and I were about to partake of a small libation. You'll join us?"

"Ye have to ask?" McPherson placed his stick to one side, took off his hat and coat and rubbed his hands together. "It's not exactly mid-summer out there and there's rain on the way, unless my old bones are mistaken."

"Then I have just the thing to warm you up! There, get that inside you."

McPherson received the cognac and knocked back half the glass with one swallow. He sighed gratefully. "By God, I needed that!"

Hawkwood smiled inwardly. All three of them might have been ensconced in an officers' mess instead of an apartment in the middle of Paris.

"Now then, Jamie," Grant said, "the captain's been telling me he's had a very productive evening. How about yourself?"

"Too early to tell." McPherson took another sip. "I've been endeavouring to get a message to L'Épine to see if he can obtain word on what fate might have befallen Captain Stuart."

"L'Épine?" Hawkwood said, wondering what thorns had to do with anything.

McPherson, cognac in hand, lowered himself into a chair and

212

stretched his legs towards the fire. "It's a nom de guerre. Best if I don't give you the fellow's real name. I can tell you he's the man responsible for all landings in the Pas de Calais area as well as transportation to and from the coast. Mademoiselle de Préville's one of his people. They all have special names. Flowers are popular. His predecessor was called La Rose so he uses L'Épine partly for that reason and also in jest; a thorn in the side of the French and so forth."

"Who said the Frogs don't have a sense of humour?" Grant grinned.

McPherson took a sip of cognac. "It may take a few days for the message to get through as he never stays in one place for too long, but I've no doubt once he's in receipt he'll put his best people on it." The old man gnawed the inside of his cheek. "It's likely to be a wee while before we hear anything."

"In that case," Hawkwood said, "I'll get my head down. It'll give me a chance to catch up on my beauty sleep. I'll need to look my best, after all."

McPherson and Grant stared at him.

"Look your best?" Grant's eyebrows lifted. "Now, that wouldn't be because of a certain lady, by any chance?"

He looked towards McPherson and winked.

"Hell, no," Hawkwood said. "The lady's got damn all to do with it. It's the general I'm worried about. I always try to look sharp when I'm meeting one of *those*."

Sheltering behind a high stone wall, the Clinique Dubuisson was set back from the street and protected from it by a border of plane trees, most of which had already shed their autumn foliage. A dignified-looking building with a weathered façade, the nursing home was smaller than most of its neighbours and, the protective wall notwithstanding, there were no towers, no grim battlements, no barred windows and, from what Hawkwood could see, no armed guards either. It was all rather refined – for a prison.

To his right, looking eastwards to where the rue du Faubourg-Saint-Antoine was at its broadest, Hawkwood could see the old toll houses

213

and above them the twin pillars that formed the Barrière du Trône. Rearing into the sky on either side of the road, they dwarfed everything in sight.

A wide variety of vehicles – mostly horse-drawn, a few steered by hand – wound their way between the columns, like desert caravans passing the ruins of an ancient Roman temple. Some trundled towards the city; others away from it, heading for the patchwork of brown pasture and autumn-stippled woodland tantalizingly visible just beyond the Barrière's outer reaches.

Dodging a couple of handcarts, Hawkwood crossed the street and made his way towards the clinic's wrought-iron gates. He could see there was a small porter's lodge inside the entrance and a handle set into a niche on the outside of the wall. Hawkwood jerked the bell pull and waited for signs of life. Looking up at the building, he wondered what he would find inside. He remembered peering through the railings at Bethlem Hospital and what his visit there had entailed. He thought about the aftermath, too, and shuddered.

Receiving no immediate response to his jangling summons he was about to try the bell again when a dishevelled figure suddenly appeared at the lodge doorway, buttoning his coat. There was no tugging of the forelock, Hawkwood noticed, as the porter ambled towards him. Evidently, in the Dubuisson clinic at least one revolutionary principle still lingered.

Reaching the gate, the porter looked Hawkwood up and down. "Help you?"

He was a middle-aged man with a large nose, red-veined cheeks and an expression of weary perseverance which indicated he'd probably been too long in the job.

"I'm here to visit with one of your residents," Hawkwood said.

"Name?"

"Mine or the resident's?" Hawkwood asked.

It had seemed a perfectly reasonable question, but the porter sighed. "Who are you here to see?"

"Maître Charles Perraux."

The porter's eyebrows rose. Imperceptibly, but enough for Hawkwood to notice. "Got your pass?"

Hawkwood reached inside his jacket. McPherson had obtained the visitor's permit from an informant at the Palais de Justice. It was genuine, he'd assured Hawkwood, as were the signatures upon it.

As the porter took possession of the document, Hawkwood heard soft footsteps and sensed a presence behind him; another visitor seeking admittance. He turned to find himself facing a woman carrying a small covered basket. She smiled politely before turning her head away.

The porter finished reading and held out his hand again. "Identification papers."

Holding his tongue, Hawkwood passed his passport through the gate. It didn't matter a jot if they were French or English, he thought. Jobsworths were all the same.

"You are Monsieur Dumas?"

"I am," Hawkwood said, thinking, *You've just taken my papers. Who else would I bloody be? An English spy?*

The porter compared the name on the passport to the name on the permit. It seemed to take an age, with the porter moving his lips as he read. Hawkwood wondered if he was having trouble with the longer words. Finally, satisfied, the porter handed the papers back, selected a key from a bunch at his belt, unlocked the gate and pulled it open.

"Don't recall seeing you before," the porter said, frowning as Hawkwood walked through. "This your first visit?"

"That's right," Hawkwood said. "Maître Perraux was my old teacher. I haven't seen him for a long time."

The porter sniffed. "I doubt *anyone's* seen him for a long time, save us lot in here." Adding cryptically, "Not that I'm surprised, mind."

"Why's that?"

Realizing he might have said too much, the porter hesitated. The surliness evaporated, to be replaced by contrition. "Not really my place to say. Probably best wait and see for yourself."

Before Hawkwood could respond, the porter had latched on to his other visitor. "Madame."

"Monsieur Lesage," the woman said pleasantly, giving no hint that she might have overheard the previous exchange. "How are we today?"

"Can't complain, madame, though the cold'll likely play havoc with my arthritis . . ."

The porter hadn't bothered to ask the woman for papers, Hawkwood noticed. Regular visitors clearly received preferential treatment, with a smattering of conversation thrown in for good measure. Hawkwood had recognized the enquiry after the porter's health as nothing more than subtle flattery. Humour the staff and they would see you were all right. Not so different from the officer class attempting to keep in with the other ranks.

Having recounted his list of ailments, the porter's voice trailed off. Hawkwood decided it was time to feign indecision.

The porter's chin lifted. Seeing a chance to make amends for his earlier indiscretion, he pointed. "It's that way. Where it says *Reception*. You'll need to sign the book."

Hawkwood moved towards the building.

"Monsieur?"

It was the woman. Hawkwood turned.

"If you would permit me?" The woman addressed the porter. "It's all right, I can show this gentleman the way."

Trying not to appear relieved that someone else was willing to take responsibility, the porter gave a brusque nod of gratitude. "As you wish, madame."

The woman smiled at Hawkwood. "Shall I lead?"

Leaving the porter to lock up, Hawkwood and his guide walked towards the clinic's main door.

"Why, Father," Denise Malet murmured, as Hawkwood fell into step beside her, "I note you're in civilian dress. Does this mean you've forsaken your vows?"

Hawkwood smiled. "I'm taking a sabbatical."

He was back in his own clothes. There hadn't seemed much point in continuing with the disguise, at least while he was in Madame Malet's company, since she'd become an accomplice to his deception. Neither had he any intention of posing as a padre in front of a genuine clergyman, to wit, Abbé Lafon. That way lay madness. One probing question or remark pertaining

216

in any way to the scriptures and Hawkwood knew that the masquerade would be doomed to failure.

"To do what? Become a highwayman?"

The comment, Hawkwood knew, was directed against his new coat, a replacement for his own riding coat that he'd exchanged for the subsequently discarded tarpaulin jacket back on the *Griffin*. Grant had directed him to a military outfitter's off the rue Saint-Honoré, where he'd made the purchase. Grey and calf-length, the cavalry-style coat bore a close resemblance to his own and he'd felt comfortable in it as soon as he'd tried it on. And he had the feeling he'd need its bulk, too, for even in the few days he'd been in the city, the weather had started to change rapidly. Rain had fallen with increased regularity and the autumn winds were beginning to nip in earnest.

As a ward against the chill she was wearing her cloak again, this time with the hood down. Her dark hair was contained beneath a neat midnight blue bonnet trimmed with feathers, one of the two that he'd seen on the coat stand behind her door.

"You saw the Barrière when you came in?" she asked.

Hawkwood nodded. "Of course."

"It's said they were executing sixty people a day there, after they moved the guillotine from the Place de la Concorde. They buried the bodies in lime pits and threw the heads in after them. They didn't care who they were killing by that time; aristos or commoners. They slaughtered soldiers and shopkeepers, even members of the clergy; it made no difference. They murdered sixteen Carmelite nuns on one afternoon alone. The sisters sang hymns as they were taken up the steps. *Some* people take their faith seriously."

Which puts me *in my place*, Hawkwood thought. He glanced down at the basket, recalling that, among his other failings, the porter hadn't bothered to check the contents.

She allowed herself a small smile. "A few provisions; that's all."

No files or pistols, then.

"Don't they feed them?" Hawkwood asked.

"Of course." She looked slightly shocked at the suggestion.

217

"But supplies can be irregular and there are never enough and so I like to take a little extra in when I can; some wine, fresh bread and cheese, sometimes a pastry and oranges. The general loves oranges." Her face clouded. "But it's difficult when we have so little to live on."

"The army's still paying him?"

"One-third pay only, and we don't know how long that will last. We have to settle the Dubuisson account weekly; so with that *and* the hotel bill, times are . . . not so easy these days. When his army pay stops, I don't know what we'll do. You can see now why we sent our son away."

They drew near to the building. Closer inspection revealed that it was showing its age in the crevices around the windows and the corners of the wall. The grounds, however, looked well tended. Flanked by trees and blanketed with fallen leaves, the lawns and shrubbery were neatly trimmed. On the far side, a gardener was attempting to scoop the rakings into a sack. On a nearby bench, two elderly men wrapped in coats with blankets over their knees were deep in discussion. It all looked very peaceful. What it didn't look like was a hotbed of sedition.

Interestingly, there still didn't appear to be any form of security in place, save for the gatekeeper. But then from what he'd observed so far and from what he'd been told, there was probably little risk of an uprising, especially given the age and physical condition of the prisoners, or, as Grant insisted on calling them, the residents.

Hawkwood wondered what he was going to find inside. He knew it wasn't going to be anything like Bedlam, where the inmates were wont to scream at the sight of a new face and where the corridors reeked like middens. He was half expecting the clinic to smell of old men waiting to die. Though what that precise smell was exactly, he had no real idea. He was, therefore, pleasantly surprised to discover, when he followed Madame Malet up the steps and through the front door, that the place didn't smell much of anything, except beeswax and fading nobility.

The lobby was uncluttered and functional with a reception area and a wide central staircase leading up to the first floor.

The atmosphere was of calm orderliness, with no screaming and no uniformed orderlies scuttling around after demented inmates, much to Hawkwood's relief.

At the reception desk, Denise Malet entered her name in the visitor's book and passed Hawkwood the pen. The desk porter, a servant of discretion compared to the gatekeeper, made no comment upon reading the identity of the resident Hawkwood was visiting. His only response, as Hawkwood put down the pen, was to say, "I believe the general and Maître Perraux are in the library."

"Thank you," Denise Malet said. She beckoned to Hawkwood. "Come, Monsieur Dumas; allow me to guide you."

"Most kind, madame," Hawkwood said, but he needn't have bothered. The porter was already turning away.

The sounds of muted conversations drifted along the corridors. A few doors were open, giving a restricted view into the rooms beyond. From the equipment within and from the charts on the wall, one looked as though it was used for medical examinations. Adjoining it was a small sickbay. Aromas issuing from another doorway indicated it was where the residents took their meals, while another, to judge from the unexpected glimpse of a pianoforte, might have been a music room. Definitely nothing like Bedlam. Maybe there were hot tubs, after all, Hawkwood mused.

Hawkwood saw that a number of the men who passed them wore the same jacket as the gatekeeper and the desk porter and he assumed that these, too, were members of the clinic's staff. A couple made eye contact with Denise Malet and murmured "Madame" as they brushed by in acknowledgement of a familiar face. Nowhere was there a sense of urgency or a sign of enforced detainment. It was a wonder, Hawkwood thought, that there weren't queues of people at the main gate trying to break in.

They were passing one of the open doorways when a voice said, "Madame Malet?"

The general's wife paused as a sedate, well-dressed and affable-looking man stepped out of one of the rooms.

"Doctor Dubuisson," Denise Malet said.

219

The doctor's eyes dropped to the basket and he smiled. "Ah, the general's favourite; Pont l'Evêque, unless I'm mistaken?"

"You are as perceptive as ever, Doctor."

"This old nose is seldom wrong when it comes to cheese, madame." Dubuisson tapped his right nostril. "One of my own little weaknesses." He looked at Hawkwood.

"This is Monsieur Dumas, Doctor. He's here to pay a call on Maître Perraux. We met at the gate. I was showing him the way to the library."

The doctor smiled. Crow's feet formed around the corners of his eyes. "In that case, I'm delighted to meet you. The maître's visitors have been few and far between. It will make a nice change for him."

Dubuisson placed a hand on Hawkwood's arm. "But do not expect too much. I take it you've not seen him for while, so you'll find him . . . changed. Though we do try our best to make his stay here as comfortable as we are able." The doctor patted Hawkwood's forearm before removing his hand. "But I must away, I have rounds to make and we've a new chef, so I need to inspect the kitchens as well. It was nice to see you again, madame. Good day to you."

"He seems sociable enough," Hawkwood commented as the doctor disappeared around the corner.

Denise Malet turned and they proceeded down the corridor.

"He is," she said drily. "For a gaoler."

The library lay at the rear of the house. It was a comfortable salon, with tall windows and a pleasant view over the grounds. A fire glowed in the hearth. With its book-lined walls, high-backed chairs, and newspaper racks, the room's quiet ambience was strangely reminiscent, Hawkwood thought, of the parliamentary reading room, which he'd had occasion to visit while on lobby duty at the House of Commons.

There were a dozen or so male occupants, in various stages of wakefulness. Half were in their late fifties or sixties. The rest looked older. The majority of the older ones were dozing, some with half-read newspapers open on their laps. A quartet, possibly a mix of residents and visitors, was engaged in subdued conversation at a corner table. There were two other women visitors present, one matronly, the other much younger; a wife and a daughter, Hawkwood presumed. Or perhaps a mistress.

"Maître Perraux." Denise Malet spoke quietly, indicating a figure seated in a wheelchair who was gazing out at the garden. At an angle to the room, only his shoulders and the back of his head were visible.

"Thank you for your help, madame," Hawkwood said. "I'm grateful."

"You're most welcome, monsieur."

Inclining her head politely, she left him. On the other side of the room, Hawkwood saw one of the residents rise from his chair to take her hand. A tall, slender, well-proportioned man with distinguished features and greying hair; the look of affection on his face told Hawkwood all he needed to know.

General Claude-François Malet in the flesh.

13

"Maître Perraux?"

The old man, who wasn't so much seated in the wheelchair as slumped in it, made no reply. Neither did he look up, but, instead, continued to stare fixedly out of the window, shoulders hunched.

Hawkwood moved nearer.

Still nothing.

He placed a hand on the old man's shoulder. There wasn't a lot to hold on to. It was like clasping a sack full of twigs.

There was an empty chair close by. Hawkwood drew it towards him and sat down. For the benefit of those who might be watching, he leaned in close. Earlier, he had wondered what the smell of old men dying might be like. Now he knew. Dust and decay and the faint yet distinct whiff of urine-soiled breeches.

"Maître? It's Dumas." Hawkwood, feeling as if every eye in the room was upon him, patted the old man's arm. "Remember me? It's been a while, hasn't it?"

This is bloody stupid, he thought.

Perraux's hair was as white as chalk. Brushed back from a high forehead, it curled in a sparse mane along the nape of his neck and nestled at the back of his collar like thistledown. His flesh was almost translucent. Over the areas where the bones lay close to the skin, across his forehead and cheeks and the ridges along the backs of his hands, it shone like waxed paper.

A pair of rheumy eyes slid sideways and Hawkwood found himself the object of a watery, unfocused stare. As he watched, a thin trickle of milky saliva emerged slowly from the corner of the old man's mouth and dribbled down on to his chin.

If Hawkwood hadn't been warned in advance it would have been obvious even before he'd sat down that the Emperor Bonaparte himself could have entered the room stark naked and taken Maître Perraux by the hand, and it was doubtful if the old man would have been any the wiser.

Fortunately.

When he'd called in at Le Moineau on the morning of the second day following his meeting with Denise Malet, there had been a message waiting. The general would be pleased to receive him that afternoon.

But there had been a condition. Their meeting had to appear inadvertent.

Included in the message was a name.

Maître Charles Gustave Perraux.

A stalking horse.

Watching the old man drooling like an infant, Hawkwood wondered if it hadn't all been an unnecessary palaver. Given the gatekeeper's reaction, there was the distinct possibility that the nomination of Perraux as a decoy may not have been the wisest move and that he'd drawn more attention to his visit, not less. Though on the face of it, in theory, a senile former professor of law at the Sorbonne had seemed a sound choice. Even if Perraux had been in full possession of his wits it was unlikely he'd be able to recall the names and faces of every student who'd appeared before him. Posing as a former pupil had therefore seemed the most appropriate ruse.

MacPherson had used his informers to make enquiries. Perraux and the rest of the teaching staff had lost their livelihoods when the university was closed because of its opposition to the Revolution. He'd later been imprisoned after siding with the disbanded Faculty of Theology in its dissent against the Convention's treatment of the Church. When the university eventually reopened not everyone had survived the purges. Against the odds, Perraux had, but time, age and the years of imprisonment had taken their toll. It had been during his time in the Sainte-Pélagie prison that the first signs of distraction had appeared.

Maître Perraux's transfer to the clinic had eventually been arranged by persons of high status within the régime. McPherson had no names, but former students with connections of their own were the most likely candidates. Men who, either through a sense of duty or quite possibly guilt, had felt the need to see their old mentor enter his twilight years with some degree of dignity. Perraux had eventually been transferred to the Dubuisson nursing home, there to live out his days in comfort instead of a rat-infested dungeon or on the streets with the rest of the dispossessed.

Maybe it wasn't so bad, Hawkwood thought, struck by the vacant expression on the old man's face. They sheltered you, fed you, probably even wiped your arse and dressed you in the mornings. There were worse ways to fade away.

At the same time, Hawkwood was also wondering how long he'd have to maintain the charade. It wasn't easy, trying to manufacture a conversation with someone who had no idea who you were, or why you were there in the first place.

Until the old man lifted his head and in a low, rasping voice enquired hoarsely, "*Donatien?*"

The utterance was so unexpected Hawkwood felt the hairs rise on the back of his neck. Feeling a slight pressure on his arm, he glanced down. A mottled claw had caught hold of his wrist. A chill moved through him. This wasn't part of the plan. Perraux was supposed to be incapable. He wasn't supposed to speak. He certainly wasn't supposed to initiate a bloody conversation! And Hawkwood knew it was a name, but who the hell was Donatien?

"He thinks you're de Sade," a voice said.

Hawkwood looked round. In front of him stood a thin, sallow-faced man, dressed in black, with a closed round collar. Hawkwood's gaze slid to the rosary the newcomer was kneading in his right hand. It held a small silver cross.

"They were in Sainte-Pélagie together. De Sade used to read to him. Hardly surprising the poor fellow's lost his mind, having to listen to the demented scribblings of *that* blasphemer."

Hawkwood had no idea who or what the man was talking about. The name de Sade meant nothing, though the newcomer evidently thought it should. Assuming what he hoped was an expression of understanding, Hawkwood nodded sympathetically.

The newcomer gazed with sorrow at the man in the wheelchair then looked up. "Forgive me, we haven't been introduced. I am Jean-Baptiste Lafon."

Lafon's eyes were very blue and set beneath a pair of heavy eyebrows that looked out of all proportion to the size of his face. He looked to be somewhere in his forties, younger than Hawkwood had been expecting. An experience that was getting to be a habit of late, he reflected.

"Dumas. Paul Dumas."

Lafon remained mute for several moments and then he said quietly. "Delighted to make your acquaintance, monsieur."

"Donatien?" The quavering enquiry came from behind him.

Hell's teeth! Hawkwood thought.

"One moment." Lafon held up a hand. His eyes alighted on the nearest catnapper who, head back in his chair, was snoring gently, a newspaper across his knees. Retrieving the paper, Lafon held it out. "There; read to him."

"What?" Hawkwood said.

"He likes being read to. It's what his friend Donatien used to do. I've done it myself a few times."

"What should I read?" Hawkwood asked, puzzled. "I doubt he'll understand any of it."

"The content is immaterial. It's the tone of your voice that matters. He'll find it soothing. You'll see. Here."

Before he could object, the paper had been thrust into Hawkwood's hands and Lafon had taken his leave and was moving towards the opposite side of the room.

Reluctantly, Hawkwood opened the journal and looked for something innocuous. The headings hadn't changed a great deal.

Most were dedicated to the glory of the Empire and the exploits of her heroes, the latest of whom was Larrey, Bonaparte's Surgeon General, who'd managed to perform over two hundred amputations in twenty-four hours in the aftermath of Borodino. Britain's war against the United States rated several column inches. Great play was made of the capture of the British sloop HMS *Alert* by the USS *Essex*. At home, bankers were reassuring everyone that they did have sufficient funds despite worrying rumours to the contrary. Several new building projects were being considered to commemorate the victories in Russia and an exhibition at the Musée had opened. Queue now, to avoid disappointment, the *Journal* urged. At the foot of the third page there was a passing mention of a new police department, the Brigade de Sûreté that was enjoying considerable success in the concerted effort to combat crime. And so it went on. It was all relentlessly optimistic, as if there were no food shortages, no potholes and no poverty on the streets.

Not having a pin to hand, Hawkwood seized upon a paragraph at random and began to read aloud, while keeping his voice low. He was two sentences in before he realized it was an opera review. At this rate, he thought, it wouldn't only be Maître Perraux's eyes that would be glazing over.

But, astonishingly, Lafon had been right. By the time Hawkwood reached the end of the second paragraph, the old man's head had fallen forward on to his chest and dry wheezing sounds were emanating from the back of his throat. Hawkwood sat back with relief.

"You see, not so difficult."

Lafon's voice came from behind him.

"No," Hawkwood agreed. He put down the newspaper.

"We should let him rest," Lafon said.

Hawkwood stood.

"I think it's time you met the general," Lafon said. "Don't you?"

General Malet topped Lafon by a good four inches. Close to, Hawkwood saw that the greying hair was due not only to age but also to a light dusting of powder, tiny specks of which had drifted on to the general's shoulders. But it was not Malet's height, however, nor his powdered hair that commanded attention. It was the strength of his gaze. The general's irises were a dark, almost reddish brown. Hawkwood had never seen such a colour before. It was hard not to be transfixed.

Lafon gestured Hawkwood forward. "Monsieur Paul Dumas, General."

"An honour, sir," Hawkwood said.

"The honour's mine, monsieur." Malet held out his hand. As Hawkwood returned his grip, a light moved in the general's remarkable eyes, which went beyond the mere courtesy of a greeting. Hawkwood recognized the signs. It made no difference if he were a private or a general, any military man worth his salt knew a fellow soldier when he saw one. Hawkwood saw the realization steal slowly across the general's face.

"You know my wife, of course."

Hawkwood inclined his head. "Madame."

"Monsieur Dumas," she said.

She had removed the cloak and bonnet. Her dress was plain, with long sleeves and a high bodice. Her hair was held up and pinned to reveal the smooth lines of her neck and throat. She looked, Hawkwood thought, as she fingered the locket chain, serene and elegant, what one would have expected from the wife of a senior officer of the Empire.

The general made no move to relinquish his hold. Instead he stepped forward, and with his left hand clasped Hawkwood's right wrist and drew him closer. When he spoke, it was almost in a whisper, so as not to be overheard.

"Thank you for what you did. I will not forget."

Giving Hawkwood's hand a final shake, he let go and stepped back. In a normal voice, he said, "You'll join us, of course. I see Maître Perraux is in Morpheus' care so I doubt you'll be missed. Our usual corner is free. Perhaps you'd care for some refreshments? Afternoon tea would be in order, I think. Though we shouldn't let the Emperor hear that, eh? He might think we've all defected to the British. What say you?"

"Thank you, General," Hawkwood said. "I could do with a drink."

"My wife tells me we have a mutual friend," Malet said.

"I believe so, General," Hawkwood replied.

"So, how is Jean-Victor?"

"He's in excellent health, sir. He sends you his warmest regards."

"That's most kind of him. And his family?"

"Also well."

"Splendid." The general sipped tea. "Still enjoying their estate in Virginia, I take it?"

Hawkwood shook his head. "No, sir; Pennsylvania. Morrisville, it lies on the Delaware River."

Admonishing himself for his mistake, the general tutted. "Ah, but of course. How could I forget? A rather grand house as well, I understand. They must rattle around in it."

"They did until it burned down," Hawkwood said. "Unfortunately, it wasn't rebuilt and the general and his family had to move into a smaller property."

A look passed between Malet and Lafon. The general took another sip of tea, and smiled apologetically. "That *was* rather clumsy of me, wasn't it?"

"Not so much, sir," Hawkwood said. "But I'd probably have done the same in your shoes."

Hawkwood offered up a silent prayer in appreciation of McPherson's attention to detail. McPherson and Grant had banked on Malet's knowledge of Moreau's circumstances being limited due to his time in prison and, latterly, the clinic, but the old Scot had plied Hawkwood with as much information as he'd been able to gather, just in case. It was intriguing, therefore, to find how up to date Malet was with Moreau's domestic arrangements. Hawkwood wondered how Malet received his intelligence; through Lafon and the Congrégation, possibly. Hopefully, the sum of their information wasn't *that* current. It then occurred to him if that was the case then Malet knew of Lafon's allegiances. He laid that thought to one side.

"My wife informs me that General Moreau might not be as far away as we were led to believe." Malet placed his cup in its saucer and stirred the liquid with a spoon. He looked up and smiled beguilingly.

Hawkwood took a slow sip of tea. It was lukewarm and devoid of flavour, though it left an after-taste reminiscent of long marches and home-made brews concocted over army camp fires using ingredients picked out of hedgerows whenever supplies ran low. It reminded him why he'd never taken to the habit.

"General Moreau's in England, sir."

Lafon stopped toying with his rosary. His head came up sharply.

Malet leaned forward, his tea forgotten. "And *what*, may I ask, is he doing in England?"

"He's on his way to Sweden at the invitation of Prince Bernadotte."

Malet frowned. "Bernadotte? I'm not sure I follow."

Which was what Hawkwood had said, until Grant had enlightened him.

Bernadotte, a former Marshal of France, was another in the growing list of disillusioned commanders who'd turned against their Emperor. After a glittering army career that had seen him rise from enlisted man to a general of division and a hero of Austerlitz, a series of flawed military judgements and increasing disagreements with his leader had resulted in a conspicuous fall from grace.

A court martial and obscurity had threatened, but two factors had come to his aid. The first was his good fortune to have married Joseph Bonaparte's sister-in-law. The second was that the Swedish King, Charles XIII, was looking for an heir. Ever pragmatic, the Swedes had seen the advantage of electing a king Napoleon would accept. Bizarrely, and with the blessing of Bonaparte, who'd seen it as a convenient way of getting the marshal out of his hair, they'd offered Bernadotte the post by virtue of the kindness he'd shown to Swedish prisoners during the last coalition war. As an adopted Crown Prince, Bernadotte was the Swedish King in waiting.

230

"He's joining the *Swedish* Army?" Malet said, aghast.

"No," Hawkwood said. "He's joining the Russian army."

There was a long pause as the words sank in.

"You cannot be serious?" Lafon said eventually.

"Alexander has asked Prince Bernadotte to make overtures to the general on his behalf. The Tsar's in need of a commander who knows how Emperor Bonaparte fights. General Moreau was the obvious choice."

"You're telling us General Moreau is in England, bound for *Russia*?" Malet said, his shock still evident. "He intends to take up arms *against France*?"

"Against *Bonaparte*," Hawkwood corrected, pausing before adding, "Unless he receives a better offer." He left the statement hanging.

Malet and Lafon exchanged looks. Malet turned to Hawkwood. "You told my wife you had a message for me?"

"Yes, sir. Although the general's most interested in Tsar Alexander's proposal, he feels there might be a less . . . adversarial . . . way of achieving a change of régime. He's very much aware of the people's growing desire for peace, and he believes the time has come to seek an accommodation with our enemies. He wanted to remind you that he was willing to act as mediator before. Should an opportunity become available, he's ready to do so again."

"I see. And why does the general think that would be of interest to *me*?"

"Because if anyone *was* in a position to seize the initiative, General, it would be you. You were General Servan's appointed successor, after all."

Malet's head came up.

A little flattery never hurt, Hawkwood thought. He saw that Lafon was regarding him closely. The soft click of the rosary beads continued unabated.

Malet resumed stirring his tea. He smiled wryly. "As you may have noticed, monsieur, while my imagination is free to take flight, I regret the rest of me does not enjoy the same luxury. Did you think I could just come and go as I please?"

231

"With respect, General," Hawkwood said, returning the smile. "There don't appear to be any bars on the windows. No one's patrolling the grounds except a gardener with sack and a broom. It's not the Bastille. I'd wager a determined man could probably find a way to slip out of here without too much trouble."

"You think so? Tell me, Monsieur Dumas, would you be looking at the defences here from a military perspective, by any chance? Correct me if I'm wrong, but you *have* worn a uniform in the past, have you not?

"It was a while ago, sir."

"For you and me both. May I enquire which regiment?"

Careful, a voice inside Hawkwood's head warned.

"The 34th."

It was the same regiment he'd used for his biography when he'd posed as an American volunteer during his internment on *Rapacious*. The regiment had only been in existence a little over a year. Malet, according to Grant, had never served in the Peninsula and he'd been locked away for the past four years, so while he might have been kept appraised of General Moreau's circumstances, it was unlikely he'd be familiar with regimental deployment.

"What rank?"

"Captain."

"You fought in Spain?"

"Yes, General."

Malet nodded, subdued. "Not our finest hour."

"No, sir."

Malet put his head on one side. "You believe we're losing?"

"That's not for me to say, General."

A flash of irritation flitted across the pale face. "Of course it is. You fought there. That entitles you to an opinion. What's your opinion?"

"We're losing," Hawkwood said.

Malet's jaw flexed. "And Russia?"

"Winter's not far off. From what I've heard, no one in his right mind would think of waging war in the Russian snows."

Malet's lips continued to form a thin line. He nodded.

"I remember the Rhineland. That was hellish enough." Regarding Hawkwood thoughtfully, he said, "And does General Moreau share your sentiments?"

"I wouldn't be so presumptuous as to speak for him, but I *believe* he does, sir, yes."

Malet's eyes moved around the room. He looked at his wife and then at Lafon. An unspoken message passed between the three of them before the general turned back. He eyed Hawkwood shrewdly.

He's still wary, Hawkwood thought. *For all he knows, I could be a government lackey.*

But then, after what seemed an age, the light of decision flared in General Malet's eyes. He smiled.

"I think the game's gone on long enough, Captain Dumas. Don't you?"

Hawkwood nodded. "Yes, sir, I'd say so."

General Malet rose to his feet. "In that case, why don't we adjourn to the garden? I don't know about you, but I'm finding it rather stuffy in here." In a lowered voice, he added, "Besides, I've always preferred to discuss intrigue in the open air. It's so much more civilized than all that whispering behind closed doors. Wouldn't you agree?"

Hawkwood stood. "I would indeed, General."

Unless you're up to your neck in a Chinese bathtub, he thought.

"So, Captain, does General Moreau have any suggestions on *how* this . . . change of régime . . . might be achieved?"

General Malet, hands thrust into his pockets, kicked a twig from his path with the toe of his boot.

"He's rather of the opinion you'd have a notion or two of your own, General."

"Really?" Malet pursed his lips. "But you're not telling me he hasn't shared a few close thoughts with you, eh? Come now, Captain, you're among friends. You can speak freely. After all, what did you *think* we'd be talking about?"

Hawkwood looked a few paces ahead, to where the abbé was

exchanging quiet words with Malet's wife. They looked at ease in each other's company. It made Hawkwood wonder idly if Lafon had ever taken confession from either of them. He dragged his thoughts back to the task in hand.

"It's General Moreau's belief that with the army weakened by having to fight on two fronts and with attention focused on Alexander, there could well be an opportunity to take advantage of the Emperor's absence from Paris."

"And did he say in what way?"

"The general was reminded of the previous occasion when His Majesty accompanied his troops abroad."

"You're referring to Spain?"

"Yes, sir."

"While the cat's away, you mean?"

"I seem to recall General Moreau using that very phrase, General."

Malet smiled. "It does carry a certain inference, doesn't it? And did he mention any particular mice by name?"

"The general's maintained a regular correspondence with a number of senior officers, sir. Generals Masséna, Donzelot, Liebert . . . and General MacDonald, too."

"MacDonald?" Malet's eyebrows lifted. "I thought he was in Russia."

"He is, sir. General Moreau did express concern over what might happen if they were to find themselves on opposing sides."

"I can see how that would trouble him."

"The general hopes it won't come to that, of course."

"As do we all, Captain. So, I'll ask again; did General Moreau have a particular course of action in mind?"

Hawkwood hesitated. "He told me to tell you that what is whispered into the ear of a man is often heard one hundred miles away.'"

Malet stopped walking. "General Moreau said that?"

No, it was actually said to me by a Scotsman, Hawkwood thought. *In the pay of a half-Irish viscount, but you wouldn't want me telling you that.*

"Yes, sir. He also told me you'd know what it meant."

Grant's voice echoed in Hawkwood's ear.

We don't want to make it too easy for him, bonny lad. He needs to think it's been his idea all along, which it has, of course. All we have to do is chivvy him along a little.

They proceeded in silence, with Malet deep in thought. To a casual observer they were just two men enjoying a stroll in the fresh air, or as fresh as it could be, given the smells that enveloped the city. Hawkwood saw that the gardener was having a hard time trying to keep the lawn clear of leaves. There were just as many blowing in from the street as there were falling from the trees within the clinic's grounds. It looked to be a thankless task, like trying to stem the tide.

Hawkwood noticed a couple of oak trees that were growing close to the clinic's boundary. There were enough convenient branches handy to help a moderately fit man scale the wall without any problem. The obstacle would probably be the drop to the ground on the other side. It still looked a lot easier than trying to escape from a prison hulk, though, that was for sure.

Lafon and Madame Malet had stopped and were waiting for Hawkwood and the general to catch them up. Sensing that his wife was looking at him in a quizzical manner, the general came out of his reverie.

Madame Malet held up the basket.

"I thought we might enjoy a picnic if there's no one in the summer house. I persuaded one of the attendants to let us have some glasses. What do you think, Claude-François?"

Malet nodded, though he looked preoccupied. "An excellent suggestion, my dear. It would be a shame for us not to try and enjoy the last of the clement weather. In the meantime, perhaps you'd like to keep Captain Dumas company and lead the way? There's something I need to discuss with Jean-Baptiste."

"Of course."

The general's wife smiled and Lafon and Hawkwood changed places. It occurred to Hawkwood that since their first meeting the abbé's hand had stilled only once – when Hawkwood had told him that Moreau was in England. The rest of the time it had remained in constant motion, clicking the rosary beads back and forth between fingers and thumb. It made Hawkwood wonder how many prayers a devout cleric could get through in a day, or whether the manipulation had become an unconscious way to steady the nerves. When the abbé was in his bed with the rosary beside him on a night stand, did his hand still twitch like a wounded spider while he slept?

The summer house sat at the far end of the garden. It wasn't much; a four-sided, rough wooden structure with one open side facing the lawn and the house. A table and chairs, equally rustic, were contained within it.

As they walked towards it, Hawkwood said, "The general and the abbé seem to have forged quite a friendship."

Denise Malet took a look over her shoulder to where her husband and Lafon were in conversation. Her gaze softened. "Yes, and I thank God for it. It's not good for a man to be without a confidante in a place like this."

"A place like *this*?" Hawkwood smiled. "It's hardly the Conciergerie."

"You think that makes it any more palatable?" There was an unexpected edge to her voice.

"I didn't notice anyone in shackles," Hawkwood said.

He knew he'd struck another nerve when he saw the spark of anger in her eyes. In a controlled tone, she said, "You say that, and I know you see the library and the gardens and people walking around at their leisure, but this is still a prison when all's said and done."

She took a breath before turning to face him. "There are two reasons why men are confined in this place instead of the Conciergerie or L'Abbaye or any of the other foul dens in this city. The first and foremost is because they can afford the fees. There are no low-bred criminals inside these walls, Captain. All residents are of noble birth. Either that or they once enjoyed positions of privilege, like Maître Perraux. Half the men snoring in the library are barons. Most of the others are marquises and dukes. There are very few exceptions."

"And the second reason?"

"It's something else they all have in common. They hate

236

Bonaparte. Every resident of the Dubuisson clinic has been judged an enemy of the State."

"I can see why the authorities would want to keep them in one place," Hawkwood said.

"And Doctor Dubuisson also benefits, don't forget. He has high-placed friends, too; within the ministries and the police. As long as he keeps the residents in line and reports any aberrant behaviour, he's left alone, so it's in his best interest to provide comfort and care."

"Keep the residents happy so they won't want to escape, and the good doctor makes a very nice living. He looked well on it. No wonder he was smiling."

"That's right. Beyond these walls, their titles don't count for a great deal in any case. In here they can rest on memories and past glories."

"They're all loyalists?"

"I believe my husband's the only one who supports the idea of a Republic. Because of that it hasn't been easy for him to fit in. When he arrived it was as if he had to prove his credentials to the rest of the residents. What his family background was, what his political views were, why he'd been admitted. Even now, I'm still not sure they've accepted him."

Grant was right, Hawkwood thought. *It is a gentlemen's club, or as good as . . .*

"With Abbé Lafon, there was none of that. Neither asked questions of the other. There was no need. It was as if they'd each found a kindred spirit."

They arrived at the summer house. Subdued, Denise Malet, began to remove items from the basket.

"I'm sorry," Hawkwood said. "I meant no offence. It can't have been easy. All this . . ."

She did not look at him but spoke over her shoulder, her voice still brittle. "No, Captain, it hasn't been easy. It's been hard; very hard. I've lost count of the letters I've written, begging that my husband be granted a pardon. Petition after petition, first to Fouché then to Savary and even Bonaparte himself. There have been days over these past four years when I thought I'd never be able to wash the ink from my hands. In the end, the only leniency my husband received was his eventual transfer from Sainte-Pélagie."

"He was in the same prison as Maître Perraux?"

She turned then and faced him. "For a year, but not at the same time. Before that he was in La Force. As was the abbé, incidentally, though not until after my husband had left. It's something else they share. We think Savary only agreed to the final transfer because his predecessor destroyed most of his files and so full details of my husband's so-called crimes were lost. Savary couldn't afford to have a state prisoner released, but he did relent to sending him here." She gave a bitter laugh. "He probably got tired of all my letters and did it to keep me quiet. I suppose we should be thankful for small mercies."

She fell silent. Hawkwood looked up and saw that the general and the abbé had arrived.

In a calmer voice, Denise Malet addressed Lafon. "Some wine, Father?"

"You spoil me, dear lady." Lafon smiled.

"General," Hawkwood said, handing Malet his drink.

The general took the glass and stole a look inside the basket. "You've brought, oranges! Splendid!"

"So," Lafon said. "To what shall we drink? Claude-François?"

Malet smiled. "It's been said that the supreme art of war is to subdue the enemy *without* fighting." The general raised his glass, eyeing Hawkwood over the rim. "The art of war."

They drank. When they'd lowered their glasses, Hawkwood said, "Would that be Sun Tzu by any chance, General?"

Malet looked surprised and then pleased. "How did you know?"

"A wild guess," Hawkwood said.

General Malet, with Hawkwood at his shoulder, stood in the doorway of the summer house and gazed across the leaf-strewn grass towards the rear of the clinic. Hawkwood realized they were facing the library windows. On the other side of the glass a motionless form was slumped in a wheelchair.

Without turning, Malet said, "I have to tell you I found General Moreau's offer most interesting, Captain."

Hawkwood said nothing.

"Knowing that Jean-Victor's remained steadfast, even in exile, and to discover that many of my old comrades feel the same way, is most heartening."

Malet turned. "I'm assuming you're familiar with the events of four years ago?"

"Yes, General."

Malet nodded. "Then you'll know we were on the threshold of something momentous. To see the possibility of change snatched away at the last moment was almost unbearable. If anything good has come out of the intervening years it's the sure and certain knowledge that the resolve of patriotic men has not weakened. Some of us may have had our freedom curtailed, but one cannot say the same for our dreams.

"I don't know if you've any understanding of how serious the situation has become, but you should know that our country is poised above an abyss. There's still time to prevent her from sliding over the edge, however. General Moreau's right when he speaks of a great opportunity, but we must act swiftly if we're to take advantage of it. Knowing there are brave men willing to make a stand against tyranny gives me hope that we *will* succeed in bringing order out of chaos."

"Yes, sir, General."

Malet took a deep breath. "And what about the British?"

"The British?" Hawkwood said.

"If Jean-Victor's in London, that implies the British are prepared to offer him their support. I assume he's been in negotiations with them regarding a potential cessation of hostilities?"

"Meetings have been held on a number of matters, sir, yes," Hawkwood said carefully.

"And would these . . . meetings . . . have included discussions of a financial nature, do you know?"

Hawkwood's heart skipped a beat. This was a consideration

that, surprisingly, Grant had overlooked. When Hawkwood had pointed out that if Malet believed the British were prepared to offer a hefty financial inducement to those willing to topple Bonaparte from his throne – as they had before – it could help tip the balance in their favour, the Scot had agreed swiftly that it was a seed worth planting.

"I believe an understanding has indeed been reached, General. I regret I don't know the full details but General Moreau did say the British government was aware that the Empire's coffers were in a perilous state and that it was prepared to be generous in its contribution to the cause."

"I see. Well, that is most gratifying." Malet fell silent. After several long seconds he turned. "I take it you have the means to correspond with General Moreau?"

"I do, sir, yes." Hawkwood's heart began to pound.

"Then you may inform him that I accept his offer and that he's to await word. Tell him also that the wait will not be long. We know Bernadotte is sympathetic to our cause, from past dealings with him, so to allay suspicions that anything is afoot it would do Jean-Victor no harm to proceed to the Baltic. It might be advisable for him to delay his onward journey to meet with Tsar Alexander, however. Stockholm's a lot closer than Morrisville, fortunately. It won't take long for a message to reach him."

Malet smiled. "You know, one of my main concerns was always how we might persuade General Moreau to return. It would appear that fate is dictating events. It's Jean-Victor who's extended his hand first. A portent, perhaps?"

"There are stranger things, General," Hawkwood said.

"Indeed there are, my friend." Malet looked at him.

There was a light deep in the general's eyes. "Tell me, Captain, will you stand with us?"

"Sir?"

"We could do with an officer of your experience." Malet smiled. "The reward for success will be substantial."

"And for failure?" The words were out before he could stop them.

"Oh, we will not fail, Captain." Malet clenched his fist. "We *must* not fail. Not this time. There's too much at stake."

"Then I'm at your service, sir," Hawkwood said. "General Moreau told me I was to offer any assistance you thought fit."

God help me.

Malet gripped Hawkwood's shoulder. "Good man." For a moment Hawkwood thought he saw a glint of moisture at the corner of Malet's eye, but then the general blinked and whatever had been there was gone.

Malet turned to Lafon, who was seated. "Did you hear that, my friend? We have ourselves a new recruit. Captain Dumas has agreed to join us."

"Has he indeed?" Lafon uncoiled from his seat. "In that case, you are most welcome, Captain." The abbé looked towards Malet. "So, my General; what's our next move?"

Malet placed his glass on the table.

"Our task's become easier now we know that Jean Victor has offered us his support. The promise of a hero who's ready to make a triumphant return adds legitimacy to our cause and with MacDonald and the others guarding our flanks we're almost ready."

Instantly, Hawkwood knew that he was missing something and that some kind of threshold had just been crossed, but leading to what? He wasn't sure he was going to like the answer, but he knew he had to ask the question.

"Forgive me, General. You said: 'Almost ready' – what does that mean?"

"It means the moment of truth is upon us."

"I gathered that, General. But . . .?"

Malet smiled. He suddenly looked a younger man. "What? Did you think we'd been whiling away our days partaking of afternoon tea and oranges? Sorry to disappoint you, Captain, but the abbé and I have been engaged in much more industrious pursuits. We've been drawing up our battle plans for some time."

"Battle plans?" Hawkwood repeated hollowly. "What battle plans?"

"Why, to capture Paris, Captain. What else?"

PART III

14

"Well, by God," Grant said. "It seems we severely under-estimated the man. He didn't need prompting at all. He was already champing at the damned bit."

Hawkwood took a sip of coffee and placed his cup back in its saucer. "It looks that way. Mind you, fooling him into thinking that Moreau was close to hand and ready to come to his aid didn't do any harm. In fact, I'd say it was definitely an added spur. My guess is he was looking for some kind of validation for his and Lafon's private campaign. And we provided it. Letting him think that London's prepared to supply funding, though; that was the deciding factor; no question. He was already primed. He was just waiting for someone to light the damned touch paper."

Grant nodded. "That's probably why he was so trusting. You'd have thought he'd have been a mite more cautious."

"What can I say? I've obviously got that sort of face."

Grant smiled. "And Madame will have put in a word for you as well, don't forget. Never underestimate a woman's powers of persuasion, especially when she's strong minded *and* good looking. You are her knight in shining armour, after all, *and* you passed those little tests he threw at you."

"Thank God for McPherson," Hawkwood said.

Grant raised his cup in salute. "I'll drink to that."

Hawkwood looked around. They were in La Colombe Rouge, a café behind the rue du Rivoli. The place was busy. There weren't too many empty tables. There were enough fellow diners making sufficient noise to mask their own conversation.

"He said whoever controls Paris controls the Empire."

Grant nodded. "Well, he's not wrong. So did he say *how* he was going to gain control?"

Hawkwood shook his head. "Not specifically."

Grant's right eyebrow lifted in query. "And no indication as to when this might happen?"

"Sooner rather than later."

"What the devil does that mean?"

"He said the reason he couldn't delay any longer was that he's not sure when he's going to be struck off the army roll. He knows the day can't be too far away. When that happens, he'll lose his pay and he and Madame become penniless. They'll evict him from the clinic and send him back to a regular prison. It'll be impossible for him to do anything then."

A waiter passed them, heading for the kitchen. Grant leant forward. "He said that? He said *any* longer?"

Hawkwood frowned. "I'm not with you."

"'*Any* longer' implies imminent; a readiness to proceed. If he'd said '*much* longer' that would suggest they might still be thinking about it."

Hawkwood wondered if Grant wasn't splitting very minute hairs. Either that or clutching at a very tenuous straw.

"He said '*any*'."

Grant sat back and scratched the side of his jaw. "I'd like to see those battle plans of his. No hint of what *they* might involve, I suppose?" he enquired hopefully.

"No. But then you can hardly blame him for keeping them close to his chest after what happened the last time. You said it yourself: there were too many cooks."

"Well, that and General Servan's bloody last will and testament."

"It's no different to what we're used to. It's how armies work. The senior staff keep the rank and file in the dark until it's time to fix bayonets. Then they let them loose and pray they do the job. The clinic's become Malet's brigade headquarters."

"T'ain't much of a brigade," Grant countered. "There're only two of them."

"Three," Hawkwood corrected.

"Three?" Grant frowned. "Who's the other one?"

"Madame."

"Ah." Grant smiled. "Of course." He looked Hawkwood in the eye. "You seem quite taken with her."

Hawkwood shrugged. "If it wasn't for *her* efforts, Malet would still be rotting in La Force and we wouldn't be having this conversation. You can't fault her dedication. From what I've seen of her, she'd put most adjutants I've met to shame. She's Malet's eyes and ears on the outside. She keeps in regular contact with friends from their army service. They provide her with information which she then passes on to the general. The rest, he and Lafon have gleaned from visitors at the nursing home. A snatch here, a smidgen there; it all adds up. They're fortunate in that the rules are pretty lax. There don't seem to be many restrictions."

"What's your opinion of Lafon?"

"He looks more like a lawyer than a priest. He didn't reveal a whole lot; he was content to let Malet do most of the talking. But they're close. There's no doubt that Malet values his opinion. There was one point where they went into a huddle. It was pretty clear Malet wanted to know what Lafon thought of my credentials. Fortunately, they were in agreement."

"Father confessor, you think?"

"That's not a bad description. Madame's certainly taken a shine to him. Though, from my conversations with her, I'd say she's more spiritually inclined than her husband. She's taken me to task a couple of times. You know my feelings on padres and prayer meetings."

The Scot grinned again. "Don't I just? I always said you had the whiff of brimstone about you. Anything else about the abbé that struck you?"

"He's intelligent and shrewd. I'd say he and Malet complement each other, but that Lafon's more of a manipulator, the man behind the scenes. He's the one with the political savvy. The general's the straight talker, the practical one."

"Sounds like Malet's own éminence grise," Grant mused. "Any thoughts that Lafon might be manipulating him?"

"It's possible, but my guess is Madame would have had some sense of that if it were so and warned her husband off, unless she's fallen under the spell, too. From what she's told me and from what I've seen, as far as she's concerned, Lafon's been a Godsend . . . no pun intended."

"So, when's your next visit?"

Hawkwood took another sip of coffee. The beverage was growing cold. He looked around for a waiter to order another.

"There isn't going to be one."

"Eh?"

"The general doesn't want me calling there again. He says it's too risky, which makes sense. He thinks I'm the main link to Moreau. He won't want to jeopardize that. To anyone looking on, I was visiting the old man and I just happened to get into conversation with Lafon and he introduced me to Malet out of politeness. A pleasant afternoon was had by all, after which I said my goodbyes – to Perraux as well, in case anyone was paying attention – signed out and left. Besides, it's not as though I could continue being the dutiful student. That well's run dry. And let's face it; the poor devil wouldn't miss me. As far as the nursing staff's concerned, I did the decent thing; I paid my respects, saw the maître's mind was too far gone to hold a respectable discourse, and buggered off back from whence I came."

A waiter arrived and apologized for the delay. He took Hawkwood and Grant's order for a refill and departed briskly.

"I suppose so," Grant agreed. "But it'd help our side if we knew what the general and Lafon were planning. How will you liaise with them now?"

"Through Madame."

Grant looked sceptical.

"It's Malet's idea. She's his strong right hand, more so than Lafon. She has his complete trust, and anyway it was you who told me the best way to the general was through his wife."

"Maybe you can use your masculine charms to ask *her* how far along they are with those plans."

"I'll do my best. I can tell you they're far enough advanced for them to have undertaken their first reconnoitre."

There was a pause. The clatter of a falling tray came from the direction of the kitchen.

"Their first *what*?" Grant stared at him. "Are you saying they've been *outside* the walls?"

"That's exactly what I'm telling you."

Grant lowered his voice. "When was this?"

"Five nights ago. Two days before *I* got here."

"Good God! They just *walked* out?"

"No. It wasn't *that* easy. They climbed out."

Grant's eyes opened wider.

"There are a couple of trees which they used to give them a leg up over the wall. Our general and padre are obviously a lot more limber than we took them for."

"I'll be God damned," Grant said. "So, this little reconnaissance sortie – did he give details?"

"Only that it involved scouting the enemy's strength and position."

"Hardly illuminating," Grant said drily. "Be good to find out the rest," he added, and then frowned. "I wonder how they got back in."

"They didn't say. Maybe they took a bottle back with them and bribed the gatekeeper."

"Maybe," Grant said thoughtfully.

Both men fell silent as the waiter returned. When he'd left, Hawkwood said, "You do know there's a limit to how long we can do this, don't you?"

"This?" Grant stirred his cup.

"Hold Malet's hand."

Grant nodded. "We go for as long as we can. We need to keep a close check on our investment. Any intelligence we come up with on Malet's tactics and his intentions has to be of benefit to London, especially if this provisional government they're planning on setting up wants to negotiate a peace. At the moment we – you – are the go-between. Anything you learn is going to be useful. When's your next rendezvous with Madame?"

"When I know, you'll know," Hawkwood said.

"I'm assuming that'll be sooner rather than later," Grant responded drily. He raised his cup and then his hand stilled and he sucked in his breath and a wary look came into his eyes.

Hawkwood made no attempt to turn. There wasn't any need. The café's mirrored walls provided him with a perfect view of what was happening behind his back. He looked past Grant's shoulder and watched in the reflection as a pair of cross-belted, blue-jacketed men entered the salon and took up positions, one on either side of the door, muskets in hand.

As the conversation died, Hawkwood kept his eyes on the mirror. Two more uniformed men entered. Between them appeared a narrow-shouldered, sallow-faced civilian in a black overcoat that looked at least one size too large for his frame.

The civilian paused on the threshold and looked about him. Smiles slid from faces, laughter became muted and a subdued atmosphere descended like a cloud upon the room. Diners dropped their gaze and began to pay more attention to the contents of their cups than to their table companions. It was as though eye contact had become contagious.

A nerve twitched in Grant's cheek. "Police," he said quietly, almost without moving his lips. "Are you armed?"

"Not enough to make a difference."

"Gently does it then," Grant murmured.

"Know him?"

Grant gave an imperceptible shake of his head. "No, but I know the type. You do, too."

Hawkwood's attention was held by the glass. The civilian, flanked by the second pair of gendarmes, had stopped alongside one of the tables close to the door. He thrust out his hand. As the first diner passed over his papers, Hawkwood looked towards the rear of the café, searching for an alternative exit. The door behind the counter that led into the kitchens was the closest escape route. He turned his attention back to the mirror.

The civilian was clearly aware of the effect his presence was having. From the way he'd beckoned for the papers to the arrogant manner in which they were studied and returned,

250

he knew he was the one with the authority and he was making sure everyone else knew it, too, as if they didn't already.

Documents examined, he moved on to the next table and the procedure was repeated.

The customers weren't the only ones made uneasy by the visitation. The attitude of the staff had also undergone a marked change. Service was continuing, but idle chatter had ceased and the interaction between waiters and clientele, though still efficient, had become noticeably distant, while the rattle of crockery had taken on a new, more abrasive resonance as orders were delivered and empty cups and platters removed without acknowledgement.

Within a matter of seconds, the mood had changed from convivial to apprehensive and in some cases, to judge from facial expressions, almost fearful. But no one seemed inclined to draw attention to themselves by getting up and leaving, or attempting to.

The over-coated man moved to another table and Hawkwood saw Grant tense. The Scot had noticed what he'd seen for himself. Male customers were the only ones being questioned. The women were being ignored.

It meant they were looking for someone.

The over-coated man moved from table to table, working his way around the room, his predatory expression as uncompromising as it had been upon his entrance. Several diners, not yet questioned, were reaching towards their pockets in nervous anticipation.

Hawkwood thought about his own papers. They had passed muster at the customs post but would they hold up under the scrutiny of a police official, who, by the looks of him and from the way he was studying each document, was already suspicious and on the hunt for discrepancies?

Hawkwood watched as the relief spread across the reflected faces of those individuals whose papers had been examined and judged to have been in order. His gaze moved back to the visitor, who was now only two tables away and drawing ever closer.

He took a sip of coffee. The beverage was stone cold; the same temperature that was spreading rapidly through his insides. He looked towards Grant. The Scot's face was unmoving, but his eyes were monitoring the room.

And then it was their turn.

Hawkwood dropped his eyes from the mirror, in time to feel the presence at his back.

"Papers," a voice said.

Hawkwood looked round.

Thin face, thin nose, thin lips, small eyes; Grant had been correct. He did know the type: an insignificant, officious toad-eater, who, in another life, if he hadn't been a policeman would probably have made a career as a tax collector or an inquisitor for Mother Church; a breed whose arrogance was matched only by his lack of manners, humour and a formal education, but who, by virtue of his office, had the ability to instil fear into the hearts of men and women through no more than an enquiring glance or by the simple crooking of his forefinger.

Hawkwood reached towards his pocket.

The thunderous crash that rocked the room as the adjacent table hit the floor sending cups and cutlery in all directions startled everyone, as did the sight of the table's two occupants, who were trying to extricate themselves from their upturned chairs.

Swiftly, the man in the overcoat turned.

"Seize them."

Waiters scattered and diners stared as the duo scrambled through the debris. Crockery was smashed underfoot as the gendarmes moved to cut them off.

It was over in seconds. The men went down, pinned under the knees of the gendarme escort. They continued to struggle violently. A flurry of blows to the backs of their skulls and kidneys brought them to heel. A woman yelped as a cut opened up on one of the men's brows and blood splattered. Under the thin man's direction, they were then dragged to their feet.

The civilian stared at them hard and then turned on his heel.

"Bring them."

With no word of explanation or apology for the chaos that

had ensued, the police official and his escort left the café the same way they had entered, dragging their captives with them.

As they passed Hawkwood and Grant's table, Hawkwood caught sight of one of the captured men's faces. The man's expression was exactly the same as Seaman Fitch's in the final seconds before his body was snatched away by the wave and dragged over *Griffin*'s starboard rail. It was the look of a man who knew that his time had just run out.

For a brief moment, there was silence. Then, gradually, conversation resumed in hushed tones. A waiter materialized with a broom. The table and chairs were righted. The broken crockery was recovered and removed. As the mood lightened, the tension that had held the room in Limbo began to evaporate.

Hawkwood looked down at his hand. To his surprise there was no hint of a tremor. Taking that as a positive sign, he looked up and caught Grant's eye.

"Well, that was interesting."

Grant nodded. "Poor bastards."

Hawkwood looked around. Had he not been a witness to events, there was nothing to show that anything untoward had happened. It was proof, he thought that life was transient and nothing could be taken for granted. It had also been a stark warning to them both.

Turning, he pointed to his cup and the empty coffee pot.

"Another?"

Grant considered the offer and then took a deep breath and shook his head. Calling the waiter, he stood and pushed back his chair.

"I don't know about you, old friend, but I think I'd prefer something a little bit stronger."

"Well, in that case," Hawkwood said, rising to his feet. "You lead and I'll follow."

Anne-Jean Marie René Savary, Duke of Rovigo, brushed an imaginary speck of dirt from his shoulder and regarded himself in the mirror. His gaze was keen and critical.

Taking his time, he searched for imperfections: another

grain of dust, a fold in his collar, a crease in the shoulder of his well-fitting jacket. Running a hand over his smooth-shaven jowls, he noted with concern the slight fleshiness beneath his jawline and his brow furrowed. Was that a grey hair? He reached for the offending follicle with a slender finger and thumb. One quick pluck and it was gone. Feeling a sense of accomplishment, he stepped back, and with a final study of his reflection, he turned and strode towards the window.

The view of the river hadn't changed much over the two years he'd held the post of Minister of Police. His eyes were drawn to the bathing boats moored against the nearside quai, eyesores in dire need of renovation, though scuttling them would probably be just as efficient, Savary had often thought to himself, not to mention deeply satisfying. The unedifying spectacle of thread-bare towels flapping in the breeze only yards from his office had never appealed to a man who was as particular about the aspect from his window as he was about his own appearance.

Swallowing his distaste, he looked downriver, past the Musée on the opposite bank and on towards the Tuileries Bridge and the palace and the vast ornamental gardens that lay beyond it. Now, there *was* a view much more pleasing to the eye.

His thoughts were interrupted by a knock on the door.

Savary turned. "Enter." He did not raise his voice.

The door opened to admit a nervous-looking man clutching a sheaf of documents. Mortier, Savary's secretary. Shadows played across his face as he advanced into the room.

"The latest surveillance reports, Excellency." Mortier placed the sheaf of documents on the corner of the desk and backed away.

Savary nodded curtly.

"Will there be anything else, Excellency?"

"No, you may go."

Mortier departed. Savary stalked to the desk and sat down. He drew the pile of papers towards him.

Receiving surveillance reports was part of the Minister's daily routine. Savary looked upon them as an unending chore.

The reports came from a wide variety of sources. Their contents varied. A large number were nothing more than denunciations; neighbours and even family members telling tales to the authorities, generally as a result of some minor difference of opinion, the origin of which had long been forgotten but which had escalated into a ludicrous vendetta that would have done justice to the Borgias. What better way to dispose of a rival, whether it be in love or business or a sibling feud, than by making up some scurrilous lie about them and have the police cart the would-be offender away to some dark and fearful place, never to be heard of again?

Others were of a more serious nature: genuine crimes against the Empire; consorting with the enemy, the printing and distribution of counter-government literature, attempting to subvert the course of justice. The list of crimes was extensive and exponential.

Before any reports reached Mortier's desk the bulk of them had already been siphoned off and processed by a score of minions further down the pecking order. It was part of Mortier's duties to filter the remainder and to bring only the ones he considered to be of the utmost significance to the Minister's attention. It was then up to Savary to decide what action needed to be taken. Unfortunately, as Mortier had discovered on more than one occasion, there was no way of knowing what Minister Savary's definition of significant might be from one day to the next; hence the secretary's trepidation at having to deliver the most recent batch.

The method of sorting the wheat from the chaff was based largely on name recognition and the ability to cross reference against the lists of persons whose misdemeanours had seen them branded, metaphorically at least, as disruptive to the smooth running of the State.

Not all the individuals listed were at large. Many were already languishing in prison. But, tainted by their past, wherever practical, all were monitored in their movements and associations by a web of police spies and informers. No strand of society was immune; high or low, rich or poor; from his lair on the

Quai Voltaire, Savary's tentacles extended far and wide, though it had been his predecessor, Joseph Fouché – a man for whom the word devious had been invented – who'd created the first dossiers. Savary had merely refined the system.

He drew a candle towards him and began to read.

As usual, the reports varied, not only in content but also in legibility, with some of them bordering on the indecipherable. Sadly, not every informer employed by the various arms of the Ministry nor every drone who converted verbal reports into written text was possessed of a tidy hand. Thus the quality of transposition varied enormously.

Within twenty minutes, Savary's eyes were straining. There didn't appear to be anything noteworthy in any of today's dispatches and most if not all of them could have been dealt with at a lower level of authority. In fact, it was debatable whether any of them should have reached Mortier's desk, never mind his own. He would have to have words. Mortier needed to understand that no one, not even the Minister's secretary, was indispensable. Savary emitted a hiss of annoyance as he continued to read. The best that could be said of the current selection was there weren't that many of them left to wade through.

He was almost at the bottom of the pile. The light in the room was bad. The grey skies outside ensured there wasn't much illumination coming in through the window, and if he'd blinked he'd have missed it. But he hadn't blinked and a name caught his eye.

Malet.

Savary paused. He wasn't sure why. No specific warning bells had sounded but as he tilted the document towards the candle flame, it occurred to him that the name did have a vaguely familiar ring.

The report was part of a collation obtained from hotel files for the past week. Hotels were required to pass names of registered guests to the authorities as a matter of course. If any name came up as being on the list of known seditionists, the hotel staff were directed to monitor the guest's activities; this included details of visits paid to the guest's room.

The brief note – it was no more than that – had been submitted by the concierge of a hotel in the 10th Arrondissement – the Hotel Patrice – and concerned a female guest by the name of Malet. Madame Malet had returned to the hotel in the company of a priest, who had then accompanied Madame to her room. The visit had lasted less than an hour. Unhelpfully, the name of the priest was not mentioned. In the absence of a name an inadequate description noted that he appeared to have been above average height. Which wasn't a lot of use, Savary thought. Attached to the report was a notification aligning the report to a second document that lay beneath the first.

The second surveillance memorandum had been submitted by an informer at the Clinique Dubuisson on the rue du Faubourg-Saint-Antoine, two days later. The Ministry employed informers in all places of detention as a matter of course; often detainees themselves, who were either coerced into spying upon their fellow prisoners or who'd volunteered, thereby hoping to improve the conditions of their sentence. They even had their own prison nickname; *sheep*, because of their habit of pretending to graze while listening to the talk going on around them.

The Dubuisson sheep's contribution to Savary's store of information wasn't much more informative than that of the concierge at the hotel. It amounted to little more than an observation; a recent visitor to the clinic had spent time in the company of the State prisoner Claude-François Malet. The visitor's name was Dumas. He'd signed himself in as a visitor to another of the clinic's residents, Charles Gustave Perraux. There had been no indication that Malet and Dumas had met before. They were seen to have been introduced to each other by a third resident, Abbé Jean-Baptiste Lafon.

Savary pursed his lips. On the face of it both reports were pretty innocuous. It looked like nothing more than a coincidence that the name had turned up twice, but, presumably, someone had deemed that sufficient cause to pass the reports further along the chain of command; most likely in an attempt to cover their backs, Savary suspected. He was well aware of his own reputation.

He was about to drop the reports on the discard pile when he considered the name again. Over the years there had been so many reports, so many names; it was almost impossible to recall them all, so what was it about this one? He paused. And then he remembered.

Letters; endless letters, from a Madame Malet – it surely had to be the same woman – trying to secure her husband's release from prison and later, when her requests had been denied, petitioning to have him transferred to a less oppressive institution. It was coming back to him. The name hadn't meant anything when he'd first heard it two years before, he recalled; his predecessor having made a point of removing many of his files before Savary had taken office. And at the time Savary had had no intention of releasing anyone whose history he didn't know. The transfer from Sainte-Pélagie to the Dubuisson facility on compassionate grounds had been an acceptable compromise to both parties.

Savary regarded the surveillance material. The observation that Madame should be talking to a priest or that her husband had been seen conversing with a visitor at his nursing home was hardly earth shattering. It was moderately interesting that both the Malets were in the company of clergy, but that was about all.

He was about to reject the reports for good but then hesitated once more. He wasn't sure why. After a few seconds he reached for the bell.

"Excellency?" Mortier was in the office almost before the summons had faded.

Savary did not look up from his desk.

"Tell Desmarest I wish to see him."

"Yes, Excellency." Mortier hovered by the door.

"Was there a particular word in my request that's causing you difficulty?" Savary still did not look up.

Mortier reddened. "No, Excellency."

"Good. Then you'd best be on your way, hadn't you?"

"Yes, Excellency."

Twenty minutes later, the secretary returned.

"Chief of Security Desmarest, Excellency," Mortier announced, stepping aside.

The man that brushed past Mortier into the room was small, only a few inches above five feet tall, but what he lacked in height, he made up for in girth. Given his rotund frame, at first sighting the uninitiated could well have taken Pierre-Marie Desmarest for an innkeeper or a pastry chef who'd sampled too many of his own creations. What they wouldn't have taken him for was a policeman, until, perhaps, they looked into his eyes, at which point they would have realized their mistake very quickly.

Savary had inherited Desmarest from Joseph Fouché, who'd appointed the former priest and army provisioning officer to head the Bureau Secret, the security division of the State Police; his remit being the investigation of all plots and conspiracies. Savary had been told, shortly after his own appointment, that Desmarest's orders from Fouché had been succinct: "Watch everyone but me, and that includes the Emperor." There were those who said that he had taken to the job like a duck to water, as he'd had no personal regard for Bonaparte to begin with, but no one had ever had the nerve to ask Desmarest if that was true. Or if they had, none had lived to talk about it.

Desmarest waited until the secretary had left the room.

"Excellency?"

Savary indicated a chair. "You may sit. Tell me, does the name Malet mean anything to you?"

Desmarest's broad rump was halfway into the seat. As he lowered himself the rest of the way he frowned. "If you're referring to Claude-François Malet, then, yes, Excellency, I'm familiar with the name."

Savary reached for the surveillance reports.

"Remind me," he said.

When Desmarest had finished talking, Savary sat back. He passed the surveillance documents across the desk. "Should I be concerned?"

Desmarest chewed a fingernail as he read. He looked up and favoured Savary with a thin smile. "I doubt it's worth calling out the National Guard, Excellency."

Savary did not return the smile. "Did you ever meet him?"

"Malet?" A guarded look came over Desmarest's face, then he shook his head. "There was a time, a few years ago, when our paths might have crossed."

"How so?"

"It was shortly after the Emperor declared himself Consul. He was preparing for the Italian campaign and due to inspect the army at Dijon. Minister Fouché . . ." Desmarest hesitated at the mention of Savary's predecessor ". . . received word there was a nest of republicans – one of those damned Philadelphian societies – who'd set themselves up and were planning to disrupt the Consul's visit. There were rumours of a possible assassination attempt. I was sent to investigate."

"And?"

"I had a quiet word in a few ears."

Savary's eyebrows rose.

"It wasn't that difficult," Desmarest said. "I can be very persuasive."

Of that, Savary thought, *I have no doubt whatsoever.*

"What did Malet have to do with it?"

"He was garrisoned at Dijon. Several army officers were reputed to have joined the group, Malet being one of them. Called himself Leonidas." Desmarest shook his head at the absurdity of it. "I ask you. Grown men. You'd think they'd have found better things to do."

"Leonidas?" Savary's face lost some of its sternness. "The King of Sparta?"

Desmarest nodded. "That's the fellow; died making a final stand at Thermopylae. You know what these factions are like. They take on all sorts of ridiculous names. The Philadelphes liked to think of themselves as Greek heroes. There's a few still around, hoping for their day of glory. Anyway, as I said, the threat didn't come to anything. I nipped it in the bud."

"It sounds to me as if a nursing home's the best place for him," Savary mused.

Desmarest nodded. "The man's a complete fantasist. I can't say he hasn't had his moments, though," he added.

"The Servan thing?"

Desmarest nodded. "There was also the incident when he was in La Force. I didn't mention that."

Savary's head came up. His gaze hardened ominously. "No, you didn't. What happened?"

"He escaped."

"From La Force? And how did he manage that?"

"Nobody's entirely sure. He was only free for a couple of hours. There was a Te Deum at Notre Dame to celebrate the capture of Vienna. He managed to disrupt that for a while before he was rounded up."

"Disrupt how?"

"He hid in the crowd and when the troops filed out he closed the doors behind them and trapped the congregation inside. Then he started yelling, 'Down with the Corsicans! Long live liberty!' – that sort of thing. Gave himself up when he ran out of breath."

Savary frowned. "Why am I only hearing this now?"

Desmarest shrugged. "It was before you took office, Excellency. At the time it seemed wise not to draw attention to the incident. We didn't want to give people ideas. In any case there were no injuries save for a few citizens whose pride had been dented. It was pretty much over before it began."

"Nipped in the bud, you mean?"

"Indeed, Excellency," Desmarest responded evenly, refusing to be baited. He suspected Savary was being sarcastic rather than humorous. Sometimes, it was hard to tell. "It was also thought advisable not to let people know that La Force wasn't escape-proof."

Desmarest slid the surveillance reports back on to the desk. "Which was also why Malet was transferred to Sainte-Pélagie. The place wasn't – isn't – as strict, but it's a lot harder to get out of. From what I've heard, he's been as good as gold ever since. In fact, Excellency, it was you who sanctioned his move to the Dubuisson establishment, I believe?"

The question was couched innocently enough, but Savary suspected Desmarest had enjoyed a shiver of pleasure from asking it. Instead of answering, he retrieved the reports and studied the names once more. "And the wife? Anything there, do you think?"

Desmarest shook his head. "Married to a lunatic? I'd probably want to talk to a priest, too, if I was that unfortunate."

"What about this . . . Lafon?"

"The name doesn't mean anything personally. A minnow caught in the net, I expect. If you recall, we've rounded up several troublesome clergy over the past few years."

"To encourage the others?" Savary quoted archly.

"Indeed, Excellency."

"The strategy would appear to have worked."

Desmarest shrugged. "Between you and me, I don't think many people have the stomach to protest any more. They've other things to occupy their time." He almost added, *As has my department*, but he bit his tongue instead.

Savary sat back and looked thoughtful. Finally, he nodded. "Yes, well, you're probably right."

Desmarest let go a quiet sigh of relief, only to hear his hopes for an uneventful departure dashed in the next breath when he heard Savary add artfully, "Whatever *you* think is best."

You devious bastard, Desmarest thought, knowing full well he'd just received his come-uppance for the comment he'd made about Savary's decision to move Malet to the clinic. It might not have been a directive in so many words, but the meaning behind Savary's last utterance had been as clear as day. Determined not to lose face, even though he knew that was unavoidable, Desmarest contrived to make it appear as though he was still capable of independent reasoning.

When he felt he'd paused long enough, he feigned a reflective expression and said nonchalantly, "Well, it probably wouldn't hurt to keep our eyes open. In the unlikely event I hear anything, I can always let you know."

"Well, if you're sure . . ." Savary said, sounding unconcerned, as though the notion might not be that important, which immediately put the onus back on Desmarest's shoulders for hinting it might be.

"Better to be safe than sorry," Desmarest said, just as coolly. He pushed himself out of the chair and immediately felt his left knee pop. "If there's nothing else, Excellency . . .?"

"No, that's all. You mustn't let me keep you. I'm sure you've important duties to attend to, keeping us safe in our beds. You'll see yourself out?"

"Of course, Excellency," Demarest said dutifully, trusting that Savary wouldn't notice he was speaking through gritted teeth. "Perhaps if I may take the reports as reference?"

"You may."

As Savary returned to his paperwork, Desmarest made his way to the door, the surveillance reports under his arm. Leaving the office, his mind was filled with one all-consuming thought.

Come back, Fouché; all is forgiven.

The apartment lay in the Marais quarter, north of the river, hidden within a maze of streets that made the rue Serpente look like a freshly scrubbed cloister. Hawkwood had lost track of the blind alleyways he'd had to negotiate before he found the right one. The sign above him read rue Saint-Pierre.

The place stank like a bog. He moved slowly, boots squelching; through what, he wasn't sure. He looked up at the windows set high above him; some were shuttered, others were so encrusted with dirt they might just as well have been. A few betrayed the dim flicker of a candle flame but there were no accompanying human sounds. A narrow, low-ceilinged passage appeared to his left. He ducked into it. At the end of the passage a tottery stairway led up to a small flagstoned courtyard. A circular stone well occupied one corner. A doorway led into the rear of the tenement. Entering, Hawkwood found himself faced by another flight of stairs. He made his way up to the third floor and on to a narrow wooden landing with a doorway to his right. He approached it cautiously.

The man who answered his knock looked as if he hadn't seen daylight for at least a week. He was gaunt, almost to the point of emaciation. The candle he was clutching illuminated a pair of hooded eyes and a cadaverous face riven with pockmarks. His dark clothing and unkempt hair only served to accentuate his pale, unhealthy features. It was, Hawkwood thought as the door opened, like being confronted by the keeper of the dead.

"Captain Dumas?"

The greeting came from within.

Hawkwood entered the apartment. The door closed behind him and he took in the view. A shabby room with a low, slanted ceiling, linked to the bedchamber by a half-open doorway; furniture that looked as if it might be hard pushed to support itself never mind a person's weight; peeling walls and a smell that could have been over-cooked cabbage or fish that had lain too long on the slab. The Hotel Patrice was as luxurious as the Chinese Baths in comparison.

"Don't worry, Captain. The accommodation is purely temporary; a place to meet without the fear of a concierge or a gatekeeper looking over our shoulders."

"That's a relief, madame," Hawkwood said drily. "I was afraid you might have fallen on hard times."

She walked forward into the light. "It's good to see you, too, Captain."

She looked tired, he thought, despite the welcoming smile, but her grey eyes, caught by the candle glow, were still captivating.

She turned to indicate the man who'd let Hawkwood into the room.

"This is Father José Cajamaño."

"Father," Hawkwood said, thinking the name sounded Spanish rather than French.

Another damned padre, too. How many more were going to come out of the woodwork?

The priest placed the candle on the table. As if sensing Hawkwood's antipathy, he made do with a curt nod.

"Father José was in La Force with Abbé Lafon," Denise Malet said. "And the apartment is rented in his name, by the way, so no one will know the connection."

As she explained, the priest reached for a long coat hanging behind the door. His movements were ungainly; all arms and legs. Turning to Denise Malet he made a strange gesture with his hands and opened his mouth to speak.

What emerged wasn't like anything Hawkwood had heard before. The words were familiar, with the bulk of them Spanish rather than French, but they were all uttered as if the priest's tongue was stuck to the roof of his mouth, giving them a curious nasal resonance.

"There's no cause for concern, Father. Captain Dumas and I have business to discuss."

Denise Malet spoke in French. Watching her look the priest full in the eye as she gave her clearly enunciated reply, Hawkwood saw the reason for the man's way of speaking. Cajamaño was either partially, or totally, deaf.

The priest put on his coat, gave Hawkwood another unsmiling tilt of the head and let himself out of the room. His boots clumped unevenly on the landing before fading into the night.

"If you were wondering about his impairment . . ." Denise Malet said, ". . . he had an accident as a child and has difficulty communicating. His family is from Saint-Jacques-de-Compostelle. Four years ago he was on his way to Rome when he lost his money and papers. The authorities in Chambéry took him for a spy and, because he wasn't able to explain himself properly, they sent him to Paris where he was placed in prison. He was only released on Abbé Lafon's recommendation. The treasurer of Notre Dame, Abbé Sombardier, holds a weekly Mass at the clinic and Jean-Baptiste pleaded Father José's case to him. As a result Father José now works as a sub-deacon at Saint-Gervais church. Sadly, he still doesn't speak very good French; only a mixture of Spanish and slang that he picked up in prison; some Latin, too. But he gets by, and it's better than being among the thieves and swindlers of La Force."

Her face took on an expression of regret. "And I'm not a little ashamed to say that his loyalty to the abbé has suited our purpose very well." She fell silent, smoothed down her dress, and then in a formal tone said, "Forgive me, I've been most inconsiderate. May I offer you some wine?" She moved towards the table.

"Thank you, no . . ."

She paused, unsure. "As you wish . . ."

"But if that's coffee . . ." Hawkwood indicated the hearth, where a blackened enamel pot with a wooden handle and curved spout rested on a hinged metal grate.

Recovering, she smiled. "Of course; allow me. Please . . . sit."

"There's no need," Hawkwood said, taking off his coat and laying it across a chair, "I'll do it."

She made no protest and watched as he helped himself to a battered mug from the mantelpiece.

"Are you married, Captain?" she asked.

Hawkwood poured the coffee and regarded her over the mug's chipped rim. "No, madame."

"And yet you're a man who's very much at ease in the company of women. Am I right?"

An odd question, Hawkwood thought.

"That's true, madame, but then, why wouldn't I be? Besides, I'm not sure what one has to do with the other."

She smiled. "My apologies. That was rather forward of me; only it's been my experience that men who wear uniform and who reach a certain age without marrying are more often than not either incorrigible rakes or confirmed celibates. You strike me as being neither, which would make you a rarity, I think. I was intrigued. That's all."

Hawkwood returned the smile. "A certain age? I'm not sure how I should take that. And just how much experience are we talking about, madame? If you don't mind *me* being forward."

"I'm the wife of a general, Captain. I've known a great many soldiers."

Hawkwood arched an eyebrow. "Then it's just as well Father José didn't hear you say *that*, given his fears for your virtue."

She almost blushed but instead acknowledged the play on words with another curve of the lips. "Shame on you, Captain. You know very well what I meant." She regarded him with renewed interest. "You speak Spanish?"

"Some," Hawkwood said. "But then he is a priest and he *was* about to leave a married lady alone in a room with a man he'd never met. You wouldn't have to be fluent to understand his worries."

"Ah, but as I told you before, I've more important things to worry about than the loss of my reputation."

"Like other people's, for instance?" Hawkwood took a sip of coffee and waited for a response. The beverage was lukewarm and left a dull, metallic taste at the back of his tongue and he suspected the beans had been put through the brewing process more than once.

"I was seventeen when I married the general." Her fingers played with the curve of her wedding band. "Though he wasn't a general at the time, of course. My father supported the Bourbons and he didn't approve of a republican lieutenant paying me court, especially one who was twice my age and virtually penniless. He warned me never to see Claude-François again." Her face softened into another wry smile. "But we married anyway; and here we are, still penniless."

She teased out the creases in her dress once more. It had become a habit, Hawkwood realized; a means by which she could gain time to collate her thoughts.

"How is your coffee? I suspect it may have cooled somewhat."

"It's fine," Hawkwood lied.

Endeavouring to appear composed, she gave a nod of satisfaction. "Good. I don't believe there is anything quite as unappetizing as cold coffee."

"No," Hawkwood agreed. "I don't suppose there is."

She looked at him, one eyebrow raised. "Are you making fun of me, Captain?"

He felt the short hairs lift across the back of his neck. They were the same words Maddie Teague had used before he'd left London.

"Perhaps . . . just a little."

He could see she wasn't sure how to take that. Looking slightly disconcerted, she lifted a hand to her throat and dropped her gaze.

An awkward silence beckoned.

"You left a message for me," Hawkwood said.

By way of Fabien at Le Moineau, the café having become their means of correspondence.

She looked up and nodded, as if grateful for the continuance. "Yes." There was another brief pause which stretched into several seconds before she said, "There's a favour the general would ask of you."

Hawkwood lowered his cup. She regarded him speculatively. "The general assumes, given the nature of your mission and the fact that when *we* first met you were dressed as a priest, that you, in fact, travelled here on false papers, which would include the passport I examined. Would we be right in thinking there are people in the city who've been providing you with assistance?"

"Why do you ask?"

She hesitated before moving towards the table and indicating a document pouch that lay upon it. "As my husband told you, he and the abbé have been making . . . preparations."

"I remember."

"They include the crafting of certain papers."

"Papers?"

"Documents relevant to the enterprise; produced in secret with Abbé Lafon. It's become too much of a risk to keep them at the clinic. Doctor Dubuisson permits the residents a good deal of freedom but every so often he receives a visit from a Ministry representative to make sure all is in order, so one cannot be too careful. If the documents were to be discovered it would be disastrous for us all. After your meeting, my husband felt you were the best person to take responsibility for their safety."

She hesitated and then said, "All are handwritten. The general was thinking that they would appear much more legitimate if they were printed. The difficulty has been finding a printer we could trust. As one officer to another, he directed me to enquire if you might have access to someone capable of carrying out the work."

"You're asking me if I know a good counterfeiter?"

"Do you?"

It wouldn't be prudent, Hawkwood thought, to tell her that his passport was not a fake but the genuine article, at least according to Stormont Flint of the Alien Office. The only fraudulent components were the signatures attached to it, but if she was looking for a forger and if the future of Grant's plan hinged on his reply, then he was not about to disappoint her.

"Yes," Hawkwood said. "As it happens, I believe I do."

"And he's trustworthy?"

"*I* trust him," Hawkwood said.

She held his gaze for several seconds. "Then you'll help us?"

Hawkwood nodded. "Yes."

The tension left her face.

"Thank you," she said.

It occurred to him that negotiating the streets – whether it had been on foot or by cab – with the documents in her possession, must have been a nerve-wracking journey after her experience the other evening. Though she still looked a little apprehensive, he thought, which meant there was something else occupying her mind.

"There is one requirement," she said.

"What's that?"

"It would benefit the general greatly if the documents were ready by the end of the week. The twenty-second at the latest. That's five days from now."

"Am I permitted to ask why?"

She smiled. "I regret I'm not at liberty to say any more."

Hawkwood remembered their original conversation in her hotel room.

Touché, madame, he thought.

Her face turned serious once more. "Can you guarantee that?"

"I think so, yes," Hawkwood said. He put his cup down.

Wordlessly, she lifted the pouch from the table and held it towards him. "Then here."

"Why are you doing this?" Hawkwood felt the tremor in her hand as he took the papers from her.

"I'm sorry?" She stared at him.

"I meant, why do you stay? The nursing home's not a fortress.

The general and the abbé have proved that. The two of you could have fled the city, taken your son and left France; gone into exile. It wouldn't be impossible. The authorities would probably prefer it if you did escape. It'd be one less agitator for them to worry about. If Bernadotte can broker a commission for General Moreau in Alexander's army, he can surely do the same for your husband."

She regarded him levelly. "We remain because we love our country. Do you think we'd abandon her in her hour of need? Without men of honour willing to stand up for what they believe, what chance does she or the rest of us have? Bonaparte has brought her to the edge of ruin. We must protect her from him." She laid her hand on his arm. "Let me ask you a question in return. Why are *you* here, Captain?"

She was standing very close. Her touch was warm and the heat from the hearth seemed suddenly to expand and fill the room.

"I'm fighting for my country, too," Hawkwood said.

"Then you knew my answer before you asked the question."

She was right, Hawkwood thought.

She took her hand away. As she did so, her features softened. "It doesn't stop me thinking about what might befall us, though." She took a deep breath. "Sometimes I'm so afraid of what might happen I believe my heart may stop beating altogether."

Hawkwood said nothing, struck by the forlorn expression on her face.

"I try to visit my husband every day. We kiss when we meet and again when we part, but it is a chaste liaison in the presence of strangers. We are never alone, so we cannot embrace as a husband and wife should. There is no opportunity to hold each other as lovers do, to talk of our hopes or how we may overcome our doubts. My husband's a good man, Captain, but he's also a proud man. Too proud, sometimes. I know he dreads what might happen if we should fail, but we never speak of it. I fear it is the abbé to whom he confesses his inner fears; not to me."

She started to turn away.

270

"Perhaps he's trying to protect you from them," Hawkwood said.

"Them?"

"His doubts."

She paused to consider the possibility and nodded absently. "Perhaps." Turning, she gazed up at him, a question in her eyes. "Have you ever known fear, Captain Dumas?"

Hawkwood nodded. "Many times."

She looked slightly taken aback by his answer. "What are *you* afraid of?"

"Dying alone."

Immediately, Hawkwood wondered how it was that the response had come so easily to him. He couldn't recall making the admission to anyone else, not even Jago, or Maddie Teague.

A shadow moved across her face.

"Me, too," she whispered.

Hawkwood watched as a small tear emerged, unbidden, at the corner of her eye. Without thinking, he reached across and wiped it away with the edge of his thumb.

Wordlessly, eyes closed, she took hold of his wrist and pressed her cheek against his palm. It was the reverse of the gesture he'd seen exchanged between Stuart and the girl at the bridge.

He could feel her breath, soft against his skin.

"Sometimes . . ." she said ". . . a woman just wants to be held and be told everything is going to be all right, even if it isn't. Is that a foolish wish?"

"No," Hawkwood said. "It's the same with men, though I doubt they'd admit it."

She opened her eyes and looked up at him.

"On the battlefield, when a soldier falls and he knows he's beyond help, it comforts him if a comrade is there to hold his hand and tell him he isn't going to die, even if he is."

"And you've done that?"

"Yes," Hawkwood answered truthfully.

She regarded him for several long seconds. "Then will you hold *me*?" she said softly. "*Please*."

Hawkwood laid the papers on the table and she moved into

his arms and nestled her head against him. As she did so a small shudder ran through her. Hawkwood wasn't sure if the thudding he could feel was coming from her heart or his.

After several moments, when he felt her hands press against him, he released her. She did not pull away immediately, however. Leaning towards him, she placed her mouth against his. Her lips were soft and pliant. It was a deep kiss, full of promise, but one he knew would never be repeated. Stepping away, she looked up at him. She did not smile. Reaching behind her, she picked up the documents and gave them to him once more.

"Guard these well, Captain. The future of France lies in your hands."

Now that, Hawkwood thought, as he gathered up his coat, *wasn't something you heard every day.*

15

"Come!"

Hearing the summons, Inspector-General Lucien Paques took a deep breath. He always took a deep breath when he was about to report to a higher authority. He liked to think it helped steady his nerves.

It didn't matter that he was a tall man who, had he been of a more belligerent disposition, might well have used his height to intimidate those smaller than himself; when it came to meeting with Chief of Security Desmarest, above whom he towered by at least seven or eight inches, he still managed to feel as though he should be apologizing every few minutes for the size of his feet.

Entering the chamber, Paques, not for the first time, asked himself why it was that small men invariably seemed to commandeer the largest offices. One would have thought they'd choose a more modest space in which to conduct business, if for no other reason than it'd be a lot easier to find them, especially in Desmarest's case, given his lack of stature and the meagre amount of daylight filtering into the room. Desmarest was well known as a man who didn't believe in squandering candle wax if he could help it.

Paques looked towards the only source of illumination and was relieved to see his superior seated behind his desk by the window. A pale, plump hand beckoned impatiently. Paques approached with caution.

Desmarest was demolishing a chicken leg. It wasn't the most edifying sight. A half-empty carafe of red wine stood on the desk before him next to an almost full glass and a platter containing a thick slice of crusty bread and a pat of what might have been either melted butter or runny cheese. A napkin was tucked into his collar.

Pointing to the chair on the opposite side of the desk, Desmarest took a bite of chicken and sucked the juice from his fingers with relish. Grease dribbled down his chin. He dabbed at it ineffectually with a corner of the napkin and reached for the glass. "So," he said, as Paques sat down. "What do you have for me?"

Besides contempt? Paques thought, as he watched a blob of gravy drip on to Desmarest's well-upholstered paunch. Extracting a small notebook from an inside pocket, he took another deep breath. "I paid a visit to the nursing home, as you directed."

"And?"

Watching Desmarest pare the flesh from the bone with his incisors was like watching an overweight vulture devour its young. Paques looked away and picked a point three inches above Desmarest's head upon which to concentrate.

"And I spoke with the clinic's director with regards to the political detainee Claude-François Malet."

"And what did you discover?"

"According to Doctor Dubuisson, there have been no issues with the staff or any of the other residents. He receives a visit from his wife most days of the week. She likes to take him oranges and cheese and he likes to take *her* for walks around the garden. It's all very civilized."

"It sounds like it. Anything else? What about other visitors?"

"Nobody of any consequence. No one on our lists, at any rate. They'd have shown up in the reports. It confirms what Doctor Dubuisson told me from his own recollections," Paques added.

"What about this fellow . . . ." Desmarest put down his snack, wiped his hands on the napkin without removing it from his

274

shirt front, sifted through papers on his desk until he had found the page he was looking for: ". . . Dumas? Find anything out about him?"

Paques nodded. "According to the register, he was there visiting one of the other residents." Paques checked an entry in his notebook. "A Maître Perraux. He was a professor at the Sorbonne. Dumas was one of his old students."

"Patient or prisoner?" Desmarest asked. The report Savary had shown him hadn't been specific in that regard.

Paques blinked in confusion. "Who? Dumas?"

Desmarest just looked at him.

"Ah, you mean Perraux," Paques said, cursing silently. "Both, as it happens. He was another transferee from Sainte-Pélagie. Got sent there during the suppressions back in the nineties. He was moved to the nursing home on compassionate grounds on account of his health. He's failing fast, according to the doctor; mind's almost completely gone. So it looks like his days are numbered as well."

"As well?" Desmarest responded sharply. "What does that mean?"

"I took the liberty of making enquiries at the War Ministry. General Malet's army pay has a little over two months to run. After that he'll be required to vacate the home. Which means he'll be returned to a State prison to see out the rest of his days."

"His age again?"

Paques checked his notes. "Fifty-eight."

"That's a lot of days," Desmarest murmured, trying to prise a piece of chicken from between his teeth with his tongue.

"Yes, sir," Paques said. "Rather him than me."

He was rewarded with a disapproving look.

"Quite. So what about this Dumas having been seen in conversation with Malet during his visit?"

"I enquired about that, too. The impression gained by observers was that neither had met the other before. Dumas spent time visiting with the professor; even read the newspapers to him. He was introduced to the general by one of the other residents and the general invited him to take tea. He stayed a couple of hours and left. There was nothing to suggest anything untoward had been taking place. The consensus is that Dumas received his invite from the general only because he was a new face."

"This other resident – this was the cleric, yes? What do we know about him? What's his name . . . Lafon?"

"He's a Gascon originally. Been a resident since . . ." Paques glanced down at his notebook ". . . July. Before that, he was at La Force. He –"

"La Force?" Desmarest's eyes narrowed. "Malet was there, too."

"Yes, but not at the same time. I checked."

Desmarest sighed. "So, remind me what Lafon was in for."

"He wasn't happy about the Holy Father's removal to Fontainebleau. Insisted on venting his displeasure during Sunday Mass. He was also suspected of spreading rumours of His Majesty's excommunication. If you recall, that was never made public, officially."

In other words, Desmarest thought, the man *was* a trouble-maker, as he'd suggested to Savary. Despite being a former cleric, Desmarest felt no empathy. Lafon would have known only too well the consequences of spreading sedition and thus had no one to blame for his situation other than himself. Justice had prevailed. There was an end to it.

Desmarest tossed the remains of the chicken leg on to the platter. Removing the napkin, he wiped his hands, pushed the uneaten food to one side and reached for his glass of wine. He could report back to Savary with a clear conscience. Paques' enquiries hadn't turned up anything that wasn't known already. It had all been a series of random occurrences; nothing more sinister than that. It was almost worth a celebratory swallow.

He was suddenly struck by a random thought. He had no idea where it came from. He paused, the glass halfway to his lips.

"Just as a matter of interest, what did this Dumas look like?"

"From the description I got from Dubuisson, he was tall and well set, with a couple of interesting facial scars, whatever that means. Seemed personable enough, though he didn't say much when Malet's wife introduced them."

"Malet's wife?"

"It was Dumas' first visit to the clinic. Madame Malet was showing him the way to the library. They'd met at the entrance gate, apparently."

And Desmarest frowned. *Apparently.* He thought about that word. It carried so many connotations. He put down his glass.

"Sir?" Paques said, struck by the furrowed brow on the other side of the desk. "Was there something else?"

Desmarest did not reply. Silently, he reached for the surveillance reports, not quite sure what was prompting him to do so, save for the faint tickle at the back of his mind. His eyes searched for the report submitted by the concierge at the Hotel Patrice.

He picked it up, read it carefully.

The priest who'd visited Denise Malet in her room. He'd been above average height. That could be taken as a definition of tall, Desmarest thought. *Wonder if he had any interesting scars?*

But so what if he did?

"Sir?" Paques asked again.

Desmarest closed the report; considered what he'd just read. *I'm seeing shadows where there aren't any*, he thought. *They'll be sending me to a nursing home next.*

But the doubt lingered.

Apparently.

The moment Hawkwood re-entered the apartment he sensed something was wrong. Grant and McPherson were standing by the fire in the main room. Facing the door, their subdued expressions made it clear they had been awaiting his arrival with some trepidation.

He stared back at them. "What's happened?"

Grant and McPherson exchanged doleful glances. Grant turned to him. The Scot's face remained bleak.

Suddenly, Hawkwood knew.

"Stuart?"

McPherson nodded. "I received a message from L'Épine. It's not good."

"Define 'not good'," Hawkwood said.

"They didn't make it," Grant said.

Hawkwood absorbed the statement. "Dead?"

Grant nodded.

"All three?"

"Weight of numbers. They were overwhelmed."

A vision of Stuart's boyish face flashed through Hawkwood's mind. He tried to recall his history. Horatius was supposed to have survived *his* battle at the bridge. Stuart, buoyed by false optimism, had not. He thought about the girl and how she had looked and hoped her death had been quick.

Not that there had ever been much hope, Hawkwood knew. Not from the moment he'd let Alain lead him away from the fight, when he'd heard the sound of the musket shot ring out across the dunes, and the fusillade that had followed soon after.

"L'Épine's people told him that, according to witnesses, Stuart and the other two managed to put up quite a fight," Grant said heavily. "When it was over the soldiers collected the bodies on carts with their own casualties and took them back to the fort."

"For burial?"

McPherson shook his head. "It's more likely they'd have waited for high water and then dropped them over the wall into the sea and let the tide carry them out."

As the anger rose like a torch in Hawkwood's chest Grant's hand fell upon his shoulder. "Though it grieves me to say it, Matthew, there's a good side to this."

"Really? And just what the hell might that be?"

"The Frogs never knew Stuart was from an English ship. They still don't know about you."

As the words sank in, Hawkwood knew the Scot's surmise was, in all likelihood, correct, though the knowledge was of small consolation. As he had calculated once before, his continued freedom was being won at great cost, in the curtailed life spans of brave and determined men and, now, one indomitable young woman. Seaman Fitch's outburst, bellowed in a moment of rage on *Griffin*'s pitching, storm-lashed deck echoed in his mind.

By Christ, I hope you're worth the bloody trouble!

Hawkwood wondered how many times the words would come back to haunt him.

"Get that down you," Grant said gently. He held out a glass.

As he tipped the cognac down his throat, Hawkwood felt the chill fingers begin to retreat. He raised a silent toast to the young British commander. Stuart would never see an admiral's pennant fly from his masthead now, that was for certain.

He thought about *Griffin* and her crew, holding offshore for their captain who would never return. He wondered how long Lieutenant Weekes had waited before the realization had set in and he'd made the decision to return to safe harbour.

"So," Grant probed gently, "what news from Madame?"

Hawkwood dragged his thoughts back to the present.

"She gave me these." He put the glass down and removed his coat. Taking the document wallet from the inside pocket, he passed it to Grant. "It's what the general and the abbé have been working on. They want them made up to look like the real thing. Madame asked me if I knew a good counterfeiter. I told her I did." He looked at the elderly Scot. "Was I right?"

McPherson's eyes widened behind his spectacle lenses. Before he could reply, however, Hawkwood heard Grant say in a hushed voice, "Have you taken a look at these?"

Hawkwood shook his head. "Not yet. All she told me was that they were documents relevant to the enterprise. Her words, not mine. What are they?"

Grant stared down at the papers in his hand. "They're the keys to the God-damned kingdom, laddie, that's what!"

"May I?" McPherson held out his hand. Grant passed some of the documents across.

"Care to enlighten me?" Hawkwood said, as Grant and McPherson continued to read.

"It's all here, by God!" Grant exclaimed. "Looks like the man's thought of everything. We've got proclamations for the garrison, orders for corps commanders, warrants for troop movements.

There are even prison arrest and release forms and what look like promissory notes. The only things missing are dates, names and signatures. They'll obviously be added once the documents have been printed."

"It'd be interesting to know which names are going on those arrest and release papers," Hawkwood mused.

Grant gnawed the inside of his cheek. "No hint from Malet?"

"No. He's obviously leaving it until the last minute."

"Oh my word," McPherson said, in a voice that sounded as if he'd been struck by wonder.

"What is it?" Grant asked, alerted by the old man's tone.

"They've drawn themselves up a Sénatus-Consulte."

"What's that?" Hawkwood asked. Latin had never been his strong point.

"It's a decree issued by the Senate. It –"

"It's their bloody battle plan, is what it is!" Grant cut in excitedly, as he looked over McPherson's shoulder. He turned to Hawkwood. "Malet's going to make out there was a special meeting of the Senate and that this was the result."

Grant retrieved the paper from McPherson's hand. "This one *is* dated."

Grant's eyes ran down the pages. "The twenty-second of October. They've drawn up a list of articles, all to take immediate effect. It says here there's to be a provisional thirteen-man government, with Moreau as President. The rest are listed, too. There's a few I recognize. Augereau – he was Commander of the Army of Catalonia, and there's Prefect of the Seine, Frochot. There's a slew of senators as well." He glanced across at McPherson, who was listening intently. "I'm not familiar with either de Montmorency or de Noailles, though. Help me out, Jamie."

McPherson's eyes flickered. "Mathieu De Montmorency was deputy in the States General. Alexis de Noailles is a former aide of Bernadotte. They're both members of the Congrégation."

"Explains why Lafon's entered the game," Grant said archly.

Hawkwood frowned. "What about Malet?"

"He's assigned himself to be the new commander of the Paris garrison. That makes sense, given his background."

Grant turned a page. "By God, they're not wasting any time. The rest of the proclamation lays out the order of business; everything from the withdrawal of troops from foreign lands to the abolishment of conscription and a pardon for all political prisoners."

"That explains the release orders," Hawkwood said.

Grant's mouth split into a grin.

"Something funny?" Hawkwood said.

"It also says, among other things, that they're going to abolish the death penalty."

"What's so amusing about that?"

"For all crimes except cases of rebellion. You've got to admire the irony, laddie."

"That date you mentioned –" Hawkwood said.

Grant looked back over what he'd read. "The twenty-second?"

"That's the latest date Madame wants me to return the documents."

"That doesn't give us much time," McPherson interjected.

Grant looked thoughtful. Suddenly, he frowned. "Wait a minute; what day is that?"

"Thursday," McPherson said. A light appeared in his eyes. He looked at Grant.

"It's too much of a coincidence," Grant said. "It has to be."

"What has to be?" Hawkwood asked. "Talk to me, gentlemen."

"You remember that conversation we had about whether Malet said 'any' or 'much' longer?"

"Vividly," Hawkwood said drily.

"Well, your meeting with Madame has just confirmed that Malet definitely plans to move sooner rather than later. A hell of a lot sooner, in fact."

"I gathered that," Hawkwood said. "Otherwise she wouldn't have wanted the documents back so quickly."

"Ah, but it ain't just the date, bonny lad, it's the day that's significant, too, and the time."

"How so?"

"The decree. It refers to the Senate having convened on October twenty-second, at eight p.m. *This* Thursday."

"All right, I'll bite. So?"

"So, every Friday, without fail, the Paris garrison conducts its weekly review. Now, if you wanted to disguise the fact that you were moving troops into position, what day would you pick? My guess is you'd do it on a day when troops were being deployed anyway. No one'll think it unusual if they see uniformed men marching through the streets. They'll just assume they're part of the parade. Well, wouldn't you?

"Look at the documents the general was working on. We've even got a letter here to Colonel Soulier, the Commander of the National Guard, ordering him to assemble his men for special duties. Take a look."

Grant held out his hand and McPherson passed him the letter.

"See?" Grant said, showing it to Hawkwood. "It's the only other document that has a date and time. October twenty-third, one a.m. – that's only five hours after the time of the decree being issued. Malet must know, if he's to have any chance of his coup succeeding, he's got to keep up the momentum, before anyone starts questioning the orders. Friday has to be the day."

Hawkwood stared at the document. It was as Grant had said. It was starting to make sense.

Apart from a name which suddenly caught his eye.

"Who the hell is General Lamotte?" Hawkwood asked.

"What?" Grant said.

"The letter's from the newly appointed General of Division, Commandant of the Main Army of Paris. I'm assuming Malet will put his own signature above that title, but the letter begins: '*I have given orders to General Lamotte, with a Police Commissioner, to attend at your barracks and to read before you and your Cohort the decree of the Senate consequent on the receipt of the news of the death of the Emperor and the cessation of the Imperial Government.*'"

Hawkwood handed the letter back to Grant. "See for yourself. Who's Lamotte?"

"Not to mention the Commissioner of Police," Grant said, frowning. "Maybe Lamotte's one of those prisoners they're planning to release. Either that or Malet's attracted a few extra souls to his banner that we don't know about. This is starting to make me wonder what else he hasn't told us."

"Bleedin' generals," Hawkwood said softly.

"What?"

"It's something Jago once said: 'The trouble with generals is that they never tell you anything. They treat you like bloody mushrooms. They keep you in the dark and feed you on shit.' Reassuring to know that French generals are no different to English ones."

"'Cept in their case, it's champignons," Grant murmured. "And I'm sorely tempted to point out that the general ain't the only one who's keeping people in the dark. Isn't that what we're doing to him?"

Hawkwood wondered if he was supposed to laugh. He shook his head. "Any more quips like that and I'll start to wonder whose side you're on."

Grant grinned but the concern at what Malet might or might not be holding back was still there in his eyes.

Hawkwood turned to McPherson. "Either way, it's first things first. Which means it's down to you, Mr McPherson. Can you get the documents finished on time?"

McPherson spoke through pursed lips. "Aye, I think so, but it'll be a close-run thing."

"We need this," Hawkwood said. "Otherwise we're dead in the bloody water."

"Then I'll have to make damned sure," McPherson said, "won't I?"

The house lay on the rue d'Hautville. It was a large house and, as befitting the home of a senior prosecutor, rather grand, with a pleasing aspect and an attractive garden to the rear which was surrounded by a high wall to deter intruders.

Deluc and his men had been watching the place for over two hours. It was a few minutes after midnight and so far there had been next to no signs of life. Deluc was growing increasingly impatient; stamping his feet, he huddled into his coat and tried to ignore the chill that was worming its way into his bones.

"How much longer do we have to wait?" The query came out of the darkness to his right.

"Until I say we don't," Deluc snapped back.

The response was an indecipherable mumble which Deluc knew was his fellow Inspector, Jules Peuchet, cursing under his breath.

Deluc and Peuchet were covering the front of the building. Four more members of the Division Deuxième were keeping watch at the rear.

"Wouldn't surprise me if the bastard's pulled a fast one," Peuchet muttered morosely. "Who's to say he's not helping himself to the contents of some mansion over on the rue Paradis while we're standing here freezing our balls off? That's the trouble when you recruit from the bloody slums, you can never trust the sods. Once a lag, always a lag."

Deluc hit back: "I'm from the bloody slums, too. As are you, if I remember rightly. We all are, come to think of it."

Peuchet sighed. "You know what I mean."

Deluc shook his head wearily, but as he stared across at the house, he wondered if Peuchet's cynicism might not be too close to the mark. Maybe Peuchet was right and Vidocq *was* half a dozen streets away, robbing a banker instead of a prosecutor and laughing himself silly.

There was no sign of life. There had been a rain shower earlier and the cobbles were slick and shiny. They'd seen a couple of cats jink past and a few drunks weaving unsteadily in the distance but, apart from that, the night had been uneventful and quiet.

Too quiet, Deluc thought moodily. But then the weather was hardly conducive to late-night promenading.

Suddenly, from his darkened doorway, Deluc caught a glimpse of movement. At first he'd taken it to be a dense patch of shadow, but when it shifted again he saw it was the figure of a man, which then broke into the shapes of four men trotting in single file. Like rats scurrying along a gutter, Deluc thought, his pulse quickening.

He heard Peuchet emit a soft grunt; a sign that he'd spotted

284

them, too. Both police officers pressed their bodies back into the brickwork and watched as the four men veered off the street, striking out determinedly for the narrow path that bordered the mansion, separating it from its immediate neighbour.

"They're going for the side gate," Peuchet whispered.

Deluc waited until the men had been swallowed up.

"We'll give them time to get inside. I'd rather we caught them *with* the spoils, not while they're thinking about them."

Deluc and Peuchet let a couple of minutes pass before they stepped out from the doorway and crossed the street. Moving quickly, they proceeded along the path, following the line of the wall. After fifty paces the side gate came into view and they paused to take stock.

"Doesn't look as though they've left a lookout," Peuchet murmured, adding scathingly, "Amateurs."

Just then there came the noise of a twig snapping underfoot and both men froze as four shadowy forms padded into view from the opposite direction.

Deluc's throat turned to sand.

"It's Sergeant Brienne," Peuchet whispered, his voice catching with relief.

As his breathing resumed, Deluc stepped out of the shadows, allowing himself to be seen. Identities established, the six officers converged stealthily upon the wrought-iron gate that guarded the gap in the wall.

Deluc patted one of the men on the shoulder.

"Your turn, César. Make your way to the front. Wait five minutes then hammer on the door and announce yourself. You know the drill. Plenty of noise. Pretend you're taking part in a raid on the Cabaret."

César grinned and loped away.

Deluc pushed the gate open. It moved freely, with no sound of a rusty hinge. They entered the garden and the back of the house rose before them, dark and still. The prosecutor and his family were away for the evening and there were no staff in residence. To all intents and purposes, there was nobody home.

Until now.

"There!" Peuchet hissed, his eyes suddenly bright.

A dull light had appeared in one of the downstairs windows; only for a couple of seconds but it was the signal Deluc had been waiting for.

He kept his eyes trained on the building and watched as one of the first-floor windows was illuminated by a passing candle flame.

Deluc pulled a pistol from his coat. The others drew batons.

Silently, the five officers crept forward, using the cover of the shrubbery to mask their approach. Their caution was well founded. The last time this particular gang had staged a robbery, at the home of a linen merchant on the rue de Richelieu, they'd bludgeoned the merchant to death in full view of his wife and child. Deluc wasn't taking any chances.

Even before they reached the house, Deluc could see the broken window pane shining in the moonlight and the kitchen door propped open. Emboldened by the knowledge that the building would be empty, the robbers had made no effort to conceal their point of access. Their belief that an unoccupied property would provide easy pickings had made them complacent.

The night was suddenly broken by a colossal thud which seemed to rock the entire house, causing Deluc, despite the fact that he'd been expecting it, to nearly leap out of his skin. César had begun his assault on the front doors.

"POLICE! OPEN UP!"

"Jesus!" Peuchet gasped in awe.

Deluc had chosen César as their beater because he was a large man with a deep, stentorian voice, but even he was shaken by the bellow that reverberated through the lower floors like a bull elephant in must.

"Stand by," Deluc hissed. "And remember your orders."

Cries of alarm rang through the house, followed by the sound of feet clumping down a staircase. All attempts to stifle noise had been forgotten in the gang members' haste to make themselves scarce. It sounded, Deluc thought, as though it was every man for himself. He raised the pistol.

The first two men broke from the back door like mice scampering away from a granary cat. They had half-full sacks slung over their shoulders and cudgels in their hands, suggesting they'd not been prepared to abandon their haul in favour of an unencumbered and speedier escape. Their greed was their undoing.

The pair were given no chance to fend off attack. Taken completely by surprise by a flurry of baton blows across the backs of their skulls, the two robbers were sent sprawling, cudgels dropping from their fingers, while the contents of the sacks spewed out across the rain-dampened grass.

As their companions were overpowered and handcuffed, the last two gang members seized the moment to make a run for it. Deciding it was to their advantage to split the opposition's forces, they separated. Neither of them was weighed down with booty, though Deluc could see that one of them – the shorter of the two – was armed with a long-bladed knife. Moonlight flickered along the serrated edge.

Deluc levelled his pistol. "Halt! Police! Drop your weapon!"

The man continued running.

Deluc fired. The fugitive threw up his arms and with a wild cry pitched forward and lay still. Deluc turned quickly and saw that the last man had almost reached the gate.

Then a dark mass appeared as if out of nowhere: César, returning to add reinforcements.

One second the man was running full pelt, the next he seemed to stop in mid stride. César had used his full weight to swing the wrought-iron gate into the robber's path. The man went down as if poleaxed. Taking hold of his collar, César turned him over and unceremoniously secured the handcuffs around his wrists.

As the captives were hauled to their feet, Deluc walked over to the body on the ground. After squatting to examine it, he straightened, returned the spent pistol to his belt and called to the others: "The bastard's dead. We're finished here."

He watched impassively as the three house-breakers were led away, noting, beneath the layers of grime and the multiple patchwork of mending, the familiar cut of military tunics. It had been some considerable time since any of them had seen a parade ground, Deluc mused.

He waited until the garden was clear before returning to the prostrate body. He gazed down at it dispassionately.

"You can get up now," he said. "They've gone."

For a moment nothing happened, then the corpse stirred and lifted its head. "Is that you, Deluc?"

"Who else?" Deluc said, reaching out.

The man on the ground took the proffered hand and climbed to his feet. "Did you get all three?"

Deluc nodded. "Like shooting fish in a barrel."

The corpse brushed himself down. "Talking of which; you think they fell for it?"

"I don't see why not. You convinced me."

The corpse grunted, bent down and retrieved his knife. "There weren't many of you."

"Six was all we could spare. We thought two to one odds and the element of surprise would be enough. Fortunately it was."

Sticking the knife in his belt, the corpse nodded. "You took the loot as well?"

"We'll need it for evidence."

"Excellent. Another good night's work, then."

"I'd say so," Deluc said. He regarded the man standing before him, taking in the sandy-coloured hair that was already showing signs of grey above the pierced ears and at the sides of the broad forehead. His gaze moved down to the short stubbled beard and the scar on the right upper lip that might have been the result of an old knife wound. It was a face, Deluc thought, that had seen more than its fair share of trouble.

"In that case, I'll bid you good night."

"Actually, it's morning and I wouldn't get too comfortable if I were you, Officer Vidocq," Deluc said.

The bearded man put his head on one side and viewed Deluc with a jaundiced eye. "And why is that?"

"I was asked to give you a message."

An eyebrow lifted.

"Your presence is required."

"Where?"

Deluc gave a small smile. "Jerusalem."

The bearded man grimaced.

"Don't be late," Deluc said.

16

McPherson's shop was located off the rue Montmartre. There were several similar establishments ranged along the street but, compared to some of the bold frontage employed by the competition, McPherson's premises were refreshingly unadorned. The sign above the modest window, inscribed in fine gilded lettering, read simply: *McPherson's – Bijoutiers.* The combination of Scottish and French struck Hawkwood as rather an odd mix but because of the contrast to its more ostentatious neighbours, the unpretentious frontage hinted that a more bespoke clientele was catered for.

Hanging a closed notice on the inside of the door, McPherson led Hawkwood and Grant past the counter and through the shop towards the rear of the building.

Hawkwood was quite prepared to admit that his knowledge of the jewellery trade was rudimentary at best. He did know that people were prepared to pay ludicrous sums for the most hideous of baubles. He was also familiar with the larcenous tendencies of the miscreants he'd had cause to arrest for the theft of such items during his time as a Runner, when he'd discovered that more often than not the more delicate the item, the greater its value. Beyond that, he was a mere student.

Entering McPherson's workshop, Hawkwood saw, laid out upon the cramped surfaces, the materials and fine tools the old man used to produce his commissions. From the tiny brass wheels, cogs, combs, spindles, cylinders and discs that lay exposed on the benches, it would have been logical to assume they were the working parts of clocks and watches. It wasn't until Hawkwood caught sight of the finished examples of McPherson's craftsmanship on the adjacent shelves that he realized what he was looking at. What he hadn't known beforehand and what he'd failed to gather from the understated window display was McPherson's speciality. He made musical boxes.

Some of the instruments were small, not much bigger than a snuff box, while others were the size of tea caddies. In all cases, the decorative work on the outside of the boxes, from the marquetry to the engraving and the enamelled inlays, was as intricate as any piece of jewellery.

A few of the instruments were open and recessed within them Hawkwood could see exquisitely fashioned replicas of brightly plumed songbirds and miniature human figures, which he presumed either turned their heads and fluttered their wings or revolved like dancers in time to the music whenever the key was turned or the box opened. From the evidence before him, Hawkwood was left in little doubt that the elderly Scot had a rare gift.

Trailing McPherson across the floor towards a large display cabinet set against the wall, he and Grant watched as the old man inserted the toe of his shoe into the gap beneath the cabinet and pressed down. There was a sharp mechanical click. McPherson stepped back and, in oiled silence, rolled the entire cabinet to one side, revealing a doorway concealed behind it.

"In ye come," he said as he ducked through the opening. "Mind your heads."

Hawkwood and Grant followed and found themselves descending a hard stone stairway. After a dozen or so steps, the floor bottomed out. McPherson went round lighting candles and gradually the contents of the cellar emerged from the gloom.

Hawkwood took in the shelves, the benches and the equipment stored around him. It was a second workshop; only this time there wasn't a musical box in sight. He looked to where McPherson was standing in front of a tall object covered by a large sheet. McPherson pulled away the sheet and all was revealed.

"Meet Mathilde," McPherson said. "She's no youngster, as you can see, but a wee dab of lubrication here and there does wonders for the old joints. A bit like me," he added, removing his spectacles and polishing them vigorously with a handkerchief. Replacing the spectacles on his nose and the handkerchief in his waistcoat pocket, he blinked and regarded the machine with a look of affection.

It struck Hawkwood that the wood-framed printing press bore a macabre resemblance to illustrations he'd seen of a guillotine. There were the sturdy uprights which, in the guillotine would have held the blade, but which in a printing machine supported the huge threaded screw as it descended through the main beam and on to the platen beneath. The bed of the press also looked like the platform upon which the victim of the guillotine was laid and which could be rolled into the optimum position for carrying out the decapitation, not unlike the printing bed, which could slide out from under the platen so the type could be placed upon it in readiness for the operation. He tried to erase the off-putting image from his mind by looking around at the rest of the cellar's contents.

Close by, a long bench supported all the paraphernalia integral to the production of the printed word; from trays of metal lettering to printing blocks, moulds, matrices, ink-pads and equipment Hawkwood couldn't begin to identify. Some of the tools suspended on the racks above the bench were as delicate as any of those he'd seen in the outer workshop. Stored beneath the bench were receptacles of various shapes and sizes which, Hawkwood presumed, contained the ingredients necessary for keeping the machinery oiled and for making ink. Cubbyholes along the back of the bench held sheaves of blank paper.

Several stacks of paper on another shelf drew Hawkwood's attention. Most were composed of blank pages, but others contained text. He chose one at random. Printed across the top of the page was the inscription: *Pour voyager dans L'intérieur de L'Empire.* It was a blank passport form, identical to the one

293

Stormont Flint had provided at the Alien Office, prior to Hawkwood's physical characteristics and relevant signatures being added. Hawkwood put the form back and chose another; this time, a travel warrant. He didn't bother to inspect the rest, knowing he'd find similar documental forgeries, though he did wonder, if he continued delving, whether he'd chance upon a supply of prison visitor permits.

Turning away, he caught sight of a small heap of papers at the back of the shelf which looked distinctly grubbier than the rest. He could see that they, too, contained text, but unlike the others they were covered by a thin patina of dust. Intrigued, he drew closer. The top sheet had the appearance of a newsletter. He blew away the dust and held it up. The heading jumped out at him: *Citoyens! Prenez garde!* – Citizens! Beware!

Not a newsletter, he realized, but a pamphlet. As he read the diatribe below the warning, he recalled what Grant had told him the other day back on the bridge. This had to be an example of McPherson's counter-Revolutionary literature and the reason the wily old Scot had been picked up by the authorities and committed to the Conciergerie for interrogation.

He chose another page and saw that instead of text there was an illustration in which a bewigged man with an excessively pointed nose, long spidery fingers, and fangs for teeth was prancing with glee around a basket full of severed human heads. Beneath the drawing were the words: *Est cela un autre Être Suprême? Non! C'est seulement Citoyen Robespierre!* Is it another Supreme Being? No! It's only Citizen Robespierre! Hawkwood had seen similar caricatures before, though perhaps not so cruel, in the English newspapers, mocking prominent establishment figures, in particular members of parliament and even, on occasion, the king himself.

If the Tribunal had got wind that McPherson was distributing this kind of material, Hawkwood reflected, it was small wonder the old man had been hauled in for questioning.

"I'd have thought you'd have got rid of these," Hawkwood said, holding up the pamphlet.

McPherson turned; the candlelight reflecting in his spectacles. "I like to keep them as mementos."

"I take it the authorities never found this place, then?" Hawkwood said.

"You think I'd be here to talk about it if they had, Captain?" the Scot responded drily.

Hawkwood knew it had been a stupid question, even as he'd voiced it, for there was no way the Tribunal would have left the premises intact, or McPherson alive, for that matter, had the workshop been discovered. He looked at the capering man in the picture and wondered if, allowing for exaggeration, the artist had come close to capturing Robespierre's likeness.

McPherson regarded the image in Hawkwood's hand. His expression hardened and when he spoke it was as if he was trying to rid himself of a sour taste at the back of his throat.

"The man grew too fond of the blood-letting. In the end it was the death of him, lucky for me. They kept me in the Conciergerie for five days, on suspicion. Normally that would have been enough to see me dead, but the odious bastard had just tried to give his speech at the Convention when the crowd turned on him. They'd had enough of the killings. He was arrested and the day after that he was executed and they forgot all about me in the mêlée. One old Jacobite? What was I to them, other than more paperwork? Someone decided I wasn't worth the bother of raising the blade and so they let me go, along with a handful of others they'd taken in. We were a hair's breadth away from boarding the carts when the word was sent down. You've never seen men sink to their knees to give thanks like they did that day. So, no, Captain; in answer to your question, they never did find Mathilde, thank the Lord."

"Lucky for me, too," Grant said, grinning. "If it wasn't for Jamie, I'd still be walking the streets as Major Hawkwood."

"God save us," Hawkwood said.

Grant chuckled. Hawkwood put the illustrations back where he'd found them.

"Aye, well it helps me keep my hand in," McPherson said quietly. He began to busy himself, sorting through the rows of type, selecting odd ones that caught his eye and checking the defined edges of each letter, making sure to put them back in the right sequence. "Sometimes, I've been able to get hold of the genuine article, but when I can't, I improvise. As long as they're accompanied by plenty of stamps and signatures, they generally pass for the real thing."

Grant let go a snort. "Hell, half the fools who ask you for papers probably can't bloody read anyway. Right, Jamie?"

McPherson did not turn but continued his examination of the trays. "Aye, that may be true, right enough, but I'd rather not take the chance." The old man sniffed disdainfully. "Some of us take pride in our work."

Grant looked towards Hawkwood and made a face. Putting his arm around the old man's shoulders, he smiled. "We all do, Jamie. Now, how can we help? Captain Hawkwood and I are yours to command."

Wordlessly, McPherson removed an apron from a peg on the side of the press. Tying it about himself, he held out his hand. Hawkwood passed him General Malet's documents.

McPherson began to lay them out carefully on top of a clear section of bench as if they were a deck of cards and he was about to play a game of patience. He took his time studying each one in turn. Eventually, he sighed, nodded to himself and looked up. His eyes were bright with anticipation.

"Right, then, gentlemen. Let's get to work, shall we?"

Situated at the western end of the Île de la Cité, the rue de Jerusalem owed its name to travellers who, in years past, had overnighted there on journeys to and from the Holy Land. Since then, its appearance had barely altered. Venturing into the grubby, sunless street was like stepping back through time, though these days pilgrims were rather thin on the ground.

The surrounding buildings did little to lighten the oppressive atmosphere. All were old; some bordering on the ancient. Most were run down, with many in need of serious repair, among them the church; its steeple now a half-forgotten memory, thanks to the Revolutionary mob which, in its rage, had seen Sainte-Chapelle as a despised symbol of both royalty and religion and had taken its vengeance accordingly, gutting the interior of its precious relics and putting its medieval hangings to the torch.

At the end of the alleyway, a conical-roofed tower stood sentinel above a large, brooding edifice that looked close to collapse. The once magnificent mansion had been home to the city's ruling elite. Now, ugly and decrepit, as a prison hulk, it housed the headquarters of the Préfecture of the Paris Police and its reputation had come to match that of the Conciergerie which lay only a few lanes away.

The building's innards were as grim as the outer shell. Subsidence had taken its toll. Many of the walls were supported by huge timber stays, while beneath the high, vaulted ceilings whole rooms had been divided and then subdivided, creating a system of mezzanine floors all connected by rickety staircases and long, winding passages, some of which were so narrow there was barely enough width for two people to walk abreast; a fact Vidocq was reminded of as he followed Jean Henry, the head of the Division Deuxième, down the dim-lit corridors. Both men trod carefully. Instances of floorboards giving way under a man's weight were not uncommon.

By the time they arrived at their destination, Vidocq wasn't in the best of moods. So it didn't help to find, upon entry to the inner sanctum, that there was a further reception committee and that he was outnumbered.

In contrast to the balding, round-shouldered and slightly bookish Henry, Prefect of Police Étienne-Denis Pasquier looked more like a politician than a policeman. Tall and lean, with a high forehead and a luxuriant head of dark hair, Pasquier was a baron of the old school and it showed in both his bearing and his demeanour. It was his habit to greet every visitor, irrespective of their status, with a scowl of irritation; as though their arrival at his door was yet one more annoyance in a long line of un-welcome interruptions.

An ambitious and conscientious man, Pasquier was known as an early riser who liked to be at his desk before sun-up in order to prepare himself for the day. There were those who said that he didn't sleep at all or that if he did it was while hanging

297

upside down in a dark, windowless garret at the top of the building, coat-tails folded around him like wings; but few took that rumour seriously.

"Last night's operation would appear to have gone well," the Prefect observed, almost before Vidocq and Henry had time to enter the room. "Though it would have been advantageous to have netted a few more."

Unruffled by a compliment bestowed with one hand and undermined with the other, Vidocq shrugged. "They'd have used more men if the family had been at home, but they knew the house was going to be empty. Why involve more bodies than you need? It'd just mean a smaller share when it came to dividing the spoils. Anyway, three will do to be going on with."

The Prefect frowned. Subordinates who lacked servility were a rare breed. He stared down his nose and then nodded. "Well, I've no doubt the ones you snared last night will be singing soon enough. They'll give up the rest if they think it'll save their heads."

"Which it won't, of course." The small man standing by the fireplace bared his teeth in a wolfish smile.

"You know Chief of Security Desmarest?" Pasquier said, without altering his expression.

Vidocq turned and said carefully. "Only by reputation."

If Desmarest felt slighted by Pasquier's less than fulsome introduction, he kept his thoughts to himself. Inclining his head as though acknowledging Vidocq's response to be some kind of compliment – which was the last thing Vidocq had intended – he offered another ingratiating smile. "Forgive me for inter-rupting, but Prefect Pasquier has been most gracious in allowing me to take a look at the preliminary report on the arrests. Interesting that the thieves were identified as deserters."

Vidocq looked to Pasquier for some sort of guidance as to how much information to give away but the Prefect's aristocratic face remained impassive. Henry was even less help. Having received the summons to the Prefect's domain only thirty minutes after Vidocq had reported to the Division's offices, his face still mirrored his apprehension. Vidocq sighed inwardly. It was down to him. He turned back.

"They're part of a larger organization. Though it's not so much a gang: more of an affiliation. Most of them have military backgrounds. There are a few exceptions: draftees who've evaded the conscription but who can demonstrate a particular skill, for example. Someone comes up with a job and they recruit the number needed. That way there's no wastage. They're efficient and they're willing to use violence to get what they want."

Henry found his voice. He drew himself up, which wasn't very far; though he did have a few inches on the security chief. "The Division got wind of them after a spate of robberies over in the 5th Arrondissement. We thought it was time they were dealt with."

"And you sent your man here to sort them out," Desmarest said, fixing Vidocq with a penetrating stare. "How very apt."

This time Vidocq kept silent. He was beginning to understand the reason for Pasquier and Henry's disquiet.

"Set a thief to catch a thief, eh?" Desmarest smirked. He immediately raised a hand in mock surrender. "My apologies; I mean no offence."

Vidocq caught sight of Desmarest's fingernails; all were bitten down to the quick. The man's lapels, he saw, were streaked with food stains and a half circle of dried blood on the rim of his stock suggested a careless slip with the morning razor.

It struck Vidocq that the contrast between the Prefect and Savary's Chief of Security couldn't have been more marked. On the one hand there was Pasquier, all poise and sophistication, with, it was rumoured, an eye on an eventual ministerial position, while on the other there was Desmarest, who had all the refinement of a hod carrier. Odd, Vidocq thought, how two men could be poles apart and yet still be supremely efficient at their jobs.

"That was quite a trick you pulled, pretending to be shot," Desmarest continued.

Ignoring the flattery, Vidocq gave another shrug. "You'd be surprised how docile villains can become if they think they've seen the police shoot down one of their own in cold blood. It makes them more amenable to persuasion."

Or maybe you wouldn't, he thought.

"Even though they'll likely go to the guillotine anyway?" Desmarest hoisted a sceptical eyebrow.

"Hope's a powerful incentive. Also it helps if they think I'm dead. It means they're less likely to realize I was the one who betrayed them. And if their friends find out, it prevents them coming after me."

"Ingenious," Desmarest said. "I can see you'll go far." Another knowing smile split the security chief's face. "Though you seem to be forging quite a career for yourself already with this new department. I understand the Brigade was your idea?"

Vidocq slid another glance towards Pasquier, hoping for a sign that Desmarest had concluded his business and was only making conversation before his departure, but none was forthcoming.

"Come now, no need to be modest," Desmarest invited coaxingly.

Seated at his desk and monitoring the exchange, Pasquier swallowed his distaste. With his shabby, ill-fitting wardrobe and his uncouth manners, Desmarest really was an obnoxious creature. The annoying thing was he didn't seem to care, and that made Pasquier despise him even more.

Pasquier's attention switched to Henry. A police officer for nearly thirty years, Henry had received his appointment from Pasquier's predecessor, Louis Dubois. Devoted to his work, Henry had gained his reputation through the surveillance of released criminals and the tracking down of escaped convicts during the Revolution. Greatly respected, he was known to his staff as Father Henry and by the men he hunted as the Dark Angel.

Pasquier could only imagine how Desmarest was referred to behind his back.

And then there was Vidocq: soldier, smuggler, outlaw, thief – and those were just the fragments of his past that Pasquier was aware of. Pasquier wasn't even sure he wanted to know the rest. It was best if he let Henry worry about that. After all, Vidocq was more Henry's man than anyone else's, seeing as Henry had been the one who'd recruited him. Though, as Pasquier recalled, it had been Vidocq who'd made the first approach.

It didn't seem possible that only three years previously, the man had been a career criminal, walled up in prison, awaiting transportation to the galleys. Even harder to believe that after a so-called moment of epiphany when he'd requested an interview with Henry and offered his services as a police spy in exchange for a reduced sentence, he'd eventually risen to become head of the Division's new criminal investigation department.

There had been a time, Pasquier remembered, when the notion that he and someone like Eugène Vidocq might end up working together or even breathing the same air would have seemed preposterous, yet here they both were. His mind went back to when Henry had come to him with the idea for a new bureau, one whose officers would work under cover within the criminal underworld, unrestricted by district boundaries. When Pasquier had pressed him, Henry had admitted that it had been Vidocq's idea. At first, Pasquier had dismissed the proposal out of hand, but the more he listened the more persuasive Henry's argument had become. What better way to pursue criminals than to turn one of their own against them and to have him use his own unrivalled knowledge of the underworld to bring those criminals to justice?

"I'll provide the offices," Henry had volunteered, ". . . if the Préfecture supplies the funds."

And thus with a stroke of a pen the Brigade de Sûreté was born; with Vidocq, the former convict, in charge. Who'd have thought it; the fox becoming the hound?

Stepping away from the fireplace, Desmarest faced Henry and Vidocq and affected another obsequious twist of the lips. "No need to look so concerned, gentlemen. I thought it was about time I came and offered my congratulations. How long's the Brigade been in operation, now? A couple of months? And yet it's already proved its worth. Most impressive. The apprehension of the murderer Charpentier, in particular, was an inspired piece of detection." The security chief spread his arms expansively. "Oh, I concede there've been differences in the past, but I know

301

good police work when I see it, and we do share a common enemy, after all."

Henry blinked. Those differences, as everyone knew, were the reason the Préfecture had been created in the first place. Under Fouché, the Police Ministry had grown so powerful that Bonaparte himself broached the idea of an independent police department. Thus, while the Ministry retained its authority over public order, security, prisons, and the dispensing of justice, the Préfecture would be there to police whores, thieves and street lamps, and to keep an eye on Fouché's activities and report them to the First Consul, as ordered.

Desmarest lowered his voice. "You know, my friend, despite what you may think, there are those of us within the Ministry who've always been of the opinion that there should be greater liaison between the Quai Voltaire and our colleagues in the rue de Jerusalem. With the growing level of crime on the streets and the increasing threats to the nation, it's even more imperative that we set those differences aside and share our resources wherever possible. Wouldn't you agree?"

Henry hesitated and then nodded warily. "Of course."

Vidocq was watching Desmarest's eyes. *He's after something*, he thought.

"Splendid," Desmarest said. "I knew you'd understand. I take it, therefore, in the spirit of co-operation, that you wouldn't raise any objections if I called upon the Brigade's services to assist me with a small security matter?"

Henry stared at him.

"A minor surveillance task. That's all."

"Surveillance?" Henry said.

"Nothing too demanding," Desmarest responded airily, wafting a hand as if the proposition was of no real consequence. "Truly."

"Doesn't the Ministry have its own people?" Henry asked. The realization that he might just have been duped into agreeing to something against his better judgement was sinking in fast.

"Of course, though, regrettably, none of them have quite the expertise that I'm looking for on this occasion."

"What does that mean?"

The words were out of his mouth before Vidocq could stop them. He wondered why Pasquier seemed content to remain silent and then it occurred to him that the Prefect might already know what Desmarest had in mind, and that in itself was mildly worrying.

Desmarest's expression hardened at Vidocq's temerity. "I need a watch placed on someone. That *is* one of the Brigade's specialities, is it not?"

"The Ministry's as well, surely?" Henry countered, his annoyance at having become prey to one of the oldest tricks in the book increasing by the second.

"Does this someone have a name?" Vidocq cut in.

Desmarest turned. "Claude-François Malet. He's a State prisoner, currently resident at the Clinique Dubuisson on the rue du Faubourg-Saint-Antoine."

Henry frowned. "Forgive me, but I was under the impression that the Ministry has informers in most of the facilities."

Desmarest nodded. "It does indeed, but sometimes one sheep alone just isn't enough."

"There are only four of us in the Brigade," Vidocq pointed out. "It's hardly a flock."

Desmarest's eyes turned to flint. Pasquier's lips twitched.

"I'm still not entirely sure why you can't use your own people," Henry said stubbornly.

Pasquier shifted in his chair. He could see that Henry wasn't going to let this one go. "Perhaps I should explain. The Ministry –"

Desmarest held up his hand. "If I may?" The Security Chief paused and, at a nod from Pasquier, said, "I'll speak frankly. We're all aware what the war's doing to our country. We've seen it with our own eyes. Conscription has deprived the homeland of its finest young men. The situation hasn't only affected the civilian population but the police force, too. In short, it's becoming hard to find suitable officers. The introduction of the Brigade, on the other hand, has brought new impetus to the fight against crime, which the Ministry, at the moment, has failed to do, though it grieves me to say it. I see no reason, therefore, why your men shouldn't expand their field of investigation into matters of security; which in this case, with regards to my particular concerns about General Malet, could mean that a fresh pair of eyes will see what others have missed."

"You're saying you don't think your own people are up to the job?" Henry said, unable to believe that Desmarest was actually being that candid.

Unsurprisingly, Desmarest shook his head. "No, I'm saying that this particular task requires a slightly different approach from the way *my* people normally operate, which is usually from a discreet distance. On this occasion, in my judgement, the task requires a slightly less conventional approach."

"How so?" Vidocq asked.

"The observer will need to spend more time in *close* proximity to the subject in order to observe his actions; to note how he conducts himself; in particular, who he talks to and so forth, especially visitors. That *is* what you and your men do best, isn't it? *Close* observation? It's how you were able to apprehend the robbers last night. You spied on them, gained their trust and inveigled yourself into their organization, and then, acting as a confederate, you lured them into your trap."

"You referred to him as *General*," Vidocq said. "Is there anything else we should know? You said he was a *State* prisoner, so he's not in the clinic because he's sick. What did he do?"

Desmarest hesitated. "It's not what he *did*, so much as what he *attempted* to do."

"Which was what?"

Desmarest told them.

Henry and Vidocq exchanged looks. "So, does that mean you suspect him of being involved in something untoward now?" Vidocq asked.

"Not specifically. At the moment all I have is a feeling. It might be nothing. It's more for my peace of mind than anything, but I'd like to know for certain if I have anything to worry about."

In other words, Henry thought, might as well have the Brigade waste its time rather than Ministry personnel. Then he had another thought. Guessing what the answer was likely to be, he said, "Assuming we accede to your request; would you want a report submitted to you directly, or through Ministry channels?"

"Any intelligence gathered is to be delivered to me," Pasquier said. "I'll see that it's passed on."

Henry knew then that a bargain had already been struck. He and Vidocq were witnesses *after* the fact. Their presence in the Prefect's office didn't even amount to a courtesy; more a formality, which was another way of saying they'd been well and truly hoodwinked.

"That would be the most convenient route," Desmarest said smoothly. "Obviously the sooner you can confirm that all is well, the quicker your Brigade members can resume their regular duties."

"And when would you like us to commence this . . . observation?" Henry asked.

"As soon as possible. Naturally I'll leave it to you to assign your men as you see fit." Desmarest looked towards Pasquier for confirmation.

Naturally, Henry thought.

"I think you mean *my* men, don't you?" Vidocq said.

Desmarest stiffened. He smiled thinly. There was an awkward silence.

Time to end it, Pasquier thought quickly. He rose to his feet. "I believe this might be an appropriate time to adjourn, gentlemen, don't you?" He turned to Desmarest. "I take it you have nothing further?"

Desmarest hesitated, then, realizing the question had been a none-too-subtle hint, he shook his head. "Not at this time. You'll keep me informed?"

"Naturally," Pasquier said. He caught Henry's eye.

"In that case, I bid you good day." Desmarest nodded towards Henry and Vidocq. "An honour, gentlemen."

As the security chief left the room, Henry stared after him before turning and addressing Pasquier. "Spirit of cooperation? We are talking about the same Ministry, aren't we? You'd already agreed to this?"

"Much as it pains me to admit it, the man has a point. Perhaps there are occasions when we should combine our resources."

"He turns my stomach," Henry said. "I trust him and his Ministry lackeys about as far as I can spit."

"Ah, but it's not *his* Ministry," Pasquier pointed out. "He might like to create the illusion that it is, but it's Savary who pulls the strings."

"You think Savary knows anything about this?" Henry asked.

"Now that," Pasquier said, pursing his lips in thought, "is a very good question."

"It'd be interesting if he doesn't," Henry said ruminatively.

"Indeed it would."

"So, maybe this is one way we can learn about some of the Ministry's dirty laundry," Vidocq said.

Henry and Pasquier both turned. Henry's head lifted. He looked at Pasquier. "Is *that* why you offered him our services?"

"A bargain runs both ways. I made him aware that the Préfecture expects something in return for our assistance."

"Such as?"

"That hasn't been decided. Rest assured, it will be commensurate to the current circumstances and not something to be squandered on a whim. It also occurred to me if our new friend Desmarest *is* working on his own without Savary's knowledge, that's also knowledge worth cultivating."

"You mean it may give us leverage?"

"All things are possible," Pasquier said enigmatically.

Henry, considering the implications of the Prefect's statement, brightened, and then nodded. "All right, I can live with that."

"If I might interrupt," Vidocq said. "I'll repeat what I said earlier: I have only four men. That's why I use Division officers like Deluc and the others as support."

Pasquier nodded. "Of course, but it's not as though you'll be doing the watching yourself, is it? That's one of the advantages of command, is it not? Delegation?"

"It'll mean taking men away from other cases."

"Then choose your priorities. From what our new-found friend has told us – which, admittedly, isn't a great deal – I'd venture that a possible threat to the security of the Empire is of greater importance than the rounding up of a team of pickpockets, wouldn't you? Besides, given our thoughts as to why the Chief of Security might wish to involve the Brigade, it behoves us to try and discover what the man *is* up to. Who knows where it might lead? Even if it comes to nothing, there may well come a time when we need to call in the debt."

"We don't even know what we're supposed to be looking *for*," Vidocq pointed out.

"Then we must hope . . ." Pasquier said, returning to his desk ". . . that your man will know it when he sees it."

The printing took longer than McPherson had anticipated.

A closer examination of his equipment had revealed several type pieces to be in need of replacement. Added to which, for some of the documents to appear authentic to a trained eye, they required official stamps, some of which had to be newly fashioned.

It had been painstaking work. McPherson had applied all his skills and concentration. Virgin type had been struck using the small bench-top foundry housed at the back of his premises while, by filing old blocks into blanks, new wooden seals had been produced in the workshop normally reserved for the construction of his musical boxes. Watching the old man had been an education in itself. Hawkwood and Grant had looked on in wonder as, like some ancient alchemist producing gold from base metal, McPherson had, with intricate precision, forged new tools from old.

After that had come the setting up of the press and the typeface, by which time Hawkwood never wanted to see another ink-pad as long as he lived. At the end of the process both his and Grant's arms were black to the elbows, though both were forced to admit, as the finished sheets were hung up to dry, that there had been something curiously satisfying in seeing the documents take form before their eyes. Though it also occurred to Hawkwood that having come to terms with matrices, chases, quoins, coffins and even galleys, the vocabulary of the printing world was as arcane as any nautical lingo.

It was early in the morning, after five days of toil but with the printing finally completed, when Hawkwood made his way to Le Moineau to leave a message that the documents were ready to be delivered. When he went back that afternoon for the reply, there was a note waiting for him.

"Well," Grant asked, when Hawkwood returned to the apartment on the rue Serpente.

"I'm to deliver them to the priest's house."

"When?"

"Midnight tonight."

They fell silent.

It was Thursday, October 22nd.

"And so it begins," Grant said softly.

17

Dark clouds had been gathering over the city since the early afternoon, but it was dusk before the first drizzle appeared. Showers followed a short time later, intermittent at first, and then with increasing regularity until, at a few minutes before eleven o'clock when the clinic gates were locked for the night, the rain, though still light, began its descent in earnest.

The clocks were striking midnight when the general and the abbé let themselves out of their rooms and made their way through the darkened corridors towards the kitchen. It was the same route they'd used eleven days before and neither of them had seen any sense in changing it.

The kitchen door was secured, but the scullery window was not. Climbing over the sill, Malet and Lafon dropped out into the darkness. Closing the window after them and hugging the side of the building, they made their way towards the rear garden; Malet leading the way.

Nearing their objective, they paused. There was no moon to speak of. It was obscured by cloud. The only sound was the patter of raindrops striking the leaves and the earth around them. They searched the darkness for movement – the gatekeeper, or perhaps one of the other porters performing a final check of the grounds – but with the exception of the rain, the night remained still and silent and free from threat. Stepping from cover, they crossed the lawn, heading for the perimeter wall and the oak trees guarding it.

Trusting fools, Malet thought, as he grasped the first branch. *What do they take us for – officers and gentlemen?*

He pulled himself up. He'd always been a fit man and the climb was relatively easy. Even so, clambering up trees and across walls was not something he'd expected to be doing at this stage of his life. Curiously, it was Lafon, fifteen years his junior, who was having the most trouble.

Physical exercise was evidently not the abbé's forte, though he'd survived their first nocturnal sortie without mishap. Admittedly, the weather had been a lot more charitable on that occasion. Tonight's rain, while not heavy, made it harder to maintain a grip. Boots had a tendency to lose traction on the wet bark.

Despite the obstacles, it took Malet only a few seconds to reach the broad limb that gave him a foothold on to the brickwork. Taking one last look around, he lowered himself carefully from the top of the wall until he was hanging by his fingertips. Mouthing a silent prayer, he let himself drop the last two feet, bending his knees in anticipation of his landing. A moment later, he was straightening and brushing himself down.

He could hear Lafon labouring above him. A dark form appeared at the top of the wall and manoeuvred itself towards the ground. Then Malet was aware of a body falling, succeeded by a heavy thud and a sharp exclamation of pain. Spinning round, he found Lafon clutching his left ankle.

Malet bent down quickly. "Are you all right?"

Lafon grimaced. "I slipped. I think I've twisted it."

Malet swore silently. This was not what they needed. Holding out his hand, he helped Lafon to his feet. "Can you walk?"

Lafon stood upright and took a tentative step forward and then another. He winced and nodded. "It's painful, but I think so."

"Then we should get moving. There's no time to waste."

Malet set off. Lafon followed behind, limping. By the time the general reached the first corner, Lafon was a dozen paces to his rear. The general turned. Curbing his impatience, he waited for the abbé to catch up.

"I'm slowing you down," Lafon said, breathing heavily. "You should go on ahead. You don't have to wait for me."

Malet shook his head. "We're in this together, remember? And don't worry, the more you walk on it, the easier it will get. You'll be skipping like a spring lamb in no time."

They set off once more, this time shoulder to shoulder, away from the rue du Faubourg-Saint-Antoine, towards the Place de la Bastille and on into the rain-shrouded city that lay slumbering beyond.

Fifty paces behind them and ten feet from the ground, the figure of a man emerged from the dark shadows cast by the oak branches. Crouched, unmoving, rain dripping down his face, he watched as the general and his companion disappeared into the night. As soon as the two fugitives were out of hearing distance, the watcher hung from the wall and lowered his body down. Then, moving cautiously, he set off in pursuit.

Bloody rain, Hawkwood thought.

Though it could have been worse, he supposed. He could have been at sea. That thought brought to mind the *Griffin* and, inevitably, Stuart and the other crew members who would never make it home. Guilt coursed through him. What was a damp collar in the scheme of things? He recalled Jago once telling him there was no such thing as bad weather, only the wrong type of clothing. That was Nathaniel for you; always there with the pithy comment. Hawkwood wondered if he'd ever get the opportunity to ride in Jago's new carriage, if he ever got one. Probably best not to dwell on that right now. There were more important things to worry about.

Like seizing a city, for instance.

Strange how the mind wandered at times like these, he mused. Moments of reverie often occurred in those tense minutes before a battle. No one knew why. It was as if the brain was trying to repel any thought of the true threat that lay ahead. Because if you dwelled too long on what might be waiting for you, there was always the risk that you'd run screaming from the field or freeze at the wrong moment, thus revealing your vulnerability to the enemy. And no one wanted that on their conscience, did they? God forbid.

Hawkwood crossed the river by way of the Île Saint-Louis. It wasn't as densely populated as the larger Île de la Cité, so there weren't as many dark corners to negotiate. Also it was the quickest route to his destination and, given what he was carrying, the less time he spent on the streets the better. Not that he was without protection, but there was a limit to how far he was prepared to go to advertise his presence. In that regard, ironically, despite the discomfort, the rain had become an ally of sorts for it helped to keep prying eyes indoors. But it didn't mean he relished it dribbling down the back of his neck.

The rue Saint-Pierre was as uninviting as it had been on his first visit; made even more malodorous by the stinking black ordure that clung to his heels as he felt his way along the dripping passageway, across the courtyard and up the crumbling stairs to the third-floor apartment.

"You have the documents?" Denise Malet asked anxiously as the still unsmiling Father José admitted Hawkwood into the room and bolted the door behind him.

Hawkwood handed the pouch over and as she pressed it to her breast he saw the relief spread across her face.

"Thank you," she said softly.

At that moment, a shadow passed through the gap between the hinges of the door leading to the adjacent bedchamber. Hawkwood's hand slid towards the pistol concealed inside his coat.

"No!" Denise Malet said quickly. She took hold of Hawkwood's arm.

Two men entered the room. Strangers; neither carried a weapon. Hawkwood withdrew his hand.

Denise Malet said, "Captain Paul Dumas, allow me to introduce Advocate André Balthus and Sergeant Jean Rateau."

Young; early thirties, with not many years between them, Hawkwood judged. Rateau was slim and good looking with narrow shoulders and dark hair and had the look of a junior subaltern rather than a non-commissioned officer. Balthus was the shorter of the two, with fair hair and a thinning crown. There was a serious, studious air about him which, Hawkwood supposed, matched his profession. Definitely more an academic than a warrior, though Hawkwood knew you couldn't always go by looks.

As he and Hawkwood were both in civilian dress, Rateau did not salute but placed his heels together, bowed formally and held out his hand. "Honoured to meet you, Captain Dumas."

"As am I," Balthus said, doing the same.

"Gentlemen," Hawkwood said, seeing the question in their eyes, which told him his presence was as much a mystery to them as theirs was to him, which also suggested that Grant's comment about Malet drawing disparate recruits to his flag might not have been without foundation.

Their thinly disguised looks of disappointment when they'd walked into the room had also told him they'd been expecting someone else. Given the circumstances, it wasn't difficult to guess who.

"I take it the general's running late," Hawkwood said.

"We expected them half an hour ago," Denise Malet said. Showing no surprise at Hawkwood's question, she was unable to hide the apprehension in her voice.

"Them?"

"The abbé is with him."

"I could go and look for them," Balthus offered.

"No," Hawkwood said. "That's not a good idea."

They looked at him. It wasn't hard to read their minds this time, either. They were asking themselves: despite holding a captain's rank, who did this Dumas think he was, giving them orders?

"We don't know which route they've taken," Hawkwood pointed out. "In this weather you might not see them, which means they could arrive and then you'd be the one missing. We start to send someone to look for you and we'll be here all night."

Balthus coloured and looked sheepish but then, seeing the sense in Hawkwood's argument, nodded.

Denise Malet drew herself up. "Captain Dumas is right. We will wait."

Placing the document pouch on the table, she turned to Hawkwood. "Let me take your coat, Captain. As you see, there's food and some wine," she added. A small crease formed at the corner of her mouth. "Or coffee, if you prefer."

He could tell the other two were intrigued by the intimacy of the exchange. *Let them wonder*, Hawkwood thought.

There was no improvement in the coffee's taste, but this time, at least, the brew was hot and for that alone Hawkwood was thankful. In truth, he was doubly grateful because it gave him something to do with his hands. It also helped bridge the stilted silence that had followed his veto of Balthus' offer to act as search party.

The only one at ease was the priest, who, without reference to any of the others, retired to a chair in the corner of the room, opened a leather-bound bible and began to read. His lips moved soundlessly as he followed the text with the end of his forefinger.

They did not have to suffer the lull for very long. Less than five minutes later a sharp rap on the door made everyone except the priest start. Balthus and Rateau straightened their backs. Denise Malet smoothed her dress and adjusted her hair into place.

Triggered by the reactions of the others, Father José looked up from the scriptures. At a nod from Denise Malet, he laid his bible aside and unbolted the door.

General Malet entered quickly with Lafon's arm across his shoulder. The cleric's face was creased with pain. Helped to the nearest chair, he sank down with a groan of relief.

Relieved of the abbé's weight, the general straightened and shook the rain from his coat. "God-damned ground was wet! Jean-Baptiste lost his footing coming over the wall. We'd have been here sooner, otherwise."

It was hard to tell if the vexation was directed against the downpour or the abbé's lack of athletic prowess. But then, as if remembering where he was, the general looked up and an apologetic smile appeared. Suddenly businesslike, he stepped forward and shook hands with Rateau and Balthus. "Good to see you, gentlemen." He held out his hand to Hawkwood. "Captain."

"General," Hawkwood said.

After giving Hawkwood's hand another emphatic shake, Malet broke his grip. He regarded his wife for the first time. Another smile, this time more wry than apologetic, flitted across his lips. "Hello, my dear. I trust you've been keeping our guests entertained in the meantime?"

Denise Malet made no reply. Her eyes misted. As the general opened his arms, she crossed the room to him and placed a finger against his lips. They hugged each other tightly until the general, gently and with great reluctance, finally broke the embrace.

"Come, my dear," he said, smiling. "I fear we're embarrassing our friends." He indicated Hawkwood's drink. "Is that coffee I smell?"

The tension in the room eased. Gathering herself, the general's wife moved to the hearth. She addressed the abbé: "Jean-Baptiste?"

Lafon nodded wearily. "That would be most welcome. Perhaps a little cognac, too, if you have it," he added hopefully.

As his wife reached for the coffee pot, the general took off his coat and laid it across the back of an empty chair. He turned to Lafon. "How's the ankle?"

The abbé grimaced. "Still painful but a little easier, I think."

Malet turned to his wife. "Perhaps Father José has something we could use as a compress?"

As the request was relayed, the general's gaze swept over the rest of the room and a flicker of doubt showed briefly in the russet brown eyes. It wasn't hard to see why. Of all the places a general might have chosen as the place from which to launch his plan to overthrow an Empire, a dingy, two-roomed apartment in a run-down

315

tenement was not the most auspicious choice. But then, like smoke in the wind, the doubt vanished, to be replaced by a look as determined as any Hawkwood had seen and, as his gaze alighted on the document pouch, General Malet's face came instantly alive.

He went quickly to the table and with an eager hand drew the enclosed papers from the pouch. His eyes shone with excitement.

Hawkwood heard a gasp. Turning, he saw that Father José had removed the abbé's left shoe and was wrapping a bandage around the injured foot.

Back at the table, Malet spoke over his shoulder. "This is most excellent work, Captain; far better than I could have wished for. Your man's done us proud. I wish I had the chance to thank him personally."

"I'm sure there'll be an opportunity for you to do that, sir," Hawkwood said.

"Then I shall look forward to it."

With the others watching in silence, Malet studied the documents. Finally, after several minutes, he laid the last one aside, hesitated and then withdrew a gold pocket watch from his jacket. With great deliberation he opened the casing and consulted the dial. The smile disappeared, to be replaced by a sombre pursing of the lips. With a look bordering on sorrow, the general snapped the timepiece shut and turned to his wife. "It's time."

Hawkwood watched the look of resignation steal over her face as she gathered up her coat and bonnet.

The general helped his wife button into her coat. "Best wrap up warm, my dear. We don't want you catching a chill."

Denise Malet placed her hands over his. She smiled up at him. "I could say the same for you."

Tenderly, the general reached out and tucked away a strand of hair that had escaped from the clasp above his wife's ear. "We'll be together soon," he said.

He turned to the priest. Cajamaño stared back at him.

"Watch over her, Father," Malet said. "Guard her well."

It was hard to tell if Cajamaño had understood the exact words, but the expression on Malet's face had undoubtedly telegraphed their meaning.

"Do not worry, my love," Denise Malet said. "I'm in safe hands."

She was right, Hawkwood thought. Just one look from the black-clad priest with his pockmarked face, suspicious eyes and matted hair would cause anyone's heart to turn to stone.

"He knows he's to return here afterwards?" Malet asked.

"He knows."

She turned then and held out her hand to each man. "You are in my prayers, gentlemen."

As she took Hawkwood's hand, she whispered in a voice almost too low for him to hear, "Bring him back to me, Captain."

Pausing on the threshold, she regarded her husband with affection. "I'll be waiting for you, General."

She turned quickly. The priest followed her out and she was gone.

A look of sadness moved across Malet's face. But then, after several seconds, his head lifted and a grim light showed in his eyes.

"Let us go to it," he said softly.

As a sharp double tap sounded on the closed door behind him.

Claubert pressed back into the shadows while he tried to decide his next move. There had been no activity since the general and the abbé entered the apartment; Claubert was growing restless, and not a little worried.

He knew it had only been blind luck that had caused him to spot Malet and Lafon as they'd made their escape from the clinic. No one would ever know that, of course, certainly not Vidocq. As far as posterity was concerned, it would be put down to sharp-eyed vigilance. There certainly wouldn't be any mention of an interrupted midnight rendezvous with a licentiously inclined housemaid.

He wondered if the girl was still awake and pining for him. Somehow, he doubted it. He suspected his name had already been changed to mud and that she was even now sound asleep and cursing him in her dreams; just like he was cursing the rain.

317

He'd been en route to the housemaid's room, eagerly anticipating the delights awaiting him, when his ears had picked up the sound of stealthily approaching footsteps. Fear of discovery had sent him scuttling into a nearby linen storage room from where he'd spied the two residents padding along the otherwise silent corridor like a couple of cutpurses. Small chance they were engaged on a similar carnally charged assignation. Given his orders, he'd had little choice but to follow them, which had meant abandoning the waiting housemaid to her own wanton devices.

The instructions from Vidocq had been explicit. Watch the general, make a note of everyone he talked to or received a visit from and, if possible, find out what they talked about. Claubert had been assigned to the clinic's staff as an auxiliary attendant. Only the director, Doctor Dubuisson, knew his true role. His duties, designed to keep him close to his subject, had been mostly of the fetch-and-carry variety with waiting duties in the dining room during meal periods.

Claubert had been convinced the job was a complete waste of time. While he'd been in situ, not a single incident had aroused his suspicions. Daily life in the Clinique Dubuisson was about as sedentary as it could get; not just for General Malet but for every other resident.

Most of each day was spent in conversation. The topics, from what Claubert had overheard during his eavesdropping, were many and varied; from politics and the war to literature, science and philosophy, with a sprinkling of gossip thrown in for good measure, mostly it had to be said at the expense of the Emperor and his court.

Given that the majority of the residents were leftovers from the old régime, and thus hostile to Bonaparte, discussions rarely became overheated, only veering towards the adversarial when they involved debates over the sort of rule that might emerge once Bonaparte was gone.

All of which Claubert planned to include in his report, even if it did little to distinguish General Malet or his views from anyone else in the home.

When residents did run out of breath, they invariably retired to the chessboard or the card table, usually after the last visitor had been escorted from the premises; which, in the general's case, had been Madame Malet. So far, no one else from outside had paid the general court.

So, all in all, compared to some of his other jobs, it had been a relatively easy duty. Although waiting tables on embittered remnants of the nobility had been more than enough to remind Claubert why there'd been a revolution in the first place.

Not that there hadn't been adequate compensations; his own room, for one. Cramped admittedly, but he'd known worse. On top of that, there had been the three meals a day, not to mention fringe benefits in the unexpected and comely form of one very accommodating housemaid. All things considered, Claubert had never had it so good.

Until tonight.

God knew where the two of them were off to, but Claubert, even as he followed them into the night, knew it was more than his life was worth not to find out. It was fortunate that the abbé had suffered his injury. It had made trailing the two of them a lot easier. Though Lafon wasn't the only one who'd had difficulty getting over the wall. Claubert had lost his footing climbing the tree and had scraped his shin on one of the branches. The warmness he was experiencing suggested it wasn't rain water that was oozing down his leg but blood. Claubert wondered if that counted as being wounded in the line of duty.

He'd almost lost them near the corner of the rue Saint Gilles. Thinking he'd heard a noise behind him, Claubert had taken a glance over his shoulder. When he looked back, Malet and Lafon had vanished. A moment of panic had ensued until, picking up his pace, he'd caught up with them just before they'd disappeared into the rue Saint-Pierre.

He'd stuck closer then, watching them as they crossed the courtyard to enter the tenement. The general had glanced back at one point, but Claubert had ducked down and turned his face to the wall and the fear of discovery had passed.

There had been no one in sight when he'd entered the building but he'd been in time to hear somebody – he'd presumed it was the general and Lafon – climbing the stairs above him. The difficulty had been in determining which apartment they were heading for. Then there had come the sound of murmuring voices and of a door opening and closing. After that: silence. Trying to gauge how far up the last sounds had come from, Claubert had continued his ascent.

On the second-floor landing he'd paused and listened. There had been no sound to advise him of Malet's and the abbé's whereabouts, but there was illumination, in the form of a single tallow candle set into a metal wall bracket. In the candle's weak glow Claubert had spotted two sets of muddy footprints; footprints that had not stopped at the second floor but which had continued up to the third and a similarly lit landing and a doorway close by the top of the stairs.

Claubert had paused then. The candle glow did not extend far and the end of the corridor was invisible in the dark, though a small alcove a few yards further along the landing had been revealed. It was there that Claubert, after placing his ear against the door and hearing only subdued voices, had sought shelter in order to assess the situation.

Claubert knew his options were limited. He could always knock on the door and demand entry, but that wasn't something that appealed to him. He had no idea what lay on the other side, for a start. The alternative was to wait a while and see what transpired.

It occurred to him then that he wasn't carrying any means of protection. But one didn't usually arm oneself before entering a woman's bedchamber, and there hadn't been time to acquire a weapon – or a coat, much to his annoyance – in between spotting Malet and Lafon in the corridor and following them over the wall.

He had just asked himself what Vidocq would do in the circumstances, when the door opened.

Claubert shrank back. Light spilled from the room on to the landing, revealing the figure of a woman framed in the open doorway and looking back into the apartment.

"I'll be waiting for you, General," she said.

Claubert heard the words from his hiding place and when a

side of her face came into view it was one that Claubert recognized. It was General Malet's wife. As she stepped into the corridor a second figure followed close behind; this one male. Tall and thin, dressed in a priest's cassock.

The door closed and Claubert watched as Madame Malet and the priest descended the stairway and disappeared from view. Claubert stared at the apartment door. What he'd seen hadn't made sense. Why would Madame Malet not want to remain with her husband? And who was the priest? In spite of his garb, the anonymous cleric had looked more like a demented scarecrow than a man of the cloth.

Claubert waited to see if anyone else appeared. After several minutes had elapsed he assumed they weren't going to. Perhaps if he tried listening again, he'd be able to hear what was going on. Crossing the landing and without much expectation he placed his ear against the door.

Claubert never saw the arm that came out of the darkness behind him. The first he knew of it was when it encircled his throat. At the same time, the click of a gun being cocked sounded loudly in his ear and the muzzle of a pistol was placed firmly against the side of his skull.

And a voice whispered softly, "Move and you die."

18

When the knocks sounded on the door Balthus and Rateau sprang back in alarm and the blood leached from Lafon's face. He stared at Malet, his eyes widening in fear and disbelief. "We're discovered!"

The words were barely out of the abbé's mouth when the sequence of taps came again.

"No," Hawkwood said, retrieving the pistol from his coat. "I rather think this will be for me."

"Captain?" Malet stood quickly and moved away from the table.

Ignoring the general and Balthus and Rateau's shared look of panic, Hawkwood crossed the room and drew back the bolt.

"No!" Lafon rose halfway out of his seat.

The door swung inwards and Hawkwood stepped aside as a body was flung into the room by a strong push from behind. As the figure went sprawling, a second shape appeared in the opening, pistol in hand.

"Morning, gentlemen," Colquhoun Grant said cheerily. "My sincere apologies for the interruption."

Grant had spoken in French. Ignoring the looks of stupefaction that had greeted his entrance, he continued in the same language. "Found your man there trying to listen in. Filthy habit. I thought you'd want to know."

Hawkwood shut the door quickly. The man on the floor

pushed himself to his knees. He wore no coat, and his jacket and breeches were damp and shiny with rain. He had a thin, angular face that Hawkwood didn't recognize.

Grant moved swiftly and pressed the muzzle of the pistol against the man's ear. "Best if you stay still, my friend. Preferably with hands behind your head." He looked up, smiled disarmingly at Malet and said, "Honoured to meet you, General."

Malet stared back at him, spellbound. Lafon, having regained some of his colour, had collapsed back into his seat, while Balthus and Rateau continued to regard Grant like startled rabbits.

"General," Hawkwood said into the stunned silence, "allow me to introduce my associate, Captain Rémy."

"Associate?" Malet said. He eyed Grant warily before swivelling and fixing Hawkwood with a Medusa stare. "Care to explain yourself, Captain?"

Hawkwood lowered the pistol. "Certainly, General. I didn't feel comfortable walking the streets without additional protection, so I arranged for Captain Rémy to watch my back. Seems I made the right decision, though I've no idea who this is."

With some reluctance, Malet switched his attention back to Grant and then to the man under Grant's guard. A light of recognition came on behind his eyes and the flesh around his jaw tightened. "No, but I do. It appears our departure did not go unnoticed after all."

Lafon's head lifted. Following Malet's gaze he drew a sharp intake of breath.

Grant nodded. "It was the two of you he was following, General. I spotted him when you arrived. Thought I'd keep an eye on him. Good thing I did."

"He's one of Dubuisson's attendants," Malet said, frowning. "New, as I recall, though his name escapes me."

Grant tapped the kneeling man on the side of the head with the pistol barrel. "That's what is known as a hint."

"Claubert," the man muttered. "Michel Claubert."

"There you go, Michel," Grant said amiably. "Not so difficult, was it?"

"I assume he has no weapon?" Malet enquired, looking to Grant for confirmation.

"No," Grant shook his head. "I made sure."

Malet nodded. "All right, better sit him down."

"You heard the general," Grant said. "Up you come." Dragging Claubert to his feet, the Scot pushed him towards the empty chair.

"I find it curious that he followed us," Malet said, casting an eye towards the sullen individual now slumped before him, hair hanging lankly over his brow. "It makes me wonder why he didn't sound the alarm and alert Doctor Dubuisson instead."

"How new?" Hawkwood asked.

Malet turned. "What?"

"You said he was a *new* attendant. How new?"

"I'm not sure; three, perhaps four days, I think. Why?"

Hawkwood was watching Claubert. He saw it then; the tensing of the shoulders, the slight dilation of the nostrils and the widening of the eyes. The seriousness of his predicament wasn't the only thing on the man's mind.

"I'm guessing he's not really an attendant."

Malet's head came round.

Hawkwood stood over the man in the chair. "Am I right?"

Hawkwood already had some idea of the answer. In the same way that the general had seen the soldier in him, Hawkwood had been a Runner long enough to recognize, if not a fellow police officer, then someone in a similar line of work.

Claubert remained silent, though the attempt at defiance did not extend to his eyes which remained in constant motion as they surveyed the men around him.

Hawkwood placed his pistol against Claubert's forehead. "Three seconds. One . . . two . . ." Hawkwood thumbed back the hammer. The ratchet sound was incredibly loud. "Thr—"

"Brigade de Sûreté," Claubert blurted quickly. He tried not to flinch but couldn't help himself.

Balthus let out a gasp.

"*Police*?" Lafon looked more shocked by that revelation than by Hawkwood's threat to scatter a man's brains all over the floor.

"And why would a Sûreté man be posing as a nursing home employee, I wonder?" Malet asked.

"My God!" Lafon breathed hoarsely. "They do know!"

Malet held up a warning hand.

"No, Hawkwood said, stepping away and un-cocking the pistol. "They don't. If they did, they'd be here in force."

Hawkwood's mind went back to the newspaper articles he'd glanced through when he'd been searching for something to read to Maître Perraux. There had been mention of the Brigade de Sûreté there, he recalled. He tried to remember what he'd read. Other than that it was a new department specially created to fight crime, not a whole lot.

Coincidences did happen, Hawkwood knew, but not with something like this. He wondered about the odds of the Sûreté placing a man inside the clinic a couple of days after his visit with the general.

Malet stared hard at Claubert. "So, why were you there?"

Though he was trying desperately not to let it show, Claubert's courage was ebbing fast. He'd found himself in awkward situations before, but this was different. Staring into the faces of the two armed men, he had his first taste of what it was to feel real fear. He wasn't sure if it was the cold touch of metal that was more frightening or the expression in those grey-blue eyes. What he did know was that when the dark-haired man placed the pistol against his skull, his stomach had contracted and his bowels had turned to gruel. So much for the easy assignment that Vidocq had promised him. What in the name of God had he stumbled into?

"If I were you, I'd answer the man."

It was the one who'd accosted him out on the landing who'd spoken. The suggestion was posed cordially enough, but that was what scared Claubert. The power of the arm around his throat and the threat whispered in his ear was still a vivid memory and a small, quiet voice in Claubert's brain told him that this one was every bit as dangerous as his companion.

"We're waiting," Malet prompted.

Claubert's throat felt as if it was filled with cobwebs.

"Still waiting," Malet said, sounding remarkably calm.

Claubert swallowed. The effort to clear his throat was only partially successful.

"Very well," Malet said, shrugging dismissively. "Shoot him."

Claubert threw up a hand as if to ward off the shot, but he wasn't quick enough. Grant stepped forward, placed the pistol against Claubert's temple and spread his left hand palm out above the gun barrel to prevent blood splatter.

"I was there to keep a watch on you, General." Claubert felt a bead of moisture slide down the sides of his brow. Not rain, he knew, but sweat.

Grant lowered the pistol.

"Why?" Malet snapped.

Claubert blinked.

"Answer me," Malet said, his voice growing even harder.

Claubert shook his head. "I don't know."

Grant cocked the pistol. "Wrong answer."

Claubert cringed. "I don't know, General, honestly! I wasn't told. My orders were to watch you and make a note of anyone who visited you or spoke to you."

Malet considered that. "Where did the orders come from?"

The question brought forth a puzzled look. "Brigade headquarters, General."

As if to say: *Where else would they have come from?*

"May I have a word, sir?" Hawkwood interjected quietly.

Malet turned. His expression was pensive. He nodded.

Drawing Malet to the other side of the room, Hawkwood lowered his voice. "With respect, General, knowing where his orders came *from* isn't really the point; not now. What's important is that our friend here doesn't get the chance to report *back*. My guess is that so far he's probably the only one who knows you and the abbé have absconded, so his being here means we still have the advantage."

Hawkwood waited as his words were digested.

Malet still looked unsure. "You think so?"

Hawkwood kept silent, and waited.

Finally, Malet's chin came up. He nodded. "You're quite right,

Captain." He stared thoughtfully towards the man in the chair. "So, any suggestions on what to *do* with our uninvited guest?"

Looking across the room, it wasn't hard to guess what thoughts were going through the Sûreté man's mind. He'd be berating his idiocy, knowing he should have been more careful, and he'd be ashamed that he hadn't put up more of a fight. Mostly, though, he'd be frightened.

"There's only one," Hawkwood said. "And you don't need me to tell you what that is."

Malet did not respond, though his lips formed a thin line.

"We can't keep him here, General. He's seen and heard too much."

Hawkwood didn't have to look to know that Grant was watching him, but he glanced at the Scot anyway and was rewarded with an imperceptible nod. It told him that Grant had understood why he had taken Malet aside and that there was little other course of action they could take. And the consequences would have to take care of themselves.

A resigned look spread across Malet's face. He sighed and said heavily, "You'll deal with it?"

"That's what I'm here for, General," Hawkwood said.

Malet nodded. He was about to turn away, when he said, "By the way, Captain, who gave you permission to include your friend Rémy in our plans?"

"That would be you, sir," Hawkwood said evenly.

"What? When did I do that?"

"When you employed your wife to ask me if I knew a good counterfeiter."

The general's eyebrows rose. "*Captain Rémy* is your counterfeiter?"

"You said you wanted to shake his hand, General. Looks like you're going to get your wish."

Which was one way of avoiding the question. But then Grant had *assisted* with the process, so it wasn't that much of a stretch. Hawkwood didn't think it was worth confusing the issue by confessing that it had been a British agent who'd actually printed out the documents, any more than he was prepared to tell Malet that Grant's pseudonym had been borrowed from a bottle of cognac.

Some things were probably best left unsaid.

"So he knows everything?" Malet said, with a hint of suspicion.

"He knows what I know, General," Hawkwood said, wondering how much that was and how much Malet was still keeping to himself.

Malet fixed Hawkwood with another penetrating gaze before nodding in acceptance.

On the other side of the room, Claubert knew they were talking about him. He might have been damp and in disarray from the downpour and bruised from his encounter with the clinic wall, but neither condition had affected his brain.

His fate was being discussed and he was in little doubt as to what the outcome was going to be. He could read it in their faces, and what made the situation all the more chilling was that they obviously didn't care two sous that he was in the room with them.

His first priority, therefore, was escape. He considered the odds. With six against one he didn't rate his chances very highly. But then, he thought, maybe those odds could be reduced, because the only ones that really counted were the two who were armed. Claubert doubted the general had the speed to stop him. The same applied to Lafon, especially with his injured foot. The two younger men were in better shape, but they had no weapons and looked almost as wary of the other two as he was himself. No, the danger would come from the men with the guns, but if he could catch them off guard, maybe, just maybe, he had a chance. Feverishly, he tried to remember if the dark-haired one with the scars on his face had turned the key when he'd pushed the door shut. The thought then occurred to Claubert that if he thought about it for too long, it'd be too late. There was nothing else to do but go for it.

And pray.

Grant and Hawkwood were exchanging a glance when Claubert launched himself from the chair. Caught unawares,

Grant only had time to see the alarm explode across Hawkwood's face before he was struck a tremendous blow between his shoulder blades and Claubert, using all his weight and momentum, shoved him across the room.

As Grant went flying, Claubert leapt for the door. Malet was starting to turn when Grant's body slammed into him. Hawkwood was already moving but, knocked off balance by the collision, he watched helplessly as Claubert's hand curled around the door knob.

The Sûreté man hauled back the bolt and tore the door open.

Grant raised his pistol. Instinctively, Hawkwood hit Grant's wrist, diverting his aim. "No!"

Claubert threw himself into the corridor and sprinted for the stairs.

Elbowing Malet aside, and with a sharp order to Balthus and Rateau to stay put, Hawkwood tossed his pistol to Grant and ran for the door. By the time he hit the first stair Claubert had reached the landing below and was heading down.

But Claubert, in his haste, had forgotten how treacherous a fresh layer of mud could be. Hurdling the last half-dozen stairs, he was on the ground floor and halfway through the door leading to the courtyard when his heel shot from under him. Putting out an arm to break his fall didn't help. Letting out a yelp, his hip and elbow struck the flagstones and he slid across the rain-soaked ground like an upturned turtle.

Winded, he managed to scramble to his feet. Ignoring the pain, he looked frantically for the entrance to the passage that would take him back to the street. Aware of a dark figure erupting from the tenement's doorway, he didn't dare turn around. Fear drove him on.

Hawkwood had seen Claubert lose his footing and very nearly went the same way, but as his boots started to slide he put out a hand and using the door frame to regain his balance he managed to exit into the courtyard without injury.

He'd tossed Grant his pistol because he knew it would only hamper him. He'd also been fearful of using it. Both he and Grant had been bluffing back in the apartment, each knowing that a shot was more likely to draw attention than the sound of an altercation. The ploy had worked. Claubert had been too preoccupied with survival to have seen through the deception. Hawkwood didn't want to use any firearm if he could help it. A silent kill was just as effective.

Then Claubert went down again.

He was getting off his knees, the rain teeming down his face, his clothes soaked and mud splattered, when Hawkwood reached him. The Sûreté man tried to lash out and twist away, but it was a wild swing and he wasn't agile enough.

Hawkwood deflected the blow and broke Claubert's neck from behind. He did it quickly and cleanly and without fuss, the snap of the bone almost inaudible beneath the sound of the rain. As Claubert's body went limp, Hawkwood held him close and took a cautious look around. There had been no witnesses. There was only the downpour and the darkness.

Hawkwood placed his hands under the dead man's armpits and dragged the corpse across the flagstones towards the corner of the courtyard. Then, positioning it head first, he pushed it over the lip of the well. The body made no sound as it fell. There was no way of telling how deep the shaft was; looking down it was no help. It was too dark. He listened for the confirmation of a splash or a hard landing and thought he heard a series of faint thuds a couple of seconds after he'd let go, but he couldn't be sure.

There was no rope or pail in sight. The well looked as if it hadn't been used for years. Even the rain couldn't mask the foetid smell that was rising from it. When or even *if* the body was found, with luck it would be assumed that the dead man had lost his way and stumbled over the edge in the dark, probably as a result of having had a few glasses too many. A broken neck wouldn't seem unusual under those circumstances.

Hawkwood turned. His breath caught in his throat. A shadowy form had materialized at the door of the tenement. He recovered when he saw it was Grant, holding a pistol in each hand.

The Scot's face was grim. "I was getting worried, laddie." He whispered the words in English as Hawkwood drew near.

"No need," Hawkwood said. "It's done."

There was regret in Grant's eyes. "So I saw," he murmured, returning Hawkwood's pistol to him. "Not what we needed."

"No," Hawkwood agreed. "But it could have been worse. He might have gotten away."

Grant did not smile as they made their way back up the stairs. "You think the police know about *us*?"

"I don't see how they could," Hawkwood said.

"You think it's something we have to worry about?" Grant murmured.

"Probably, but I'll cross that bridge when I come to it. I've a more pressing question."

"What's that?" Grant asked.

"I'd like to know what our friends Balthus and Rateau are for," Hawkwood said.

"You killed him?" Lafon made it sound more like an accusation than an enquiry. Hawkwood suspected it was Lafon's way of masking his relief that the threat had been averted by someone else. That way he'd be able to convince himself that, as far as responsibility for the man's death was concerned, he didn't have to wash the blood from his own hands.

Before Hawkwood could respond, Malet said, "Captain Dumas was operating under my orders, Jean-Baptiste. He did what was necessary. Let's not forget what forces the man represented and why he was here. Had it not been for Captain Rémy's swift action in the first place, we might never have known about Claubert and our mission could have been severely compromised. So, while his demise is deeply regrettable, we must not allow it to distract us from our path. God knows, there may be more casualties before the night is through. It's our duty to try and prevent that and to keep ourselves and the citizens of Paris safe so that we may live to face our new future together. Let that be our creed."

For a moment Lafon looked as if he was about to say something, but then, as if sensing that remonstration was useless or perhaps cowed into acquiescence by the strength of Malet's gaze, he nodded mutely.

Malet spread his hands. He looked around the room. "Good. We've only a short time to prepare so we'll speak no more about it. First, though, I'd like to pay tribute to you, Captain Rémy. Captain Dumas tells me it's you we have to thank for the excellent workmanship on the documentation."

Grant gave a self-deprecating smile. "You're most welcome, sir."

Malet clapped Grant on the shoulder. "I assume, by the way, seeing that he's not spoken of you, that you and Captain Dumas are former comrades-in-arms?" Malet threw Hawkwood a reproving glance.

"Indeed we are, General. We fought together in Spain."

"Then you've proved your worth thrice over, Captain Rémy. I say again, thank you, and welcome!" As he drew the document pouch towards him, his eyes swept the men gathered round. "So, gentlemen, enough talk. Shall we get to it?"

It took less than an hour to put the finishing touches to the forged paperwork, with Hawkwood, Grant, Balthus and Rateau inserting dates and the general and the abbé applying names and signatures. When the ink was dry, each document was placed in an inscribed envelope which was then sealed with a globule of red wax.

"L?" Hawkwood said, as he watched Lafon press the engraved L on his signet ring into the still-molten seals.

Malet nodded. "We thought we'd take advantage of Jean-Baptiste's personal seal because it could mean a number of things: Liberty, His Majesty King Louis, or even Secretary of the Senate, Lanjuinais. Hopefully, people will accept it as an additional stamp of authority. In any case, it's not the wrapping; it's the contents we want them to take note of."

Hawkwood had to admit the seals were an impressive touch. He looked up and said casually, "Captain Rémy and I were wondering when we get to meet General Lamotte?"

Balthus and Rateau exchanged puzzled glances. From their expressions the name was evidently new to them, too, suggesting Malet hadn't taken them fully into his confidence either, which was interesting, Hawkwood thought.

Malet smiled. "Don't worry, you'll be meeting him shortly."

He turned back to Balthus and Rateau. "Has everything else been made ready?"

Balthus, brow still creased from the mention of the imminent arrival of another, as yet unseen, senior officer, nodded. "As you instructed, General."

"Very good. In that case, if you gentlemen will excuse me, I must away to make myself presentable. I need to look my best for the troops, after all." The general nodded towards a large trunk that was standing against the wall. "You'll find everything you need in that portmanteau. I hope the fit is correct, Captain," he added, addressing Hawkwood. "My wife made the purchases, though I'm afraid the responsibility for guessing your size rests with me."

Before Hawkwood could think of a reply, General Malet had already disappeared into the bedchamber.

Balthus and Rateau moved to the trunk.

The first item that came to light when the lid was lifted was a bright tricolour sash. Beneath it was a grey bicorne hat with a white cockade. Balthus lifted out the sash and handed Rateau the hat, which had been resting on a set of grey-blue breeches, a matching tunic with sky-blue collar and cuffs, and a dark grey cloak. Rateau helped himself to the clothes. Taking them aside, he began to undress. Balthus slipped the sash over his shoulder, adjusting it so that it lay diagonally across his chest.

Hawkwood reached into the trunk and removed a sword and several pistols. He passed them to Grant who, after raising a quizzical eyebrow, checked the guns were loaded before placing them on the table.

Hawkwood turned his attention to the rest of the portmanteau's contents. He lifted out another tunic and set of breeches. There was more clothing below: another uniform with gold braid, three more cloaks and hats, including one with a cockade and a black shako.

"That one's yours, Captain," Balthus said, indicating the uniform Hawkwood was holding.

Hawkwood unfolded the garments, an indigo blue jacket with

white facings, matching red collar and cuffs, and a pair of creased white breeches.

"Infantry of the Line, 8th Regiment," Grant murmured, eyeing the insignia. "Second Battalion, unless I miss my guess. Correct rank, too. It'll suit you nicely, Captain, if I may say so."

To Hawkwood's relief, the uniform proved to be a good fit, save for a slight tightness across the shoulders and under the arms. It was fortunate, he reflected, that he already had the boots. They'd once been the property of a French lieutenant. Hawkwood had liberated them after Talavera, the lieutenant having no more use for them since most of his head had been blown off by a British artillery ball. Hawkwood's own boots had been on their last legs, literally, and Hawkwood had taken full advantage of the lieutenant's misfortune. It was also a matter of practicality. British boots were badly made; the French, on the other hand, took care of their feet – or the officers did, at any rate. The boots had served him well over the intervening years. Who'd have thought, though, that they'd have come in this useful?

Rateau had pulled on the breeches and was struggling with the top button on his tunic when his hands stilled.

The rest of them turned. Hawkwood felt the short hairs on the back of his neck lift.

General Malet stood in the doorway. His dark blue tunic, white stock and breeches were spotless. His black, knee-length boots were buffed to a mirrored shine. The broad sash around his waist matched the gold brocade of his epaulets and cord while the embellished embroidery round the hem, collar and cuffs of his tailcoat complemented the pattern of the braid along the crest of his magnificently plumed hat. His left hand rested on the pommel of a long, curved sabre. His right hand held a leather dispatch wallet. The Légion d'Honneur medal, complete with scarlet ribbon, was pinned to his left breast. His own height, added to the crest of the hat, made him look about seven feet tall.

Malet gave a small bow. "Allow me to present General of Division, Auguste Lamotte." To Hawkwood and Grant he added,

"I see you've already met my Aide de Camp, Lieutenant Rateau, and Police Commissioner Balthus."

General and commissioner. *Two more mysteries solved,* Hawkwood thought, though it would still be interesting to know where the general had found his commissioner and his aide.

"You'll forgive the intrigue, Captain." Malet smiled at Hawkwood's expression. "But I've learnt from past experience that, the less people who are privy to an enterprise in its entirety, the less danger there is of discovery. Hence my decision not to inform you of the nature of André and Jean's contribution to the cause. Likewise I did not advise them of your involvement prior to this evening. I hope you understand?"

"Perfectly, General," Hawkwood said, managing to keep his face neutral. "One can never be too careful."

"Indeed. And in case you were still wondering, André and Jean are former parishioners of the abbé. Jean-Baptiste introduced us during one of their visits to the clinic. It didn't take us long to discover we had a number of interests in common. André's brother is a priest, by the way. His family's from Rennes. It transpired that he and I have several mutual acquaintances; friends of a . . . philosophical persuasion, with a shared interest in the Classics."

Hawkwood assumed that he was supposed to know what that meant, so he nodded sagely.

"André's knowledge of the law has proved invaluable, especially with regards to the legal language we've employed in our documentation. We couldn't have done it without him. As for Jean; he's from the Gironde, like the abbé. What's more important, however, is that he's also a member of the Paris Guard. Thanks to him we have details of Guard numbers, the names of senior personnel and their deployment within the city." Malet paused and smiled. "And the daily passwords."

Rateau, smiling, gave a mock bow.

"As for General Lamotte . . ." Malet swept off his plumed hat, walked forward and laid it on the table. "Unfortunately, there are those who are still indisposed towards the name Malet, so this is a temporary precaution, at least until the city is secured.

The real General Lamotte's a former comrade of mine. He's retired now, so he'll not mind me using his identity – in a good cause, of course."

"May I enquire as to what role you have for me, sir?" Hawkwood asked, buckling on the sword and reaching for the shako that was still taking up space in the trunk. He lifted the shako out. With its gold braid, chin scales, black hackle and the eagle plate set above the peak, it was a splendid piece of headgear.

"Consider yourself my personal voltigeur, Captain Dumas."

Hawkwood suppressed a wry grimace.

Voltigeurs were skirmishers, assigned to French infantry regiments to harass the enemy. It looked as if his military career had come full circle. The twitch at the side of Grant's mouth told Hawkwood that the Scot was also appreciating the irony.

Malet smiled at Grant. "I regret we've no uniform for you, Captain Rémy, due to your, ah, unexpected addition to our ranks."

Malet looked Grant up and down. Grant had forsaken his army tunic for more subdued civilian attire though the dark greatcoat he was wearing could have passed for military wear, especially at night.

"I suggest we pass you off as another of my aides, Captain; a former officer now acting as liaison between the military and the Senate, perhaps. All you have to do is stand by my shoulder and look menacing. I can't see you having any problems with that; can you?"

"None at all, General."

"That's settled then."

Hawkwood looked around the table. He caught Grant's eye and was rewarded with a sly wink.

With the others looking on, the general divided the sealed envelopes into two piles. Leaving one pile on the table, Malet slid the other into the dispatch wallet. Fastening the wallet, he straightened. With a sideways glance towards Hawkwood, which went unseen by the others, he drew himself up and focused his attention on Balthus and Rateau.

"My friends, not long ago I informed you that I'd been approached by the Senate and told that I was to be entrusted with carrying out a special mission on its behalf. You pledged me that, when the time came, I could rely on your support. That hour is now upon us."

The general paused, as if formulating his thoughts, and then continued. "The Senate has been aware for some time that there are certain corrupt elements within the legislature who've been usurping their powers to suit their own individual ends. It is the Senate's ruling that the State must be protected at all costs. Our task, therefore, is to arrest the perpetrators, remove them from office and deliver them to justice.

"Regrettably, this necessitates the installation of a provisional administration which will remain in place until such time as the Senate confirms that the canker has been excised from the heart of government. This must be done if we are to restore France to her former glory. That is why the Senate has called upon men like myself and Abbé Lafon; loyal servants once falsely accused and held against our will but now recognized as true patriots. We may be few in number, but our cause is just and our hearts are strong and there are others who will stand with us. With God's help, we will prevail."

Malet's voice dropped. "First, however, there is something else I need to tell you. In the last few hours, I have become the bearer of momentous tidings, passed on to me by President of the Senate, Sieyès; news which places an even greater urgency on the task before us."

Malet took a deep breath. "Gentlemen, there is no easy way to say this but it is my solemn duty to inform you that Napoleon Bonaparte is dead."

The room went quiet. Their hearts still stirred by Malet's clarion call, Balthus and Rateau's jaws dropped in disbelief.

"Word has reached the Senate by messenger that the Emperor was struck by an enemy bullet two weeks ago beneath the walls of Moscow. The wound turned septic. The surgeons were unable to save him." Malet drew himself up to his full height. "The Senate has assigned me the additional and grave responsibility of announcing His Majesty's death to the troops and citizens of Paris."

A sibilant hiss came from Hawkwood's right. It was Grant. The Scot wasn't acting for effect, making it appear as if he was equally dumfounded by the news. It was because he, like Hawkwood, had seen from their faces that Balthus and Rateau had both been genuinely shaken to the core by Malet's statement. In fact they looked overawed to the point of paralysis. The realization of what he was witnessing hit Hawkwood like a hammer blow, the same way it had hit Grant.

Sweet God Almighty! The poor devils think it's for real!

"Nearly four o'clock. It's time, gentlemen." General Malet pressed the clasp of his watch shut and slid the timepiece into his pocket. "Everything is clear? You all know your assigned duties?"

The five other men around the table nodded.

"Questions?"

No one spoke.

"Good." The general gave a determined nod. "Then let us away."

One by one the men rose to their feet, but as they pushed their chairs back, one of them let out a sharp grunt of pain.

"Jean-Baptiste?" Malet turned quickly.

Lafon waved him away. "It's nothing, just a twinge. It caught me by surprise; that's all."

"You're sure?" Malet frowned.

Lafon smiled ruefully. "Of course. My own fault. I should have taken it more slowly. Lead on, my General. I'm right behind you."

"Very well." Picking up a brace of pistols, Malet tucked one into his sash and the second one inside the document wallet.

Donning his hat, and having swapped his coat for a military cloak, the general tucked the wallet under his arm and turned towards the door. The abbé moved to follow but no sooner had he taken a step forward than he stumbled to one side with a cry. Grabbing the table for support, he fell back into the chair, his face pinched with pain.

Malet swung round. "Jean-Baptiste!"

Lafon gritted his teeth. "I'm all right, really."

"Don't be a fool, man! Look at you! You can barely stand, let alone walk!"

Lafon shook his head. "I can walk. Just give me a few minutes to catch my breath."

"We don't have a few minutes. We have to leave now!"

"A moment then. That's all I ask. Please!"

Malet stared hard at him for several seconds. Finally, coming to a decision, he placed his hand on Lafon's shoulder. "I'm sorry, my friend. You're not going anywhere. You'll only slow us down. Think also what it will look like if we have an injured man in our midst. What sort of message will that send out? We have to appear strong and vigorous." Malet's face softened. He looked almost sorrowful. "Far better that you remain here, at least until Father José gets back. That will give you more time to rest the ankle. Then you can rejoin us."

"But you need me, Claude-François," Lafon begged. "We agreed. You said it was imperative the clergy should be represented. It will show the people that the Church supports the Senate's actions."

"You'll be with us in spirit."

"I don't want to be with you in spirit. I want to be at your side!"

"I'm sorry, Jean-Baptiste, truly I am, but it's for the best."

Lafon opened his mouth to protest, but Malet cut him short: "No, my friend. You stay here and rest – and that's my last word on it."

Lafon hesitated but then, knowing he'd been outmanoeuvred, he nodded resignedly. "Very well. I'll stay until Father José gets back then I'll make for the Place Vendôme and meet you there."

Malet nodded. "I'm glad you're seeing sense."

Lafon smiled wanly and clasped Malet's arm. "I should be with you, my General."

"You will be," Malet said fondly. "Very soon, I promise."

Lafon sank back into the chair. "Then go with God. I'll pray for your safety."

"And I'll pray that God's listening," Malet said.

If God was listening, Hawkwood thought, He could at least have done something about the rain, which, as they left the tenement and crossed the courtyard, was still coming down hard, hammering on to the flagstones and the surrounding slate roofs with the persistence of arrow hail. By the time they emerged on to the rue Saint-Pierre it was hard to see more than a dozen paces in front of them.

Turning east on to the rue Saint Gilles, Hawkwood, his voice lowered, said, "What have you promised them, General?"

"Them?" Malet said, frowning.

"Balthus and Rateau."

Malet gave Hawkwood a sideways look. "You don't think they're here out of a sense of loyalty?"

"To you, General?"

"To France."

"You tell me, sir."

He kept his voice low, though he knew that, despite the two men being only a few paces behind them, the rain would probably drown out his voice.

It had taken a little while for Balthus and Rateau to recover from hearing that the Emperor was dead and that France was again rudderless. Only when Malet had judged them ready to proceed had he unveiled his plan of attack.

There were three main obstacles to overcome, Malet had told them; three factions over which it was necessary to gain control if they were to have any chance of taking the city: the Guard, the Préfecture of Police, and the garrison. They could secure the second if they had control of the first, and the third if they had control of the first two.

There was a game, Malet had added, recently devised, played with small flat oblong tiles. Sometimes it was amusing to stand the tiles on end, spaced one behind the other in a line. The fun was in knocking over the first tile so that it fell against the second which in turn fell against the third tile and so on until all the tiles had fallen.

The first tile was only fifteen minutes away. They were on their way there now.

"I take it Balthus gets to be Commissioner," Hawkwood said. "What have you promised Rateau, apart from his new uniform?"

Malet smiled. "So cynical, Captain?"

"What can I tell you, General. It's a curse."

Malet paused and then said, "All he wants is to improve his position."

It took a second for the statement to sink in.

"He's after *promotion*? That's it?"

"I've promised him a lieutenancy."

"And he's happy with that?"

Malet smiled. "We're fortunate in that they're both modest young men. Their only dream is to make better lives for themselves."

Hawkwood knew his scepticism must still have showed, for Malet said, "They may be younger than you and me, Captain, but they've been around long enough to have seen the upheavals that have befallen the State; the changes that have taken place, the challenges facing us. At their age, it's *all* they've known. It's been more than twenty years since the Bastille was stormed. Since then, unrest of one form or another has become a natural phenomenon; like breathing.

"The difference here is that, for the first time, they have the opportunity to be a part of the change right from the beginning. In future years they'll be able to tell their children and their children's children that they were there, that *they* were the ones who made the difference, the ones who helped shine a light on to the darkness; the ones who changed history. What higher reward could there be? Wouldn't you want that as *your* epitaph?"

"But you didn't feel it necessary to take them into your confidence and tell them that this is all based on a lie?" Hawkwood pointed out.

"If they believe what I told them is true, they will be more convincing in the role."

The bigger the lie, Hawkwood thought.

"It's a thin line you're treading, General. What happens when they find out?"

"Then I'll pray that they'll forgive me and see that I did it for the right reasons."

"You mean they'll have got what they wanted and it won't matter anyway?"

"There is that," Malet said. "Though there's another reason why I've not confided in them."

"And what's that?"

"If we fail – and pray to Heaven we don't – it may just save them from a firing squad. It's just possible that a court will view them not as accomplices but as innocents who believed they were carrying out their duty at the command of a senior officer."

"Somehow, General, if this doesn't go as we want it to, I think that'll be the least of our worries, don't you?"

"Then we must make sure we win, eh, Captain? This time we finish what we started."

"From your lips to God's ear, General," Hawkwood said.

PART IV

19

When he saw the shadowy group of figures emerging from behind the curtain of rain, Private Pappin's first reaction was to stand up straight and try to look alert. It wasn't unknown for Garrison Command to send out patrols every so often to make sure sentries weren't sleeping on duty. Pappin was only a quarter of an hour away from being relieved and he'd been looking forward to handing over to his replacement and heading back into the barracks to the comfort of his mattress. All he needed was some supercilious clod turning up at the last minute and putting him on a charge because he wasn't holding his musket at the right angle.

Peering out of his box outside the gates of Popincourt Barracks, the private watched anxiously as the five men approached. When they were a dozen paces away, he stepped out into the wet, musket held high, and called out nervously, "Halt! Who goes there?"

Almost to his surprise, the men stopped. It struck Pappin that this didn't look like your usual garrison patrol. The hats were the giveaway. Peering closer, he realized with a start that he wasn't looking at a sergeant of patrol; he was staring at a general.

Hawkwood saw the sentry's eyes widen and the barrel of the musket start to waver, and waited, nerves stretched, for Rateau's response to the challenge.

Rateau cleared his throat. "Headquarters patrol."

The sentry hesitated and then, as if suspecting this might be some kind of test, gripped his musket more firmly. "Password?"

Hawkwood held his breath.

"Conspiracy."

He hadn't quite believed it when Rateau had revealed the countersign back at the apartment, but the sergeant had been adamant that it was the correct one for the day. Nevertheless, even as Rateau responded to the private's call, Hawkwood, still doubtful, was wondering how easy it would be to draw his pistol. His coat was already unbuttoned when the sentry signalled them to advance and be recognized. He heard Grant exhale with relief.

As they drew near to the gate, Malet moved his cloak aside, revealing his braid and sash. The sentry's eyes grew even wider.

"General Lamotte, on behalf of the commander of the Paris garrison," Rateau intoned. "Open up."

Hurriedly shouldering his musket, the sentry nodded dumbly. His hand reached for the bell pull. Hawkwood heard a distant jangle and was reminded of his entry into the Dubuisson clinic.

After what seemed an interminable delay but could only have been a matter of minutes, the gate behind the sentry box swung open and a man wearing the uniform of a National Guard sergeant emerged carrying a lantern. He had the look of someone recently aroused from slumber and didn't look best pleased. His shako was slightly askew and the top two buttons of his tunic were undone.

"You arse-wipe, this had better be import—" His voice trailed off and he stopped dead, eyes moving warily over the group of men standing before him.

"Oh, it is, Sergeant," Malet said. "I need to speak with your duty officer."

Caught in two minds, the sergeant wasn't sure what to do first, admit them or stand to attention and do up his buttons. In the end he gave the sentry the lantern and led the way through the gate, to where another uniformed figure, alerted by the commotion, was emerging from the guardroom. Helmeted and evidently more alert than his fellow NCO, he came to attention at the sight of Malet's gold braid and threw up a hasty salute.

"Sergeant-Major Rabutel at your service, General."

"You're the duty officer?" Malet asked.

"Yes, sir."

"I'm here to see the commandant. Colonel Soulier, isn't it?"

Rabutel nodded. "Yes, General."

"Where is he?"

The two sergeants exchanged glances. Rabutel swallowed nervously. "He's in his quarters, sir."

There was a noise from the doorway. Hawkwood and Grant spun quickly, only to discover it was the sentry. He was staring at them with eyes that would not have disgraced an awestruck dormouse. Hawkwood wondered if it had occurred to the man that he had deserted his post. Presumably not.

"Take me to him," Malet said. "Now."

"Sir?" Rabutel hesitated.

"Something wrong, Sergeant-Major?" Malet asked.

"Er, no, sir. It's just that the colonel's indisposed. He has influenza and the medical officer's confined him to his bed."

"And you've forgotten where he lives?" Malet said.

Rabutel looked confused. "Er . . . no, General."

"Good, you can still take me to him then, can't you?"

The sergeant-major coloured. "Er . . . yes, sir." He threw a glance towards Hawkwood and Grant but must have realized that sympathy was in short supply for he averted his eyes quickly.

Malet swung round and pointed at the sentry. "You, what's your name?"

The private blinked. Generals rarely, if ever, addressed private soldiers. He drew himself up and found his voice.

"Private Pappin, sir."

"Pappin from Popincourt?" Malet smiled. "That has a nice ring to it. Very well, Private Pappin, you can light the way. And you –" Malet pointed his finger at the hapless Sergeant of the Guard "– fasten your damned buttons."

*   *   *

Colonel Gabriel Soulier, clad in his nightshirt and dripping with fever, sat slumped on the end of his bed and stared at his visitors with bloodshot eyes. A hook-nosed man with a cleft chin and bony shoulders, it was hard to tell his age. He looked, temporarily at least, like death warmed over.

They'd been admitted into the colonel's quarters by his wife, a well-upholstered woman with premature grey hair, who after greeting and showing the visitors into the bedchamber had departed to her dressing room, leaving her ailing spouse to fend for himself.

Malet stared down at the invalid.

"I'm sorry to hear you've not been feeling well, Colonel. My apologies for arriving unannounced. However, I regret my business cannot wait. I am General Auguste Lamotte. These are my aides, Captains Dumas and Rémy, Lieutenant Rateau and Commissioner Balthus. I come bearing a dispatch from the Senate."

"Senate?" Soulier frowned. His eyes moved along the line of uniforms and faces. "At this hour? Has something happened?"

"I'm afraid it has, Colonel. I regret to inform you that we've received word that the Emperor has been killed in Russia. The Senate is in the process of forming an interim government and the 10th Cohort has been designated to help take control of the city. I have your orders here."

There were sharp gasps from Rabutel and the sentry as Malet drew the dispatch wallet from beneath his cloak and extracted several of the sealed envelopes.

Soulier stared at Malet in horror. "It's not true! It can't be!"

"I'm sorry, Colonel. There's no mistake. Here –" Malet held out one of the envelopes. "This is a Sénatus-Consulte, issued only a few hours ago. As you'll see, it's signed by both President Sieyès and Secretary Lanjuinais and witnessed by General of Division Malet, the newly appointed Garrison Commander. Read it for yourself."

Hawkwood caught Grant's eye. This was the first test of the documentation. As Hawkwood watched, Grant slowly unbuttoned his coat so that he could get to the pistol at his waist. Hawkwood found he was holding his breath once again.

Soulier took the envelope with a shaking hand, broke the seal and withdrew the contents. Fresh beads of sweat began to gather across his forehead as his eyes moved half-focused across the page.

"I don't understand, General," he said after only a few seconds, shaking his head in confusion. "What is this?"

Hawkwood tensed for a moment, until he realized that Soulier was not querying the validity of the document, he was simply in no fit state to decipher the contents, let alone appreciate the importance of the orders contained within.

"Allow me, Colonel," Malet said, almost gently. He held out his hand.

Soulier passed the document back. Although only a few minutes had elapsed since they'd entered the bedchamber, Hawkwood thought the colonel looked to be in a worse state than when they'd arrived. It was as if news of the Emperor's death had exacerbated his condition. In fact, he looked like a man who was almost on the verge of tears.

Malet said, "What it means, Colonel, is that the Senate has issued a decree expediting the formation of a provisional government under the presidency of General Jean-Victor Moreau. It is required that this interim authority watches over the internal and external safety of the State and enters into immediate negotiations with the military powers for the re-establishment of peace. A new constitution is to be drawn up and submitted to the General Assembly. As part of the negotiations, the afore-mentioned General Malet has replaced General Hulin as Commander of the Paris Garrison."

Malet smiled. "That's where you come in, Colonel. I've a letter here from General Malet which places all officers and men of the 10th Cohort under my direct command." Malet paused and extracted another document from its envelope. "It also confirms your promotion to the rank of General of Brigade."

Soulier's head came up. "I've been promoted?"

Not that ill, then, Hawkwood thought.

Malet nodded and smiled. "In appreciation of your long and faithful service, Colonel, as befits a veteran of Marengo and Austerlitz, and in anticipation of your loyalty to the new régime.

I'm also authorized to present you with this Treasury note for the amount of one hundred thousand francs, countersigned by General Malet. This will enable you to settle all pay arrears. It's also the Senate's way of showing that it has full confidence in the 10th Cohort's integrity."

Malet drew the note from the wallet and passed it to Soulier, who was starting to look overwhelmed, unsure whether to continue mourning the death of his Emperor or weep with joy at the gifts being bestowed upon him from on high.

Further dark patches of sweat began to blossom across the colonel's night shirt as the significance of the largesse continued to sink into his befuddled brain. He shook his head slowly as if to clear it. "I'm honoured, General. I don't know what to say." His chin came up. "What should I do now?"

Malet frowned. "I can see you're not yet at your best, Col—, ah, General. Why don't we get your adjutant in here? He can shoulder some of your responsibilities and it'll save me having to explain myself twice."

Malet turned. "Sergeant-Major, who is the adjutant?"

Rabutel came to attention. "That would be Captain Piquerel, sir."

"Fetch him."

"Sir." Rabutel turned for the door.

"Sergeant-Major."

"General?" Rabutel turned.

"You will not tell anyone, including Captain Piquerel, anything of what you've just heard. Is that clear?"

Rabutel nodded. "Yes, General."

"One word and you'll be scrubbing out the latrine block for the rest of your life. Understand?"

The sergeant-major paled. "Yes, General."

"Very good. Off you go. And make it quick."

Rabutel disappeared. He wasn't gone very long, finally returning with a stern-looking uniformed man with a salt-and-pepper moustache.

"Captain Piquerel?" Malet said.

The newcomer quivered to attention. "At your command, General."

An officer of the old school, Hawkwood thought immediately. Probably, like his commanding officer, a veteran and used to obeying orders without argument.

Piquerel, puzzled by the number of men gathered around the bed, looked to his commandant for guidance. "Colonel?"

Soulier rose painstakingly to his feet and gripped his adjutant's arm. "Terrible news, Captain. The Emperor's been killed."

Piquerel went white. Instinctively, he looked towards the most senior officer in the room for confirmation.

"It's true, Captain," Malet said gravely. "It's why we're here. The Senate has tasked the 10th Cohort with special duties. When the news reaches the streets it'll be the Cohort's job to ensure the people remain calm during the transition."

"Transition?" Piquerel said.

"A provisional government is to be installed. The Senate requires the support of the Guards and the garrison to make sure everything goes as smoothly as possible. There may well be some initial unrest, so I expect every man here to carry out his orders to the letter. As your colonel is currently indisposed it will be your responsibility to prepare the troops. Can I count on you, Captain?"

Piquerel flicked a quick glance towards Soulier as if seeking reassurance and squared his shoulders. "Yes, General."

"Good. There's much to do. Assemble the men. Don't sound reveille. There's to be as little disturbance as possible. We don't want to spread alarm if we can avoid it. Use your NCOs to round them up. You're not to tell them about the Emperor's demise either. That's my job. Understood?"

"Sir!" Piquerel, still standing heels together, nodded determinedly.

"Go," Malet said.

He caught Hawkwood's eye.

So far, so good.

*   *   *

Hawkwood's first thought, as he watched the barracks spring into life, was of termites disturbed in a nest, but then as the minutes went by and as the men of the cohort assembled by torchlight he decided

353

that the comparison was wrong. Termites were probably better organized.

He recalled what Grant had told him about the Guard being made up of individuals who'd been considered unfit for active service. Looking at the calibre of the men who were gathering in the courtyard it wasn't hard to see why the majority of them had been held back from frontline deployment. At first he thought it might have been the rain that was responsible for their general state of bedragglement, but as the numbers swelled and ranks formed, Hawkwood realized it was the men themselves who were the problem. There was no sense of pride or discipline. He could see it in the state of their uniforms and the way they handled their weapons and by the exasperated faces of the officers and NCOs who were trying to herd them into line. In the end, Hawkwood estimated it had taken some forty-five minutes for the twelve hundred or so men to come to order.

If every other Guard unit was of the same standard, Hawkwood mused, it'd be worth sending a message to Wellington telling him that if he were to release fifty riflemen from the Peninsula, they could take Paris in a day and the country within a week. He looked at Grant. The Scot met his gaze and a corner of his mouth turned down in dismay.

By the time the last of the men had slotted into place the rain had eased considerably, but the first ones to have answered the call were already cold and damp and wondering aloud why they'd been ordered from their beds at five o'clock in the morning, until Sergeant Major Rabutel, lit by hissing torch flames and with raindrops glittering along the rim of his shako, bellowed, "SILENCE IN THE RANKS!"

As the cohort waited expectantly, General Malet, who'd been watching from the wings, removed his cloak so that his uniform was in full view. He caught Adjutant Piquerel's eye and nodded.

Piquerel faced the assembled men. "Soldiers of the 10th Cohort! I present General Lamotte! He comes to us bearing important news from the Senate!"

Accompanied by Balthus in his Commissioner's sash, Malet stepped forward. Illuminated by both lantern and torchlight, shadows played across his long face.

"Good morning, gentlemen!"

The greeting echoed out around the yard, eclipsing the patter of the rain. Generals of Division didn't turn up on the doorstep every morning of the week. The men stared at his gold braid, his plumed hat and his sword, wondering what was so important that they had been gathered to hear him speak. He had the attention of everyone present.

Malet placed his left hand on his sword hilt and began again: "Gentlemen, it is my solemn duty to inform you that Emperor Napoleon Bonaparte is dead, killed beneath the gates of Moscow! By senatorial decree, the imperial government is hereby annulled!"

An explosion of disbelieving voices followed the announcement.

"SILENCE!" Rabutel, louder this time.

As the men quietened around him, Malet continued: "I would ask you to remain calm while Commissioner Balthus reads the Senate's proclamation." He turned to Balthus. "Commissioner . . ."

Balthus donned a pair of spectacles. Gathering himself, the lawyer began to read aloud.

"Session of twenty-second October, 1812; opened at eight p.m. under the presidency of Emmanuel-Joseph Sieyès. The occasion of this extraordinary session was the receipt of the news of the death of the Emperor Napoleon, under the walls of Moscow, on the seventh of this month. The Senate, after mature consideration of the condition of affairs caused by this event, named a Commission to consider the danger of the situation, and to arrange for the maintenance of government and order. After having received the report of this Commission, the following orders were passed . . ."

As the words of the forged Sénatus-Consulte permeated the courtyard, Hawkwood studied the ranks of men. After their initial reaction, many appeared to have been struck dumb by the news, but as his gaze moved along the lines he could see that loss and sadness weren't the only emotions on show. A fair proportion of the Guard were trying hard to suppress excitement, some even looked pleased. It wasn't hard to guess why: no more army, no more drilling, no more being yelled at, no more bloody war. When Balthus announced that the

Provisional Government would open peace negotiations with the allies and withdraw troops from the Peninsula and Italy, a good few men even let out a ragged cheer. They looked happier still when Balthus told them that four million francs were to be placed at the disposal of the newly appointed Head of the Garrison, General Malet, to be distributed among troops who displayed conspicuous loyalty to the new régime. Slowly but surely, a sense of optimism began to permeate the cohort's ranks.

But the rain continued to fall and Hawkwood knew the longer the troops stood there the quicker the good mood would evaporate. It occurred to him that the men to the rear probably hadn't been able to hear the pronouncements clearly over the rain and had been relying on the men in front to relay the news back to them. Already, the guardsmen on the fringes, wet and miserable, with no real knowledge of what was happening, were starting to shuffle restlessly.

When Balthus had finished relaying the Senate's intentions to the troops, his spectacle lenses were misted almost to the point of being opaque. As he retreated to one side, wiping them on the hem of his sash, Malet stepped forward again.

Hawkwood studied the general's face. Not a hint of deceit was visible. It dawned on Hawkwood that perhaps Malet had lived with his schemes and prepared himself for this moment for so long he'd reached the stage where he'd come to believe that he really was there with the Senate's blessing.

A good general could gauge the mood of his troops. Malet, clearly sensing the growing irritation of the men facing him, knew that if he was to have any hope of drawing them to his banner, the time was nigh. "Soldiers of the 10th Cohort!" he roared. "I can see you've had enough of the rain! Well, to tell you the truth, so have I! But I'm not God! I can't promise I can make the bloody stuff go away!"

Malet stared at them, his gaze moving along the lines, making eye contact. He smiled ruefully. A few men even smiled back. Some grinned. It was a beginning.

Malet's voice rose.

"Some things, however, I *can* promise you! No more tyranny, for one thing! The Emperor is dead, slain in the Russian snows! The Grand Army is making its way back home. Many brave men have died. Some will say they died for France, others will say they gave their lives for a needless cause: to serve the dreams of a Corsican usurper! Well, I say to you: this is not a time for recrimination! It's a time for loyal French men, and women, to come together and create their *own* destiny!

"It's time for peace, not war! Negotiations with our enemies are already under way. Before long, our armies will be stood down. Within the next seven days, any soldier of the Paris Garrison who wishes to return home will be granted travel permits. Those who decide to continue in the service will be merged into a new Corps of Guards. There will be rewards for long service and an increase in pay for all troops, NCOs and officers. Within the next twenty-four hours *all* soldiers will receive one month's wages as a gratuity for their loyalty to the motherland! This is by order of the Senate! I know that times have been hard and many sacrifices have been made, but change *is* coming! You can trust me on that! Long live the Provisional Government! Long live France!"

Hawkwood watched as shoulders lifted, heads came up and backs straightened. *Dear God,* he thought. *It's working! The man's done it!*

Malet stepped aside. "They're all yours, Captain," he said to the startled Piquerel. "I want them ready to march in fifteen minutes."

The adjutant saluted. "Yes, sir." He turned to Rabutel. "You heard the general."

"Sir!"

As the sergeant-major spun away, Piquerel enquired tentatively, "Where are we marching to, General?"

Malet was about to reply when Piquerel's attention shifted. The captain stiffened.

Former Colonel, now General, Soulier had left his sickbed. Dressed in his uniform, his face still pale and his gait as he walked towards them tentative and unsteady, there was nevertheless a determined expression on his gaunt face. Presenting himself before Malet, he raised his hand in a shaky but formal salute.

"Reporting for duty, sir."

Malet smiled. "Then you're just in time, *General*. I was about to have Captain Piquerel deploy the men."

"I await your orders, sir." Soulier clicked his heels together.

Malet nodded. In a comradely gesture, he laid his hand on Soulier's shoulder. "There are six companies under your command, correct?"

"Yes, sir."

"Excellent. Companies one through five are to come with me; 6th Company will remain here with you. Your fortitude is much appreciated, but you should still be in your sickbed. Give yourself an hour, gather your strength. Then take your Company directly to the Hotel de Ville. Present yourself to the Prefect of the Seine, Frochot. Tell him he's to make immediate preparations for the installation of the new government. You're then to wait for me there. Clear?"

"Yes, General. It will be done."

Malet turned. "Captain Piquerel, you're with me. And I need a man to accompany my aide, Lieutenant Rateau, on an errand. Arrange it, will you?"

"At once, sir." Piquerel beckoned to a passing corporal and relayed Malet's request.

Malet beckoned Rateau to him. "You know what to do?"

Rateau nodded. "Sir."

"Very good." Malet turned. "Your escort's here."

A guardsman had appeared out of the mass of men. He saluted nervously, "Private Mazarin, sir, reporting as ordered."

"You're to go with the lieutenant," Piquerel told him.

"Sir." The guardsman moved to Rateau's side.

Rateau looked to Malet and saluted. "General."

"Carry out your orders, Lieutenant."

"Sir."

Malet watched as the two men headed towards the gates. He drew out his watch and checked the dial. With a grunt of satisfaction he slipped the watch back into his pocket and turned to the waiting Piquerel.

"The rest of the men are ready?"

Piquerel nodded. "Awaiting your orders, General."

"Very good, Captain. Move them out."

"Yes, sir." Piquerel saluted. "And our destination?"

General Malet smiled. "Rue due Roi de Sicile – La Force prison."

Hawkwood was no stranger to houses of detention. He'd visited enough of them in his time as a Runner to be able to tell the difference between the bad and the unspeakable. As he drew near to its grim exterior he had no doubt in his mind that La Force would have given any of London's more notorious gaols a good run for their money, for the place wasn't just one building but a ramshackle collection of festering ruins that could have been lifted from any one of the London rookeries. In the dim light of an October dawn and with the rain still drizzling down, even the Conciergerie was a palace of light by comparison.

It had taken a little over twenty minutes to cover the distance from the barracks to the prison and the column's passing had not gone unnoticed. A thousand-plus guardsmen marching in formation are not quiet beasts by nature and the narrow streets had echoed to the tramp of marching feet. However, it was now Friday, the day of the weekly review, and the sight of troops parading through the capital, while of moderate interest to an impressive number of early risers, did not in itself incite panic or even much interest among those citizens who did go to the trouble of peering out of their windows on to the puddled cobblestones below. It was clearly nothing more than garrison manoeuvres. Nothing to be concerned about.

Entering the rue du Roi de Sicile, Malet gave the order for the column to halt. As he did so two figures stepped out from a nearby archway. Hawkwood recognized Rateau and the guardsman. They had not returned empty-handed. Each carried a bundle under his arm. Rateau also had an oilskin pouch in his hand. He held the pouch out to Malet. Malet took it, lifted the flap and sifted through the contents. Hawkwood saw they were the documents that the general had separated earlier and left behind at the apartment.

"You'd no problems, I take it?" Malet said.

"None, sir," Rateau confirmed.

"And the abbé? Has his ankle improved?"

"He wasn't there, General."

"Really?" Malet looked momentarily surprised, but then, as if aware for the first time that the sky was growing lighter and that time had moved on, he nodded. "He'll be on his way to meet us, I expect."

"How did you gain entry?" Hawkwood asked.

"Father José was back, Captain. He let us in."

"My wife's safe?" Malet asked quickly.

"Father José gave me this, sir." Rateau handed over a small envelope. "I understand it's from Madame."

"Thank you." Malet took the envelope and removed the note from inside. His expression softened as he read the contents. Without speaking he folded the letter, returned it to the envelope, which he folded and pushed up his right sleeve. He looked around.

"Private Pappin!"

The sentry, who by a dint of resourcefulness had somehow managed to remain within earshot, trotted up like a faithful gun dog. Astonishingly, he still had the lantern with him, though it was now unlit.

"Sir?"

"I've an assignment for you, Pappin."

Malet handed the soldier two packets of documents. "You're to deliver these without delay. One each to the senior officer at the Courtille Barracks and the Minimes Barracks. Have you got that?"

Still looking slightly overawed, the private nodded.

"Fast as you can," Malet said.

As the guardsman hurried away, Malet turned. "First Company! Captain Steenhouwer!"

A lean, hawk-faced, middle-aged officer stepped out of the column. "Sir?"

"Bring your men."

"Sir."

"Captain Dumas and Captain Rémy, Commissioner Balthus

360

and Lieutenant Rateau, also with me, if you please. You, too."
Malet beckoned to the guardsman who'd accompanied Rateau
to the apartment and who was still clutching his bundle. Giving
the rest of the troops the order to remain where they were,
Malet led the way towards the prison entrance.

The closer they drew to the gaol, the grimmer the place looked.
The blackened four-storey-high walls were engrained with dirt;
the barred windows encrusted with soot and grime. Filthy rain
water flowed from the guttering in torrents.

There was a wine shop close to the main entrance, its windows
hidden behind wooden shutters. Hawkwood presumed most of
its trade was dependent on the prison staff and in all likelihood
the inmates too, which meant the proprietor probably made a
steady living. There was nothing like alcohol to deaden the
senses and make palatable that which was unpalatable, even if
it was only for a few desperate hours.

Malet held up his hand. "All right, Commissioner," he said
to Balthus. "Let's see if anyone's awake."

Hawkwood wondered why there weren't any guards. He'd
expected there to have been at least one sentry guarding the
entrance. Though, given the foul weather and the lack of
adequate shelter, it probably wasn't that surprising there was
no one in sight. Whether anyone was awake inside remained to
be seen.

There was no bell pull. Balthus raised the knocker and
slammed it down as hard as he could.

He had to do it twice more before an eye-level panel in the
door slid back and an unshaven face appeared in the gap. It
didn't look happy. It looked even less happy when Balthus
commanded it to open up.

"By whose authority?"

"That would be mine," Malet said, he kept his face lowered,
but drew back his cloak.

Balthus stepped helpfully out of the gaoler's line of sight. The
gaoler blinked. The last thing he'd expected to see was a deputation,
especially one containing a fully accoutred general. His eyes ranged
warily over the rest of the uniforms on display.

The head disappeared. A rattle of keys was followed by the sounds of locks being unfastened and bolts being drawn. Finally the door swung back. The man who stood in the opening fastening his belt looked as if he'd just woken up.

"Hold your men here, Captain," Malet said to Steenhouwer. "I'll summon you if I need you."

Without waiting for an invitation, Malet stepped through the door and pushed past the gaoler. Hawkwood and the others followed him. A small vestibule lay immediately beyond. A rough wooden pallet sat against a wall just inside the door, covered by a mattress and a rumple of blankets. The foetid odour of stale sweat filled the room. Hawkwood knew it wasn't just coming from the doorkeeper. It was seeping out of the walls and the rafters: the familiar smell of too many bodies confined in too small a space. He saw Grant wrinkle his nose in disgust.

"Fetch the warder," Rateau instructed. "Now."

The gaoler swallowed and disappeared rapidly. He was back in less than two minutes, though to Hawkwood, who was counting off the passing seconds in his head, it seemed as if a lifetime had gone by. The man accompanying him was short of stature with thick eyebrows and a paunch. He looked as if he'd dressed in a hurry. He also looked worried.

"Warder Bault, at your service, General. What can I do for you?" He looked Malet up and down and frowned.

Malet nodded to Rateau, who handed Bault a sheaf of papers. "My name is Lamotte. I have release orders for two of your prisoners: General Victor La Horie and General Maximilien-Joseph Guidal. They're to be set free immediately."

Bault took the papers and sniffed disdainfully. "Who says?"

"I do," Malet said.

Bault scanned the release forms. He shook his head. "Sorry, General, can't do that; not without the proper authority."

Malet stared hard at the warder. "You've just been handed all the authority you need. I can quote it verbatim, if you like. 'The concierge of La Force prison will at once set at liberty Generals Victor Fanneau de La Horie and Maximilien-Joseph Guidal. The present order, given in virtue of Article 13 of the Senate's decision of twenty-second October shall be carried out in the presence of the Armed Forces and the concierge shall be responsible on pain of death for any delay, and the other warders with him. Signed: Malet; General in Command of the Armed Forces and the troops of the First Military Division.'"

Malet smiled grimly. "If that isn't sufficient authority, I'd like to know what is. And was the rest of the order not clear enough for you? I refer specifically to the instruction: 'On pain of death.' That would include the two of you," Malet added, pointing an accusing finger at both the warder and his subordinate. "Oh, and by the way . . ." spreading a hand to incorporate Hawkwood and the others ". . . these, in case you hadn't noticed, are my 'Armed Forces'."

Bault stared down at the release form. He seemed to be studying the stamp marks. He looked up and fixed Malet with another lingering stare.

Jesus! Hawkwood thought wildly. *He's recognized the name! He knows Malet from when he was imprisoned here!*

He threw Grant a warning look but Grant had evidently had the same thought for the Scot was already edging towards a spot behind the warder's back.

"I don't see the Minister's signature," Bault said pedantically, tapping the document with the back of his knuckles. "He's usually the one to sign these. If not him, then Prefect Pasquier." Bault shook his head. "So I'm sorry, General, but if you'd care to wait a while, I can send my man here to the Quai Voltaire to obtain Minister Savary's signature. Shouldn't be more than forty-five minutes or so."

"You're refusing the order?" Malet raised an imperious eyebrow.

"Not all, General, but this is hardly normal procedure, and it's a strange hour to come calling."

"I see. Well, it might interest you to learn that the Duke of Rovigo is no longer the Police Minister."

Bault blinked. "Since when?"

"Since around the time that release order was signed. Y'see, Bault, there's something I neglected to tell you. Not only has the Minister been replaced. So has the government."

Malet then went for the jugular.

363

"The Emperor's dead, Bault. Shot with a Russian bullet. As a result, the Senate's issuing proclamations left, right and centre. One of them grants amnesty to political prisoners. You see where I'm going with this, Bault? Changes are afoot. That includes the Minister of Police, the Prefect of Police and, if you're not careful, it'll also include the head warder of La Force prison. You saw the wording. I just repeated it to you. If you don't carry out the Senate's orders, you die. Both of you." He turned to Hawkwood. "Captain Dumas, Captain Rémy, you have your weapons primed?"

Hawkwood drew his pistol. "Sir."

Grant did the same. "Say the word, General."

Malet turned to Bault. "Your move, I believe."

"The Emperor's dead?" Bault repeated. He swallowed and took another look at the release order. Then he looked at his fellow gaoler. The doorkeeper stared back at him plaintively. It wasn't hard to decipher the silent message passing between them.

"You need to make a decision, Bault," Malet said, catching Hawkwood's eye. Hawkwood knew then that Malet was thinking the same thing he was. It was already past six, and the city was coming awake. Any further delay and whatever element of surprise they might have had would be lost.

The warder, still doubtful, gnawed the inside of his cheek.

"Captain Dumas," Malet said.

"General." Hawkwood cocked his pistol.

Bault sighed and reached for the key ring at his belt.

*   *   *

The two individuals whom Bault delivered blinking into the light couldn't have been more different in appearance. One was of middle height and slender with black hair and an aristocratic face indented by a pair of deep-set, melancholic eyes. His legs were slightly bowed as though he'd spent a lot of time on horseback. The other was a bear of a man; tall and rough hewn, with a broad, overhanging forehead, untidily cropped hair and chin stubble that was almost thick enough to be considered a beard. His huge frame was matched by his hands, which were large and callused. He looked more like a blacksmith than a general. Both men were younger than Malet; probably in their late forties.

When the smaller man saw Malet, his eyes brightened considerably, transforming his features. Malet stepped forward and the two men clasped hands.

"My dear Victor," Malet said. "It's been too long."

Which makes the other one Guidal, Hawkwood thought. *At least we know which is which.*

"It's good to see you, too, old friend!"

General of Division Victor La Horie held Malet in a warm embrace. As he did so he placed his mouth close to Malet's ear. He spoke softly; a single word.

Hawkwood, standing a few feet away, wondered if he'd misheard. It had sounded like Latin.

Leonidas.

Hawkwood looked to see if anyone else had caught the exchange. Grant gave no sign that he had.

The two men broke apart and the moment was gone as La Horie clapped Malet on the shoulder. "You were cutting it fine. You did know Savary's signed my exile order? When they unlocked my cell I thought they'd come for me."

Malet smiled. "Then it appears we've arrived in the nick of time."

As Malet and La Horie extricated themselves, the second man shambled forward and Malet extended his hand. "How are you, General?"

The big man grimaced. "All the better for being out of this shit hole."

He let go of Malet's hand and his eyes narrowed as he contemplated the rest of the gathering.

"Friends," Malet said. "There'll be introductions later." He threw Bault a sidelong glance.

La Horie regarded Malet levelly. "It's started then?"

Malet nodded. "And we should leave now. Before we do, though, I have something for you." The general beckoned the guardsman forward with his bundle.

365

"Thought you might appreciate these." Malet nodded to the guardsman, who used his bayonet to cut the strings. "Hats and cloaks. The weather's not at its best. Careful how you take them out, there's something wrapped inside them."

La Horie bent down and unwrapped the cloak to reveal two loaded pistols hidden in the folds.

"You'd think he'd have included a flask of cognac," Guidal muttered as he fastened the cloak around his neck.

La Horie looked at Malet, rolled his eyes, and grinned.

Malet turned to Bault. "When we leave, secure the doors. No one's allowed in or out unless it's on my order. That includes the staff."

Bault nodded, though he still looked apprehensive. Evidently, the wording on the release forms was still preying heavily on his mind.

Malet turned to the released prisoners. "Ready?"

Both men nodded. They'd tucked the pistols into their waist-bands and looked, Hawkwood thought, more like a couple of freebooters than senior army officers, Guidal especially.

Guidal eyed Malet's braid. "No uniforms for us?"

Malet gave a wry smile. "It was rather short notice. Besides, there might have been some trouble with the sizes." He caught Hawkwood's eye, as if to say, *Some miracles take a bit longer.*

Guidal put his hat on. He turned to Malet. "In that case can we get the hell out of here please?"

"You took the words right out of my mouth," La Horie said.

Mine, too, Hawkwood thought. As they headed for the entrance he saw that Warder Bault, forehead puckered, was still throwing suspicious glances in Malet's direction.

The second the prison door slammed shut behind them, La Horie raised his face to the rain, closed his eyes and let go a sigh of relief followed by a long, deeper intake of breath.

When he opened his eyes, he smiled, placed his hat on his head and said, "Good to know the smell hasn't improved out here either."

He took in the troops waiting in the street. "An honour guard?

You shouldn't have . . ." He regarded Hawkwood and Grant with interest.

"Captain Dumas and Captain Rémy," Malet said. "And these are Lieutenant Rateau and Commissioner Balthus."

"Of course they are," La Horie said. "So, what's the plan, General?" He eyed the waiting Cohort with a critical eye.

With good reason, Hawkwood saw. For the troops were no longer the only people on the street. Although used to seeing soldiers gathering for the weekly review a growing number of passers-by, curious at the guardsmen's presence outside the prison at such an early hour, were asking questions. A good many of the troopers had broken ranks and from the stunned expressions on faces of the civilians it wasn't hard to see what the troops had been telling them. Lights were starting to flicker on in the nearby buildings. The news was out and it was spreading.

Grant tugged Hawkwood's arm. "The devil with this! It'll be all over the bloody city before we know it!"

"Look at them, though," Hawkwood said.

Grant frowned and then looked again and saw what Hawkwood had seen. "I'll be damned," he breathed softly.

Hawkwood stared at the expressions of the people around them. There wasn't a single grieving face in sight; not one. All he could see was happiness and what might have been interpreted as joyous relief. Some people were hugging.

"Captain Dumas! Captain Rémy!" Malet beckoned, interrupting his thoughts. "We should move. It's six-thirty already and the word's obviously out. I'd like to put some distance between myself and the warder before he recovers his memory. Captain Piquerel! Get them back into line and tell the company commanders that their men are to keep their eyes forward and their mouths shut. I hear anyone conversing with a civilian and he'll be on a charge. Understood?"

"Sir."

"All right, let's go."

The column moved off, but it did not travel far. A short while later, in the shadow of the Tour de Saint-Jacques, Malet called a second halt and summoned the officers to him.

"This is where we part company. Captain Piquerel, from now on you'll take your orders from General La Horie and General Guidal. I'm giving them command of Companies two, three and five."

"Very good, sir." Piquerel nodded. A model officer; he showed neither surprise nor displeasure, merely acceptance of his general's directive.

Malet addressed La Horie. "Commissioner Balthus and Captain Rémy will go with you, Victor. Your first objective's the Préfecture; followed by the Police Ministry. When you've taken those, Maximilien will leave sufficient troops for their protection while he seeks out Savary's deputy, Councillor of State Réal. He's then to head for the War Ministry, where he'll replace Minister Clarke. After that it will be Arch-Chancellor Cambacérès' turn. With Bonaparte in Russia, He's the man left in charge."

Malet handed envelopes to La Horie and Guidal. "These are your orders and the documents to support them. You know what you have to do. No distractions. Anyone who either questions or disobeys the Senate's orders is to be considered an enemy of the Provisional Government. Use force if you have to, but only as a last resort. Though, if what I've seen on the street so far is any indication, that might not be necessary. Remember, from now on every second is vital."

La Horie nodded. "Where are you going to be?"

"Garrison Command. I'll take 1st Company with me. Once you've secured your objectives to your satisfaction you're to join me there. Questions?"

"And the 4th Company, General?"

The question came from a stocky officer with a thin face and a goatee beard.

"Your name?" Malet asked.

"Lieutenant Régnier, sir."

"You're with me, Lieutenant," Hawkwood said, catching Malet's eye. "You and I have a special assignment. We won't need all your men; a dozen at the most; enough for an escort. The rest can join with 3rd Company. I'll explain as we go."

The lieutenant drew himself up. "Very good, sir."

"What about the Palais de Justice?" La Horie said.

Malet nodded. "Secure that as well. I suggest you take care of that, Maximilien, while Victor takes care of the Préfecture. It's only a short step from there to the Police Ministry."

Guidal's eyes darkened. "My pleasure."

Malet regarded him for several seconds before nodding. "Good. Anything else? No? All right. Move out. Oh and, gentlemen . . ."

La Horie and Guidal turned.

"Long live France," Malet said.

La Horie smiled. "Long live France."

Guidal said nothing.

As he went to follow, Grant paused and held out his hand to Hawkwood. Hawkwood clasped it. Grant nodded mutely before breaking his grip.

Words weren't necessary. Each of them knew what the other was thinking.

One domino down, two more to go.

20

Prefect of Police Etienne Pasquier, seated at his desk, drew his robe close about him. The Préfecture was a damp and chilly building at the best of times. For all the heat generated by the fire crackling in the grate, on this dark and rainy morning he might just as well have been working in a barn.

Despite the discomforts, however, there were certain advantages to starting work early. It meant he had the place to himself, for one thing. There was no one to interrupt him, no minions demanding his attention or pestering him with trivialities. He drew a sheaf of papers towards him and reached for his pen.

When he heard the creak of a hinge, he paid no attention to the noise, assuming it was just the building settling about him; floorboards groaned all the time, as did the rafters and on stormy days, windows and doors rattled and you could hear the wind whistling through the eaves loud enough to wake the dead.

But when the door crashed back and a dozen National Guardsmen armed with muskets filled the opening, Pasquier sensed that a draughty office might be the least of his problems. He sprang to his feet.

The soldiers parted and three men in civilian dress entered the room. Two wore cloaks; the third had on a long military greatcoat. The oldest was wearing a hat; his companions were bare headed, their hair damp from the rain.

"Prefect Pasquier, how nice to see you." It was the oldest one who spoke.

Pasquier frowned. His eyes flickered towards the door in the corner of the office. It led to his private apartment.

"Don't," the one in the greatcoat warned. "You'll never make it."

Pasquier eyed the muskets. All had bayonets attached and all were pointed at his midriff. Forcing himself not to show fear, he faced his visitors squarely. "Who are you? What do you want?"

Where were the police guards? he wondered.

"We want you, Baron. I've a warrant for your arrest," the eldest one said.

Pasquier stared at the speaker. "On what grounds?"

"On the grounds that the Empire's been annulled, as of this morning, by order of the Senate." La Horie walked forward. "Bonaparte's dead, Baron. The eastern army's on the retreat and the Senate's issued orders for any minister it considers a threat to be taken into custody."

Pasquier's jaw dropped. "What?"

He gazed at them blankly. The Emperor dead? The notion was preposterous. Then, a realization of what else had just been said pierced his brain.

"What do you mean 'threat'? To whom?"

"The Provisional Government."

Pasquier stared at La Horie. "Now I *know* you're mad!" He stepped out from behind his desk and held out his hand. "Show me the warrant."

La Horie reached into his jacket. "I think you'll find it's all in order."

Pasquier snatched the document from La Horie's grip. His eyes moved unerringly to the signature at the bottom of the page. When he read the name he thought his heart might stop.

"*Malet?*" He looked up. "General Malet's an enemy of the State! He's in detention!"

"Not any more," La Horie said. "The Senate's reinstated him; and not before time, if you ask me."

It can't be true! Pasquier thought feverishly. *Can it?*

He stared down at the signature, at the official stamps. It wasn't possible. None of this was.

"This warrant's not legal!"

"I had a feeling you'd say that," La Horie said, smiling. "Lieutenant Lefèvre!"

A young, blue-coated officer stepped into the room. "General?"

General? Pasquier thought. He realized the civilian was still smiling at him. He also had his hand outstretched.

With a calmness he did not feel, Pasquier handed the warrant back. "It seems you have the advantage of me, sir. In more ways than one. To whom am I speaking? You owe me that courtesy at least."

"I don't think that matters," La Horie said curtly. "Do you?" He eyed Pasquier's robe. "You might want to change, Baron. I'm assuming you don't want us to take you into custody in your gown?"

"My coat's in my dressing room," Pasquier said stiffly. He was unused to being rebuffed and realized even as he said it how mundane the statement sounded.

La Horie nodded to Lefèvre. "Go with him, Lieutenant. Take a couple of men. Don't leave him alone and make sure he hurries back."

His mind spinning, Pasquier led the way, uncomfortably aware of the armed escort walking beside him. As he passed the mirror he caught sight of himself and remembered he hadn't shaved. So much for appearances.

Collecting his coat, he returned to his office to find that the rest of the guardsmen had been sent outside into the corridor, leaving the three civilians by themselves.

"What now?" he asked.

"We wait while Lieutenant Lefèvre goes and finds a carriage," La Horie said. He nodded to Lefèvre, who saluted and left the room. The remaining two guardsmen took up positions on either side of the door.

"Where am I being taken?"

"La Force."

Pasquier felt a ripple of unease. He looked at the two other men. The youngest one had taken his place at the desk. He looked as if he was trying the chair out for size.

La Horie followed the Prefect's gaze. "Perhaps this would be a good opportunity to introduce you to your successor. Allow me to present Commissioner Balthus."

Balthus stood, bowed politely and began to remove his cloak. "Baron."

Pasquier stared at the tricolour sash and his eyes widened. *This is insanity,* he thought.

Balthus sat back down and Pasquier turned to the man in the coat and found himself perused by a pair of pale blue eyes.

"May I know *your* name, sir?" Pasquier said.

"It wouldn't mean anything if I did give it to you," Grant said. "So what would be the point?"

Pasquier tried to think of a suitable response and couldn't come up with anything.

Lieutenant Lefèvre appeared in the doorway. He caught La Horie's eye.

"Your carriage awaits, Baron," La Horie said. "When you're ready."

Leaving Balthus going through his papers at the desk, the bewildered Prefect allowed himself to be escorted from his office. Outside, he saw that the corridor, stairway and lobby were lined with guardsmen.

A door opened suddenly at the end of the passage and a woman appeared in a nightgown and robe. "I heard a commotion," she said. She stared at the guardsmen in confusion and fear. "Etienne, what's happening?"

Pasquier manufactured a smile. He wasn't sure how. "It's all right, my dear. Nothing to worry about. Just something I have to attend to. I won't be long."

Eyeing the troops, he wondered if that was true.

His wife looked equally unconvinced. "Where are you going?"

But the baroness found she was talking to herself. As she

stared after her husband it struck her as odd that he wasn't the one who appeared to be in charge. It looked as though it was the soldiers who were wielding all the authority.

Outside, Grant and La Horie waited as Lefèvre showed Pasquier to his seat in the carriage and then they watched as the vehicle pulled away, flanked by a dozen guardsmen; muskets held at shoulder arms.

Grant stared after it. "Should have made him walk, too," he muttered. "They'd likely be there a damned sight quicker."

"Probably forgotten how to walk," La Horie said. "That's the thing about barons. They tend to ride everywhere."

Grant turned. La Horie met his gaze and chuckled. "We, on the other hand, are soldiers. We walk all the bloody time. Are you ready?"

Grant nodded.

"Excellent," La Horie said. "Next stop the Police Ministry."

Lieutenant Régnier looked like a man who was still contemplating the wisdom of his next move. He bit his lip, drew his sword and stole a quick glance at the officer by his side.

"On you go, Lieutenant," Hawkwood said.

Régnier took a deep breath. He stared up through the darkened stairwell. At his shoulder a dozen guardsmen fingered their muskets anxiously and waited for the order to proceed.

Hawkwood hoped the lieutenant wasn't going to let the situation get the better of him. It was clear that Régnier had been beset by misgivings from the moment Hawkwood had given him the outline of their mission.

As he followed Régnier up the stairs, Hawkwood wondered how Malet had come by the address, for the building lay behind the rue de Varenne, which was tucked away south of the river. More footwork by Madame, he presumed.

Arriving on the second floor, Régnier, at a nod from Hawkwood, hammered on the apartment door with the hilt of his sword.

Hawkwood drew his pistol.

*   *   *

375

Colonel Frédéric Rabbe, Commander of the Regiment of the Paris Guard, could never get used to wearing civilian clothes. They always made him feel under-dressed. Travelling in uniform by public diligence for long periods, however, could be a gruelling experience and so on this occasion he was prepared to compromise. The trip to Beauvais was liable to be uncomfortable and very muddy, and he didn't want to arrive at his destination and take his place on the Conscription Board wearing a tunic and breeches that looked as if they'd just returned from a twenty-mile route march. He was all set to leave his lodgings when his batman announced that he had two visitors: his adjutant, Sergeant-Major Limousin, and a soldier of the National Guard, whose name his batman had temporarily forgotten.

Rabbe sighed. "No rest for the wicked. All right, Vincent, better show them in. You can take my bags downstairs in the mean time."

When Rabbe trailed his batman down to the hallway he found his adjutant waiting for him. The sergeant-major looked disconcerted to find his colonel out of uniform. He threw up a hasty salute. "Sorry to call at such an inconvenient moment, sir," Limousin wheezed. He looked and sounded as if he'd run all the way from the barracks to be there.

Rabbe eyed the guardsman, who was small and half hidden by the sergeant-major's bulk. "Who's this?"

The guardsman saluted. "Private Pappin, Colonel; National Guard."

Rabbe frowned. "What's going on, Sergeant-Major?"

Limousin hesitated.

"The diligence to Beauvais isn't going to wait," Rabbe said testily.

"Private Pappin has an urgent dispatch from the garrison commander, Colonel."

"And Borderieux couldn't have dealt with it?"

Captain Borderieux was the officer Rabbe had left in charge of the Minimes Barracks.

"Not this time; no, sir. With respect, I thought it too important. Soon as I read it, I came straight here."

With the private still in tow? Rabbe thought warily. *Why was that?*

"All right, man. Spit it out."

Limousin handed the envelope gingerly to his colonel. "It might be quicker if Private Pappin explains, sir."

"Somebody better had," Rabbe said, opening the envelope. "Private?"

As Pappin stepped forward and launched into the morning's events, Rabbe opened the letter and began to read.

Seconds later, he held up his hand. His face had turned very pale.

Pappin's voice trailed off.

Rabbe yelled for his batman.

He wasn't going to Beauvais after all, he told him. He could take the bag back upstairs and start laying out his uniform.

He turned to Limousin. "Return to barracks. Fast as you can. I want the men assembled by the time I get there."

As the door closed behind them, Rabbe, unbuttoning his coat, headed for the stairs. He took them two at a time as fear rose like a torrent into his chest.

General Guidal was drunk.

Not roaring drunk but just tipsy enough to make it apparent to anyone who approached to within a couple of feet of him. The slight tremor in his hands and the tilt of his head as he walked were the first giveaways but up close it was the wine on his breath and the cast in his eye that confirmed he might have been enjoying something slightly stronger than the mere whiff of a cork.

The man had seemed sober when Grant and La Horie had left him on their way to confront Pasquier in the rue de Jerusalem. While they'd been removing the Prefect from office Guidal's task had been to take Piquerel and his squad of guardsmen to secure the nearby Palais de Justice, and this he'd done, leaving half a company to guard the access routes in and around the Palais before rejoining the column on the Quai des Orfevres. In Guidal's eyes that had evidently been cause for celebration; much to the disquiet of Captain Piquerel, who'd presented himself to La Horie and Grant upon their return and given them the news.

"Where did he get the damned stuff?" had been Grant's first question, though he knew the answer was academic.

Piquerel didn't know. He was aware only that the general had slipped off the street a couple of times, supposedly to relieve himself, and that ever since then, not long after Grant and La Horie had left him in charge, he'd been taking regular swallows from a flask and the effects were beginning to show.

The booze, Grant knew, could have been acquired from any number of places. There were drinking dens around every corner and most of them kept irregular hours. For a determined man, finding a watering hole at seven-thirty in the morning down one of the ink-black alleyways wasn't a problem. And from what he'd seen of him so far, Grant had little doubt that, where pleasures of the flesh and palate were concerned, General Guidal was a very determined man.

"Who the hell do you think you are – my God-damned wife?" Guidal growled as La Horie confronted him.

They were on the approach to the Pont du Neuf. The rain had thankfully stopped a while back and on the other side of the river the long dark building that housed the Police Ministry was starting to take form against the slowly brightening but still murky sky.

"Better that than your widow, old friend," La Horie warned. "There'll be time enough to enjoy a drink or two *after* we've gained our victory, not before. We need you sober, not in your cups."

Guidal fixed La Horie with a lopsided smile. "Don't worry, General. It's only small sips. You'll get your victory." He patted the butt of the pistol tucked in his belt. "Where to now?"

La Horie hesitated, then said, "We have the Préfecture. Commissioner Balthus is in charge there. The Police Ministry's next. Captain Rémy and I will take care of that. Your objective is to seize the War Ministry and remove Henri Clarke. After that you're to go to the apartment of Arch-Chancellor Cambacérès on the rue Saint Dominique. When you've arrested them, we start rounding up the councillors. Take two companies. We'll rendezvous with you and Claude-François at garrison command."

"You're going after Savary?"

"Yes."

"Not without me, you're not."

"That's not the plan," La Horie argued.

"The hell you say. I've a score to settle with that son of a bitch."

"Not a good idea, General," Grant said.

Guidal paused. A vein throbbed in his temple. "I don't recall asking your permission, *Captain*."

"I mean no offence, sir. I'm only reiterating General Malet's orders."

"Are you? Well, last I heard, a general outranks a God-damned captain, so I'm countermanding General Malet's orders. Which means I'm coming with you, whether you like it or not. I'll take care of Clarke *after* we've taken care of Rovigo. Now, if nobody objects, I'm going to take a piss."

Without another word, he left them and headed unsteadily towards the edge of the quai, unbuttoning his breeches as he went. With his back to them, he emptied his bladder into the still black water below, his body slanted to one side as if leaning against an invisible wall.

La Horie pursed his lips.

"He's a liability, General." Grant spoke softly, knowing it wouldn't do for Piquerel and his lieutenants to hear two out of the three senior officers discussing the third of their number in such derogatory tones, though he suspected the general's condition was already a topic of discussion.

"He's just been delivered from a prison cell," La Horie said. "You can hardly blame him."

"I can if he gets us killed," Grant said. "You're saying it's all right?"

La Horie gave Grant a sharp look. "I'm saying I can understand his need. I didn't say I supported his efforts to quench it. I would also remind you, Captain, that the general's right. He is your superior officer. As am I. You would do well to adhere to the strictures of rank."

"My apologies, sir. My only concern is the success of our mission; as a consequence I have a tendency to forget my place. However, if you don't mind my asking, what *has* General Guidal got against Savary, apart from the fact he's the Prince of Darkness?"

La Horie allowed himself a small smile before he replied.

"It was Savary who had him arrested. And a couple of weeks ago Maximilien received word that Savary had signed his transfer papers; they were sending him to Aix to face a Tribunal. He'd more than likely have been found guilty and shot."

"You sound sure of that."

La Horie pursed his lips. "That's the usual penalty for passing information to the enemy."

"Enemy?"

"You don't know his story?"

Grant shook his head. "Rumours here and there."

"Maximilien's a royalist. He offered his services to the British in the hope they'd help return a Bourbon to the throne. He became the main connective between loyalist rebels in the Midi and the English fleet. It was his information that enabled the English admiral, Collingwood, to maintain his blockade off Toulon. They arrested Maximilien in Marseilles and brought him here while they gathered further evidence of his activities."

Grant looked across to where Guidal was leaning over the water. The man looked an unlikely candidate for a British-paid spy. But then, that was probably the point. *And I can talk*, he thought.

He turned back. "It's your decision, General. What do you want to do?"

La Horie sighed. "I don't think we've much choice, do you?"

"You mean it's better if we keep him with us?"

"You wouldn't want to see him when he's really drunk, Captain. At least this way we can keep an eye on him, make sure he doesn't get into any more mischief."

"Hopefully, he'll walk it off, you mean?"

"Hopefully," La Horie agreed.

La Horie's eyes moved to a point over Grant's shoulder. Grant turned. General Guidal was on his way back, wiping his hands on his jacket, his imposing figure slightly more upright than before.

Watching him, Grant was sure of one thing: this wasn't a man to argue with, drunk *or* sober.

"Right," Guidal said, his bearded face splitting into a lupine grin. "What are we waiting for? Let's go and get the bastard."

Desmarest came awake in a tangle of blankets, gasping for air; a whale breaching inside a whirlpool. He continued to thrash confusedly for several seconds. There was some sort of shimmering glow ahead of him, beckoning him towards the surface. As he rose from the darkness and his eyes focused, he realized the light was coming from a candle held by his manservant who was hovering over his bed with a worried look on his face.

Groggily, Desmarest tried to sit up. "What is it?"

The manservant looked down on him, apprehension on his face.

"There are soldiers . . ." he said.

At the La Courtille guardhouse, the Commander of the 2nd Battalion of the Paris Guard, Captain Émile Rouffe, finished reading the dispatch handed to him by Private Pappin. He fixed the guardsman with a steely glare.

"You've just delivered the same instructions to the Minimes, you say?"

"Yes, sir." Pappin nodded. His chest rose and fell rapidly. He was still out of breath from his rapid transit from the 1st Battalion's barracks. He hadn't had this much exercise for weeks, he reflected painfully, and his boots were pinching something chronic.

"The 1st Battalion were about to depart the barracks when I left, sir," Pappin volunteered. But he found he was talking to himself. The commander was already calling for his adjutant.

"Assemble the men! Company Commanders, report to my office at the double!"

As with the soldiers at the Minimes, the Courtilles garrison was composed of regular troops: grenadiers, voltigeurs and fusiliers. Standing nervously in the colonel's shadow, Pappin watched as the battalion gathered on the parade ground. It was impossible not to compare its deployment with the way the 10th Cohort had assembled. Unlike his fellow guardsmen, these soldiers were lining up without fuss or fluster.

The colonel looked at his watch. Despite the earth-shattering news, there was no time to address the men properly. The chain of command would have to suffice. As soon as his officers were through the door, he began issuing orders.

In no time at all, or so it seemed to Private Pappin, the 2nd Battalion of the Paris Guard was on its way out of the main gate.

At which point, it dawned on Pappin that, having accomplished his task, he had become instantly surplus to requirements.

What to do now?

Pappin decided his best option was to return to Popincourt. Fascinated as he was by the news and all the commotion, from the untimely death of the Emperor to the deployment of troops on to the streets, he was suddenly overwhelmed by a desire to find somewhere quiet to sit down and take off his boots.

Wearily, Private Pappin, a slave to his fallen arches, shouldered his musket and headed home to his barracks.

For someone who was reputed to be the most feared police officer in the country, the man didn't look much, Hawkwood thought as Desmarest emerged from his bedchamber, puffy-eyed, stubby fingers struggling to fasten the robe around his waist.

But then, wasn't that always the way? Reputation invariably added inches to a man's stature, but the moment the pedestal was removed that individual became just another mortal, which in Desmarest's case meant a short, overweight, fleshy-faced minion with a bad complexion, a double chin and questionable taste in slumber wear.

Desmarest blinked as he took in the uniforms. Interpreting the difference in rank, he fixed his gaze on Hawkwood.

"This had better be important. I don't take kindly to being disturbed at this hour of the morning without good reason."

"You're under arrest," Hawkwood said. "That good enough for you?"

The manservant's jaw dropped. The candle in his hand wobbled alarmingly, sending shadows scampering around the room.

Desmarest's eyes bored into Hawkwood's own. "*What* did you say?"

"And if I were you," Hawkwood added, "I'd go and put some breeches on. You look ridiculous."

The manservant seemed on the verge of fainting. Desmarest considered Hawkwood for several seconds. His eyes hard as flint. "And your name is?"

"Captain will do for now," Hawkwood said. Régnier's face, he noticed, seemed to have lost several shades of colour.

There was another lengthy silence. Finally, Desmarest said, "Do you have *any* idea who you're talking to, *Captain*? Any idea at all?"

"You think we'd be having this conversation if I didn't?" Hawkwood said evenly.

A nerve ticked along Desmarest's cheek. His eyes narrowed. "Who sent you? Was it Rovigo?"

An odd question, Hawkwood thought.

"We're here on the orders of General Lamotte," Lieutenant Régnier said.

"And who," Desmarest asked, head swivelling like a turtle about to snap, "is General Lamotte?"

"General Lamotte's acting for the garrison commander, on the instruction of the Provisional Government."

"The *what*?" Desmarest said.

"The Provisional Government," Régnier said again. The lieutenant's left hand played with the hilt of his sword, which had been returned to its scabbard when the manservant had admitted them into the apartment.

"*What* Provisional Government?"

"The new one," Hawkwood said. "Best get a move on. It doesn't like being kept waiting."

Desmarest turned quickly.

"And you, *Captain*, would do well to keep a civil tongue. I'll ask you again, Lieutenant; what Provisional Government?"

Hawkwood sighed. "You'd better tell him. Then we can get out of here."

Régnier, having first considered that a man in his nightshirt might not constitute much of a threat, was clearly beginning to have second thoughts. He came to attention. "I regret to advise that the Empire has been annulled by order of the Senate."

"Annulled? You're speaking gibberish, Lieutenant. The Senate can't annul the Empire."

"It can if there's no Emperor," Hawkwood said.

Desmarest froze.

"The Emperor's dead," Régnier said woodenly "The Senate's installing an interim government and has issued orders that all former ministers and their subordinates are to be arrested."

Not strictly true, Hawkwood thought. But close enough for the sake of argument.

"You'd be one of the subordinates," Hawkwood said.

Desmarest ignored the gibe and stared instead at the lieutenant. "Did you just say that the Emperor was *dead*?"

Régnier, faced with the police chief's cold glare, swallowed nervously. "Yes, sir."

"And this was supposed to have happened when, exactly?"

"Two weeks ago. It's taken that long for the news to reach the capital."

Desmarest's brain was spinning. He stared at Hawkwood. "Rovigo?"

"He'd be one of those ministers we mentioned earlier," Hawkwood said. "Now, are you going to get dressed? It makes no odds to me, but you might be more comfortable in a decent pair of trousers. I wouldn't want you blaming me if you catch your death."

Desmarest's eyes darkened but he made no reply. He was too busy considering the possibilities.

Bonaparte dead? If that were true, what were the ramifications? If the Senate was setting up a Provisional Government, what came next? And then Desmarest corrected himself for he realized he was asking the wrong question.

The question wasn't what came next.

It was who.

A thought occurred.

If Bonaparte had really been dead for two weeks, what about the intervening period? Had the Emperor's senior staff all been slaughtered, too? Surely the lieutenant or the captain would have hinted at something if that were the case? The likely consequence had probably been an agreement between Alexander and the surviving generals; an amnesty, to allow the Grand Army to make a strategic withdrawal from the Russian steppes.

Which brought him back to the question he'd asked himself earlier.

Desmarest addressed Hawkwood. "Has the Senate nominated a successor?"

"It's to be General Moreau," Régnier said, before Hawkwood could reply.

Moreau? Desmarest thought desperately. Moreau was in America. There had to be someone closer to home, at least for the period of talks. A person of equal status who was capable of negotiating with Alexander. And then it came to him.

Bernadotte.

Rumours had surfaced back in the summer hinting that Bernadotte had been in league with Alexander to discuss the possibility of Moreau's emergence from exile. It would therefore make sense if Bernadotte was the guiding light behind the Senate's action. And Bernadotte was a man with scores to settle, so who better to dictate which ministers were to be removed from their posts in preparation for the prodigal's return? There had even been stories that Fouché had been corresponding with Bernadotte. Now, there was a man who knew how to feather his own nest.

And then Desmarest thought, *Perhaps that wasn't such a bad idea.*

Moreau, Bernadotte, Fouché – a powerful alliance, and one worth siding with if a person knew what was good for him.

So it wouldn't do to antagonize the wrong people. But how was he to avoid falling into that trap?

A sigh of reluctance, he decided, was probably his best gambit.

He made it sound as realistic as he could and then nodded sagely, as if accepting his fate.

"All right; seems I've little choice. I'll come with you. I assume it's General Hulin's signature on the warrant? I'm sure, once I've spoken with him, we can get this unfortunate matter cleared up."

"Sorry to disappoint you," Hawkwood said. "But I'm afraid General Hulin's no longer the garrison commander. He's also been replaced."

Desmarest frowned. "By whom?"

"General Malet."

The room went very still.

"*Claude-François* Malet?" Desmarest said.

"Correct."

Pins and needles began to spread their way down Desmarest's arms and across the back of his neck. He had the awful feeling that his problems, far from becoming resolved, were only just beginning.

He stared hard at the captain, at the dark hair beneath the shako and at the blue-grey eyes and the scars etched across the strong cheekbones and he sucked in his breath as the realization hit him like a kick to the stomach.

"You're Dumas," he said.

21

The first thing that entered Savary's mind when he awoke to the sound of the apartment door splintering was that the Ministry building was on fire. He could hear yelling, too. He remembered then that he'd locked the doors to his office and his private rooms. Some of his staff were obviously breaking them down in order to effect a rescue.

He'd only been in bed for two hours. Still weary after a night spent completing his daily reports to the Emperor, he managed to push the blankets back and sit up. As he looked for his robe it occurred to him that he couldn't smell any smoke. Groping his way across the floor of his bedroom he opened the connecting door to his office.

He saw immediately that the window shutters were still closed and the bulk of the room lay in darkness. The only light was coming from the splits in the broken outer door, which were widening rapidly under the onslaught not of fire axes but of musket butts and boot heels. As he watched, an entire panel fractured before his eyes and a bellow of triumph sounded from the corridor beyond. The next second the lock gave way. Splinters flying, the door crashed back on its hinges. Before he could protest, Savary found himself lifted off his feet and thrust back into the room. He tried to break free but there were too many of them. His nostrils were filled with the smell of wet uniforms and of unwashed bodies.

"Release him!"

The order came from outside.

Savary felt the hands drop away. A figure appeared in the shattered opening and walked towards him through the wreckage.

"Hello, René," General La Horie said.

Savary stared. "Victor?"

"Seems like only yesterday when we said our goodbyes, doesn't it?" La Horie said, taking off his hat and looking about him. "Very impressive. You've done well for yourself."

"What is this?" Savary's face was a pale orb in the half-lit room.

"This?" La Horie said. "This is a friend paying a morning call on a former comrade in arms."

"You're supposed to be in prison," Savary said. Even to his own ears, his voice sounded hollow.

"No. If you remember, I'm supposed to be on my way to the coast and a ship to Philadelphia. Don't tell me it's slipped your mind. *You* signed the papers."

"I don't understand." Savary eyed the guardsmen warily. They weren't the smartest soldiers he'd ever seen. In fact, some of them looked quite slovenly and they were regarding him like a pack of hungry dogs eyeing their next meal.

"Evidently," La Horie said. "Allow me to explain. It's over. Your lord and master is no more."

"What are you saying?"

"He's dead, René. The Corsican's gone, and you're under arrest. That clear enough for you? Oh, this is Captain Rémy, by the way. Captain Rémy, allow me to introduce His Excellency the Duke of Rovigo. I'm assuming you haven't met?"

Grant was thinking that he'd seen enough of men in nightshirts. The damned things did nothing for the figure or the dignity. Savary would not have warranted a second glance were it not for the fact this was the man to whom he was supposed to have been delivered back in June. The man who, according to Captain Fosse, would happily slaughter his own family if the Emperor asked him to. He didn't look so dangerous now, in his bare feet and with his hair flattened by restless sleep.

Savary tightened the sash of his robe. His brain reeled. "How? When . . . when did this happen?"

"A fortnight ago; the seventh."

Savary frowned. "That's impossible. I've had a dispatch from him dated that very day. Your information's wrong."

"No," La Horie said firmly. "It's not."

"But I have it to hand. I can show it to you."

"That won't be necessary." La Horie looked around for Piquerel. "Send someone to prepare the transport. His Excellency's leaving shortly."

"Sir!"

Piquerel turned, pointed to a nearby sergeant and said, "You, quick as you can."

"You're not listening to me!" Savary protested.

The sergeant saluted and disappeared. Savary was suddenly struck with a premonition.

"No . . . you lie!" Savary looked at the guardsmen clustered around the room. "This is a trick! You, Captain!"

"Excellency?" Piquerel said tentatively.

"What's your name?"

Piquerel told him.

"You know me?"

"We've not met, Excellency, but I recognize you."

"What do you know of this man?" Savary pointed to La Horie.

Piquerel's eyebrows lifted. "General La Horie's my commanding officer."

"Wrong, Captain. I take it these are all men of your own corps?"

"Yes, Excellency: 10th Cohort, National Guard." Piquerel glanced towards La Horie, who was regarding Savary with a faintly bemused expression.

"And you'd consider yourselves loyal to France?"

"Of course, Excellency."

"Then I'll tell you now that General La Horie is far from loyal. He's a former Chief of Staff to the traitor Moreau. Like Moreau he was tried and found guilty of treason. He's under sentence of exile. He was confined to La Force and should not have been released without my authority. I demand that you arrest him immediately!"

The first snort of laughter came from behind Savary's back. Savary turned to confront the offender. His look was savage. "You dare to mock?" He jabbed a finger around the room. "I'm telling you all now that this man is deceiving you. I'm also warning you that, unless you do as I say and arrest him, you will all be considered traitors to the Empire. When the day of reckoning comes – and it will, mark my words – justice will be swift and final."

Many faces maintained their wide grins. Others turned more neutral, while a few went several shades paler.

"Enough!" La Horie snapped. He walked forward. "We were friends once, René, back in the Rhineland. When you served with Moreau as well, or had you conveniently forgotten? And you dare talk of treason? You forfeited the right to pass judgement on others when you commanded the troops who shot Condé's son at Vincennes. How many innocent men and women have you condemned since then? How many have you sent to the galleys and the scaffold?" La Horie leaned in close. "Be thankful it's me who's talking. If it wasn't for our past association, I'd happily hand you over to these *loyal* men. There are more than a few here who'd see you dead for the crimes you've perpetrated – the brothers, sons and fathers you've sent to the blade; wives and mothers, too, I've no doubt."

Not just French men and women, Grant remembered, as he watched the anger turn La Horie's face dark.

Grant had landed in the Peninsula in '09, a year after the Madrid uprising, but talk of the brutality inflicted by the French had not subsided, even amongst the most hardened British troops. Savary had been one of the commanders tasked with wreaking vengeance on the Spaniards who had dared to aim a blow for freedom against the hated invaders. Survivors described streets running with the blood of the men and women slaughtered under the swords and hooves of the French cavalry.

Grant gave a silent prayer for Captain Fosse and his brother officers who'd defied their commander's orders and given him the chance to evade the clutches of the man standing before him.

"Where the hell's that sergeant?" La Horie turned towards the corridor. His eyes brightened as a shadowy figure appeared, but his relief was short-lived.

"Rovigo! You whore's son! You in here?"

General Guidal had arrived.

It had been La Horie's and Grant's plan to have Savary sent on his way before Guidal could get to him. In an attempt to stall the increasingly irascible general from launching his own pre-emptive assault on the Ministry, they'd managed to persuade him that they first had to secure the area in case the Minister tried to evade capture. One of the streets that had to be blocked was the rue des Saints-Pères. The suggestion that it was the most logical escape route had been enough to convince the semi-inebriated Guidal that it would be a good idea if he took half a company with him and set up a perimeter.

At least, it had seemed like a sound strategy at the time. What they hadn't allowed for was a tardy sergeant and Guidal's capacity to seek out yet another wine shop on the very street he'd been sent to guard; which, with the rapidly dawning realization that he'd been bamboozled, had only served to increase General Guidal's ire. Worse, he'd managed to commandeer a sabre.

Guidal stormed into the room like a berserker looking for plunder. His massive frame dwarfed the men around him. Somewhere along the way, he'd mislaid his hat. His hair was plastered to his head and there was a wild look in his eyes, which blazed with alcohol-fuelled intensity as he spied the Minister in his night clothes.

Guidal's anger and the wine he'd imbibed had not improved his reflexes. The bad light in the room didn't help. The crash as his shin connected with the corner of a low, unseen table could probably have been heard three streets away. Grant and several others winced at the sound of it.

"Christ Jesus!" The bellow of pain rebounded off the walls.

391

It was followed, as Guidal righted himself and rubbed his shin, by a volley of invective. Still brandishing the blade, he lurched painfully towards his target and, before La Horie could intervene, jabbed the point of the sabre against the Police Minister's chest.

Savary recoiled.

"Do you know me?" Guidal demanded. Flecks of spittle landed on the shoulder of Savary's robe.

Savary looked terrified. He shook his head vehemently.

"Well, you bloody well should, you bastard! I was arrested on your orders! I'm Guidal!"

The sword point rose. "You're thinking I should be in Aix, right? I'm not though, am I?"

Guidal grinned, revealing yellowing teeth through the gap in his beard. Savary backed away, only to find his retreat stymied the moment his spine hit the wall. Guidal pressed the blade against Savary's throat. Blood welled.

"Maximilien!" La Horie said warningly.

Guidal paused. The smell of drink was coming off him in waves. The sabre tip hovered at Savary's Adam's apple, which contracted alarmingly. "By rights I should stick the bastard."

"Which would make you a murderer, my friend," La Horie said gently. "If you become that, then we've lost."

A tear welled suddenly at the corner of Guidal's eye. A snarl broke from his lips. He drew the weapon back, bracing himself as if to thrust the blade home. Savary gasped and closed his eyes.

"No!" La Horie cried.

Guidal slammed the point of the sabre into the wall four inches from Savary's right eye and let go. Embedded in the panelling, it continued to vibrate as if on a spring.

Guidal stepped back. Savary looked as though he was about to pass out.

"I hope you rot in hell, you bastard!" Guidal hissed. "In fact, it'll be my pleasure to escort you there myself." He looked to La Horie, who nodded silently.

Grant let out his breath.

From the door a voice called, "Transport's ready, General."

"Thank you, Sergeant," La Horie said, without turning. He looked at Savary, who was staring at Guidal, chest heaving, his face as white as a sheet.

"I suggest you call your valet to bring you something suitable to wear, Minister," La Horie said calmly. He beckoned to Grant and said quietly, "Go with them. The sooner the man's behind bars, the better I'll feel. I don't want Maximilien to have second thoughts about killing him. See the bastard's delivered to La Force in one piece. You and Maximilien can go from there to the War Ministry. Maximilien's still tasked to take care of Clarke. He can't do that if he's drunk, so I'm relying on you to keep an eye on him. Can you do that for me, while I remain here?"

Grant nodded.

"Good man." La Horie clapped Grant on the shoulder. "All right, let's get them moving."

They waited until Savary's valet had brought his clothes and watched as he put them on. There were titters from the guardsmen as he rolled the stockings over his milk-white calves. Then they took him downstairs to where the carriage was waiting. A detachment of guardsmen stood in formation before it.

"Christ," Guidal muttered when he saw the transport. "Where the hell did they find this pile of shit?"

It was fortunate the rain had petered out, Grant thought. The *fiacre*'s roof had obviously been damaged at some point and only extended halfway over the passenger compartment. Guidal shook his head, held the carriage door open and showed his teeth. "After you, *Excellency*."

Grant and Guidal waited until Savary was seated and then climbed in after him. Guidal sat on Savary's left. Grant took the seat opposite, his back to the direction of travel.

The convoy moved off.

Five minutes after that, Savary made his escape bid.

Colonel Gabriel Soulier still felt like death, but he and his aide, Captain Verdet, and the 6th Company of the National Guard had finally arrived at the Hotel de Ville. It was a little after seven-thirty.

Leaving Verdet to set up a cordon, Soulier, running his finger inside his collar to try and ease the discomfort of it chafing against his skin, made his way into the building. His breeches were too tight around his thighs and the sweat brought on by his fever was hot and damp in the small of his back and beneath his arms. After the march from Popincourt, he was starting to wish he'd stayed in bed.

The Senate papers that he was carrying and which he'd been directed to hand to the Prefect of the Seine were sticky from the moisture that coated his palms. The ink had rubbed off on to his fingers. It looked as though his veins had broken through his skin.

Prefect Frochot wasn't there, which was galling.

"Who *is* here?" Soulier enquired of the clerk who had greeted him. He took off his hat and mopped his forehead.

"Deputy Villemsens," the clerk replied.

Never heard of him, Soulier thought. "All right, he'll do. Fetch *him*."

Villemsens, a small, reed-thin man, with an ill-fitting wig and a web of broken capillaries across his nose and cheeks, viewed Soulier with polite enquiry and explained that the colonel might have a wait as His Excellency Count Frochot didn't live in the city but rode to work each morning from his house on the banks of the Marne. He was undoubtedly on his way, but it could be a while.

"You might want to send a messenger," Soulier advised. "It would help if he was here sooner."

"And why's that?" Villemsens asked innocently.

Soulier told him.

Five minutes later a mounted messenger was on his way.

Hawkwood arrived at the church of Saint Roch to find General Malet and the 1st Company lined up along the street outside.

The general was standing on the church steps, Rateau and Captain Steenhouwer by his side. Malet was staring up at the huge main entrance doors and the columns and statues that framed them. There were very few sharp edges to the architecture save for the apex roof, which looked as if it would have been more at home atop a Roman temple, had it not been for the simple cross that rose above it.

"Captain," Malet said by way of greeting. "It's done?"

"Yes, General."

Hawkwood returned Rateau and Steenhouwer's nods of welcome and was struck not for the first time by the Dutchman's narrow shoulders and willowy frame. His upper body also looked out of alignment with his legs, giving him a vaguely comical look, like a sapling trying to remain upright in a strong wind.

"Lieutenant Régnier acquitted himself well?" Malet enquired.

"Yes, sir."

"And our friend Desmarest offered no resistance?"

"None, sir."

"A pity." Malet allowed himself a thin smile.

"He knew who I was, though," Hawkwood said. "He knew my name."

There was a pause, then Malet's head came up sharply. He turned to Steenhouwer. "Have the column ready to move out, Captain."

As the Dutchman turned away, Malet drew Hawkwood aside.

"First our friend Claubert's presence at the clinic, now this. I wonder what else they might know," he said pensively.

"If they knew anything, General, we'd be knee-deep in gendarmes. They were fishing, that's all. In fact, when we arrested Desmarest, he asked if it was Rovigo who'd sent us."

"Did he now? That's even more interesting. I wonder . . ."

He looked at Hawkwood and smiled. "'*Quis custodiet ipsos custodes*?', eh, Captain?"

"Sir?"

"'Who will guard the guardians?' It was penned by Juvenal, a Roman satirist. It considers the impossibility of dealing with corruption when the dispensers of justice are themselves corrupt. It sounds, from what you've said, as if there's a degree of intrigue in the palace corridors that goes beyond our endeavours. Also, Claubert's allegiance was to the Préfecture as I recall, whereas Desmarest's loyalties would tend to lie with the Ministry. They rarely work hand in glove. It's all rather odd. It smacks of certain individuals pursuing their own agendas."

"To what end?"

"There you have me. Who knows?" Malet looked thoughtful.

"We took Desmarest by surprise," Hawkwood said. "He might have known who I was, but it's as I said: if he or the Préfecture had even the slightest inkling of what you and the abbé were planning, we'd never have got this far. Hell, you and the abbé wouldn't even have made it over the wall. You'd have been arrested in your beds and taken away for interrogation."

Malet looked at him.

"There's been nothing to suggest that anyone knows what we're up to. There have been no sounds of alarm," Hawkwood said. "From what I've seen, the city's still half asleep."

"But the longer we delay, the greater the risk of discovery, eh? That's what you're saying."

Hawkwood nodded. "We're close, General. We're almost there."

The general took out his watch and studied the dial.

"Rovigo should have been delivered to La Force by now. If we assume Real, Cambacérès and Clarke are on their way there as well, that only leaves Hulin and the Garrison."

Looking up, he studied the sky, and snapped the watch shut.

"It's getting light. We'll no longer have the darkness to cover our deeds. But the rain's helped keep the streets empty, so you're right. We still hold the advantage."

"And it would be a shame to lose it," Hawkwood said.

"Not a shame, Captain – a crime." Malet favoured Hawkwood with a piercing stare. "You saw nothing untoward on your way here, you say?"

"Not a thing, General. Apart from our deployment of the Guard, the city's as quiet as a tomb."

Hawkwood hoped that wasn't the wrong choice of words.

Leaving Régnier and the Guard detail to escort Desmarest to La Force, Hawkwood had returned to join Malet and the others by way of the Pont Royal. It had been an uneventful journey. The only thing of note had been the view along the river when he'd crossed the bridge. The sight of the dawn spreading out behind the towers of Notre Dame had been quite spectacular, despite the overcast skies.

The city was stirring, of that there was no doubt, but the number of people venturing forth was still relatively small. Hawkwood had passed shopkeepers pinning back shutters and setting out their produce and there had seemed to be no sense of urgency to the preparations.

"But not for long, eh?" Malet said.

"No, sir. The word is out there and it will be spreading fast."

Malet nodded briskly. "Then we must make even more haste! Lieutenant Rateau!"

"Sir?" Rateau stepped forward. The parcel he'd retrieved from Father José's apartment was still slung awkwardly over his shoulder. Part of it had split, Hawkwood saw, the wrapping disintegrating due to the rain and rubbing against Rateau's shoulder. Through a rip, parts of a dark tunic and a gold epaulette were visible.

Malet grasped Rateau's shoulder. "Time for your next assignment, Lieutenant. You know what you have to do; deliver the parcel to General Desnoyers. Give him my compliments and tell him it's time and that he's to meet us at garrison headquarters as soon as he's able."

"Yes, sir."

Saluting crisply, Rateau set off up the street. Malet gazed after him.

"You think he'll join us?" Hawkwood said.

"The general's an old friend. He's been on the retired list for some years, due in no small measure to his hatred for Bonaparte, but he still has many friends within the army. He's been helping my wife these past few months with details of the garrison and its personnel. He knows there's a position waiting for him in the office of Chief of the General Staff, if he wants it."

"Then let's hope he does," Hawkwood said.

"We'll find out soon enough. He lives close by."

Malet paused, then said, "You know, it didn't occur to me before, but it's rather apt that we regrouped here." Smiling, he indicated the church. "Treize Vendémiaire. It's where Bonaparte and Murat defeated the royalist forces and saved the Republic. They were outnumbered six to one. The man had principles then." Malet smiled. "Mind you, he also had the use of forty cannon, so it wasn't that one-sided."

The general stared up at the closed doors and then nodded towards the patiently waiting Steenhouwer. "All right, Captain; when you're ready."

Steenhouwer saluted and gave the order for the column to move out.

The men fell into step and Hawkwood felt the excitement move through him.

Garrison headquarters lay less than five hundred yards ahead.

Lieutenant Verdet had just finished deploying his troops when he heard the clump of hoof-beats and the rattle of springs. He stood and watched as the coach slithered around the corner, drawing to a halt outside the Hotel de Ville.

The coachman's assistant got down. After speaking briefly with the passenger concealed within the vehicle's interior, he made his way up the steps into the building. A few moments later he reappeared.

Verdet watched as the assistant conferred with the passenger before re-boarding. As soon as he had settled in his seat, the coachman flicked the reins and the coach moved away across the Place de Grève, heading for the river, finally disappearing out of sight as it turned on to the Quai Pelletier, leaving no record of its passing save for a trail of hoof prints and the indentations from its wheels in the mud.

Life goes on, Verdet thought.

From the window of the Prefect's office on the first floor, Deputy Villemsens watched as the coach drove out of sight, and called for an usher.

"We've just had a visitor. Find out who it was."

The usher disappeared. Villemsens turned to Colonel Soulier, who was seated in a chair by the desk, wiping his neck with a handkerchief. His hat rested on his knees. A fading red weal caused by the hat's brim was still visible across the breadth of the colonel's forehead.

"I'm sorry, Colonel. I'm sure Count Frochot won't be long. He's rarely late, even in bad weather."

Soulier curbed his irritation. Villemsens had been reciting the same apology for the past half hour. The mantra had become wearisome.

There was a knock on the door. Soulier brightened, but it was only the usher returning with the news that the carriage had contained the Minister of Police, who'd come to see the Prefect.

Villemsens frowned. He thought the coach had looked familiar. "There was no message?"

"No, sir."

And Savary wasn't a man who'd be prepared to sit and wait, Villemsens thought. *Which, this morning of all mornings, was probably just as well.*

Villemsens dismissed the usher. He viewed Soulier with concern. The colonel didn't look at all well. He was perspiring copiously and his hands, Villemsens noticed, were shaking, as if with palsy.

"A cognac, Colonel?" Villemsens offered. "It's early, I know, but you look as though you need it, if you don't mind me saying so."

Soulier nodded his thanks.

As Villemsens began to pour, he wondered nervously how ill Colonel Soulier might be.

Hopefully, it wasn't anything catching.

As the carriage trundled along the Quai Pelletier, General La Horie stared out at the river passing beside him. The water looked cold and depressing.

He'd grown restless in Savary's office and had driven to the Hotel de Ville to check on progress. On learning that the Prefect had yet to arrive, La Horie decided there was no point in lingering. The National Guard were lined up in front of the building, clearly Soulier had everything under control. Curbing his impatience, he had ordered the driver to return to the Ministry, planning to remain there until he received confirmation that the coup had succeeded when he could rejoin Malet at the Place Vendôme.

His eye moved to the walls and towers of the Conciergerie on the opposite side of the river and he shivered; not from the cold but from the fear of what would happen if they failed. He tried not to dwell on that. The thought of returning to prison was too terrible to even contemplate. It would be better, La Horie decided, to be put in front of a firing squad.

As the prison ramparts disappeared from view, he sat back in his seat. Struck by a sudden thought, he smiled to himself.

Better to die on your feet than spend a lifetime on your knees.

He'd lost count of the number of times he'd heard men say that.

Perhaps this was the morning he'd discover if the philosophy was true.

Savary and his escort were travelling along the Quai des Lunettes on their way to the Pont au Change, the bridge that would take them off the Île. The river lay to their right. Guidal, still befuddled by drink and lulled by the movement of the carriage, the clopping hooves and the tramping of the guardsmen ahead of them, had his eyes closed. His head had fallen on to his chest.

Despite Guidal's earlier display of anger, Savary knew the nameless man seated opposite him was the one to watch. He'd tried engaging both of them in conversation as soon as they'd pulled away from the Ministry steps, cajolingly at first, entreating them to see the error of their ways; letting on that he knew it was all some trick and the Emperor wasn't dead. At first he'd promised that the State would show leniency if they let him go. When that hadn't worked he'd tried bluster and threats, where-upon Guidal had told him to shut his mouth otherwise it would be shut for him. The other one had remained silent throughout. It was his silence that Savary found the most unnerving, that and the look in those blue eyes, which had chilled the Minister as much as Guidal's intimidation with the sword. So Savary had shut up and waited for his moment.

As the column turned left on to the Pont au Change, he seized it.

Guidal was still dozing and had begun to snore. The other one had turned his head as the bridge came into view. Savary knew it was the best chance he was ever going to get.

Grant hadn't been expecting Savary to act so impulsively. He was looking over his shoulder as they turned off the quai to cross the river. The next thing he knew Savary was scrambling over the half-open carriage door and out on to the road.

The carriage was still in motion as Savary made his leap; when he hit the ground he did so awkwardly, nearly falling full length. Putting out a hand, he managed to recover his balance. Half-winded, he clambered to his feet and ran.

Grant spun, jumped out of his seat and yelled at the driver to stop. As the reins were hauled back, the Scot flung himself from the carriage.

The men in the escort heard the commotion and looked back to see that the *fiacre* had halted and that an escape was in progress. Unharnessing their muskets they, too, gave chase.

Savary knew there was no refuge for him back at the Ministry, which left him with only one direction to flee: towards the Palais de Justice. There were bound to be people around, even at that hour of the morning. It wasn't far, less than a hundred yards.

Grant drew the pistol from his belt. His coat flapped around him. He could hear the shouts of the guardsmen running in his wake and the pounding of their boots on the cobbles. He did not turn to look but kept his eye fixed on his quarry.

Savary was panting hard. He was unused to physical exertion and even though he'd covered only a short distance his legs felt as heavy as lead. He stared about him frantically. Of the few people he could see, none looked as though they were prepared to come to his aid.

Savary tried calling out but because of his breathlessness the words emerged only as a rasping croak. To his consternation, he saw that the witnesses to his distress were already turning away or hurrying on, not wanting to become involved.

Suddenly, he saw more soldiers. A small squad had appeared from an alleyway ahead of him. A surge of hope moved through him. Lungs bursting, he staggered towards them, near to collapse. The entrance steps came into view. Once he reached them he knew he'd be safe. Ten paces . . . five . . . three. He was so close. As his rescuers – a sergeant and six troopers – fell in about him, his fingers clawed at the first stone and he sank to his knees, his lungs on fire, sobbing with relief.

Turning, he pointed to the men running in behind him. "Stop them!" he gasped.

Less than thirty paces back, Grant saw Savary stumble. His heart faltered when he saw the soldiers run out in front of the Palais entrance, but he kept going.

It was then, in a terrible moment of clarity when he saw that his pursuers had not faltered, that Savary realized, far from gaining sanctuary, he had run himself into a dead end. He heard the man in the greatcoat shout, "Leave him, Sergeant! He's mine!" and knew, even as he tried to stand, that there was nowhere left for him to hide.

The detachment left by General Guidal to guard the Palais de Justice stood back and watched unsympathetically as Grant jammed the muzzle of his pistol against Savary's right temple.

"Nice try, Excellency," Grant gasped. The weight of the great-coat had made the running hard. He was nearly out of breath himself. He grabbed hold of Savary's collar. "Up!"

Savary stared beseechingly at the ring of guardsmen but their faces showed no mercy.

Grant hauled Savary to his feet. "You can resume your duty, Sergeant. I'll take it from here."

The sergeant nodded. Hawking up a gobbet of phlegm, he aimed it at Savary's boots. Without waiting to see where it had landed, he gathered his men and the squad retraced its steps.

"I'll see you shot for this," Savary hissed after him. "All of you!"

The carriage escort arrived, breathing hard.

"Relax, gentlemen," Grant told them. "The excitement's over."

Grant's first thought was to return with Savary to the *fiacre* that was waiting by the bridge, but when the sergeant of the escort ordered his men back into formation, Grant decided a change of tactic was in order.

"We'll walk."

The sergeant's eyebrows lifted. "And the general, sir?"

Grant realized there had been no sign or sound from Guidal during the entire episode.

"Leave him," Grant said, adding drily, "He's had a hard morning."

A grizzled smile came over the sergeant's seamed face. "As you wish, sir."

"Tell the driver to continue to La Force. We'll meet him there. Better leave a couple of men with the general, just in case he wakes up and wonders where we've gone. The rest of you come with me. We'll keep to this side of the river and use the foot-bridge to the Île Saint-Louis, then the Pont Marie to cross back. It'll likely be quicker than the carriage."

"Very good, sir." The sergeant nodded. "All right. Corporal Cassalle, Private Périer, you're with the general; the rest of you into line. Sharply now!"

The two guardsmen exchanged looks, unsure as to whether they had just become the recipients of the cushiest errand of the morning or the detail from hell.

"And you," Grant said, dragging Savary with him as the pair hurried away, "you'll remain quiet and cooperative at all times. Got that? Because I'm just looking for an excuse."

Savary nodded, but there was a watchful look in his eye.

"All right, Sergeant," Grant ordered. "Move them out."

Malet halted the Company at the entrance to the Place Vendôme. Framed by magnificent colonnaded façades and with a ground floor ringed with archways, it was like standing inside a vast arena. Despite their grandeur, however, the surrounding buildings were not the most prominent feature. That privilege had been reserved for the column that rose like an erect phallus from the Place's centre. Over one hundred feet high, built of stone and covered with a veneer of overlapping bronze plates, its summit was occupied by the statue of a male figure dressed as a Roman Emperor. Bare-headed save for a crown of laurels and holding a sword in his right hand and a globe surmounted with a statue of Victory in his left, Napoleon Bonaparte surveyed his domain with haughty disdain.

The column, Grant had told Hawkwood during one of their walks, had been erected in homage to the Grande Armée and the victory of Austerlitz. Popular myth recorded that it had been made from twelve hundred cannon captured after the battle.

"They must have been bloody small cannon," had been Grant's pithy comment; the true number, it was said, having been closer to one hundred and thirty.

Malet called Hawkwood, Steenhouwer and his two lieutenants to him.

"The final phase, gentlemen. Pray that our good fortune stays with us. Lieutenant Prévost, I'd be obliged if you'd take two dozen men on to garrison command headquarters."

Malet did not point but nodded towards the immediate left-hand corner of the Place and a trio of archways where a single guard stood before an iron gate.

"You're unlikely to be challenged. The guard will assume you're an advance party for the morning review. Once inside, take the right-hand stairway. You will deliver a letter to Colonel Doucet, Chief of the General Staff. While the colonel's carrying out his orders, you are to return to the entrance where you're to deploy your men and await my arrival. Do you have that?"

"Yes, sir." Prévost clicked his heels.

Hawkwood knew the type: young, keen, clear-eyed, anxious to impress. He wondered if he'd been like that once. He couldn't recall. The lieutenant would soon learn.

As Prévost studied his objective, Malet turned to the second section commander. "Lieutenant Gomont?"

"Sir?"

Malet pointed to the opposite corner of the square. "You and the rest of your section will proceed directly to number 22. That's where General Hulin has his quarters. Place your troops outside the building. The captains and I will join you shortly. I'll be requiring the services

404

of four of your men. I'll leave you to choose, so long as they have brains."

"Sir."

"And, gentlemen . . ."

The lieutenants turned.

"Keep the noise to a minimum. We don't want to alarm the citizenry."

"Sir."

Malet handed Prévost the dispatch. The lieutenants divided their sections and moved off.

"As a matter of interest, sir," Hawkwood said, "does General Hulin know you?"

"Not by sight, if that's what you were thinking."

"It was," Hawkwood admitted. He stared across the square. It was still quite empty, but it wouldn't be long before spectators began arriving in earnest for the morning review.

Malet smiled. "Fortunately, I know *him*. Captain Steenhouwer, are you ready?"

The Dutchman drew himself up "Awaiting the word, sir."

Malet nodded. He looked to the guardsmen Gomont had left behind. "You four stay close."

Hawkwood drew his pistol, checked the flint and powder and replaced it in his belt. "Lead on, General."

22

Chief Warder Bault slid back the hatch. He looked like a man who was having an eventful and far from enjoyable day. Grant had no trouble guessing why.

"Don't tell me," Bault said as he tried to peer through the gap over Grant's shoulder. "You've brought us another one."

"How many have you had so far?" Grant asked.

"Two," Bault said wearily. He'd been looking for a carriage but there was no vehicle in sight, only guardsmen and a second, unhappy-looking, civilian.

"That would be Baron Pasquier and former Chief of Security Desmarest?"

"It would," Bault confirmed. He felt a flutter inside his chest.

"Well, so now you've got three," Grant said cheerfully. "Open the door."

Bault grimaced. His face slid away. The hatch scraped shut and the door was unbolted. As it creaked open, Grant beckoned to the sergeant. "Bring him in."

They marched Savary forward and the door was closed after them.

"So, who's this?" Bault asked warily. He stared hard at the civilian and wondered if he was supposed to recognize him. He looked slightly familiar, but Bault couldn't place him. He still hadn't entirely gotten over the shock of learning the identities of the first two men who'd been brought to the prison earlier that morning. La Force hadn't seen this much illustrious traffic since the conspiracy trials back in '08.

Grant handed the warder the prison admittance order. When Bault saw the name on the form, his eyebrows nearly took flight. With a sense of trepidation, his attention moved to the signature at the bottom of the page. There it was again: *Victor-Fanneau de La Horie, Minister of Police.*

When he'd first seen it, on the order for Prefect Pasquier's detention, he hadn't quite believed it. Now, with the arrival of Savary, Duke of Rovigo, it was beginning to make a kind of sense, though how La Horie could go from prisoner to Minister of Police in not much more than an hour was something Bault was having a hard time comprehending. Not that he dared to enquire too closely. If the heads of the Bureau Secret, the Préfecture *and* the Ministry of Police could find themselves suddenly demoted and in gaol, what chance was there for a lowly prison warder? Bault was starting to wish he was back in his bed, safe and warm and isolated from the madness that appeared to be taking place on the other side of the walls.

He studied the prisoner with renewed interest. Unshaven and pale, his hair uncombed, at first glance the man didn't look like a duke, any more than Pasquier had looked like a baron – but then, no one was at their best when they walked into La Force for the first time and saw what was facing them. Entering gaol did that to a man, whether he was a Prefect, the Minister of Police or a pauper.

Desmarest, the second one to arrive, had been different. He had no title and didn't look like the sort of person who was likely to be in receipt of one any time soon and therefore of the three he looked to be the one most likely to survive the ignominy. There was something about him that suggested he was no stranger to duplicity and deceit; in prison, those were attributes that would serve a man well, if he knew how to use them. Based on the security chief's reputation, Bault reckoned Desmarest was probably something of an expert in that regard.

"You do realize," Bault said mournfully, "if you continue at this rate I'm likely to run out of cells."

Grant smiled. "I've a feeling you'll cope. You had two come empty just this morning. I'm sure you'll be able to find a few more."

"How many's a few?" Bault asked, his eyes narrowing with suspicion.

"Depends," Grant said.

"On what?"

"On whether anyone puts up a fight."

Grant left the sentence hanging.

Bault wondered if his day could get any stranger. He nodded towards Savary. "His Excellency will have to go in the clerk's room until his cell's ready."

"Ready?" Grant said. "Why can't you take him there now? Or are you having it cleaned first?"

Bault gave him a look. He wasn't sure any of the cells had been cleaned, ever. That wasn't how La Force worked. The place wasn't a hotel. Bault, however, wasn't about to tell Grant that the reason he was delaying transferring Savary was a far more simple one: self-preservation.

Over the years, Bault had seen a great many people come and go; their sentences determined as much by their politics as by the crimes they were alleged to have committed. And allegiances shifted all the time, with people falling in and out of favour with monotonous regularity; this morning's departures and arrivals being cases in point. Bault was often the one constant factor in their lives, and if he understood anything it was expediency. He liked to think of himself, therefore, as a facilitator.

So, in keeping with his own dubious code, he had remained polite during the registration of the first pair of unexpected inmates – he'd even apologized when he'd shown Pasquier to his cell – and he saw no reason to change his strategy as far as number three was concerned. *Especially* where number three was concerned. Savary's name and the intrigues of his ministry were known and feared throughout the country. Bault had no intention of getting on the wrong side of this one if he could help it, prisoner or no prisoner. Because you never knew when a good deed might be reciprocated, or rewarded.

All in all, though, it was turning into one hell of a morning.

Count Nicholas Frochot, Prefect of the Seine, trotted his horse beneath the twin pillars of the Barrière du Trône and into the rue du Faubourg-Saint-Antoine. The journey had been an exhausting one. The overnight downpour had turned the road from Nogent to clay. The mare's legs were caked in it, as were Frochot's boots and riding coat, which seemed to weigh heavier and press down upon him with each of his mount's long strides. During the summer months when the woods and hedgerows were dappled with early morning sunlight and alive with bird-song, and with the river glinting as though its surface was strewn with diamonds, the eight-mile ride from his house was the most enjoyable part of his day. But this morning, the going had been especially taxing and Frochot was looking forward to reaching the comfort of his office. Head down, collar high around his neck, hat pulled low, he burrowed himself into his saddle, guiding the mare lightly with the reins, allowing her to do all the work. She'd done the journey so many times, she knew the way without being told.

It was as Frochot was passing the Church of the Jesuits a mile and a half further on that he became aware of a horseman cantering towards him. There weren't that many solitary riders on the road, other than military couriers, so another lone civilian at this hour was noticeable. As the rider drew closer and he heard his name called, he realized with a start he was being hailed by one of the Préfecture's stable hands. Frochot reined in his horse. "Bertrand? What are you doing here?"

The stable hand guided his horse alongside. His hair was stuck to his face and there was mud on his cheeks. "Forgive me, Excellency. I wasn't sure it was you."

Frochot unfastened the top button of his coat and peeled the collar back so that his features were revealed. The strands of grey hair that poked from beneath the brim of his hat were curly and damp. He smiled. "Well, it is."

The stable hand reached inside his coat. "Deputy Villemsens directed me to find you and hand you this message. He said it was most important and that you should come as quickly as possible."

Frochot frowned. An odd request, considering that his deputy would know he was en route anyway.

Bertrand passed the note across and the Prefect broke it open. The message was brief. *You are needed urgently.* Two further words were scrawled beneath and like the first sentence they looked as if they had been transcribed in haste. They were not written in French, however, but in Latin.

Fuit Imperator.

Frochot stared down at them. His heart began to thud.

Beneath him, the mare, as if sensing her master's alarm, pawed the ground impatiently. Using only his right hand – the note was still clutched in his left – Frochot brought her under control. Quickly, he thrust the note into his pocket. Then, without pausing to fasten his collar, and under the stable hand's startled gaze, Frochot gripped the reins of his horse with both hands, dug his heels into the mare's flanks and set off at a gallop towards the city.

It was after eight-thirty when Grant walked out of La Force, having gained Bault's word that the prison's three newest residents would remain segregated. Watching Bault enter Savary's details into the register had been both satisfying and oddly unreal and for several seconds the absurd desire to blurt out, "Now you know what it feels like, and by the way my name's Major Colquhoun Grant, you Frog bastard!" had hovered enticingly on the edge of his tongue.

Inevitably, common sense had prevailed, but it had been a close call.

His last view of Savary being led away by the gaolers had been an illuminating one. Savary had turned just before his departure through the inner door. He'd stared hard into Grant's eyes, the flesh around his jaw drawn as tight as a drum skin. There had been no trace of self-pity in his expression, no sense

411

of a man resigned to his fate. There had only been arrogance and contempt, as if, in his own mind, at least, he was the deity and the rest of humanity was subject to his divine will.

Outside, a *fiacre* with a broken roof was drawing up. When it stopped, two guardsmen stepped down. They did not look the happiest of souls. Neither did the driver. Grant soon saw why, though the fact that the guardsmen had been riding *inside* the carriage had already aroused his suspicions.

"Where's General Guidal?"

The question drew an awkward silence, guilty looks and a shuffling of feet from the guardsmen.

"Someone had better spit it out," Grant said. He pointed to one of them at random. "You; what's your name?"

"Corporal Cassalle."

The other one looked thankful he hadn't been chosen.

"All right, Corporal. Where is he?"

"Don't know, sir." The corporal shook his head helplessly.

"Not the answer I was hoping for. When did you see him last?"

The general had woken up, Cassalle told Grant, just as the carriage was approaching the Quai Pelletier on the far side of the Pont au Change from where Grant had elected to finish the journey to La Force on foot. Following the general's discovery that he had, to use his own words, been abandoned like a leper, several minutes of high drama had ensued, during which the hapless guardsmen had been reduced to near quivering wrecks by a verbal onslaught that would have put a battery of howitzers to shame, interspersed by the general taking frequent swigs from a flask of cognac he'd removed from his pocket within seconds of letting rip.

The guardsmen had had little option but to stand and suffer the abuse, which had increased in ferocity with every sip the general had taken. The name of one Captain Rémy had also started to bear the brunt of Guidal's wrath, at which point the driver had taken his life in his hands by pointing out that in the time the carriage had been stopped, they could have picked up the pace and intercepted Captain Rémy and the escort as they crossed the Pont Marie back to the other side of the river.

Which hadn't gone down well. It was then that the general had finally lost his head, hurling his empty flask on to the cobbles, where it had shattered, spraying shards of glass in all directions.

It had been an odd thing, Cassalle then told Grant nervously. It was almost as if the smashing of the glass had acted as some kind of snapping finger, for at the sound of the breakage the general had suddenly fallen mute, as if he'd spied himself from a distance and been subdued and ashamed by what he'd seen.

Whereupon, in no uncertain terms he'd ordered the guardsmen to get the hell out of his sight and to take the driver and his flea-bitten nag with them. He had better things to do than help deliver a God-damned son-of-a-bitch aristo into Purgatory when he'd been there once already and hadn't liked it much the first time. His parting words as he'd staggered off had been, "And you can tell that God-damned Rémy that I'm away to find myself a drink. They can finish their God-damned rebellion without me!"

General Guidal had last been seen stumbling away in the direction of the rue Saint-Denis with the guardsmen having little option but to watch him go, because no corporal or private in his right mind was going to argue with a general of the Empire, especially one the size of a bear, with a temper to match. Add the fact that he was drunk and spoiling for a fight and the potential for mayhem was there for all but the blind or the witless to see. The guardsmen weren't blind and neither of them was *that* clueless, so they'd chosen the less confrontational option and left the general to his own devices while they'd hitched a ride in the carriage to rejoin their company at La Force. The driver hadn't been sorry to see the general go either.

Listening to the guardsman's account, Grant wondered what he should do next. General Guidal on the loose, whether he was in a foul mood or merely maudlin or drifting between both states, was not something he wished to consider. Bault had told him that Pasquier and Desmarest had arrived and were in his

413

safekeeping. With Savary's arrest, that meant the unholy trinity was now under lock and key, so the first part of the plan had been achieved without mishap or bloodshed; the sabre nick to Savary's Adam's apple notwithstanding.

Guidal's next allotted tasks had been to arrest Savary's deputy, Réal, and secure the War Ministry, but that part of the plan looked as if it might now be in jeopardy. It didn't help that Guidal had in his possession the documents necessary for the accomplishment of his orders. Without them, irrespective of their legitimacy, it was unlikely that Réal or Clarke could be unseated unless force were used, which, admittedly, had always been an option, though one to be considered only as a last resort.

The most crucial objective by far, after each of the police departments, was the garrison, and that was a responsibility Malet had reserved for himself, aided by Hawkwood and the 1st Company. Guidal's condition and his errant behaviour could not be allowed to interfere with that phase of the operation.

The best place to head for, Grant decided, was the Place Vendôme. General Malet needed to be informed of Guidal's actions as soon as possible. On the way, he could call in on the newly incumbent Commissioner Balthus and General La Horie in the hope that Guidal had made a re-appearance either at the Préfecture or the Police Ministry.

He nodded to the guardsmen. "All right, gentlemen, you can rejoin the rest of the escort."

Trying not to look too relieved at having been dismissed, the guardsmen turned away. As they did so, unseen by either of them, a small dark object fell from the corporal's musket and bounced across the cobbles. It made no sound as it hit the road surface.

It should have.

Grant stared at it. Bending down, he picked the object up, cupped it in his palm and studied it closely. It was a semi-circular, wedge-shaped piece of wood a little less than an inch across. As he rubbed his thumb across its surface, his blood ran cold. He looked up.

"Corporal Cassalle, you've dropped something."

The two guardsmen stopped and turned.

"Sir?" Cassalle said.

Grant walked towards them and held out his hand. "I believe this is yours."

The corporal frowned and then stared at the object in Grant's palm.

"Tell me this was an oversight, Corporal," Grant said.

The corporal said nothing.

Grant looked at the second guardsman. "Show me your musket."

The guardsman slid the musket strap from his shoulder and held out the weapon with both hands. Grant stared down at it. His insides twisted.

"Is it the same for the rest of the men?"

The guardsmen looked at each other and then nodded.

Sweet God Almighty, Grant thought. *How did we not notice?*

Grant handed the wedge back to the corporal. "Don't let it come loose again."

"No, sir."

"Dismissed," Grant said.

As the guardsmen walked away, Grant summoned the sergeant of the escort to him. He forced himself to remain calm.

"You're to rejoin your company at the Ministry, Sergeant."

"Sir."

"I suggest you return by the route we came. It'll be quicker."

"And you, Captain?"

"I'm due to rendezvous with General Lamotte. He's expecting a progress report."

"Very good, sir."

As the sergeant gathered his men, Grant walked quickly to the *fiacre* and climbed aboard.

The driver turned in his seat and looked at him. "Where to?"

All thoughts of calling in at the Police Ministry and the Préfecture were now abandoned.

"Place Vendôme, quick as you can."

The guardsmen were already on the march as the carriage

415

moved off. It was only as the horse broke into a trot leaving the soldiers behind that Grant looked down at his hands.

They began to shake violently.

Shrugging off his coat, Frochot took the stairs two at a time and met Villemsens on the landing coming down to meet him. The deputy had clearly been watching for his arrival from his office window.

"Well?" Frochot asked breathlessly. "Is it true?"

The note that Villemsens had penned was fresh in his mind. *Fuit Imperator.*

Imperator could be translated in a number of ways, but Frochot had understood the intended meaning immediately: *The Emperor is no more.*

"It would appear so, Excellency," Villemsens said, his face grim, adding, "Rovigo called to see you earlier. He went away when we told him you hadn't arrived. There's a Colonel Soulier here though, from the National Guard. He's been waiting for a while. It was he who brought the news."

"I saw the troops outside," Frochot said. "Where've you put him?"

"He's in your office."

Frochot folded his coat over his arm and followed his deputy up the stairs. When he entered the room he was relieved to see that a fire had been lit. Hanging up his coat, he shook hands with Soulier.

"What can you tell me, Colonel?"

Soulier recounted the morning's events, wasting no time in presenting Frochot with copies of the documents entrusted to him by General Lamotte.

The name meant nothing.

"I don't know a General Malet either," Frochot said. "Who's he?" He glanced over at Villemsens, who looked perplexed and shook his head.

Soulier pointed to the document in Frochot's hand. It was a copy of the Sénatus-Consulte. "It's his signature at the bottom of the page. He's the Garrison Commander."

"What's happened to Hulin?"

"The Senate's replaced him."

"Since when?"

"Does it say when the Senate met?" Soulier asked, indicating the document.

Frochot looked at the date. "Last night. The twenty-second."

"Then that's when he was replaced," Soulier said. His eyebrows lifted. "Did you not read that part? It's near the bottom. After the list of names the Senate's chosen for the new government," Soulier added pointedly.

Frochot chewed his lip. He knew what Soulier was getting at. Why was he, Frochot, bothering to question the Senate's decision when he was a beneficiary of it?

Which was a valid point, Frochot could not deny. His gaze moved back up to the list. There it was; *his* name, in the same paragraph as Moreau, Augereau, and the rest. But he'd still never heard of General Malet.

Not that the omission was especially significant. There had to be scores of officers on the general staff he'd never heard of. What were two more?

The names of the thirteen men nominated by the Senate to form the Provisional Government were an intriguing mix: aristos, military men, senators – republicans *and* monarchists. All of them anti-Bonapartists, with one noticeable exception: Prefect Nicholas Frochot. Why had he been included? Continuity, he suspected, which was probably why Rovigo had called by, to offer his allegiance. Which was reassuring, Frochot thought. He eyed Soulier.

"What do you need from me, Colonel?"

"General Lamotte wants meeting chambers made ready for occupation. The Senate will require quarters for both the members of the Provisional Government as well as the general staff."

"I can do that," Frochot confirmed. He turned to Villemsens. "Gather the porters and the ushers. Tell them to prepare the great hall."

"And the general staff?" Villemsens asked.

Frochot smiled. "The army can have the basement."

Soulier mopped his brow. His job was done. All that remained was to wait for General Lamotte to return.

It took a little over fifteen minutes, following Savary's arrival at La Force, for Bault to perform his first facilitation of the day.

He'd been on the point of escorting the former Minister of Police from the clerk's office to his new accommodation when he'd let slip in a conversational aside that Savary's wasn't the first arrival of note he'd had that morning.

Savary, not having heard Grant's opening conversation with the warder, had, with feigned nonchalance to cover a feeling of impending dread, asked Bault who those other people might be. Bault, sensing an opportunity for remuneration, had duly obliged.

The gleam of avarice in Bault's eyes may have been in the foetal stage, but for Savary, master of guile, it might as well have been emblazoned across the warder's forehead.

Within minutes, Pasquier and Desmarest had been delivered from their cells to the clerk's office. All three men had gazed at each other in awe as the significance of their incarceration had struck home.

"I can give you twenty minutes, Excellencies," Bault told them, securing the door and leaving two gaolers outside for added security.

By which time Savary was already pacing the room.

"So, let me see if I have this right: Malet, La Horie and Guidal have gained control of the National Guard, the Préfecture and the Ministry, and that's all without a shot being fired. That's quite an achievement for three criminals who are supposed to be behind bars."

He stabbed a finger at Desmarest.

"I seem to recall asking you if I should be concerned about Malet. Your answer – if I remember correctly – was: 'I doubt it's worth calling out the National Guard.' Well, that's ironic, wouldn't you say? Seeing as it's the Guard that's supporting him!"

Desmarest said nothing. He knew better than to interrupt.

"Do we know how much support he has?" Pasquier enquired.

Savary considered the question. "If he has the Guard then he has more than enough men to help him seize total control. There are only seven thousand troops in the entire city. That's nothing. If he now has the police, as would appear likely, then he has the gendarmerie, too. His next goal has to be the garrison. After that, there'll be no stopping him."

"How loyal are they?" Desmarest asked.

"The garrison troops? You tell me," Savary said. "It's no secret, the Russian campaign's sapped the army's will. You're aware of the rumours of discontent as much as I am. In all likelihood, the regular troops will follow their commanders; even against the Emperor, if Malet provides the right incentive. He's already proved it's possible with the Guard."

"You don't think the Emperor's really dead?" Desmarest posed the question.

"If he is," Pasquier said, "then this conversation is irrelevant."

"Of course he's not dead!" Savary spat. "There was no special Senate meeting either. It's all lies! They tried before, remember? This is the same thing."

"Servan," Desmarest said.

Savary nodded. "Only this time His Majesty's a lot further away than Spain."

"Malet's managed to fool a lot of people so far," Pasquier said. "The documents I saw looked genuine, and I've dictated enough in my time."

Desmarest chewed a nail. "So, what do we do? We have to warn people. We can't just sit here. We have to get the word out. We know the warder's malleable. Maybe we can persuade him to pass a message."

"To whom?" Pasquier said.

"Réal, for one," Savary replied. "If they haven't got to him first. He's got to be on Malet's list."

"And tell him what? To run and hide?"

Savary shook his head. "Alert the garrison."

"There's no time. Dumas told me Hulin had already been replaced," Desmarest said. "Maybe it's too late. Maybe Hulin's going to be the next one through the door."

Desmarest saw that Savary was staring at him.

"*Dumas?*" Savary said, his eyes darkening. "You've *met* Dumas?"

Desmarest realized his mistake. "He was the one that arrested me."

Savary saw that Pasquier was giving Desmarest an odd look, as if the name meant something to the Prefect, too. How was that possible? Unless Pasquier knew something he as Minister didn't, or else the Prefect and Desmarest had already been in discussions. If so, when did that happen? It must have been before this morning's debacle, because both of them had been surprised to see each other. Unless that had been an act – and Savary didn't think so. There was definitely something going on here.

To the other two he said silkily, "I think it's time we compared notes, gentlemen; don't you?"

General Malet, the document wallet under his left arm, ran his right hand down the buttons of his tunic as if to reassure himself they were all fastened correctly, and in a quiet aside to Hawkwood murmured, "How do I look?"

"I'd march with you," Hawkwood said.

The corner of the general's mouth lifted. He nodded at Steenhouwer. "Ready, Captain?"

Steenhouwer turned to the four guardsmen who'd accompanied them from the street. "Guard the landing and stairs."

As the soldiers spread out, Steenhouwer rapped loudly on the apartment door.

The servant who answered the knock looked startled to see a fully plumed general standing on the threshold. Senior officers didn't normally drop by to pay homage at this hour of the day.

"I've an urgent dispatch for General Hulin," Malet said. "From the Senate."

The servant looked apologetic. "The general's still sleeping, sir."

"Then I suggest you go and wake him," Malet said.

"Sir?"

"Wake. Him," Malet said, enunciating each syllable with icy precision.

The servant bridled. Realizing this might involve more than just an early morning courtesy call, he stood aside and allowed Malet, Hawkwood and Steenhouwer to enter. Still determined to maintain some semblance of protocol, the servant then announced formally, "If you'd care to wait, gentlemen. I'll advise the general you're here."

"No need," Malet said, smiling. "We'll come with you. It'll save time."

The servant's eyebrows rose. "The countess is with him, General."

"Perhaps you didn't understand the word *urgent*," Malet said.

"No, but *I* do," a voice said from the doorway.

The man who advanced into the hallway wore a velvet collared robe over a cream-coloured night shirt. He was well over six feet tall and might easily have equalled General Guidal in height. Beneath the robe, however, in contrast to Guidal's stouter bulk, General Hulin's torso was powerful and muscular. His face, strong-chinned and framed by a pair of long and well-trimmed side whiskers, matched his impressive physique. He was the embodiment of everything a Count of the Empire and holder of the Grand Cross of the *Légion d'Honneur* should be.

Hawkwood's knowledge of Hulin stemmed from what Malet had told him. Despite his rank, the count was from modest beginnings. He'd been a lowly private when he'd taken part in the assault to liberate the inmates of the Bastille. Now, not much more than twenty years later, he was the commander in charge of the 1st Division of the Paris garrison which, to all intents and purposes, made him the Governor of Paris. A zealous Bonaparte supporter, it was rumoured he'd presided over the council that had condemned the Duke of Enghien to death.

No one, Hawkwood knew, could rise from the ranks to that sort of prominence without having a steel core buried deep in the heart of him. Even so, the general looked more puzzled than annoyed at the unexpected arrival of early morning visitors and he regarded the three officers standing before him with interest. He stared at Malet, taking in the uniform. "I don't believe I know you, sir."

"We've not met, General," Malet confirmed. "My name is Lamotte."

Hulin looked at Hawkwood, at the tunic showing beneath his great-coat. His eyes narrowed. "So, gentlemen, what can I do for you at this hour?"

Malet eyed the servant, who was still in the room. "If we might speak in private?"

Hulin nodded. "Very well, as you wish."

"Wait here," Malet told Steenhouwer.

Voicing the same instruction to his manservant, Hulin led Malet and Hawkwood through the doorway by which he'd just entered and into the adjoining office. "So, gentlemen," he said as he closed the door behind them, "this looks serious. What can I do for you?"

"I bring news from the Senate, General," Malet said.

"The Senate? Must be important for you to come calling at this hour." Brow creasing, Hulin walked towards his desk.

"It is, General," Malet said. "You've been relieved of your command. I'm here to secure all your papers. I'll also need the 1st Division's seal."

"Excuse me?" Hulin stopped in mid stride. He turned.

"His Majesty's been killed. The Senate's issued a decree dissolving the Empire. A new government's been established which means that you're being replaced."

"What the hell d'you mean, dead? The hell he is! And the Senate's met? Since when? I haven't heard anything, and I'm Commander of the damned garrison. You're telling me the Senate didn't think to include me in its deliberations?"

Hulin paused. His eyes became slits. "It's because I've always taken the Emperor's side, isn't it? God damn it! Is that why? Afraid I might kick up a fuss? Sons of bitches! What sort of trick is this?"

Hulin reached his desk and stood behind it; a proud captain at the helm of his ship, preparing to repel boarders. He frowned once more. "Are you sure we haven't met?"

"Positive, General." Malet smiled. "I think we both would have remembered."

Hulin nodded, though it was clear he was still aggrieved. He held out his hand. "Well, if we're going to proceed with this farce, show me your orders."

"Of course, General. Allow me." Malet slid the document wallet from under his arm.

Whether it was the expression on Malet's face that speared the warning into Hulin's brain or his doubt over the Emperor's death and the idea that the Senate had convened without him, or whether it was the partly concealed pistol in his own belt, Hawkwood would never know, but as Malet's hand dipped out of view he saw the flash of consternation pass across the garrison commander's face and even as Hulin snatched the pistol from the open drawer, Hawkwood was pulling his coat hem aside.

As General Malet drew his own pistol from the wallet and pointed it directly at the Garrison Commander.

Hulin, judging that the main threat lay with the man facing him, already had his pistol aimed at Malet's breast. Shock flooded his face as he realized Malet was also armed.

There was a bright flash as Malet squeezed the trigger. Powder smoke obscured his face.

Hawkwood fired at the same second.

The pistol ball blew out Hulin's cheek and jaw, propelling a red mist across the front and shoulder of his robe. As he toppled backwards behind the desk, the pistol fell from his hand and clattered across the floor.

Even before the echo of the report had died away, the door crashed open. Steenhouwer burst in, followed by the manservant. With the reek of powder clogging his nostrils, Hawkwood ran to the other side of the desk.

Hulin lay on his back. His eyes were closed. A red tide of blood was spreading slowly out from beneath him.

A frantic cry sounded from the doorway as a thin, middle-aged woman clad in a nightgown and with her hair in disarray, rushed in. When she saw her husband on the floor, covered in blood, the countess fell to her knees beside the body, her face pale and stricken with grief.

Malet stared down. "Why did he do that?"

Ignoring the woman's bleating sobs, Hawkwood retrieved Hulin's pistol. The moment he picked it up, he could see it wasn't loaded. Hulin had only been planning to use the weapon as a threat.

The flash, linked to the lack of a report from Malet's pistol, had told its own story. A misfire. It could have been the rain, Hawkwood supposed, though that would have been unusual. A primed gun could still fire in the wet as long as it was well maintained. Alternatively, there may have been a weakness in the powder or the touch hole could have become clogged. Whatever the reason, it didn't matter now. The damage had been done.

Hawkwood rounded on Steenhouwer, who was clutching his sword and staring at the scene before him as if in a trance. "Get the men in from the landing, now!"

Steenhouwer hesitated and then, nodding quickly, he disappeared. Hawkwood turned to the servant.

"You! Fetch bandages! Something to staunch the bleeding!"

A low keening sound was issuing from the woman's mouth. Hunched over her husband's prostrate form, the countess stroked his hair and the uninjured side of his face. Her hands and nightdress were smeared red.

Hawkwood looked for Malet. "Time to go, General!"

"We need the seal!" Malet protested.

The seal of the 1st Division of the Paris garrison. It was the garrison commander's ultimate badge of office.

"Then find it!"

A clatter of boots came from outside. Steenhouwer was back, the guardsmen with him. Having been alerted by the gunshot, they pulled up short when they saw blood.

"You four," Hawkwood snapped. "You're to stay here. No one's to enter or leave the apartment. You – what's your name?"

The servant had also returned, with a bowl and bandages. He looked bewildered and terrified at the same time. He stared at Hawkwood, at the four soldiers with muskets. "Pascal."

"All right, Pascal. We're locking you in for your own safety. If you make any sound, if you try to call for help, and if either

424

you or the countess try to leave, these men have orders to shoot you. Do you understand?"

The servant's hands shook. He nodded mutely.

"There's a lot of blood, but the general's wound isn't fatal. A doctor will be sent. Have you got *that*?"

Another nod.

"Then assist the countess. General, have you found your damned seal yet?"

"I have it!"

"Then we go, now! You four, remember what I said. You do not leave the apartment. No one in or out. I'm locking the room and taking the key with me. I hear you've disobeyed my order and I'll have you up before a firing squad. Captain Steenhouwer, you're with the general and me. Move!"

Pushing Malet and the captain ahead of him, Hawkwood locked the door of the office and the three men hurried for the stairs.

23

Grant's mind was in turmoil after his discovery at La Force. As the carriage rattled along the street he cast his thoughts back through the morning's events, to the suborning of the Guard at Popincourt Barracks. How could they have missed it? It didn't seem possible. He blamed himself as much as anyone. Why had there been no inspection? Answer: because he and Hawkwood and General Malet had taken it for granted that when Colonel Soulier and Captain Piquerel had deployed the Guard, the men had assembled with battle-ready equipment. Grant cursed his stupidity. He and Hawkwood had crossed glances over the quality of the guardsmen when they'd lined up. That should have been warning enough. Between them, they'd managed to break one of the first rules of warfare: Never assume anything.

What it meant, of course, was that speed was now, more than ever, the critical factor. The risk of the blunder being spotted by the forces that opposed them was increasing with every passing second. Grant wondered if Hawkwood and Malet had made the same discovery. It struck him then that if they had and the opposition remained oblivious and victory was still achieved, it would surely go down as one of the greatest bluffs in military history.

Grant braced himself as the carriage bounced across a pothole. He looked to his left. They were passing the Hotel de Ville. In front of the building, on the Place de Grève, a company of

National Guardsmen stood in formation. Soulier and the 6th Company had arrived from Popincourt.

A premonition made him look to his right. At the far end of the rue du Temple, Grant spotted movement. It was the head of a marching column. Grant recognized the green and white uniforms. Fusiliers of the Paris Guard; from La Courtille Barracks, most likely, which meant that Malet's orders had been delivered. It was a sign that the first regular units were on their way. By now, if the commanders had relayed their orders correctly, other companies of the Paris Guard were spreading out like tentacles to guard the city's strategic buildings and main gates.

As the carriage approached the junction with the rue Saint-Denis, Grant looked about him keenly, though he knew it was a forlorn hope that General Guidal, drunk or otherwise, might just be passing that way. There were scores of wine shops and drinking cellars in the vicinity, but it would take hours to visit them all. A search was out of the question. And for all anyone knew the man could just as easily be sleeping it off face down in an alleyway.

Grant took a deep breath. The warm aroma of baking bread drifted on the air, mixing uneasily with the sweet, sickly stench of human sewage being emptied from half-lit doorways into gutters that steamed like cooking fires.

There was no dawn chorus; no birdsong to herald the damp grey light of morning; only the wailing of children, the barking of dogs and the squeaking of the carriage as it trundled over the cobblestones; intrusive sounds that grated on the ear like nails raked across a slate. While from a distance there came the pervasive and relentless tramp of marching feet.

The sound faded as the carriage moved on and Grant wondered if it hadn't simply been his own heart that he had heard beating. He shivered, despite his heavy coat. Someone, he thought, had just walked across his grave. In a single moment the full nature of the drama he was engaged upon rose into his mind with a force that was as overwhelming as anything he'd experienced.

Here he was, on his way to seize the Paris Garrison, with a

renegade general and little more than a handful of National Guardsmen who hadn't a hope in hell of defending themselves if the final phase of the plan fell apart.

Because it was impossible to fire a musket if there was no bloody flint.

Grant knew, as he'd known from the moment he'd picked up the small wedge of hardwood that had fallen from Corporal Cassalle's weapon, what its significance was. It was a practice flint, for use in drills and exercises when the regular flint was removed from the musket jaw and a wooden flint of the same dimensions substituted. It enabled the musket to be fully functional without wearing down the steel of the frizzen. Unfortunately, it also rendered the musket completely useless, unless it was swung as a club; a woefully inadequate weapon with which to try and subdue an Empire.

Hawkwood and Malet were armed. They had swords and pistols. That much Grant knew, but they wouldn't be enough. So Grant was doing the only thing he could think of in the time allowed. Limited though his resources were, he was going to provide Hawkwood and General Malet with the only reinforcements he had to hand.

Himself.

It was Lieutenant Prévost's first visit to Garrison Headquarters. As he led his men through the entrance gate and into the courtyard he tried not to let his apprehension show. The general had told him that they would probably gain admittance without being challenged by the guard on duty and so it had proved. The sentry hadn't given them a second glance, though it still felt to Prévost as though he was entering the lion's den. Very few officers chose to visit Number 7 Place Vendôme voluntarily.

Officially, the building housed the offices of the Army's High Command. In reality, the place had become synonymous with activities of a far darker shade. The men who worked within its walls may have worn army uniforms, but few of them had ever trodden a battlefield. Most were agents of the police; their speciality: the maintenance of order through surveillance of the military. At their head, nestling like a spider in his web, sat General Hulin's Chief of Staff, Colonel Jean Doucet.

Doucet was at breakfast. A glass of cognac and an egg were arranged on a plate before him. Doucet took the egg, cracked it against the rim of the glass and emptied the raw contents into the drink. Downing the mixture in one, he returned the glass to the plate and dabbed his lips with a napkin, which he then folded and set down by his right elbow.

He motioned to his orderly to serve him his coffee. Doucet did not add milk or cream. He took a sip, rolling the liquid around his tongue for several seconds. Finally, he nodded and watched in silence as the orderly took the plate, the empty glass and the broken egg shell, and left the room.

His ritual completed, Doucet placed his coffee cup in its saucer and looked up. "Well?" he said.

Prévost stepped forward. He swallowed nervously. "My apologies, Colonel. Lieutenant Prévost. I've important dispatches for your attention."

"From whom?"

"General Lamotte."

Doucet frowned but said nothing. A vain, tight-lipped man with a face as sharp as a flint and more than a dozen years of military and police work behind him, he had little time for subordinates, particularly those with whom he was not personally acquainted and who had the temerity to interrupt his morning routine; a prejudice that was even more pronounced when it came to members of the National Guard. He took another sip of coffee. Then, making no effort to bestow a glance in Prévost's direction, he held out his hand. "Show me."

Taking the package from the lieutenant, Doucet put his cup down, opened the first document and began to read. He was surprised to discover it was a personal letter signed by the Commander of the Armed Forces of Paris, composed and dated that morning at the Hotel de Ville.

The opening paragraph drew his attention immediately. He was being promoted; to the rank of General of Brigade, as a reward for outstanding service. It wasn't something he'd been expecting. Intrigued, he read on.

By the time he'd reached the bottom of the letter, the temperature of Doucet's coffee had deteriorated from steaming to below tepid. He picked up the next document, trying to keep his hand steady as he did so. It was a copy of a Senate decree. The third document was a bank order for one hundred thousand francs. The fourth was a proclamation issued by the new Head of the 1st Division, General Malet, which Doucet was to read out to all Staff officers and troops under his command.

After setting the last document aside he sat back and laid his hands palm down on the table. His face remained perfectly still. Inside, his nerve ends were on fire.

"Tell me everything," he said.

He listened in silence as Prévost described Lamotte's arrival at the barracks, the mustering of the Guard and the announcement of the Emperor's death, the march to the prison and the freeing of Generals La Horie and Guidal.

"It sounds as if you've had a rather busy morning, Lieutenant," Doucet observed. "Where's General Lamotte now?"

"He's with General Hulin, sir."

Doucet picked the letter up from the table. "To place him under arrest, it states here; by order of the new garrison commander."

Prévost hesitated before giving his reply. "That's my understanding, sir. Yes."

"Have you met General Malet?"

"No, Colonel."

"It also says that a General Desnoyers is being assigned to the office of the General Staff. I seem to recall that Desnoyers has been on the retired list for several years."

"I'm afraid I wouldn't know, Colonel," Prévost said. "I'm sorry. Perhaps it would be better if you saved your questions for General Lamotte himself?"

The colonel's interrogation was making Prévost nervous. He wasn't comfortable being grilled by senior officers, especially those of Doucet's status. They had the uncanny knack of making you feel guilty when you hadn't done anything.

Doucet fixed Prévost with a cold glare. "Thank you, Lieutenant. Your advice is noted. So, do you know when I can expect to receive the general?"

Prévost let his gaze drift towards the window and gave up a silent prayer of thanks. "He's on his way now, Colonel. I can see him from here."

Doucet pushed himself to his feet and strode to the glass. His view of the entrance to Hulin's apartment was partially blocked by the Austerlitz column. But as he watched, the group of four previously hidden officers walked out from behind the column's shadow.

"There," Prévost said, pointing helpfully.

Doucet watched as the officers broke apart and, with the Company at their shoulders, headed towards the headquarters' entrance. The general was easy to spot from his uniform. His height also made him stand out. Of the three men with him, two were dressed in uniforms identifying them as officers in the National Guard. The fourth wore a military greatcoat, open to display an infantry officer's tunic.

"Who are the others?" Doucet asked.

"The Guards officers are Captain Steenhouwer and Lieutenant Gomont. The officer on the general's immediate right is his aide, Captain Dumas."

Doucet stared down at the approaching soldiers. "Then I should make myself ready. We wouldn't want the general to gain a bad impression of his staff, would we?"

"No, sir," Prévost agreed quickly. A shiver of pleasure moved through him. It had felt, just for a moment, as if the colonel had forgiven him his previous gaffe and was taking him into his confidence.

Prévost's sense of worth was short-lived. Doucet turned away from the window. He looked surprised to see that Prévost was still there. "That's all, Lieutenant. You may rejoin your men."

"My instructions from General Lamotte were to remain downstairs and protect the entrance, Colonel," Prévost said, emboldened by the fleeting sensation of intimacy.

Doucet nodded curtly. "Very good. Dismissed."

"Yes, sir. Thank you, sir."

Don't grovel, Prévost thought as he saluted, but Doucet was already turning away.

As the lieutenant left the room Doucet returned to the table. The taste of cold coffee lingered at the back of his throat. It was a perfect complement to the trepidation that was moving through him as his brain struggled to comprehend the onus that had just been placed upon his shoulders. He thought about General Hulin. In his letter, General Malet had written that he appreciated how difficult it would be for Doucet to arrest his own commander, a man with whom he'd enjoyed a close rapport over the past few years, so to spare Doucet that disagreeable duty he'd assigned General Lamotte to the task.

The letter had contained another instruction. Doucet was to place his own adjutant, Major Etienne Laborde, under house arrest. The reason, Malet had outlined, was that Laborde's activities had made him too many enemies among the ranks of the military. It would be detrimental to morale if he were to remain in his current post.

General Malet hoped that Doucet would understand and that, irrespective of his personal feelings for General Hulin and Major Laborde, he was confident the colonel would fulfil his duty. The general had gone on to add that in the spirit of cooperation he was certain their shared experience of carrying out duties in the public service would only enhance their future working relationship.

Doucet moved back to the window. General Lamotte and his staff were approaching with purpose. He only had a few minutes. Calling his orderly to him he issued rapid instructions.

Before summoning the unsuspecting Major Laborde to his office.

Lieutenant Gomont looked nervous. When Malet, Hawkwood and Steenhouwer stepped from Hulin's building he did everything except bound up to them wagging his tail.

"Are you all right, General? I thought I heard a pistol shot."

"Strange," Hawkwood said, making a play of looking around the square. "We did, too. You've seen no sign of trouble here?"

"None, sir," Gomont answered, looking relieved.

"Nothing to worry about then," Malet said, glancing towards the headquarters' entrance. "We must have imagined it."

Hawkwood ordered Gomont to fall the men in. He followed Malet's gaze. According to Malet's information, there was minimal guard presence in the building, other than a handful of gendarmes and perhaps half a dozen dragoons who were employed as couriers. He looked up. A shadow moved across one of the first-floor windows, but it was too far away to make out who it might have been.

Place Vendôme was slowly filling up. Small knots of people were gathering. Most of them – the unsuspecting ones – Hawkwood guessed, were there to secure a good view of the morning parade. The others – and he could tell from their faces who they were – had obviously come to see if the rumours were true. It was already becoming clear, from the way the crowd was congregating, that word of the Emperor's death was spreading fast, like ripples from the centre of a pool. Soon, the news would begin to insinuate its way into the surrounding streets and then out across the entire city. And from there . . .

Time to move, Hawkwood thought.

They were halfway to their objective when a figure came hurrying towards them. It was Rateau. He was no longer carrying the package containing the spare uniform but he was alone and looking contrite.

"I'm sorry, sir. I called on General Desnoyers. He sends his respects, but . . ."

"He's decided not to join us after all," Malet finished. Disappointment clouded his russet-coloured eyes and a wry smile flitted across his lean face.

"No, sir. I mean yes, sir."

"Did he give a reason?"

Rateau hesitated. "I regret he was not . . . specific . . . in that regard, General."

Malet nodded thoughtfully. He looked at Hawkwood. "I think we can guess why, don't you?"

Because he doesn't believe we can succeed, Hawkwood thought.

"Then we'll just have to prove him wrong, General," Hawkwood said. "Won't we?"

He looked for Prévost. The lieutenant should have reappeared by now. He could hear rising chatter from the Cohort behind them. He turned and fixed Gomont with a look.

"Keep the men quiet, Lieutenant! They're not going to a regimental ball!"

Gomont coloured. "Yes, sir."

"No sign of Jean-Baptiste either," Malet murmured, as Gomont relayed Hawkwood's order to his sergeant.

Hawkwood had forgotten all about Lafon. Rateau had told them that there had been no sign of the cleric at the priest's apartment, which meant that, by rights, he should have been waiting for them in the square. Unless the injury to his ankle had flared up again and he was either incapacitated somewhere en route or else he'd returned to Cajamaño's garret. On a positive note, at least there'd be no risk of him getting in the way.

They were drawing closer to the headquarters' building. Hawkwood caught sight of Prévost then. The lieutenant was the other side of the gate, forming up his men in the courtyard.

Malet saw him at the same time. "It all looks peaceful enough," he said softly to Hawkwood. He turned to Gomont. "Hold the Company here, Lieutenant."

Gomont saluted and Malet, Hawkwood, Steenhouwer and Rateau headed for the entrance.

Prévost saw them. He did not approach but came to attention at the vanguard of his men and saluted.

Passing through the gate, Malet ignored the sentry on duty. Without stopping, he acknowledged Prévost's gesture with a nod and led the way towards the stairs, walking quickly.

They entered the building.

Not as impressive as Horse Guards, Hawkwood thought. The lobby looked more suited to the Alien Office than a military headquarters.

There were no milling uniforms, no harassed clerks scurrying to and fro. Apart from the orderly standing at the foot of the wide stairway leading to the first floor, there were no other staff members in sight. Hawkwood presumed Malet knew the way. It would be embarrassing if they had to stop and ask a clerk for directions.

A pair of dragoons appeared from a doorway to their right, smart in their green tunics. Hawkwood tensed but they paid no attention to Malet's group and walked on down the corridor. The sight of uniformed officers in command headquarters was hardly an irregular occurrence. Hawkwood let out his breath.

"Colonel Doucet?" Malet addressed the orderly sharply without breaking stride. "Office or apartment?"

The orderly's chin rose. "His office, General."

"Thank you."

Two armed gendarmes flanked the top of the stairs but, other than giving Malet's braid a sideways glance, they were as inanimate as gargoyles. Looking straight ahead, ignoring them as he had the sentry at the gate, Malet turned on to a broad corridor. A copper plate attached to the wall by each door gave the identity and role of the room's occupant.

Malet marched to the door marked *Chef de L'État-Major: Colonel J. Doucet.*

"Wait here," he told Rateau. He smiled at Hawkwood. "Let's find out if God *was* paying attention."

Giving Hawkwood no chance to reply, General Malet, without bothering to knock, opened the door and strode into the room.

There were two men present; a colonel and a major. The colonel was seated at the desk. The major was standing by the window, staring down on to the square below.

With Hawkwood and Steenhouwer at his shoulder, Malet addressed the man at the desk. "Colonel Doucet, good morning. You've been expecting me. I'm General Lamotte. These are my aides, Captains Dumas and Steenhouwer."

He's too slow, Hawkwood thought. *He should be on his feet. A senior officer enters the room, the first thing you do is stand up.*

436

Doucet rose languidly from his chair.

"General," he said. His attention moved to Hawkwood and then to Steenhouwer. "Gentlemen."

"Colonel," Hawkwood said.

It was a fact of life, Hawkwood thought. No matter which army they fought for, there were always officers who held the firm belief that they were superior in every way to the men under their command; not just by virtue of rank but in every fibre of their being, morally and intellectually. Doucet was one of those. Hawkwood could see it in the colonel's expression, that aura of loftiness, as if Doucet considered himself the chosen one, designated by the Almighty to transport the tablets down from the mountaintop.

The officer standing by the window turned to face the room and Hawkwood found himself confronted by one of the most dissolute-looking men he'd ever seen in a uniform. The officer's face was pitted with tiny fissures; the ravages of some childhood disease, Hawkwood could only assume. His louche expression, accentuated by a pair of drooping eyes and petulant lips, hinted at a life in which pursuance of the pleasures of the flesh had taken dominion over all other pastimes. As he took in the three visitors, his mouth formed a goatish smile.

"My adjutant," Doucet said amiably. "Major Laborde."

There was a pause.

"You are in receipt of the orders, Colonel, are you not?" Malet said sharply. "Perhaps they weren't clear enough? You were told to place Major Laborde under house arrest. Or could it be there are two Major Labordes in command headquarters? Is that possible?"

Doucet shook his head. "Only the one, General. That's more than enough, believe me."

"Then why is he here?" Malet demanded. He turned to Laborde. "You'll oblige me by confining yourself to your quarters with immediate effect, Major."

Laborde smiled. "In that case, General, the least I can do is return to my own apartment."

Laborde walked to the door. When he got there he turned.

"But then, why should I do that, when the order carries no legitimacy?"

Doucet moved out from the desk. "There's someone else I think you should meet, General. Allow me."

A side door opened and Lucien Paques walked in.

"You know the Inspector-General of Police, of course," Doucet said.

As Malet clawed for his second pistol, Laborde thrust past the astonished Steenhouwer and yelled through the open door, "Dragoons, to me!"

Hawkwood started to turn but he knew he was about a thousand years too late.

Laborde hurled himself towards Malet. As the two men crashed to the floor, wrestling for possession of the pistol, Doucet launched his own attack.

Hawkwood pivoted towards the threat. He'd seen the glint of steel. From somewhere Doucet had retrieved his sword. It must have been concealed behind the desk, Hawkwood realized.

Reacting instinctively, he moved inside the swing, seized Doucet's sword arm, locked the wrist and raked his boot heel down Doucet's shin. As the sabre dropped from Doucet's hand Hawkwood drove his elbow towards Doucet's jaw. Doucet fell back against the desk with a grunt and Hawkwood snatched up the fallen sword.

But time had run out.

The room was suddenly filled with bodies; green-uniformed dragoons summoned by Laborde's cry for help and blue-clad gendarmes alerted by the call to arms and the sounds of the struggle that had ensued because of it.

As he grasped the sword hilt, Hawkwood saw Steenhouwer go down, forced to his knees by two of the dragoons, his face still frozen in shock at the sight of Laborde's attack on a senior officer.

And then, as Hawkwood pushed himself up, sabre in hand, they were on him. He saw the gendarmes' muskets coming round, the muzzles as wide as cannon maws. As he drew the sword back he heard Doucet bellow from the desk: "I want them alive!"

Hawkwood had only enough time to see the nearest gendarme

reverse his musket and slam the butt towards his face. As he turned his head to avoid the strike, he felt a jarring pain in the small of his back, followed by a crushing blow to the base of his skull. As he heard Malet shout, "Listen to me!" the world went black.

Grant abandoned the *fiacre* at the corner of the rue de Castiglione and the rue Saint-Honoré. He knew he'd be less conspicuous entering the square on foot than he would be arriving by carriage.

At the entrance to the Place Vendôme, Grant saw that civilians, despite their growing number, were still in the minority. To his right, fifty paces away, a column of National Guardsmen had been drawn up, with Lieutenant Gomont at its head.

Averting his face to avoid recognition, Grant made his way towards the throng of people that had gathered around the base of the pillar. All eyes, were focused on the headquarters' building in the corner of the square. Grant followed the crowd's collective gaze and saw that it was fixed upon the first-floor windows, where uniformed figures could be seen moving behind the glass.

A ripple of anticipation spread suddenly through the watchers. Voices rose in excited chatter as the doors opened and the tall figure of General Malet stepped out on to the balcony. The breath stuck in Grant's throat. The crowd surged forward and Grant felt elation move through him.

My God, he thought wildly. *We've bloody done it!*

And then, as he looked on, another officer, clad in a colonel's uniform, appeared alongside the general and Grant realized that Malet's hands were bound in front of him and that the victory was not theirs after all.

The colonel raised his arm to quieten the crowd. He stared down at the sea of faces, waited for the noise to die away and then he called out.

"I am Colonel Jean Doucet, Chief of Staff to the Paris garrison! I am here to tell you that rumours of the Emperor's death are completely false! His Majesty lives!"

Doucet took Malet's elbow and dragged him forward. His voice rose. "*This* is the man responsible. He is an impostor, who for many years has born a grudge against the Empire! As you see, he is now under arrest. Even as I speak, troops of the National and the Paris Guard are rounding up his fellow conspirators. There is no need to panic! Order is being restored! A declaration will soon be issued by the Senate! Until then, go about your normal business. Long live the Emperor! Long live France!"

The words were met with a stunned silence. For several seconds no one moved. Then, a half-hearted echo drifted up from the onlookers. As the cheers slowly built, the sour taste of bile rose into Grant's throat. He trained his eyes on the balcony. Malet stood tall and still. His attention was not on the crowd. Instead, he was staring up at the statue. There was a curious expression on his face; a mixture of sadness and resignation, followed by what might have been the beginning of a rueful smile, as if he was amused at the thought of what had so nearly been achieved.

Then, with the crowd still watching, General Malet allowed himself to be pulled back into the room. The balcony doors closed.

Leaving Grant with the burning question.

Where the hell was Hawkwood?

He looked around, hoping for a sighting, knowing that the possibility was unlikely. As he went to turn back, he thought he saw a familiar figure hurrying away at the opposite side of the square. It wasn't Hawkwood. The man wasn't wearing a uniform. He was tall and thin and dressed in black and wearing what had looked like a priest's tricorne hat. Had it not been for the fact that there was no trace of a limp in the man's stride, Grant could have sworn it was Abbé Lafon. But then the man was gone, swallowed up by the dispersing bodies. Grant knew it was useless to follow. He had other priorities now.

With the voices of the people rising as one to proclaim the glory of the Emperor, Grant turned his collar up and with his face still averted and the cheers of the National Guardsmen ringing in his ears, he made his way quickly from the square.

24

"How's the head? I heard you took quite a knock."

Hawkwood looked up, slowly. The procedure wasn't too painful, though the back of his skull was still tender to the touch. There was some stiffness in his neck and soreness around his kidneys as well, but he'd suffered worse. He wasn't pissing blood any more either, which he took as a positive sign.

He'd been unconscious when they'd transported him from Garrison Headquarters to L'Abbaye, the military prison on the Place Sainte-Marguerite, where he'd eventually come around, face down on a biscuit-thin mattress atop a wooden pallet in a stone cell reeking of substances he had no desire to think about. A small barred window set at fingertip height – measured only if he stood on his toes and stretched his arms out as far as they could reach – admitted light. A bucket in the corner served as a latrine. In the two days he'd been occupying the cell, the bucket had not been emptied. There was a blanket, but when he'd seen the state of it, he'd resorted to using his coat for warmth. He was wearing the coat now. He had no idea what time it was. He knew it was day because he could see sky through the window, though there wasn't much of it. He guessed it was close to mid morning. Sitting up, he scraped a hand down his face, feeling the stubble growth.

When the gaoler had ordered him to stand back Hawkwood

hadn't bothered moving. A small victory won. He'd assumed they'd come to escort him to the warder's room for questioning.

The man looking down on him, however, didn't seem to be a turnkey. He was too well dressed. His hair was the colour of dirty straw. He had a short beard, a long nose, pierced ears and an interesting scar on his right upper lip. He was, Hawkwood estimated, about his own age, perhaps a couple of years younger. His expression, as he gazed down, hands shoved in his coat pockets, was neither hostile nor friendly but calm and studied.

"My name's Vidocq."

"And . . .?" Hawkwood said.

His visitor frowned. "Thought I'd come and take a look at you. See for myself what the fuss was about. You're a bit of an enigma. Did you know that?"

"Is that so?" Hawkwood sat back against the wall and rested his hands on his knees. It looked, this time, as though his captors might have grown weary of taking him from his cell. This time the interrogator had come to him. A pity. He wouldn't have minded the exercise.

Vidocq nodded. "They've been doing some checking. Turns out there's no record of a Captain Dumas serving with the 8th Regiment. How do you explain that?"

The Frenchman put his head on a slant and stared hard at the blue uniform that Hawkwood was still wearing beneath the coat. It was a lot grubbier than it had been when he'd first put it on. His breeches weren't white any more either.

"A clerical error. Maybe they should take another look."

His visitor nodded sagely. "I dare say that'll do it. Not easy though, given the amount of paperwork they've got to wade through. There's cellars full of the stuff. Between you and me, I expect information gets lost all the time. A clerk puts a ledger back on the wrong shelf and the entire system falls apart. You just can't get the staff these days."

Hawkwood wasn't sure how he was expected to respond to that, so he kept quiet.

"Anyway, there it is and here you are." Vidocq shook his head. He looked genuinely perplexed. "You've got balls, I'll give you that. How the hell did you all think you'd get away with it?"

Hawkwood remained silent. That was one of the first questions they'd asked him when he'd come to.

"Created quite a stir, I can tell you," Vidocq continued, unabashed. "You've got them all in a right state. They've rounded everyone up, by the way, in case you were wondering. Well, apart from a couple, that is. They're still looking for the priest. What's his name; Lafon? Still can't find hide nor hair of him."

Vidocq offered a speculative look. "Your friend Balthus was the last person to see him. Told us the abbé paid him a visit shortly after he took up his post as Commissioner. Lafon wanted him to sign prison release forms for some friends of his. Balthus told him he couldn't do that without the general's authority. The last he knew, Lafon said he was off to plead his case to the general personally. We're not sure how far he got. I expect he fled as soon as he saw the game was up. I've no doubt he has friends who've been helping him. So most likely he's hiding out somewhere, waiting for the hunt to die down. Which it won't of course.

"Talking of friends; they've lost your friend Captain Rémy. No one's seen him either. It's as if he doesn't exist. A bit like yourself. I don't suppose you'd know where he is?"

"Can't help you," Hawkwood said. "Sorry."

"Can't or won't?"

Hawkwood said nothing.

Vidocq shrugged. "Just thought I'd ask."

"No harm in asking," Hawkwood said.

The Frenchman smiled thinly. "I've been informed that you've been somewhat unhelpful during your interviews. That might be about to change. Have you met Gabel? No? You will. They use him when all other kinds of questioning fail. He's an interesting fellow. Wouldn't think so to look at him. You could pass him on the street and never suspect what he does for a living. The word is, he likes to apply hot irons to his victim's feet. Oh, I know what you're thinking. It's barbaric, but I'm told he has quite a high rate of success."

"If I didn't know any better, I'd say you were trying to frighten me," Hawkwood said.

The Frenchman smiled. "How am I doing?"

"What do you think?"

"What I think doesn't really matter, does it? I have to say, I'm impressed so far, though. You've been here, what, a couple of days and all they've got is your name, rank and regiment. And they're not even sure those are correct."

Vidocq leant close. "Two days! The others were singing their hearts out after a couple of hours. Well, Sergeant Rateau was. In fact, they've been hard pushed to get him to shut up."

Vidocq chuckled. "You want to hear something funny? Doucet and his men were concentrating so hard on arresting you and the general and Steenhouwer that they missed Rateau. He managed to make a run for it. Got clean away, too. Or he thought he had. Damned fool reckoned if he returned to his duties with the Guard, no one would suspect him. I ask you!

"That might have worked if he hadn't drawn attention to himself when he took flight. He was in such a hurry, he took a cab back to the priest's house. He was that anxious to get out of his uniform he actually stripped off! Arrived at his destination stark naked. Cab driver couldn't forget that. Bragged to his pals over a glass and got himself overheard by two off-duty gendarmes. They took him to the Préfecture, asked him a few questions. All we had to do then was make enquiries around the area where he'd dropped his fare off. Didn't take us long to find the Spaniard after that."

Vidocq's face suddenly darkened. All trace of humour had disappeared. "Rateau told us that it was you who killed my man, by the way, in case you thought I wouldn't find out."

Hawkwood felt his insides twist. "Your man?"

"Claubert. I didn't mention that, did I? I should have introduced myself properly. I run the Brigade de Sûreté. We found his corpse when we raided the priest's apartment. The fool tried to hide Rateau's uniform and weapons down the well. They were on top of the body. The priest swears blind he didn't know

444

Claubert was down there. Pretty cold-hearted, breaking his neck like that, tossing him aside like an old shoe."

"I don't suppose you'd believe me if I told you he slipped?" Hawkwood said.

The Frenchman stared at Hawkwood in silence. Eventually, he shook his head. "No. Same way you wouldn't believe me if the situation were reversed. Tell me that's not true," he challenged.

Hawkwood didn't reply.

Vidocq nodded, his suspicions confirmed. "Thought as much."

Taking his hands from his pockets, Vidocq laced them behind his back and stared up at the window. In a more considered tone, he said, "I have to confess, I did have half a mind to punish you myself."

Hawkwood waited. He knew there was more.

Vidocq turned. "The other half wants to thank you. It's taught me not to take anything for granted. There I was, assuming it was a simple surveillance job. You can be sure I won't make that mistake again. How's the pain, by the way, or have I asked you that already?"

"It comes and goes," Hawkwood said.

"Well, the reason I ask is that you won't have to worry about it for much longer. I'm told you don't feel much when the blade hits you. They do say the brain functions for about seven or eight seconds afterwards. Gives you the chance to scream, I suppose, or tell the executioner he's a bastard. Anyway, it'll give you something to think about between now and when it happens."

He stared at Hawkwood's expression. "What? Did you think because you're an officer you'd be taken away and shot? They don't shoot murderers, my friend. They guillotine them. They'll shoot the others, though. Not sure when. They've not set the trial date yet. Should be any day now."

"If they're going to shoot them anyway," Hawkwood said, "what's the point of a trial?"

The Frenchman sighed. "Well, they have to go through the motions, otherwise the people will think there's no rule of law.

Then where would we be? They've decided on the charge, by the way: armed conspiracy. They don't send you into exile for that, or slap you in a nursing home. They put you in front of a firing squad. Well, not you, but the others. I've already told you that, though, haven't I?"

The Frenchman began to pace the cell. Resuming his conversational tone, he said, "They'll want to get it over and done with as quickly as possible, of course. You've made a lot of people very unhappy, not to say embarrassed. People don't like to be embarrassed."

"Nobody ever *died* of embarrassment," Hawkwood said. "To my knowledge."

"That's not the way they look at it."

"They?"

"Savary, Pasquier, that shit Desmarest . . ." Vidocq stopped pacing and raised his eyebrows. "What? A man's not entitled to his opinion? Desmarest really has it in for you, by the way. Not that the others haven't. It can't do much for your dignity being arrested in your nightshirt. That was all over the city faster than you could blink. They've become a laughing stock, as you can imagine.

"That's the other thing. The Senate's worried. It's not sure who it can trust. It's concerned as to how deep the conspiracy went. That's what they'll be asking you next, if they haven't already. Were there any ministers involved? The way Savary, Pasquier and Desmarest were taken, it's got people wondering. It was all remarkably easy; how they surrendered without a fight. La Horie was at school with Desmarest, for example, and he served with Savary in Germany. Well, you can see the Senate's dilemma."

"Maybe you should be asking them the questions then, not me," Hawkwood said.

Vidocq made a face. "Well, *somebody* will certainly be asking them. You can be certain of that. His Majesty, for one. They've sent a message to inform him of events. I expect his first question when he gets back will be why didn't they have Malet under surveillance?"

"They did," Hawkwood said.

"Ah, well, I know that and you know that, but I suspect Savary and the others won't want anyone else to know, least of all His Majesty or the Senate. It might get them wondering how vulnerable the Empire is if the suspect being watched still manages to come within a cat's whisker of seizing power. The bastards are closing ranks. I'll probably have to watch *my* back now, come to think of it."

The Frenchman fell silent for several seconds. Then he looked up. "The Senate's also concerned about the apparent willingness of senior army officers to believe the lie that the Emperor was dead. It suggests the army might not be as loyal to His Majesty as he supposes. What's to stop another disaffected general leading his troops to meet the Emperor on the field? Intercepting His Majesty on his way back from Russia, for example, when his forces are likely to be at their weakest? All they'd need to do then is approach Britain and sue for peace."

Raising his hand, the Frenchman made a small gap between his thumb and forefinger. "You and General Malet came this close, by the way. If Doucet hadn't taken a proper look at those documents, who knows what might have happened? Though the date didn't help."

"Date?"

Vidocq looked at Hawkwood askance. "Haven't they told you *anything*?"

Hawkwood allowed himself a smile. "Not much, but then, I rather think they'd prefer it if *I* did all the talking. What about the date?"

"Malet told everyone the Emperor had been killed on the seventh. It just so happened that Doucet was in receipt of a message from His Majesty dated the ninth. It was as simple as that. Paques being on hand, by the way, was pure chance. He was at headquarters to arrange Guidal's transfer to Aix. Half an hour later, and it might have been a different story. Oh, did you hear about Guidal, or are you in the dark about him, too? He was found in a friend's house in the Faubourg Poissonniere, drunk as a knave. La Horie was arrested at the Ministry.

Commissioner Balthus was tracked to a house in Courcelles. They found him hiding in the cellar. No one put up a fight, if that's what you were hoping.

"They're saying they were duped, of course. Though La Horie's known Malet for years, so I'm not sure he'll be believed. And talking about putting up a fight, turns out the only casualties were you and Hulin. They've managed to save his face but he'll be on liquids for quite a while. Malet was lucky he didn't kill him, otherwise he'd be for the blade, too, as opposed to the bullet, that is."

"Malet?" Hawkwood said cautiously.

"General Malet." Vidocq cocked his head and smiled. "You do remember him, don't you? Tried to take over the Empire? Maybe that bang on the head did more damage than you thought."

This time, Hawkwood did not return the smile. Not because it hurt to do so – which it did – but because he was thinking back to the moment he and the general had loosed off their pistols. It had been the general's weapon that had misfired, not his, and yet Malet had apparently taken responsibility for the wounding.

"It's just that it happened so quickly," Hawkwood said.

"Yes, well, I've no doubt that when General Hulin's able to speak, he'll have something to say on the matter. Though that might not be for some time – if at all. The doctors say the ball went in that deep, they might never get it out. His wife will be ordering their cook to make lots of soups, I suspect."

The Frenchman patted his pockets as if he'd forgotten where he'd placed his gloves. "Anyway, enough of this. I have to get on. I've a funeral to attend. At least Claubert didn't leave a wife or children behind. Though he had a mother." His eyes hardened. "Thought you should know that, Captain. I can call you Captain, can't I?"

"Does it make a difference?"

"Not especially. Though I suppose it lends your allegiance with General Malet and his enterprise some weight. It supports the ludicrous theory that you all believed you were only following

448

orders, that you thought His Majesty really had been killed and the Senate had chosen Malet as the anointed one. I'm assuming that's your story, too? You were only doing as you were told?"

"I'm a soldier; that's what I do. Captains obey generals."

"If you really are a captain," Vidocq said, smiling. "That's Malet's defence, by the way, as if you didn't know. He's saying the Senate decree was delivered to him at the clinic and he was acting on the mistaken assumption that it was authentic. He'd no idea he was acting illegally."

Vidocq shook his head. "Poor Soulier's been telling them he was so ill with the fever he couldn't think straight. Said if he'd really been in on it he'd have released the powder and cartridges that were in the barracks armoury."

Hawkwood stared at him.

"Ah, don't tell me you didn't know that either? You didn't. My God! Well, it's true; your weapons were useless, you might as well have been carrying broom handles. No flints, no cartridges. It would have been a blood bath. Just as well you were able to trick the Guard into joining you."

While Hawkwood's brain reeled, the Sûreté man chuckled. "Rabbe's blaming his subordinates. He said that, as he received the orders second-hand and not directly from the Senate or garrison command, it wasn't his fault. The orders were delivered according to regulations. His adjutant should have checked, if there was any doubt. In any case, being ordered to man positions around the city wasn't any different from the daily routine anyway. Why would they question that? He says he only found out the truth when he went to report to garrison command. It'll be interesting to see if that line of defence works. Personally, I have my doubts."

Vidocq rubbed his palms together. "Someone told me this place was like an oven, but it's freezing in here. Good thing they left you your coat. Well, like I said, I should get on. Can't stand and chat all day. You've probably got things to do as well. There'll be more questions, no doubt, though I'm pretty sure they must have all the information they need by now. Save for the whereabouts of Lafon and Rémy, of course. You sure you don't want to clear your conscience, before it's too late?"

"I've told you already. I can't help you."

Vidocq nodded. "I had a feeling you'd say that. Oh, well . . ."

The Frenchman hesitated, turned to go and then paused. "We tracked down the real Lamotte, by the way. Turns out he was a guest at the Hotel Patrice. He's under arrest, too. Funny thing, for a time we thought he was in league with Malet and that he actually was the one who recruited the 10th, until we presented him to Soulier, who had no idea who he was.

"And I don't suppose they told you, but they arrested Madame Malet, too. Attractive, I'm told, for her age. She's in the Madelonnettes. She has a cell to herself, at least. That's something."

Hawkwood willed himself not to show a reaction.

Why hadn't she left the city and joined her son?

"So," Vidocq said. "You're sure there's nothing I can get you? I've some influence with the prison staff: old acquaintances, you might say. No? In that case, I'll bid you good day. We'll be seeing each other again, though. I'll be there when they fasten you down. I promised Claubert's mother that mine would be the last face you'd see."

"I'm not sure I find that particularly reassuring," Hawkwood said. "And I still don't understand why you've been telling me all this."

"Call it professional courtesy. Oh, but don't worry; I'm not offering to shake hands. And there's no need to get up, either. I can see myself out."

As he reached the door, the Frenchman turned. "You know, I'm glad we've had this talk. It's been most . . . illuminating. You're not at all what I expected. I can't help thinking that, if it were in any other circumstances . . . well, you know how it is."

Hawkwood nodded. "Until next time."

Vidocq smiled. With a final curt nod, he knocked twice on the door. It opened and he was gone.

"On your feet!"

The turnkey's mouth twisted.

Hawkwood stood, held out his hands and the manacles were

fastened about his wrists. With an armed gendarme marching in step behind, he was led out of the cell and along the candlelit passageway to the stairs. The route had become a familiar one.

During the days he'd been held, no physical coercion had been applied to extract information. Hawkwood had been surprised by this, until his visit from Vidocq, whose willingness to expound on the revelations uncovered during the questioning of the others suggested that Hawkwood's unconscious state had probably spared him from a more rigorous form of interrogation, at least in the beginning.

Also, if what Vidocq had told him was true, his fellow conspirators had been only too eager to unburden themselves, if only to prove that they'd all been innocent victims of General Malet's duplicity. It was likely, therefore, that by the time he'd recovered sufficiently to be able to give testimony, most of the plot's entrails had already been laid out and dissected.

Nevertheless, Hawkwood had no doubt that, from the State's point of view, there were some details of the insurrection that were still a mystery; such as the possible complicity of the army and the police departments, and the whereabouts of Abbé Lafon and the mythical Captain Rémy. Which begged the question: to what lengths were the authorities prepared to go in order to uncover what they might suspect but had so far been unable to prove? Vidocq's mention of the interrogator, Gabel, had revealed that extreme methods were available. Was that how the others had been made to confess their sins?

Hawkwood had the uneasy feeling that the tone of the questioning was about to change. A memory of something Grant had mentioned swam into his mind; the supposed suicides of the English naval commander, Wright, and Moreau's fellow general, Pichegru, in the Temple prison. By the time the turnkey halted him outside the warder's office, unease had given way to apprehension over what was to come.

The turnkey opened the door and pushed Hawkwood forward. "Prisoner Dumas, Excellency."

Councillor Pierre Réal, Director-General of the State Police, did not look up from the table but continued writing. The man

451

standing beside him watched in glowering silence as the turnkey escorted Hawkwood to one of the two wooden chairs that occupied the centre of the room. The gendarme had already taken his position to the left of the door. A second gendarme stood guard on the right. The turnkey remained at the back of Hawkwood's chair, keys in hand.

"You're acquainted with Chief of Security Desmarest," Réal said, putting his pen down. He nodded towards the turnkey, who left the room.

"Intimately," Hawkwood said.

He saw by the security chief's expression that his deliberate use of the word had hit a nerve. The last and only time they'd met, Desmarest had been in his nightclothes. Clearly the memory was still raw. His face was as dark as a thundercloud.

Réal regarded Hawkwood with a similar cold intensity. An obdurate-looking man in his fifties, his greying hair was long and wavy and combed back from his high, broad forehead. The set of his mouth suggested he was an individual short on humour. As Savary's deputy, this was the man Guidal was supposed to have arrested. Hawkwood presumed both Desmarest and Réal were aware of that and wondered how the knowledge sat with Desmarest, who would be conscious that while he'd suffered the indignity of abduction and imprisonment Réal had been one of the few to have emerged unsullied by events.

"You had a visitor this morning," Réal began.

Hawkwood said, "Is that a statement or a question?"

"An observation. What did you and Vidocq talk about."

"He's decided not to kill me," Hawkwood said. "He'd rather leave it to the guillotine."

"You did murder one of his officers."

"He seems to think so."

"You deny the charge?" Réal said sceptically.

"Would you believe me if I did?"

Réal made no comment. Desmarest snorted derisively. The security chief moved to the window and stared out at the grey skies as if disinterested in the scene behind him. Over his shoulder,

Hawkwood could see the curve of a tower; part of the Abbey of Saint-Germain, to which the prison was connected.

"What else did you talk about?" Réal asked after a short pause.

"Nothing," Hawkwood said. "I lost interest after that and I didn't want to annoy him in case he changed his mind."

He wondered what Desmarest was doing there. The man hadn't been around during the previous periods of questioning, which Réal had conducted on his own, with only the gendarmes present. He also wondered about the other chair. That hadn't been there either.

Réal addressed Hawkwood once more. "You'll be interested to know the inquiry's almost over. The trial will then begin. There's a situation that's arisen, however, that puts a rather different perspective on events. We thought you might assist us in shedding some light on the matter."

Assist? Hawkwood thought.

The door opened.

Desmarest turned. "Say hello to an old friend."

Three men entered. The turnkey and another man Hawkwood hadn't seen before were supporting a third man between them. As they half-dragged, half-lifted their charge towards the adjacent chair, Hawkwood caught sight of a gaunt face framed by matted hair and indented by a pair of eye sockets so dark it looked as if holes had been drilled into the prisoner's skull. A thin, uneven beard covered the lower part of his jaw. A bruise, as wide as a palm print, marred his right cheek.

As the turnkey left the room the prisoner turned his head. Light from the window spilled on to his face. His right eyebrow was heavily swollen. Both eyes glistened with tears.

A cold hand clamped itself around Hawkwood's heart as he found himself gazing helplessly into the pain-racked features of Lieutenant Jonathan Stuart, commanding officer of His Britannic Majesty's cutter, *Griffin*.

"We were wondering why there was no record of a Captain Dumas in the regimental lists," Desmarest said. " Now we know. You can imagine our surprise."

Hawkwood forced himself to ignore Stuart's bloodied face. "Am I supposed to know this man?"

Desmarest took a step forward. "You know full well who he is. His name is Stuart. He's an officer in the British Royal Navy. Two weeks ago, the two of you came ashore from an English ship, supposedly wrecked during a storm. You were picked up by a patrol from the Fort Mahon garrison near Ambleteuse. You identified yourself as Captain Vallon, of the . . .?" Desmarest paused.

Réal consulted a document on his desk. "The 93rd Regiment of Infantry."

"Thank you," Desmarest said. He turned back. "You told the officer commanding the patrol that you were an escaped prisoner of war and that Lieutenant Stuart was an English smuggler, hired to deliver you back to France."

"And I've told you," Hawkwood said, "that my name is Paul Dumas."

"No!" Desmarest spat. "You lie! Do you take us for idiots?"

"We know everything," Réal said. "We know how your Chouan friends intercepted the patrol. We know about the skirmish on the bridge, your escape . . ."

Hawkwood felt his innards contract.

"But you mustn't place *all* the blame on Lieutenant Stuart," Desmarest said. "Lieutenant Malbreau's contribution shouldn't be underestimated." A smug grin spread across the security chief's face. "Ah, of course, but you didn't know, did you?"

"It's true," Réal said. "Contrary to your expectations, Lieutenant Malbreau survived, though not without serious injury, it has to be said. Unsurprisingly, due to the gravity of his condition, he wasn't always lucid, so it took a while before he was able to furnish the garrison commander with an adequate account of what happened."

Hawkwood heard Stuart let out a low moan.

Réal ignored the interruption. "When he was taken prisoner, Lieutenant Stuart also thought Malbreau was dead, so there was no mention of a Captain Vallon. It wasn't until Malbreau became more coherent that the name emerged. Which had the garrison commander asking himself, quite rightly, why a French army officer would attempt to shoot a fellow officer dead and then disappear, leaving a British smuggler and a handful of French rebels to fight a rear-guard action to help him escape. Odd that, don't you think?"

"Which was why," Desmarest said, folding his arms, "the commander decided to send his prisoner to Paris for further questioning, accompanied by Lieutenant Malbreau's very precise description of the man who shot him, even down to the scars on his face. Subsequent discussions with Lieutenant Stuart yielded additional, more pertinent information."

Desmarest regarded Stuart with the sort of fond expression a benevolent uncle bestows upon a favourite nephew. "I have to say, since we discovered his true role, your lieutenant's been of immense help." He turned to Réal. "Isn't that so?"

Réal nodded. "Thanks to him, we've expanded our knowledge of British involvement in the transportation of *emigrés*, the location of the landing grounds, the vessels employed, the delivery of weapons and the links to local rebel groups – all manner of wondrous things."

Desmarest smiled. "Sadly, the lieutenant wasn't much help when it came to determining Captain Vallon's whereabouts. In spite of Gabel's best efforts, it seems he had no prior knowledge of your intended activities."

Desmarest smiled at the man who'd helped the turnkey carry Stuart to the chair.

Hawkwood turned his head. Vidocq was right, he thought. You wouldn't have given him a second glance. Average height, neither slim nor fat, with an even cast to an unassuming face that showed no outstanding characteristics; no scars no blemishes. He had a receding and slightly greying hairline, suggesting he might be approaching middle age, but other than that it would have been hard to pick him out in a crowd. Ordinary would have been an accurate description.

Until he smiled, which he did now in response to Desmarest's praise. In an instant the man's features changed. The bland mask slid away, to be replaced by a grin of such feral intensity that

Hawkwood was left in no doubt that here was one individual who found pleasure in his work.

Studying Gabel gave Hawkwood an opportunity to steal a glance at his fellow prisoner. There was severe bruising around some of the fingertips and knuckles of Stuart's left hand, he saw. They looked to have bled heavily.

What did they do to you?

Desmarest unfolded his arms and picked at a stain on his lapel before glancing up. "Obviously, we continued the search. We were able to establish that a man fitting Vallon's description travelled by diligence from Wimereux to Paris."

The bastard's enjoying this, Hawkwood thought. He willed himself to ignore Stuart and look straight ahead.

"We picked up your spoor," Réal went on, "when an official at the Chapelle Gate remembered checking the papers of a man who matched the description of the individual we were looking for and who arrived on the Beauvais diligence three days after the date Captain Vallon fled from the bridge." Real paused, then said, "He remembered the scars and, rather more conveniently, he remembered the name. Not Vallon . . . Dumas."

Desmarest smiled. "I suppose you're going to tell us it's all a coincidence?"

"They've been known to happen," Hawkwood said. He looked at Réal, but the Director-General seemed content to let Desmarest continue.

"Yes, they have," Desmarest said, "but not, I feel, on this occasion. So, Captain Vallon disappears into thin air and Captain Dumas, who bears a striking resemblance to the aforementioned Vallon, arrives out of nowhere. Literally, according to army records. And what do we find? We discover that, shortly after his arrival, Captain Dumas pays a visit to the Dubuisson nursing home, where he spends most of his time in the company of General Malet and his wife and their good friend, Abbé Lafon. A week later, the same Captain Dumas is arrested while attempting, in the company of General Malet, to lead an armed revolt against the Empire."

The security chief shook his head in amusement. "Are you

456

really going to persist in this ridiculous charade? That you're Captain Dumas of the 8th Regiment and that you were only obeying orders? Or are you going to admit to the truth?"

Desmarest cocked an eyebrow expectantly. "Well?"

A throaty rattle came from the man in the adjacent chair; an attempt to speak, the words faint and indistinct. Abandoning pretence, Hawkwood turned his head. Stuart's face was angled towards him. It was full of pain. The lieutenant's lips parted.

"I'm s-sorry," he whispered.

The words were spoken in English.

Hawkwood knew that his next words would alter everything.

Fixing Stuart in the eye, he replied softly in the same language, "Don't be. It's not your fault."

A broad, self-satisfied smile spread across Desmarest's face; the expression of a man who had just seen all his suspicions confirmed in one fell swoop. "How wonderfully touching."

Reverting to French, Hawkwood turned to him and said, "What is it you want from me?"

Desmarest's smile receded. "Well, I think a confession would be somewhat academic at this stage, don't you? We know you're an envoy of the British government and that you were sent here to support the traitor Claude-François Malet in his attempt to overthrow the Empire. So, why don't we settle for information? By the way, does General Malet know you're a British spy?"

Hawkwood hesitated, thinking about the possible consequences of his answer. Several seconds passed. Then:

"No."

Desmarest gave a conciliatory grunt. "You know, I do believe that's the first honest answer you've given me. I'm rather looking forward to seeing his reaction when I tell him he's been standing shoulder to shoulder with his country's oldest enemy. He'll go down in history not only as a misguided fool but as a traitor in the pay of the British.

"Not that we should be surprised, since we know London's been financing the Comité for years. The audacity of the British government to think it can meddle in the internal affairs of France never ceases to amaze!"

457

Réal looked thoughtful. "Clearly, this goes beyond a handful of disgruntled generals. We know British correspondents are working within the city. We want their names. You can start with the people from whom you received assistance. We're especially interested in the person who printed the documents. We know from Sergeant Rateau that your associate Rémy was involved with that. Is Rémy his real name, by the way?"

"I can't help you," Hawkwood said.

Desmarest shook his head and let out a weary sigh. "Just when I thought we'd reached an agreement. Like a whore who promises so much, you close your legs at the last minute." He looked towards Réal.

"We've been tolerant up until now," Réal said. "So far you've been treated very fairly, as befits an officer, even a deluded one. That's about to change, now that we know what you really are."

Desmarest addressed Gabel. "Secure him."

With the gendarmes' muskets aimed at his head, Hawkwood's wrists were removed from the manacles and bound to the chair's arm rests. They did the same to Stuart. Desmarest nodded to Réal.

The Director-General rose to his feet. He gave Hawkwood a speculative look. "Do you pray?"

"Hardly ever," Hawkwood said. "There's never seemed much point."

Réal gathered his papers.

"You might want to reconsider that," he said, as he left the room.

"Leave us," Desmarest told the gendarmes. "But remain within call."

The gendarmes followed Réal out, closing the door behind them.

"Now," Desmarest said, "I'll ask you again: where are Rémy and Lafon?"

"I've already told you," Hawkwood said. "I don't know."

Gabel, he saw, was the only other one who'd remained in the room. He was standing to one side, motionless, his face serene, waiting.

"Why is that? You told General Malet that Captain Rémy was your friend."

"I lied about that, too," Hawkwood said.

Desmarest sighed. "It really would be best if you told me what I want to know."

"Why?" Hawkwood said. "You're going to execute me anyway."

Desmarest looked thoughtful. "We might show clemency."

"*Might?*" Hawkwood said. "That's not much of an incentive. And I think you're overestimating my importance. All I did was obey orders and make myself known to General Malet to see if there were any advantages in assisting him. I'm just a poor foot soldier, nothing more."

Desmarest's eyebrows rose. "Oh, I think you do yourself an injustice. I've a feeling you're a lot more than that. I don't believe your name's Smith, either, given your propensity for aliases. By the way, I never complimented you on your fluency, did I? Your command of French is excellent. Another reason why I don't believe you're *just* a foot soldier."

"You must really be worried," Hawkwood said. "Is that why you don't want Captain Stuart or me on trial with the others? That's it, isn't it? The last thing you and Savary want is for anyone to know that one of the people involved was a British correspondent. You want all this buried before the Emperor gets back, because if he finds out and thinks that perhaps you could have prevented all this, your heads are going to be joining mine in the basket.

"And I wonder how it's going to look when His Majesty finds out we nearly took the Empire without a working musket between us. How are you going to explain that? Letting yourselves be taken by unarmed men? You think he'll be impressed when he hears you were caught with your breeches down? All you're trying to do is protect your arses. You think I'm going to help you do *that*? Why the hell should I?"

"What if I *did* offer a stay of execution? Imprisonment instead? What then? There's every probability you'd be exchanged, perhaps in a few months."

459

Hawkwood heard another echo of Brooke's words:

If you were to be apprehended, you would be on your own and left to your own resources.

Which meant there would be no exchange, and without the possibility of an exchange there would be no future and no hope. He looked towards Stuart and knew his answer was about to condemn them both.

"I don't think so. I've heard what happens to English prisoners in your care."

There was a pause.

"Then you leave me no choice," Desmarest said, sounding almost apologetic. He nodded to Gabel.

Gabel leant over Stuart's chair. The lieutenant shrank back and tried to clench his fists, but Gabel proved to be the stronger. Taking hold of Stuart's left hand, he prised open the fingers one by one until the lieutenant's palm was splayed out flat on the arm rest. Then he reached behind his back.

The implement was made of metal and had a pair of wooden handles; it looked like an elongated nutcracker. It took a couple of seconds for Hawkwood to realize what it was he was looking at. It was a hand-held mould for making pistol balls.

"Gabel used to favour a musket lock," Desmarest said matter-of-factly, "but it was too cumbersome. This is much more convenient. It's unusual, as you can see. Most moulds can only cast one or two balls at a time. This one can do four."

A whimpering sound broke from Stuart's lips. The damage to the lieutenant's fingers was suddenly explained. He was anticipating what was to come.

"He doesn't know anything!" Hawkwood said desperately. "I told you, for Christ's sake!"

"You misunderstand," Desmarest said. "Gabel's not going to hurt the lieutenant to make *him* talk. He's going to hurt him to make *you* talk. I'll ask you again: where are Rémy and the abbé?"

"I don't know," Hawkwood said. "I keep telling you!"

With great care, Gabel isolated the little finger of Stuart's right hand – one of the two that were undamaged – and closed the mould around it until the tip of the finger was held fast. Stuart writhed in his chair.

"Are you sure?" Desmarest said. Anticipation shone brightly in his eyes.

"I told you. I don't bloody know!"

Desmarest nodded.

"No!" Hawkwood yelled. "God damn you!"

Gabel squeezed the two halves of the mould together.

The shriek that erupted from Stuart's lips wasn't human. The only time Hawkwood had heard anything like it was during his fight with William Lee, on board the American's submersible beneath the waters of the Thames, when Hawkwood had plunged an auger into Lee's right eyeball.

The sound seemed to go on for ever, rebounding around the walls, before Gabel finally opened the mould and released the finger, by which time Stuart's terrible cry had been reduced to a low, bubbling moan. His head had sunk forward on to his heaving chest.

"You bastard!" Hawkwood yelled. "You rotten, shit-eating Frog bastard!"

Desmarest let the insults wash over him. "Once more," he said calmly: "where are Rémy and Lafon? It's a perfectly simple question."

"I don't know. Can't you understand that? I don't bloody know! Neither of us does, God damn it!"

Desmarest sighed. "Very well, then," he said, and nodded. "Again."

This time it was the thumb of Stuart's right hand. The lieutenant's cry was as piercing in its intensity as the one that had gone before. Hawkwood clamped his eyes shut but there was no escape from the ghastly ululation.

"Christ Almighty!"

"You can end it," Desmarest said softly, as Gabel stepped away, the blood-stained instrument hanging loose in his hand. "All you have to do is tell us what we want to know. What could be simpler? In fact, I'll make it even easier for you. I'll give you the opportunity to experience what you've been

461

putting your friend through. That seems fair, doesn't it? Gabel."

Hawkwood tried to do as Stuart had done and clench his fist, but tied as he was to the chair frame, he was powerless to prevent Gabel from opening his palm and positioning the mould around the little finger of his left hand. He realized, too, that neither his nor Stuart's struggles had had any effect on their chairs. They were bolted to the floor.

Hawkwood braced himself.

He needn't have done. It wouldn't have made the slightest difference. When Gabel clamped the mould shut, the scream burst from his lips like an explosion. There were no words to describe the pain. It invaded every part of him. The room swam. A coppery taste filled his mouth and he knew he'd bitten through his tongue.

"You see?" Desmarest said, as Gabel eased the mould apart.

Hawkwood thought he might pass out. He didn't dare look at his finger. Stuart was still slumped in his chair, eyes closed. Tear tracks stained his hollowed cheeks. A low puling sound was coming from his lips. At that moment, Hawkwood's agony was eclipsed by self-loathing at the thought of what he was forcing Stuart to endure.

But, God help them, Grant was still out there somewhere. McPherson, too. They had to be protected at all costs. Their survival was what mattered; not his own, nor Stuart's. The degradation he and the lieutenant were experiencing would end eventually, one way or another. Sooner, preferably. He'd told Réal that he no longer prayed. But perhaps the Director-General had been right and it was time to make his peace.

Then he heard Desmarest say, "Once more, Gabel."

In that instant Hawkwood knew that Desmarest's motive for the torture went beyond a desire for information. The man was acting out of spite, in revenge for his humiliation at Hawkwood's hand. He was determined that Hawkwood was going to suffer the consequences of making him look like a fool at best and a collaborator at worst, and he wanted Hawkwood to know it. Whether Hawkwood had information or not wasn't the issue.

Gabel isolated the second finger of Hawkwood's left hand. Grinning, he brought the two halves of the mould together.

Hawkwood screamed again.

After that, Gabel turned his attention to Stuart's knuckles.

When the door eventually opened and he heard Réal say, as if from a great distance, "You can stop. They've had enough", Hawkwood had no clear perception as to whether hours or only minutes had passed since they'd placed him in the chair or whether it had been his own screams he'd been hearing throughout the ordeal or Lieutenant Stuart's.

"No," he heard Desmarest say in reply. "I don't think they have."

"If they knew anything," Réal said, "they would have told you by now."

There was a lengthy silence. Then Desmarest sighed. "Perhaps you're right."

"And the trial has to take precedence. The Senate's orders."

Desmarest sighed again. "Very well, so be it. In that case, we may as well get it over and done with. Dawn tomorrow?"

"I think that would suit all concerned, don't you?"

"I'll make the arrangements," Desmarest said.

Hawkwood raised his head slowly.

"I'm impressed," Desmarest said, looking down at him. "I didn't think you'd show this much resilience."

If he had any nails left on the fingers that had suffered the brunt of Gabel's attention, Hawkwood couldn't see them for the blood and the torn flesh. The tips looked like purple grapes that had been left out too long in the sun. The sensation was beyond pain; bordering on the exquisite.

Lieutenant Stuart had stopped moving. It looked as if he'd fainted. Once more Hawkwood was overcome by an onslaught of guilt. He might just as well have applied the bullet mould himself, he thought.

He'd interpreted Desmarest's motive for subjecting them to torture as a means of vengeance, but was his own refusal to surrender to the interrogation not the other side of the same

463

coin? Had his determination to outlast the security chief's questions been as much about his desire to frustrate the man as his need to save Colquhoun Grant from capture? How much of Stuart's pain had been caused by his own obstinacy?

Desmarest called to the turnkey and gendarmes.

"Getting rid of us so soon?" Hawkwood heard himself say. "Just when I was starting to like you."

"Enjoy the humour while it lasts," Desmarest retorted smugly. "I doubt you'll be laughing in the morning."

"You mean I don't get to meet His Majesty after all?" Hawkwood wanted to rip the man's face off there and then. Gabel's too.

Desmarest smirked. "He'll never know you existed. No one will. At sunrise tomorrow, you'll go to the guillotine. You'll die and no one will even know your name. Your remains will be thrown into an unmarked grave. There'll be no headstone, nothing to mark your passing save for weeds and thistles. Spies do not die heroes' deaths. There's no guard of honour to see them on their way. They die alone, forgotten by their enemies and by the men who sent them. There is no glory. Your employer and your friends in England will receive no word of your demise. You will simply fade from memory. It will be as if you never existed. The same will apply to Lieutenant Stuart."

Desmarest drew himself up. "So, you see, despite your efforts, the Empire will endure. His Majesty will emerge stronger than ever and he will lead our armies to victory."

"You're wrong," Hawkwood said. "You're losing in Spain. You won't win in Russia and the Royal Navy rules the seas. And his own people have had enough of him. It's only a matter of time. Whether I'm here or not won't make a sou's worth of difference. So do what you will, you gutless little shit. Let's get it over with."

"As you wish." Demarest smiled.

The turnkey and gendarmes re-entered the room. They looked around nervously.

"Replace the manacles," Desmarest told them. "You can put

them both in the one cell. It's their last night. They might as well spend it together."

Desmarest stepped away as Hawkwood and Stuart were shackled. As Stuart was pulled out of the chair he came round and made a brave effort to push himself upright and lift his chin. He swayed slightly before finding his balance. The ends of his fingers looked like pieces of raw meat.

Hawkwood felt nothing but shame. Stuart had been prepared to die at the bridge so that he could continue with his mission and this was how he had repaid him. The man hadn't deserved this.

Gabel was standing close to Stuart's vacated chair. As Hawkwood watched, he spat into a rag and began to wipe the blood from the bullet mould. Engrossed in the task, he did not look up.

Hawkwood rose to his feet and the turnkey pushed him towards the door.

"You," Hawkwood said as he passed the interrogator.

Gabel looked up.

Before the gendarmes could react, Hawkwood snapped his wrists apart and, ignoring the pain in his injured hand, drove the taut connecting chain up and into the interrogator's throat. It struck with the force of a steel bar. By the time the gendarmes had wrestled Hawkwood to the ground, Gabel was on his knees, fighting to draw breath through his crushed larynx. His eyes were wide and rolling and filled with terror. A harsh rattling sound came from his lips.

The gendarmes dragged Hawkwood to his feet. Desmarest and Réal's faces were frozen in shock.

Desmarest stared down to where the turnkey was crouching over Gabel, who was now on his side, his hands clutching his neck. Suddenly, the interrogator shuddered and lay still. The turnkey looked up and slowly shook his head.

"You killed him!" Réal said in utter disbelief.

"Well, it's not as if I had anything to lose, is it?" Hawkwood said. His hand was pulsing violently. His fingers felt as if they'd been torn out at the roots.

Desmarest turned his head. His look was dark and savage. "I could order you shot," he hissed. "Right here, right now."

"But you wouldn't want that," Hawkwood said. "Would you? It'd be too easy and it wouldn't give you half as much satisfaction as what you have planned."

Desmarest's eyes glittered. "And it would be a pity to deprive the Widow. It's been a while since she tasted blood."

"I'll be sure to give her your regards," Hawkwood said.

25

Was there ever a good day to die? Hawkwood wondered.

He suspected the Chinese general, Sun Tzu, would probably have had thoughts on the matter, very likely just before the moment of his demise, if his other pronouncements were anything to go by. No doubt it had been something singular and profound, as befitting his status. Another passing thought slipped into Hawkwood's mind: how come there were never any death-bed speeches by corporals?

He heard the creak of a pallet and the rustle of straw and turned. Stuart was sitting with his back propped against the wall, his arms across his knees.

"Is it dawn?" he enquired hoarsely.

"Soon," Hawkwood said.

Stuart stared up to where a grey light had appeared between the bars of the window. Then, wearily, he closed his eyes, and lowered his head on to his chest.

Hawkwood turned away.

There'd been a time when he'd expected that his death would take place on a battlefield, if not with a rifle in his hand then at least a sword or pistol. Face down on a wooden board was something he couldn't possibly have envisaged. He remembered what McPherson had told him about Robespierre. Better to be face down than face up, he decided. At least he wouldn't see the blade coming towards him.

He wondered how long they had before the guards came for them. Now that death was certain, he wasn't even sure what he was supposed to do. Think of the happy moments in his life? The sad ones? Or, as Réal had suggested, say a prayer. But for what? Mercy? A quick and painless death? Forgiveness for past crimes? It was a long list. The chances were that he'd never get to finish the bloody thing.

His thoughts turned to Grant and McPherson. There had been nothing to connect McPherson to Malet and it was more than likely that the old Scot would remain safe in his anonymity and survive the aftermath of the coup attempt. Grant, on the other hand, was a wanted man so he'd be in hiding somewhere, or else he'd already made either for the coast or the nearest border. Hopefully, the three days since the insurrection had been enough time for him to make good his escape.

He thought then about Maddie Teague, the way she'd looked when they'd last been together, her green eyes watching him as he'd prepared for his journey. He wondered how long she would keep the room. Sooner or later she'd realize he wasn't going to return. Would she weep for him? Would she contact Jago and ask him to collect the battered war chest, his sword and his rifle? At least they'd be going to a good home.

Just so long as he doesn't name the bloody horse after me, Hawkwood thought.

And what of James Read? Eventually, he'd discover what had happened, either through Brooke or some other nameless department that operated in the shadows. Would there be a moment's reflection on the loss of one of his men? Perhaps it was best not knowing.

"They say it's quick," Stuart said, lifting his head, "due to the weight of the blade."

"So I've heard. How're your hands?"

"Hurting like hell," Stuart said. "Yours?"

"Hurting like hell," Hawkwood said.

"Can't be long now," Stuart said. He stole a glance at the cell door.

The prison was unusually quiet. Gaols, in Hawkwood's experience, were seldom quiet. There were always noises coming from somewhere. A minute couldn't go by without some sound echoing down a corridor: footsteps or someone yelling or coughing or spitting or weeping. Sometimes there'd be singing, occasionally there'd even be a burst of laughter – although those moments were rare – but there was always something to break the silence.

Yet this morning, L'Abbaye seemed the quietest place on earth. Even the rats were keeping out of sight.

They know, Hawkwood thought. *They know the tumbril is coming.*

"I wonder if they'll serve us breakfast," Stuart said with a forced smile.

Why waste the food? Hawkwood thought.

Then they heard the sound of a key in the lock.

The guards, Hawkwood noticed, were giving him a wide berth as they led them out of the cell. Even though both he and Stuart were manacled for the journey, the prison staff were evidently taking no chances, Word of Gabel's death and the means by which he'd died had clearly spread. Curiously, they had allowed Hawkwood to keep his coat.

The vehicle waiting for them in the prison yard wasn't an open tumbril but a dark painted, four-wheeled, closed wagon with a hard bench along each interior wall and a barred window in the rear door. It was drawn by two black horses.

There were no formalities. Hawkwood and Stuart were herded into the vehicle in silence and the door was bolted after them. Hawkwood had half expected Desmarest to be there to see them off with a gloating farewell, but the only people in attendance were the turnkey, the head warder and the uniformed escort, which consisted of two new and unsmiling gendarmes, one of whom sat in the front seat next to the driver, while his colleague stood on a fold-out wooden platform affixed to the back of the wagon, next to the door. From their expressions, they were not newcomers to the duty.

Significantly, no mention had been made of their destination.

When Grant had first shown him around the city their walks

had taken them to the Place de la Concorde, the former Place de la Révolution, and Grant had pointed out where the guillotine had stood and where the King and Queen had been executed in full view of the howling mob. The machine, Grant had revealed, was easily dismantled and had undergone several changes of location since its inception on the Cour du Commerce Saint-André, where it had been tested on calves and sheep. From there it had moved to the Tuileries, the Place Saint-Antoine and on to its current site in front of the Hotel de Ville, though it hadn't been seen there for several months.

There was also, Grant had told him, more than one guillotine. The authorities liked to use them in rotation, with the mechanism being tested, away from the eyes of the public, before each fresh deployment.

Desmarest had promised Hawkwood their deaths would go unrecorded. It looked likely, therefore, that they were on their way to a private location where their bodies would be used to test the efficiency of the next machine to be rolled into place.

Small bloody comfort in that, Hawkwood thought, as the wagon bumped through the prison gate and out on to the deserted street. Maybe the thing would jam. He wondered why the idea amused him.

"Bloody Malbreau," Stuart murmured, shifting on his seat. "Who'd've thought it?"

They were the first words the lieutenant had spoken since they'd left their cell. Bent forward, his bruised face looked tired and strained. "I was sure you'd killed the bastard."

"That's the trouble with French muskets," Hawkwood said. "Even when they *are* loaded, they're next to useless."

Stuart frowned at the emphasis in Hawkwood's voice and then winced as the wagon rocked over a pothole and his elbow slipped, jarring his hand. "Jesus!" he hissed.

Hawkwood fought to ignore the pain that was coursing through his own damaged fingers. The blood was trying to circulate and not getting anywhere and the pressure was excruciating.

Not that it's going to last for long, Hawkwood thought.

"I was sure that evil little bastard was going to order the gendarmes to shoot you," Stuart said.

"He'd promised us the guillotine. He wasn't going to change his mind on that. It would have made him look contrary. He's lost enough credibility as it is."

Stuart shook his head in admiration. "God, you were quick! Scared the devil out of *me*, never mind the Frogs. Served the bastard right, though. I hope he rots in hell. I hope they *all* do."

The lieutenant straightened, his expression contrite. "I meant what I said. I'm truly sorry. I tried to hold out as long as I could."

"I know," Hawkwood said. "But it shouldn't be you apologizing. It should be me; for what I put you through, refusing to answer their questions . . ."

Stuart shook his head. "No. You did what you had to do. I understand that. In any case, it didn't seem to occur to the buggers that after the first couple of times it tended not to hurt so much. You got used to it."

Hawkwood stared at him. "Speak for yourself, Lieutenant. *My* hand's bloody killing me."

And, incredibly, a grin rearranged Stuart's battered features. "I don't know what you're complaining about. Another hour and it won't really matter much anyway, will it?"

"No," Hawkwood said. "I don't suppose it will."

An awkward silence fell between them. The only sounds were the rattle of wheels and the rhythmic clomp of hooves on the road outside, drawing death closer.

After a few minutes, Stuart sat up and turned to him. "I should very much like to know your real name, sir, if that sits well with you."

"It sits very well with me, Lieutenant. It's Hawkwood, Matthew Hawkwood."

Stuart nodded. "It's a fine name; a lot more interesting than Smith, if I may say so. I'd offer to shake your hand, but I'm not sure either of us could stand it."

Hawkwood smiled. Deliberately, he held out his left hand. "It's been an honour, Lieutenant."

471

Stuart returned the smile. With his swollen eye, it made him look even more lopsided. "No, Mr Hawkwood. The honour's mine."

They shook awkwardly, manacles clinking, maintaining the hold for several seconds as if reluctant to lose the bond, both of them ignoring the pain.

"I understand they took the girl as well," Hawkwood said when they'd released their grip. "Is that true?"

Stuart hesitated before nodding. "She was struck by a musket ball here." Stuart raised his hands, touched his forehead tentatively and winced. "But she was alive when they took us to the fort. They wouldn't tell me what happened to her, though. I never found out."

"I'm sorry. She was dear to you, wasn't she?"

"Yes." There was a catch in Stuart's voice.

"And the others; Raoul?"

"Dead."

"Alain?"

"I don't know." Stuart said bleakly. He shook his head then, frowned at Hawkwood and said, "You could have lied."

Hawkwood looked at him.

"When you were being questioned. Why didn't you lie?"

For a moment Hawkwood thought Stuart might be chastising him and then it struck him that the lieutenant looked genuinely intrigued.

"I didn't have to. All I had was the truth. I really don't know where anyone else is."

"Truly?"

"Truly."

"I'll be double damned." Stuart turned and peered through the rear window. He remained silent for several seconds and then said wistfully, "They say there are parts of Paris that are quite splendid to behold. I should have liked to have seen some of them."

"We can change seats, if you like," Hawkwood said. "I'll ask the guard to move aside. I'm sure he won't mind."

Stuart chuckled. Then he took a deep breath.

"I'm exceedingly glad of your company, Mr Hawkwood. Were I alone, I do not think I could bear it."

A lump formed unexpectedly in Hawkwood's throat. The lieutenant's words were an instant reminder of his conversation with Denise Malet when she'd asked him what he feared the most.

Hawkwood smiled. "And I'm glad of yours, Lieutenant."

Stuart held his gaze and gave a small satisfied nod, as if everything had been said and settled between them and then, to Hawkwood's astonishment, he cleared his throat and began to intone softly, "*Come cheer up, my lads, 'tis to glory we steer. To add something more to this wonderful year; to honour we call you, as free men not slaves, for who are so free as the sons of the waves.*"

Stuart turned. The boyish grin was there once more as, in a still low but more determined voice, he took up the chorus.

"*Heart of oak are our ships, jolly tars are our men, we always are ready; Steady, boys, steady! We'll fight and we'll conquer again and again . . .*"

Tears pricked Hawkwood's eyes. He concentrated on staring at the floor by his feet. Slowly, he reached down towards his right boot.

As the wagon came to an abrupt halt.

Instantly, the lieutenant's voice dropped away.

"Oh, dear God," he breathed.

There was a silence, followed by a sudden sharp crack and then a cry. A horse whinnied.

Something struck the side of the wagon, hard.

Twice in quick succession followed by a gap and the same pattern repeated.

Hawkwood's heart leapt. He saw a flash of uniform as the gendarme moved past the window and then there came a grunt of pain and the dragging of a bolt and the door opened. A figure dressed in a ragged army tunic and a filthy pair of grey breeches appeared in the opening, brandishing a pistol.

"All right, bonny lads, time to go! D'ye not know a bloody rescue when y'see it?"

Hawkwood grabbed Stuart's arm. "Move!"

Grant stepped aside quickly as Hawkwood and Stuart jumped down on to the road. The Scot frowned and his expression hardened when he saw the manacles and the state of Hawkwood's hands and the bruises on Stuart's face.

Stuart gaped at their rescuer.

"Close your mouth, laddie," Grant said. "It's rude to stare. You'll be Lieutenant Stuart, I take it?"

They were on a side street. It didn't look like anywhere Hawkwood had been before. It was still early. There was no other traffic on the road and no pedestrians in sight. The sound of the shot had not brought anyone running, yet. The rear guard was lying face down on the cobbles, his musket next to him. At the front of the wagon, the driver was seated with his arms at the back of his head. The gendarme who'd been sitting next to him was slumped in his seat, leaking blood from a wound in his chest. A few feet away, a man with a bald crown and an unsmiling face, in similar grubby attire to Grant, was holding a pistol aimed at the driver's head. Another pistol was tucked under his belt.

The Scot jabbed a thumb at his companion. "That's Guillaume, by the way." Reverting to French, he called out, "You'll keep them here?"

The other man nodded.

"As long as you can," Grant said.

The order was followed by another nod.

"Then let's go, gentlemen," Grant said. "Smartly now."

"Wait!" Hawkwood said, and ran to the front of the wagon. Ignoring the petrified driver, he took hold of the dead gendarme's foot and pulled the body down on to the road. There was a sickening smack as the gendarme's skull hit the cobbles.

Grant looked on in puzzlement. "What the hell are you doing?"

"He's got the key to the manacles. I saw the warder give it to him before we left."

With his good hand, Hawkwood rifled the dead man's tunic pockets.

"Got it! Here, you do the honours." He tossed the key to Grant.

Grant unlocked the manacles and tossed the key in the gutter. "*Now* can we go?"

With Hawkwood and the still bewildered Stuart trotting

quickly in his wake, he led the way towards an alley on the other side of the street.

They were almost at the entrance to the alley when the shot rang out.

Stuart grunted and staggered against the wall. Hawkwood spun towards him. As he did so, he saw that the gendarme who'd been guarding the back of the wagon was up and on one knee, his musket set against his shoulder. His face was wreathed in powder smoke.

The gendarme was given no time to rejoice in his aim, however, for Grant's companion, Guillaume, without ceremony, shot him in the head. As the gendarme fell, Guillaume coolly replaced the discharged pistol with the one from his belt and took a fresh aim at the driver, who'd barely had time to lower his hands.

"Keep moving!" Grant urged.

Supporting the wounded lieutenant between them, Grant and Hawkwood entered the alley. A wooden cart was parked a dozen yards from the corner, a bony horse harnessed between the shafts. The back of the cart was piled high with rags.

They lifted Stuart on to the back of the cart. He groaned as they laid him down.

"No time to examine him here," Grant said. "We'll do that later. Up you go."

He waited as Hawkwood lay down beside Stuart and then piled rags on top of them both. Hawkwood gagged at the stench. Grant ran to the front of the cart, clambered on board and picked up the reins.

"Hang on," he said. "Anyone falls off now and we're all buggered."

Hawkwood soon lost track of the number of turns Grant made as he steered the cart through the labyrinthine streets. He couldn't tell how Stuart was faring, either. Every time the cart hit a rut, the lieutenant let out a grunt, but as to the seriousness of his wound, Hawkwood had no clue. He fumbled beneath the rags and placed his good hand reassuringly on Stuart's arm and his spirits lifted when he felt Stuart's injured fingers touch the back of his own in response.

Hawkwood guessed they'd been travelling for some twenty minutes when the cart creaked to a halt. He heard Grant step down and then his ears picked out the sound of a gate latch being lifted. They set off again but stopped within seconds so that the entrance could be closed behind them. Shortly after that, Grant halted the cart for the third time and announced they had arrived.

Hawkwood cast the rags aside.

They were in a small paved courtyard. Through an archway, Hawkwood could see part of an ivy-covered wall, the corner of a garden and some trees which might have been the edge of a small wood. There was an arbour, too, beneath which was a statue of the Madonna and child, the marble stippled with age. The grass was strewn with fallen leaves, reminding Hawkwood of the clinic's tended grounds.

"What is this place?" Hawkwood asked.

"The Mission of the Infant Jesus. Or it used to be. It was a hospital for incurables, until the Revolution, when Robespierre and his cronies had it shut down. The holy sisters who ran the place were sent to the guillotine and the patients were cast out on to the streets. It's a private residence now. The Congrégation use it as a meeting house. The present owner's a senior member of the Chevaliers. We're safe here, don't worry. Jamie made the arrangements. Come on, we should get your man inside so that we can have a look at his wound."

"Is Guillaume a member of the Congrégation?"

Grant shook his head. "The Chouans. We thought we might need more . . . practical . . . assistance. James called in a wee favour."

As they helped Stuart down from the cart a familiar figure emerged from the door of the house.

"Captain Hawkwood," James McPherson said. "It's good to see you again."

"Not half as good as it is to see you, Mr McPherson," Hawkwood said.

The old man peered at Hawkwood over the top of his spectacles. "I think it's time we dispensed with the formalities, Captain, don't you? James or Jamie will do just fine." McPherson stared at Stuart. "What do we have here?"

"One of the gendarmes managed to get off a musket shot. We don't know how bad it is."

McPherson's expression softened. "Then you'd best bring him inside. This way." He saw Hawkwood's hands then and his face clouded even further. "Looks like you've been in the wars, too, Captain."

"Not as much as this man," Hawkwood said. "He needs the attention, not me."

They helped Stuart into the house and McPherson led the way down the hallway and into the kitchen. He pointed to a long table. "Take off his jacket and set him down there. Easy now."

Removing Stuart's jacket, Grant and Hawkwood lifted the by now semi-conscious lieutenant on to the table. He let out a groan as they did so.

While Grant and Hawkwood propped the wounded man on his side, McPherson cut away his blood-soaked shirt. The musket ball had struck Stuart just under his right shoulder blade. McPherson probed the skin gently around the entry wound and then felt around Stuart's breastbone, under his arm and down his side. Finally, he straightened and clicked his tongue.

"Verdict?" Grant said.

"I'm no expert, so I don't know how much damage has been done, but from what I can tell the ball's ended up by his right armpit. I can feel it under his skin. See this lump here." McPherson lifted Stuart's arm and indicated the protrusion with the tip of his finger. "Which means we might be in luck."

"You mean you can remove it?" Hawkwood asked.

McPherson looked surprised. "You'd be better off with a surgeon, Captain."

"I don't think that's an option," Hawkwood said. "Do you?"

"It's up to you, Jamie," Grant said. "We trust you."

McPherson stared down at the man on the table. "He's not much more than a boy," he said softly. He stroked Stuart's forehead. "All right, I'll need boiling water and a sharp knife. You shouldn't have any difficulty finding one of those. And something to use as a bandage – linen or muslin wrap. See if there's any alcohol, and honey, too. Oh, and light a candle while you're at it."

"Honey?" Grant and Hawkwood chorused, thinking they'd probably misheard.

"It will help prevent infection. If it was good enough for the Egyptians, it's good enough for this wee lad. I can use it on his hands, too."

Hawkwood took off his coat. While he and Grant searched for the required items, McPherson reached into his pocket and extracted a small metal tin. Placing it on the table, he opened the lid and searched the contents before lifting out a pair of tweezers and a jeweller's loupe. Sliding his spectacles on to the top of his head he used the loupe to conduct a closer examination of the entry wound, murmuring to himself under his breath. "Looks clean; no material in there, at any rate." He straightened, replaced his spectacles and patted Stuart's arm.

Stuart's eyes flickered open. "How bad is it?"

"Och, I've dealt with worse," McPherson said.

Hawkwood wondered when and where that had been.

"Are you a surgeon, sir?" Stuart enquired groggily.

"Not exactly," Hawkwood said as he passed McPherson a pair of chopping knives. "He makes music boxes."

"Oh, God," Stuart said, closing his eyes.

"Hot water and bandages," Grant announced, adding in a surprised tone, "There *was* honey, too. I found a small pot. And I don't know what's in this, but if it tastes as bad as it smells, it's more likely to kill than cure." He held out a corked bottle. "Cheap cognac, I'd say. I'll let the sawbones decide."

While Hawkwood found and lit a candle, McPherson examined the knives. "I might need something with a finer blade."

Both Hawkwood and Grant reached down.

Grant stared in wonderment as Hawkwood removed the stiletto from the inside of his right boot. "Are you telling me they didn't search you? How is that even possible?"

"I have no bloody idea," Hawkwood said truthfully. "I've been asking myself the same damned question. They took everything else. I don't think it even occurred to them to check."

"Useless bloody buggers," Grant said, shaking his head in contempt. "And so were you thinking of using it at all?"

"I was usually outnumbered. There was only the one time . . ."

Grant raised his eyebrows. "And when was that?"

"Just before you banged on the side of the wagon. I had a plan that I might try and persuade the rear guard to open the door."

"Just as well I happened along then, wasn't it?" Grant said drily.

"I can't argue with that," Hawkwood said.

"When you've quite finished, gentlemen," McPherson said sternly.

With Grant and Hawkwood holding Stuart down, McPherson cleaned the flesh around the wound, making doubly sure that no material had been forced into it by the impact from the musket ball. If an infection were to occur, it would more likely be caused by dirt from the cloth than by the projectile itself.

When he'd done that, the old man turned his attention to the lump beneath Stuart's arm.

McPherson could have been a surgeon, Hawkwood thought as he watched the elderly Scot go to work. Taking Grant's knife, McPherson swabbed the blade with the cognac and ran it back and forth over the candle flame. Next he made an incision in the skin above the place where the musket ball had come to rest and pared away the flesh. It was at that point, much to the others' relief, that Stuart finally passed out.

Taking swift advantage, using the point of Hawkwood's heated stiletto and the tweezers, McPherson manipulated the musket ball to a position where he was able to prise it out into his fingers. The whole procedure hadn't taken more than twenty seconds.

"Grand job, Jamie," Grant said, as McPherson dropped the musket ball into a basin and cleansed away the blood from the cut he'd made. "D'you need any more help?"

"I'll tend to his hands and face as well. Then we can put him to bed. He'll need rest. What about you, Captain?"

"I can wait," Hawkwood said.

By the time McPherson had attended to his face and cleaned

and applied salve and bandages to his hands, Stuart had regained consciousness. He'd not lost a lot of blood but the trauma had left him very pale. Under McPherson's supervision, Hawkwood and Grant helped him upstairs and into one of the bedrooms.

"You can leave him with me," McPherson said. "I'll see he's comfortable."

Hawkwood and Grant left the room.

"It's time we talked," Hawkwood said.

They made their way downstairs and out into the garden. The sky was the colour of pewter but the air was mild and the fresh smells of the morning cut through Hawkwood's memory of the prison stench and of the rags he'd hidden beneath on the back of the cart.

"I thought you'd be on your way to England, Col. Though I'm damned glad you're not."

Grant's eyebrow lifted. "You didn't think I'd leave you here, surely?"

"The people in London have to know what happened."

"And they will, all in good time. Besides, you wouldn't have left me."

"No," Hawkwood agreed.

"Well, then. And we got Lieutenant Stuart out as well. I'd say it's been a good day, so far, wouldn't you?"

"For us, maybe. What about Malet and the others? Have you heard anything?"

"You never saw them?"

Hawkwood frowned. "No, why?"

"They were taken to L'Abbaye as well; Malet, La Horie, all of them."

"I didn't know," Hawkwood said.

"But you do know about the trial?"

"Begins the day after tomorrow, according to Réal."

"The twenty-eighth; it's to be a military commission with General Dejean chairing." Grant smiled grimly. "You'll be pleased to know the buggers are still running around like headless chickens. The authorities have no real idea who to believe."

Which confirmed what he'd been told by Vidocq, Hawkwood thought.

Grant scratched the side of his jaw. "They've confined the entire National and Paris Guards to barracks. The only forces left in the city with any credibility are the Imperials, whom we didn't involve."

"Savary's blaming the military," Hawkwood said.

Grant grinned. "There's a surprise. It's put him at odds with Henri Clarke, as you can imagine. There's never been any love lost between those two. I'd like to be a fly on the wall when His Majesty gets back and has each of *them* in his office. I'd say Clarke has the stronger position because he wasn't compromised and it was the High Command that defeated us, not the police. But then, this is Savary we're talking about – the man's as slippery as an eel."

They walked a few more yards and then Grant put his head on one side. "Aren't you going to ask me about Madame?"

"I already know," Hawkwood said.

"Ah," Grant said. "I'm sorry, Matthew."

"What do you think will happen to her?"

"Hard to say."

Grant's expression implied he didn't want to put into words what both of them were thinking.

"Rateau's sure to have mentioned her role," Hawkwood said.

Grant nodded. "Yes. I hear he's been rather fulsome in his cooperation. But then they'd have known about her anyway. It's not as though she kept herself hidden away. Far from it, in fact."

The Scot threw Hawkwood a penetrating look. "Please tell me you're not blaming yourself?"

Hawkwood shook his head. "No. She knew full well what she was doing. She loved him and she believed in him. We should all be as fortunate to have someone like her by our side."

"It could cost her dear," Grant said.

"That's what makes her all the more remarkable," Hawkwood said.

Grant thought about that. "There's no one waiting for *you* back home?"

Hawkwood thought about Maddie Teague.

"I hope so."

Grant laughed. "I'm assuming you don't mean Jago."

"Well, him as well," Hawkwood said. "Someone has to keep him on the straight and narrow."

They continued their walk. There were darker clouds towards the east, Hawkwood saw. More rain looked to be on the way. Grant nodded towards Hawkwood's wounded hand.

"Anything you want to tell me?"

Hawkwood shrugged. "A minor difference of opinion. Nothing serious."

Grant stared at him. "Now there's a tone I recognize. May I assume the other person was made to see the error of his ways?"

"You may and he was," Hawkwood said. "Comprehensively."

"That's all right then," Grant said.

"I had a visitor, too," Hawkwood said, after a pause. "Called himself Vidocq."

Grant frowned. "That name has a familiar ring."

"He's head of the Brigade de Sûreté. He was the one who sent Claubert to watch the general."

"And you killed his man. That must have been an interesting parley."

"It was."

"Care to expound?"

Hawkwood did so.

"He sounds a most intriguing fellow," Grant said.

"Who will not be pleased when he discovers the lieutenant and I failed to attend our morning appointment."

"Which means you'll have the Brigade on your trail, as well." Grant smiled. "You don't do things by halves, laddie, do you?"

"So, what happens now?" Hawkwood asked.

"Jamie's already making arrangements to get you out of the country."

Hawkwood stopped. *You?* "Don't you mean *us?*"

"Oh, I'm not leaving," Grant said firmly. "At least, not for a while."

"What? Until this morning, you and Lafon were top of the authorities' wanted list. I doubt they're about to give up the hunt. What's happened to the abbé, by the way? You told me this house was used by the Congrégation. That's a link with Lafon right there. Won't this be one of the first places the police will look?"

"Jamie assures me they neither know about the connection to the mission nor do they have the imagination to figure it out. Even if they do, you – we – will be long gone from here."

"That's if Lieutenant Stuart's well enough to be moved."

"Jamie has friends. They'll alert him to any sign of danger. There'll be plenty of time."

"You didn't answer my question about Lafon."

"He's no longer in Paris, I can tell you that. His chevalier brothers were able to smuggle him out of the city. They're moving him to the south, apparently."

"Which leaves you," Hawkwood said.

"Well, not quite. There's you and Lieutenant Stuart now," Grant said wryly. "You escaped, remember? Leaving a stack of dead bodies behind you. I'd say there's a very good chance that you've just replaced me at the top of the list."

"I wasn't forgetting. I don't understand why you're staying, though."

"I still have work to do. Boney's going to be returning from Russia. I have to be here when he gets back. Our little escapade may not have had the direct result we were after, but we've added to the brew of discontent. Savary and Clarke will be jockeying for position, which means His Majesty will likely have to pick sides. And that means there will be divisions. Divisions our government will be interested in exploiting. I need to be in close range to observe what happens and then report to London."

Hawkwood looked sceptical.

"Don't worry. I'll be keeping out of their way. Captain Rémy doesn't exist, remember. He's a figment of the imagination. Major Connor Grey, however, is real. I've papers to prove it. I'll be back in my old uniform and keeping my ear to the ground as usual. As I said, I'll be careful. I'll know when to turn my head.

Most of them won't even remember what I look like, anyway."

"Savary bloody well will," Hawkwood said. "He's just itching to meet up with *you* again."

"Then I'll make sure our paths don't cross. Christ, Matthew, if they couldn't spot your bloody knife down your boot, do you seriously think they'll chance upon one wily Scot who doesn't want to be found? Think on, bonny lad."

Hawkwood sighed. "You always were a cocky bugger. Don't let it be the death of you, that's all I'm asking."

"It won't. I'll make sure of it."

"What about McPherson? How safe is he?"

"Jamie?" Grant looked surprised by the question. "He's smarter than the two of us combined. He outlived Robespierre *and* survived the Conciergerie. Besides, he has protection."

"Protection? What the hell does that mean?"

"Ah, now there you have me. I've no idea. But it's what he told me when I expressed my doubts about this place, same as you, and I've no reason not to believe him."

"And it might be best not to delve too deeply; is that it?"

"You've said it, bonny lad."

The Scot smiled suddenly and rubbed his hands together. "Now, what about some breakfast? All that exercise has given me an appetite. And you, if you don't mind me saying so, are in need of a bath. You're not on a bloody forced march now, Captain Hawkwood. The fire's been lit, there'll be hot water and there's even honey for your wounds. What more could a man ask for?"

Hawkwood scratched his four-day-old stubble, looked down at the uniform he was still wearing and sniffed.

"A clean shirt wouldn't go amiss."

"Follow me," Grant said.

26

On the afternoon of Hawkwood and Stuart's second day at the house, Grant and McPherson returned from the city bearing news.

Grant was still in civilian dress. He'd told Hawkwood he was waiting until the authorities had calmed down and stopped jumping at shadows before he redonned his uniform.

Hawkwood remained unconvinced by Grant's strategy for reverting to his previous persona but he knew better than to broach the subject. Besides, Grant had been in the city for a lot longer than he had and therefore it could be assumed that the canny Scot would know when it was safe to resurrect Major Grey. But it didn't mean that Hawkwood had to like or agree with it.

"The trial started this morning," Grant said. "In the old Convent of the Good Shepherd on the rue Cherche-Midi. The building was taken over by the military for use as a warehouse for the Paris Guard. It's where they hold their war cabinets."

"They're conducting it behind closed doors," McPherson cut in. "No members of the public allowed and the accused have been denied legal counsel."

"They say that Clarke entrusted the formation of the firing squad to members of the Imperial Guard four days ago," Grant said. "So the verdict's never been in doubt."

"We knew that anyway," Hawkwood pointed out.

McPherson nodded. "They don't expect the proceedings to last long. They'll likely be finished by this evening. Tomorrow morning at the latest. They're not planning any adjournments."

"They want it over and done with by the time Bonaparte gets back," Hawkwood said.

"Poor bastards," Grant murmured.

"If it's a military commission," Hawkwood said, "what about the civilians, Balthus and Cajamaño –"

"And Madame," Grant finished.

"Yes."

"Jamie?" Grant said.

"There'll be a separate trial. They're still being questioned. As for Madame Malet, I'm not sure. She's likely to remain in the Madelonnettes for quite some time, I fear."

Grant caught Hawkwood's expression. "Don't even think it, bonny lad. We can't get to her."

"It wasn't that. I was thinking that the last thing she said was 'bring him back to me'. I didn't do that."

"He knew the risks. We all did. He's accepted his fate."

"It doesn't make it any easier. He told the inquiry that he shot Hulin. He didn't. I did."

"You think that would have made any difference for either of you?" Grant frowned and then sighed. "You think we failed, don't you?"

"Of course we bloody did," Hawkwood snapped.

Grant shook his head. "You're judging the outcome in the wrong terms. Look, we may not have emerged victorious, but by God, we came damned close! We showed that, with the right leverage, the Empire *can* be defeated from within. We proved it's vulnerable. We've had the Police Ministry, the National Guard *and* the army chasing their tails and circling each other like rabid dogs. If we thought there was mistrust before, there's a damned sight more now! We helped kindle that – you and me! *British* officers!

"Clarke's so determined to discredit Savary he's seeing conspiracies behind every corner, and with Savary hell-bent on blaming everyone but himself, they'll be sniping at each other until doomsday. And d'you not remember the faces when the good citizens thought their Emperor was dead? If someone had brought a fiddle there'd have been dancing in the streets."

"Tell that to Malet and the others. I'm sure that'll raise their spirits"

"As I said, they knew what they were getting into. Don't you weep for them, laddie. They're grown men."

"At least they were able to get their son out," Hawkwood said, thinking aloud.

"Then be thankful for that," Grant said, "if nothing else."

McPherson nodded in agreement. "Indeed."

There was an expression on the old man's face that Hawkwood couldn't interpret. "What?"

"It's time you were on your way as well, Captain."

"You have a plan?"

"Our first task is obviously to get you out of the city, too. Then once you get to Orleans –"

"Orleans?" Hawkwood cut in. "Why Orleans? That's in the wrong direction. Why not north to the Channel?"

"Because after Captain Stuart's interrogation the northern coast is being closely watched, not just for Royal Navy ships making night landings but for smuggling vessels and Chouan activity. It's also the place they'll be expecting you to make for. Far safer if you head further west. Our man in Orleans will arrange your onward journey. The river's the safest option. That'll take you all the way to the coast."

"Curtis's man," Hawkwood said, remembering.

"Monsieur Ouvrard," McPherson confirmed, nodding.

"When do we leave?" Hawkwood asked.

"As soon as we can arrange transport," McPherson said. "And you'll be travelling alone," he added.

"What about Lieutenant Stuart?"

"Regrettably, he's not yet well enough."

"Then I'll wait. We can go together."

Immediately, McPherson shook his head. "No. That's not a good idea. We've since learned that the search for you has intensified. Desmarest is most vexed at your escape and by the killing of the two gendarmes and his interrogator. He's rather anxious to make your reacquaintance. So's Vidocq. He has a score to settle and he does not intend the deed to go unpunished. It's best, therefore, that you're sent on your way as soon as possible. While we consider Lieutenant Stuart to be important, he's a much smaller cog. The authorities see you as one of the main instigators of the insurrection. You have to leave. Besides, they'll be expecting you to stay together, so far better that you travel separately. If the net does start to close in, we'll move Lieutenant Stuart to another location."

Hawkwood knew the old man was right. It made sense for Stuart to remain where he was. While his wounds were healing, the abuse he'd suffered at the hands of his captors had taken more out of him than had first been supposed, a factor not helped by McPherson discovering that the cut he'd made to extract the musket ball had become enflamed. In examining the incision, he'd found a minute piece of metal which had become detached and which he'd missed during his initial examination. Draining the wound, McPherson had expressed cautious optimism that further infection had been averted but, to remain on the safe side, Stuart was to rest for at least the next few days.

"Does he know I'll be going on alone?" Hawkwood asked.

"Not yet. We thought we'd leave that to you."

Hawkwood nodded.

McPherson's face softened. "Don't worry, we'll take good care of him."

"I know," Hawkwood said. "But it doesn't make *me* feel any better."

"That's splendid, sir!" Stuart exclaimed when Hawkwood broke the news of his imminent and solo departure, though there was no hiding the disappointment in the lieutenant's eyes.

He was propped up on pillows, a bandage wrapped around his chest. His hands had been left exposed to speed the healing process. There was no suppuration, but they still looked raw and were very painful to the touch; another reason to delay the lieutenant's departure, Hawkwood reasoned, when Stuart expressed his frustration at being left behind.

"You'll be home soon enough," Hawkwood said. "As soon as you're on your feet. In the meantime, you'll be well looked after."

"You don't have to tell me that, sir."

"Listen to Major Grant and you won't go far wrong."

"I'll do that." Stuart hesitated then said, "Forgive me, sir, I haven't mentioned this before, but I heard Mr McPherson refer to you as 'Captain'. I wondered what he meant by it. I've been calling you 'Mister' and you did not correct me. Major Grant's a military man. You're clearly friends. I wondered –"

"I *was* in the army. Not any more."

"May I enquire as to what regiment?"

"The 95th."

"The Rifles! That explains the shot at the bridge and your comment about French muskets!" Stuart's face lit up and then he winced. Leaning back he closed his eyes and took a long breath. "I think Mr McPherson may be right in his diagnosis. I'm not as ready as I'd thought I was."

"It won't be long," Hawkwood said.

"The lad needs his rest," McPherson said from the doorway. "'Else he'll never get better and then we'll never be rid of him." There was a smile on the old man's face.

"I heard that, Mr McPherson," Stuart said, without opening his eyes.

"That's why he'll never make a *real* physician," Hawkwood said. "No bedside manner."

"And I heard *that,* Captain Hawkwood," McPherson said.

But Stuart wasn't listening. His head had fallen to one side. His chest was rising and falling gently. His expression was serene.

Hawkwood left the room and closed the door softly behind him.

"Three o'clock," McPherson had told him. "Be ready."

It was the next day, 29th October, and the trial was over.

It had ended at 2 a.m., after nineteen hours of examination. Fourteen of the accused had been found guilty and sentenced to death. The executions were to be carried out that afternoon on the

489

Plaine de Grenelle, an open stretch of ground adjacent to the military academy. A crowd was expected. The authorities – the army and police – would be preoccupied with co-ordinating the day's orders and controlling the spectators. There was never going to be a more opportune time to slip away, McPherson told him.

At a quarter to the hour, the transport arrived. A large wagon loaded with sealed barrels was parked in the courtyard. The man holding the reins was Guillaume. He recognized Hawkwood and nodded a greeting.

Hawkwood suddenly became aware of the stench. He stared at the cargo.

"What the hell is that smell?"

"Night soil," Grant said cheerfully. "They collect it from the city and deliver it to the local farms."

"The farms don't produce their own shit? What are you trying to do, kill me?"

"Spoken like a true namby-pamby Sassenach," Grant said, shaking his head. "I've always had my doubts." He grinned at Hawkwood's pained expression. "Well, would you want to search the things if *you* were manning the barrier?"

Hawkwood stared at the barrels and then at Grant in horror. "You're not bloody serious?"

"Och, would I do that to you? Don't worry. You'll be travelling up front as Guillaume's mate. Right, if you want to say goodbye to the lieutenant, best do it now."

Hawkwood, thinking he might just shoot Grant if he had a gun to hand, made his way to Stuart's room, but when he looked in the lieutenant's eyes were closed and he was sleeping soundly. Hawkwood watched him for a few moments and then closed the door and went back downstairs to where Grant and McPherson were waiting.

"Change into these," Grant said.

The tunic and breeches looked suspiciously like the ones the Scot had been wearing when he and Guillaume had intercepted the prison detail.

"You're a bloody night-soil driver," Grant said. "What do you think they wear? Full dress uniform? You can change back

490

once you're outside the city."

Mindful of his injured fingers, Hawkwood sighed and unbuttoned his shirt. He should have become used to wardrobe changes by now, he thought. He'd given up wondering what had become of his own clothes. He'd left them at Cajamaño's apartment; there was no retrieving them now. The clothes he was changing out of were the ones he'd received from Alain. Grant had brought them with him from McPherson's apartment, along with his razor, though he'd advised Hawkwood to delay using the latter as his unshaven state could aid his disguise, which made Hawkwood wonder, as he changed breeches, if Grant had been given some forewarning of the means by which he was to begin his flight for freedom. No wonder he'd kept it quiet.

"There's this as well," Grant said, making poor play of keeping a straight face.

Hawkwood stared down at the object Grant was holding out to him. It was a black leather eye patch.

"I suggest you put it over your right eye. It'll draw attention away from the scars on your other cheek. If you recall, they were what got you into trouble in the first place."

When they went out into the courtyard, Grant said, "I'd dirty yourself up a bit, too. This should help."

Grant ran his hand round the wagon's rear-wheel rim and dropped the gathered mud into Hawkwood's palm. "Rub it into your hands and face. With what you're carrying in the barrels, they'll be anxious to keep you at arm's length."

Hawkwood daubed the mud into his skin, concealing the scars. He threw Grant a glare. "One day, Col. One bloody day."

Grant grinned. "Looking forward to it, laddie." He tossed the canvas bag containing Hawkwood's clothes to Guillaume, who caught it expertly and stowed it in a box beneath the wagon's front seat.

Hawkwood wiped the surplus mud from his hands. Grant surveyed the result.

"Very fetching."

"You'll tell the lieutenant I wished him a safe journey," Hawkwood said.

"Aye." Grant nodded. "I will. He'll be sorry he missed you."

"Better that he gets the rest," Hawkwood said. "He'll understand. You'll see he makes it, won't you?"

"On my honour," Grant said. He held out his hand. "God speed, laddie."

They shook.

"You, too, Col."

Hawkwood turned. "Mr McPherson."

"*Slàn leat*, Captain."

Hawkwood looked to Grant.

"He says 'Farewell'."

"*Slàn leat*, Mr McPherson," Hawkwood said.

A rare smile hovered at the corner of the old man's mouth.

"I told you, Captain. There's no need to be so formal."

"Maybe next time," Hawkwood said.

The old man muttered something under his breath.

Hawkwood waited for a translation.

Grant grinned.

"He said, 'That'll be the bloody day.'"

Hawkwood climbed up next to the patiently waiting driver.

"Trust Guillaume," Grant said. "You're safe in his hands. It's his job to pass you on to the next link in the chain. Oh, and one more thing," Grant added. "You'll be going out through the Grenelle barrier. Make sure you're there as close to four o'clock as possible."

"Why then?"

"Because it's next door to the military academy and the executions are set for 1600 hours. You think anyone'll be paying attention to a wagonload of shit?"

Hawkwood was thankful it was late in the year. In midsummer the smell from the barrels stacked behind them would have been horrendous. As it was, every time they hit a pothole – which seemed to be rather too often for comfort – Hawkwood caught a fresh whiff of the contents. It made him wonder how securely the lids were fastened down. The prospect of the casks toppling and swamping them in a tidal wave of excreta was not a pleasant one. He hung on grimly, ready to leap aside should the circumstances demand it.

The other worrying factor was the number of troops on the streets. It had become impossible to ignore them, though they were paying no attention to civilian members of the public. All were heading relentlessly in the same direction; towards the south-west corner of the city. There was none of the excitement that usually accompanied a parade, however. The collective mood from both troops and bystanders was sombre, in keeping with the weather and the colour of the afternoon sky. No one waved or cheered. It was like watching a funeral cortège, Hawkwood thought, then, given the reason why everyone was on the move, but, that wasn't so far perhaps from the truth.

Guillaume halted the wagon at a crossroads to allow a column of National Guardsmen the right of way. He spat into the road and regarded the marching soldiers with ill-disguised contempt.

"They've been on the parade grounds since early morning. Every barracks has been ordered to attend."

The soldiers' faces bore no meaningful expressions. Most had the look of sleepwalkers. A good proportion of them were out of step. Significantly, none of them were armed. Hawkwood saw that wasn't the only odd thing about their appearance.

Every one of them was wearing his uniform inside out.

It was the mark of a detachment in disgrace. Only their shakos identified them as members of the Guard. Hawkwood didn't recognize any faces. Nevertheless, he turned his collar up and kept his chin low, although it would have been doubtful if anyone could see past the dirt and the ridiculous eye patch.

He almost felt sorry for the soldiers. Their only crime had been to follow their officers. Had they not done so, they'd probably have been put on a charge and shot for their trouble. They were paying the price for their obedience. A soldier's lot, it appeared, no matter to whose army he belonged, was seldom just.

The last of the column filed past and the way became clear. Guillaume jostled the reins and the wagon moved slowly on. After a short distance, the road began to widen and it wasn't long before they had left the urban sprawl behind them. An avenue bordered by tall poplars appeared. Through the gaps in the trunks Hawkwood could see the beginning of open heathland. They were nearing the city limits.

Guillaume turned the wagon on to a long tree-lined avenue. Streams of people were moving steadily along it. At the far end, directly ahead of them and a half a mile or so distant, was a large building fronted by massive Greek columns. A huge grey dome rose above it. A clock was set into the dome's base. As they drew closer, Hawkwood was able to read the numerals. The hands were set at ten minutes to four.

By the time they arrived in front of the building the streams had merged into a single, slow-moving flow of bodies wending its way towards an arena of open ground, where Hawkwood could see troops lined up in columns. A chain of cabs was parked along the side of the road. Next to them were two flat-bed wagons, the horses waiting patiently.

"Hearses," Guillaume muttered in a gravelled voice, as the wagon rumbled past. "They're bound for the cemetery at Vaugirard."

A murmur ran through the growing crowd. It was the sound anxious spectators made when they thought they were going to miss the main event. People quickened their pace.

"Right on time," Guillaume muttered, and nodded up the road towards a pair of squat, cube-shaped buildings; the gatehouses that formed the Grenelle barrier. A handful of carts and carriages were waiting to go through.

Hawkwood looked over towards the execution ground. He could see that the troops had been drawn up on three sides, with the open end of the U facing the academy wall. It was hard to tell how many men were assembled, but it must have been at least a thousand; composed of National Guardsmen and units of the Paris Guard. In front of them were several officers on horseback.

The crowd had swollen considerably. People were craning their necks to see over the tops of heads. The more agile among them had scaled nearby trees to get a better view.

Guillaume steered the wagon towards the end of the queue of vehicles and Hawkwood's view of the troops became obscured. He turned to face forward, aware of the eerie silence that had descended like a cloud around them. A solitary cry sounded from the field, breaking the tension, but the NCO was too far from the road for his words to carry clearly.

Hawkwood adjusted the eye patch and willed himself to direct his gaze straight ahead at the open country beyond the toll stations. Guillaume nudged the wagon forward, bringing it to a stop in the lee of a cart piled with what looked like empty milk churns. A distant and extended drum beat rolled out across the field behind them. The cart in front moved on and the barrier guard gestured impatiently, his face wrinkling as his nose picked up the smell from the wagon bed. Hawkwood discovered that his own fists were tightly clenched. The throbbing pain in the fingertips of his left hand as they pressed into his palm was an agonizing reminder that, had it not been for his killing of Claubert, he could just as easily have been one of the men standing with his back to the Academy's wall.

Another shout came from the execution ground. A split-second later a ragged volley of musket fire shattered the afternoon. The barrier guard's attention swung towards the sound of the guns as a flock of starlings, wings beating in unified alarm, erupted like a burst of black shrapnel from the Academy roof. The guard stood still, his attention temporarily diverted. There was a long pause then a second volley crashed out. The birds, still squawking vociferously, wheeled and dived in even more confusion. Finally, as the echoes from the fusillade drifted away, the guard turned back and gestured impatiently and Guillaume, glancing neither right nor left, flicked the reins and the wagon rolled forward towards the barrier.

Hawkwood let out a slow breath and unclenched his fists.

His relief was short-lived.

"You there! Halt!"

Guillaume tensed. The order had come from behind them.

"Halt, I said!" The order was shouted again, more insistent this time.

Hawkwood turned and glanced back over his shoulder.

The barrier guard was walking towards them.

Christ! Hawkwood thought wildly.

"*Merde*," Guillaume swore under his breath and adjusted his grip on the reins.

Hawkwood was not carrying a pistol. He didn't know if Guillaume was armed. He reached down towards the knife concealed in his boot.

The guard approached the wagon and glowered up at them. "Are you deaf? When I tell you to halt; you damn well halt."

"Didn't hear you," Hawkwood said, cupping his hand over his ear. "Lost my hearing at Jena; damned Prussian cannon. There a problem?"

The guard drew closer and jabbed a grubby thumb in the direction of the tailgate. Clearly, the reminiscences of a wounded veteran were of no interest.

"I don't have the problem. You do. One of your stinking barrels is losing its lid. That spills over and I'll make you come down and lick it up. You think I want to spend what's left of my shift wading through your shit? Get back there and fix it. Now! Move it. There's been enough of a delay already. You're holding up the traffic!"

Hawkwood and Guillaume exchanged looks. Guillaume rifled under his seat, finally coming up with a heavy wooden mallet. "You heard the man. Make sure it's on tight."

He held the mallet out.

Hawkwood took it, clambered over on to the back of the wagon and, under the guard's watchful eye, sucked in his breath and tamped down the offending lid. The reek coming from the barrel was eye-watering. Job completed, he climbed back and re-took his seat. By the time the mallet had been re-stowed, the guard was already yelling at the next vehicle to get into line.

Guillaume spat over the side of the wagon, urged the horse forward and as they passed on to the road beyond, Hawkwood finally allowed himself a deep, fresh intake of breath.

They were through.

The church lay to the east of the village. Built of dark, rough-hewn stone with a small square tower, it looked as though it had seen better days. Before the Revolution, Hawkwood guessed,

496

before the building had been desecrated and vandalized by the mob. It was a wonder any of it was still standing.

"The church of Saint Lambert," Guillaume said. "This is as far as I go."

Retrieving the bag containing Hawkwood's clothes from its hiding place, he smiled. "You didn't expect to travel all the way by shit cart, did you?"

Hawkwood climbed down and looked around. He did so with both eyes. The first thing he'd done when he and Guillaume were well clear of the barrier was toss the leather patch into a ditch.

They hadn't travelled much more than a mile or so from the barrier and yet the contrast between the city's hemmed-in streets and the tiny huddle of houses surrounded by vineyards couldn't have been greater.

"You might want to try confession," Guillaume said, nodding towards the entrance. "I hear it's good for the soul." He winked and tapped the side of his nose.

And with that parting suggestion drifting in the air, the wagon moved off.

Hawkwood entered the church. It was dark and quiet and full of shadows. A row of black stained pews occupied the centre of the nave. A wooden rail separated the body of the church from the altar, behind which was a small circular stained-glass window. A raised pulpit was situated against the wall to the altar's left. To the right: a statue of the Virgin with child. To one side of that, partially visible behind a supporting pillar, was the confessional.

He walked towards the altar, his footsteps echoing on the cold stone floor. There was no sign that anyone was around.

Trust Guillaume, Grant had told him.

Hawkwood looked towards the confessional and saw that the left-hand window was curtained. The right-hand side was not. Feeling self-conscious, he walked to the right-hand stall, opened the panelled door and stepped inside.

As soon as he sat down he knew he was not alone. He tensed. If it was a trap, he thought, it was an elaborate one. He wondered what he was supposed to do. It was the first time he'd been in a confessional. He was only dimly aware of what was required.

The decision, however, was made for him.

A wooden panel on the other side of the dividing wall slid back, revealing a latticed screen and a shadowy figure seated beyond it. A voice spoke softly in French.

"I suspect both of us are feeling unease at having to resort to such a tiresome ritual, but one should never underestimate the danger of prying eyes. We haven't met. Allow me to introduce myself. My name is Fouché . . ."

27

"How would you prefer to be addressed? As Dumas or Smith?"

Hawkwood suppressed the urge to open the door and bolt. He kept his voice steady. "Dumas will suffice."

"Excellent," the darkened shape said. "Captain Dumas it is then. It makes it so much easier when one knows to whom one is speaking. I trust you'll forgive the melodramatics, by the way; a regrettable necessity. One of the penalties of being exiled from one's own country. It would benefit my enemies greatly if my presence here was to become known. I'd rather that didn't happen."

"And that's supposed to make me feel safer?" Hawkwood said.

"I would hope so. I mean you no harm. In fact, now that our credentials *have* been established, so to speak, why don't we dispense with this nonsense and make ourselves more comfortable outside? I have people keeping watch and Father Thomas is the model of discretion. Would you care to join me?"

Without waiting for an answer, the shadow moved and Hawkwood heard a stall door open followed by receding footsteps. Reasoning that if someone was going to kill him, they'd have probably done it by now, he got to his feet and let himself out. His eyes moved to the hunched figure dressed in dark clothes seated in the second row of pews.

The figure turned, eyebrows raised at the state of Hawkwood's attire and the dirt that was still on his face.

Hawkwood sat down.

Close to, Fouché was a small, slight man, with thinning grey hair, a narrow face and a weak mouth. His grey eyes and pallid complexion gave him the appearance of someone recovering from a long and debilitating illness spent mostly in rooms with the curtains drawn. Hawkwood had to remind himself that this had been Savary's predecessor and one of the most powerful men in the country after the Emperor, so he probably wasn't as sickly as he looked.

"I understand you arrested Desmarest in his nightshirt," Fouché said, his mouth forming a pout. There was a soft, sibilant quality to his voice.

"We arrested everyone in his nightshirt," Hawkwood said. "We didn't want anyone to feel left out."

The thin lips twitched. "And only one fatality."

Hawkwood assumed he meant Claubert, as Hulin was still alive, but he decided a little contrariness wouldn't go amiss.

"Not if you include General Malet and the rest."

"Ah, yes, indeed; your fellow conspirators. You witnessed the executions?"

"From a distance."

Fouché nodded thoughtfully. "And I was forgetting the two gendarmes, of course. One mustn't forget them."

"No," Hawkwood agreed. "One mustn't."

A look of irritation flashed across the pale face only to fade just as quickly.

"You did know the general and the others are being buried locally?" Fouché said. "The cemetery's not far from here."

"Does that mean you'll be paying your respects?"

"Not publicly, no."

"Privately, then."

Fouché smiled. "A little later, perhaps, when the excitement has died down."

"If I didn't know any better," Hawkwood said. "I'd say you're sorry we didn't succeed."

Fouché's thin fingers caressed the top of the pew.

And suddenly, it became clear.

500

"My God," Hawkwood said. "That's why you're here. You've been waiting in the wings all along. General La Horie was never going to be Savary's true successor – you were."

The grey eyes narrowed. "A change of régime for any country is a defining event. Serious consideration must always be given to the aftermath. One cannot expect the transition to go smoothly unless there are competent people ready to take office. Had General Malet's plan been successful and had Moreau returned as head of the provisional government, he would have required men of experience to help him govern. With Savary removed, logic dictates that his replacement should have similar ministerial experience."

"Which would be you," Hawkwood said.

"I'd already been in correspondence with the general through Prince Bernadotte to offer my support in the event he might return." Fouché paused. "You look . . . doubtful. You thought that, given my circumstances, I would no longer care about France's future?"

"Of course you would," Hawkwood said. "And perish the thought you'd be in it for personal gain. Tell me something; when you took British gold to bribe the judges at Moreau's trial, how much of the cream did you skim from the jug for yourself, I wonder?"

Fouché's hand stopped moving.

"Yes, I know about that," Hawkwood said. "And so does everyone else. But it did the trick, though, didn't it? Moreau was spared and he went into exile, which gave him the opportunity to return home at a later date if the circumstances became favourable. I'll wager you made damned sure he knew who'd saved him, too. You were looking after your own interests as much as his."

The thin face went taut.

"And you being here," Hawkwood said, "in this place, speaking with me. That tells me a lot. For one thing, it tells me you're in communication with the Congrégation."

"Father Thomas is an old colleague. We studied at the Oratory together."

"So it's a coincidence that he's a member of the Congrégation then?" Hawkwood shook his head. "I don't think so. In fact, you know what? I've just had another thought. I'm suddenly wondering if it might not have been you who put the idea of supporting Malet into the Congrégation's mind in the first place. Am I right?"

"Go on." The grey eyes had lost their gleam, but there was still a spark of interest at their core.

"I'm only thinking aloud, you understand?" Hawkwood said.

He wondered how far away Fouché's helpers were and whether, if things turned nasty, he could kill Fouché before they could stop him. He was confident he could. Escaping would be the bugger.

"Of course. But I'm most interested in your theory."

"All right," Hawkwood said. "Well, for one thing, you'd know all about the plot to replace Bonaparte when he was in Spain, from your time in the Police Ministry. You'd know about Malet's involvement and how he replaced Servan as the man the others would follow. You'd know, despite his being in prison, how much he still hated Bonaparte. How he'd do anything to get rid of him.

"Even though you were in exile, you'd have kept yourself informed so you'd know there was dissent among the generals and that the country wanted an end to the war. You knew Moreau was willing to come back if the opportunity presented itself. And if *he* came back, you could come back, maybe even stronger than before. And when Bonaparte invaded Russia, you saw your chance."

Fouché's eyebrows rose. "But it was I who urged His Majesty not to engage Alexander. I told him that was the last thing he should do."

Hawkwood shook his head. "You were protecting your arse. You were making sure that if something did happen while he was away, but he survived, you'd be able to say that it was you who tried to warn him. You'd be back in his affections.

"I think that's when you renewed your communication with Moreau, probably to remind him of his obligations. You'd helped him. Time for him to show his gratitude. But you still needed assistance. Who else was there? You were in Italy, the centre of the Faith. The Church wanted the Pope returned to Rome. That led you to approach the Congrégation. You suggested there might be a way to free the Pope, by removing Bonaparte. You told them Moreau was willing to return. You told them, if he came back, one of the first things he'd do as head of the provisional government was free His Holiness.

"If that happened, you'd have the Church as a friend for life; and with the Church behind you, who knows where you might end up? You've been using the Congrégation just like they thought they were using Malet."

Fouché stared at him intently.

"Which brings us back to the general," Hawkwood said. "You knew he was plotting in prison but that wasn't enough, was it? So you told the Congrégation about his earlier affiliation with Moreau and his dream of staging an insurrection and forming a republic, which again would result in the Pope being freed. Their man Lafon was in prison with Malet. So Lafon befriends Malet and his wife, plants the seed and Malet thinks he'd found a comrade in arms. Between the three of them, the plot starts to take shape. And then, what happens? I come along. I'm still guessing, but I think I was also part of the plan."

"You?"

"Well, not me specifically, but someone like me. Because you'd seen a way of involving Britain in this as well. You knew the British would be interested in Moreau's return, because once he was in government he'd start peace negotiations. So, you told the Congrégation to pass the word to their London paymasters about Lafon's and Malet's plot; which got London thinking that if they could persuade Malet that they supported his coup and were willing to provide Moreau's new government with financial support, that would encourage him even further. So I was sent over to stir the pot."

Hawkwood raised a hand to his cheek. His beard was starting to itch.

"Most of your people are still in place, aren't they? They never left. You still have your own agents within the police. Savary may be the Minister in charge, but you have influence. It's as if you never went away. You've been pulling the strings all along."

I'm guessing you're McPherson's guardian angel, too, Hawkwood thought. *It's your people who've been supplying him with information! No wonder the old man's kept that to himself. That's assuming he's known the true identity of the puppeteer all along, of course.*

Which could also explain something that had been preying on Hawkwood's mind since he and Stuart had been loaded into the prison cart.

Why hadn't they been subjected to more prolonged sessions of interrogation? When Réal told Desmarest that the questioning had gone on long enough, had that been an order relayed from on high? Desmarest's protest at having to curtail the questioning so abruptly had been at best weak, at worse derisory, which was curious, given his initial relish at having obtained Hawkwood's confession to being a British correspondent.

And the rescue from the prison cart – notwithstanding the deaths of the gendarmes and Stuart's wounding – had been carried off with remarkable ease in the face of not much opposition.

Had it all been just a little too easy?

Hawkwood's mind seethed with a jumble of possibilities.

"One does what one can." Fouché's reply cut into his thoughts, bringing him back to the present.

"And now it's all fallen apart," Hawkwood said. "Like a house of cards. So where does that leave you? Waiting until the Emperor returns so that you can say 'I told you so'? With Savary embarrassed, that would certainly strengthen your hand. You might even get your old ministry back anyway. What I don't understand though is why you're talking to *me*."

"I wanted to offer my commiserations."

"Well, of course you did."

Fouché smiled again. "I'm beginning to see why London chose *you*."

Hawkwood shook his head. "I already told Desmarest; I'm only a foot soldier, sent to do a job."

"Ah, yes." The grey eyes took in Hawkwood's injured hand. "Desmarest; my old protégé. I understand the two of you had quite an interesting discussion."

"That's one way of putting it."

"You know he's put a price on your head?"

"So I've heard."

"You killed his man, Gabel."

"Yes," Hawkwood said. "Now you come to mention it. I'd forgotten all about him. Was there anything else you wanted, by the way, other than to offer your sympathy? Only time's getting on."

"Which is why I thought it would be beneficial to meet."

"Beneficial for whom?" Hawkwood said cautiously. "And in what way?"

Fouché paused then said. "I'd like you to carry a message to your government; to Lord Liverpool."

"The Prime Minister?" Hawkwood said. "We're not exactly on speaking terms."

"But I've no doubt your employer is," Fouché said smoothly.

"That's quite possible," Hawkwood agreed. "And the message?"

"A private dispatch; a letter."

"Am I permitted to know the contents?" Hawkwood asked. "In case I lose it."

Fouché stared at him for several seconds. Eventually, he said, "It's to advise your government that, despite this setback, the situation has not altered. I am still available, should it require the services of an intermediary."

"Still?" Hawkwood said.

The sly smile returned. "I am a pragmatist."

"That's one word for it," Hawkwood said. "What it means is you're trying to back all sides, just in case."

"I'm offering Liverpool the same arrangement that I had with his predecessor, the unfortunate Perceval."

"Arrangement?" Hawkwood said. "And would that be of a financial nature, by any chance?"

Fouché smiled. "To show my good faith, I have an offer he may want to consider."

"And what kind of offer would that be?"

"If he withdraws his troops from Spain, France will support Britain in its war against the United States."

There was a long silence as Hawkwood tried to absorb what he'd just heard.

"But America's your ally."

"And Spain is part of our dominion."

"By right of conquest? Because Bonaparte invaded and made his brother the king? I'm not sure the Spanish see it quite like that."

"The war in the Peninsula is costing you dear. Fighting on two fronts is very expensive."

"And your Emperor should know," Hawkwood said. "But in case you haven't noticed, we're winning."

Fouché waved a hand dismissively. "The United States is a different proposition entirely. A greater distance for your navy to travel; a bigger area to supply, to control. If the war escalates, your resources will be stretched to breaking point and your Exchequer will be unable to cope. An extended conflict could well cripple your country financially."

"I'm sure my government will be touched by your concern," Hawkwood said.

"Does that mean the message will be delivered?"

Hawkwood considered the question and wondered if this was the real reason he and Stuart had been spared.

"All right, if that's what you want."

Fouché beamed. "Excellent."

Reaching into his pocket he withdrew a sealed envelope and handed it to Hawkwood across the back of the intervening pew. "Then I believe that concludes our business."

Fouché stood. "You'll find Father Thomas waiting for you in the vestry. I regret I can't stay. I'd be obliged if you'd thank him on my behalf for the use of his . . . facilities. I wish you a safe journey."

There was no offer to shake hands. Hawkwood remained seated. It was then he saw the two dark-clad figures detach themselves from the shadows at the back of the church and move silently towards the door. Fouché's watchers.

Fouché fastened his coat and turned to go.

Then he stopped.

506

"I almost forgot; there was one other thing. Do be sure to pass my regards to Superintendent Brooke when next you see him."

And with a brief nod, he was gone.

Hawkwood stared after him and then down at the envelope in his hand.

Bastards, he thought.

The priest, whom he presumed was Father Thomas, answered his knock on the vestry door and took a step back at the sight of Hawkwood's filthy clothes. Recovering quickly, he stole a wary glance over Hawkwood's shoulder before inviting him into the room.

"Don't worry," Hawkwood said. "He's gone."

The cleric, a tall man with white hair and a face as fissured as cracked leather, looked as if a huge weight had just been hoisted off his shoulders.

Not such a friend then, Hawkwood thought.

"Are you hungry, my son?" the priest asked. "I have bread and cheese and cold ham; something for the journey?"

"Water to wash and a place to change would be better, Father," Hawkwood said.

The priest showed him to a room with a jug and a basin and a mirror on the wall. Washed and shaved and wearing his own clothes, he began to feel a little more human.

He handed the filthy clothes to the priest. "For the poor."

The priest screwed up his nose and held the clothes at arm's length. "I doubt even the poor will want these rags."

"In that case," Hawkwood said. "You can burn them."

A steady breeze was blowing along the quai and the evening air was thick with the smell of tarred rope and damp timbers. The sights and sounds and the pungent smells were so reminiscent of his arrival in Dover that Hawkwood found it hard to believe there were still thirty miles of navigable waterway between Nantes and the open sea.

His conveyance from Vaugirard had taken nine days, the first of which had been by carriage; an uncomfortable over-night drive during which sleep had been next to impossible due to a lack of springs and the poor state of the road. It had been a private coach, however, not a public diligence, and Hawkwood had been the only occupant, so for that reason alone the experience had been just about bearable.

Father Thomas had not been forthcoming on the vehicle's provenance, but it hadn't taken much to conclude that it was, like the Mission of the Infant Jesus, another of the Congrégation's many useful assets.

By contrast, the second and longest leg of his journey, by wine barge from Orleans, had been much less taxing. Hawkwood couldn't remember when he'd last slept so soundly. With nothing to do except enjoy the views and watch other boats pass idly by, the sense of wanting to look over his shoulder for signs of pursuit had lessened with each passing mile.

The three-man Breton crew, which consisted of a father, Marcel, and his two sons, Luc and Olivier, had been friendly without being intrusive and for most of the voyage they had been content to leave their anonymous passenger to his own resources. Meals had been taken together in the barge's cramped but homely saloon, and in the evenings, despite the chill, it had been pleasant to sit on deck, share a bottle of wine, and watch the fields and the forests and the chateaux disappear behind the drifting banks of mist. By the time he arrived in Nantes, Hawkwood felt more rested than he had done in months. And though they were still tender to the touch, the pain in his fingers had all but disappeared.

The port proved to be a lot bigger than he'd expected. Straddling both banks of the Loire, Nantes' prosperity had been built on profits made by the sugar and slave trades, with much of the wealth being displayed in the merchants' and ship owners' houses that lined the quaysides.

When he'd first arrived, Hawkwood had thought that his week on the barge had left him with an uneven sense of balance for a good many of the houses fronting the river appeared to be leaning to one side. Until Marcel, with much amusement, had revealed at the moment of parting that it wasn't Hawkwood's lack of equilibrium that had caused him to think he was seeing things. The area around the shore was reclaimed wetland and many of the buildings had been built on sand. The houses really were sinking.

In the dark, though, the listing wasn't so noticeable, which was more than could be said for the some of the locals. It struck Hawkwood, as he made his way along the quai, that another measure of a port's prosperity, apart from the ships and the grand mansions, was the preponderance of taverns and the number of whores that were touting for business. Since he'd left the inn, Hawkwood had lost count of how many times he'd been propositioned.

The dockside was busy. The crews were anxious to see their cargos stowed in order to take advantage of the tide. Hawkwood had been told that the vessel he was looking for was moored at the western end of the dock. It was due to depart at nine o'clock. All he had to do was present himself to the captain. His passage had been pre-arranged.

Hawkwood noted that most of the moored ships were of modest dimensions, suggesting they were of shallow draught and thus unsuitable for sailing in open waters. It was an indication that the blockade was continuing to have an effect, making it hard for vessels of any notable size to evade British coastal patrols. Though, to judge by a few that were present, there were still some captains who were willing to take the risk.

A spot of rain hit the back of Hawkwood's neck and he cursed, remembering the last time he'd left a port at night. A memory of the storm that had swept him from *Griffin*'s pitching deck rose into his mind. Well, it was too damned late to turn back now.

He stopped, adjusted the seaman's bag on his shoulder and looked about him, taking stock of the numbers on the sides of the warehouses and the names of the ships lined up alongside them. In the darkness, it had become difficult to tell them apart. According to the directions he'd been given, the vessel he was seeking was berthed alongside the next stretch of quai.

He knew it was a pistol the instant he felt the pressure against his shoulder blades. And the shocking thing was that he hadn't heard a thing. The days and nights on the barge, thinking he'd left danger behind, had made him over confident, and careless.

So he had no one to blame but himself.

"Thought you'd slip away without a word of farewell, Captain? I take that as a personal insult."

It was a voice he recognized. Hawkwood sighed.

"Hello, Vidocq. I was just thinking to myself it's a small world."

"You don't seem surprised."

"Nothing surprises me much any more. It's been that sort of week."

A soft chuckle sounded. "You left a lot of chaos and unhappy people in your wake."

"Then it's good to know my time wasn't entirely wasted. I suppose you're here to take me back?"

"That wasn't my first intention. You can turn around. But do it slowly."

Hawkwood turned, letting the bag drop to the ground. The pistol was pointed at his chest.

"I'm not going back," Hawkwood said.

The Frenchman nodded. "I'd probably say that if I was in your shoes. You met Gabel, then?"

"Just the once."

A smile touched the bearded face.

"How did you find me?" Hawkwood asked.

"Bribery and friends in low places. I did wonder if I'd get here before you. It was quite a ride."

"You certainly cut things fine," Hawkwood agreed. He looked along the quai. Ships were being loaded and off-loaded, crews were embarking and disembarking, mooring lines were being cast hither and yon. No one was looking their way; which meant the gun in Vidocq's hand had either not been spotted or else no one gave a damn. Given the area, Hawkwood suspected it was probably the latter, but then Vidocq wasn't standing that far from him and to a casual observer they could have been taken for two friends having a quiet chat.

"You came all this way just to say goodbye?" Hawkwood said. "I'm flattered."

"I came all this way because you killed one of my men. Jilting the Widow didn't do your cause any favours either."

Hawkwood nodded. "What is this then; revenge?"

"No, justice."

"Ah."

Vidocq gave a rueful smile. "Can't let something like that go unpunished. I've my reputation to think of."

"You have a reputation?"

"Such as it is."

"Forgive me," Hawkwood said. "I had no idea. So, what happens now?"

"How about two for the price of one? It's been a slow night."

"The girl had appeared from nowhere, or so it seemed; petite, with dark ringlets framing a set of gamine features, above a low-cut bodice that left little to the imagination; one hand twirling a lock of hair; the other playing with her skirt. She looked about twenty years old but was probably fifteen and thought she was being provocative. She wasn't.

As Vidocq's attention shifted, Hawkwood's arm swept round, batting the pistol aside. There was a bright flash and a crack. The girl jumped and let out a screech and Hawkwood felt the wind from the ball as it passed by his cheek. The girl, eyes wide with fright, threw Hawkwood a startled look and took to her heels back into the narrow passageway from which she'd emerged, losing one of her shoes to a puddle in the process.

Vidocq whipped the pistol butt towards Hawkwood's skull. Hawkwood moved inside, slammed his left elbow against the Frenchman's upper arm to numb the muscle and block the strike and smashed the heel of his right hand into Vidocq's ribs. He heard a grunt and the pistol dropped and then Vidocq seemed to back away and spin like a top and the next thing Hawkwood saw was a boot curving towards his groin. He jerked aside just in time, and felt the burn as the edge of Vidocq's boot raked across his thigh.

A shout came from further down the quai. The sound of the

shot had carried and someone had seen the tussle and the fleeing girl. No one was hurrying to intervene, though, presumably having accepted the confrontation as nothing more serious than two drunkards arguing over a whore.

Vidocq, regaining his balance, pivoted again and with astonishing speed aimed a roundhouse kick towards Hawkwood's face. Hawkwood moved inside the kick, blocked with his forearm, hooked his right leg behind Vidocq's left knee, and tripped the Frenchman on to his back.

Immediately Vidocq rolled, giving Hawkwood no time to follow through. Springing to his feet, he looked shaken by the speed of Hawkwood's counter-attack. And then his right hand dropped to his waist and Hawkwood saw the hilt of a knife. There was no time to think. He threw himself forward, gripped the Frenchman's wrist and drove him back into the alley. Vidocq's knee came up. Hawkwood turned his hip to deflect the blow, locked Vidocq's knife arm and twisted. The knife clattered to the ground.

Vidocq broke free and clawed for Hawkwood's windpipe. Hawkwood brought his hands up, rammed his knee up into Vidocq's balls, and broke the Frenchman's grip. Vidocq went down. Locking his opponent's knife arm, Hawkwood drew the stiletto from his boot and placed the tip of the blade against the Frenchman's throat.

Vidocq went very still.

"You fight dirty," he gasped, and winced at the touch of cold steel against his skin.

"You're one to talk," Hawkwood said.

"Who taught you?"

"A Portuguese guerrilla and a Chinese holy man," Hawkwood said. "You?"

"The streets."

Vidocq's features relaxed and he let out a long resigned sigh. "I suppose you'd best get it over with."

Hawkwood nodded and pressed the blade against Vidocq's jugular. And paused.

Releasing the Frenchman's arm, he straightened, stepped back and returned the stiletto to his boot.

"It's possible I may live to regret this, but no. I don't think so. Not tonight."

Vidocq stared up at him.

"Does that mean I can stand up?" he asked finally.

Hawkwood nodded. "Be my guest."

The Frenchman rose gingerly to his feet.

"You," he said, "are a very curious man."

"It wasn't your time," Hawkwood said. "Anyone who's prepared to go to the lengths you did to avenge the death of one of his men doesn't deserve to die in a stinking alleyway with a knife in his throat. Besides, there's been enough damned killing, don't you think?"

Vidocq took in another deep breath, bent and grimaced. "Jesus, my balls hurt."

"Could've been worse," Hawkwood said.

Vidocq looked at him. "I suppose it could. But what am I supposed to tell Claubert's mother?"

"I expect you'll think of something."

"So, what? This is goodbye?"

Hawkwood smiled. "There's a ship about to sail with the tide and I've a feeling it might not wait for me. I trust you can find your own way back?"

Vidocq gave a tired nod. "I'm a police officer. I can always ask somebody."

"I won't offer to shake hands," Hawkwood said. "And don't worry, I can see myself out."

Vidocq leaned back against the wall. "I won't bother to wave you off. In fact, I think I may just stay here for a while until I get my breath back."

Hawkwood nodded, went to pick up his bag and then turned back.

"I almost forgot. There is one other thing. You might like to see that this gets into the right hands."

He held out Fouché's sealed envelope.

Vidocq frowned. "What is it?"

"Read it. You'll see. I said I'd make sure it was delivered. I didn't say who I would deliver it to."

Vidocq took the envelope, turned it over and stared at the seal. When he looked up, the man he'd known as Captain Paul Dumas had disappeared into the night.

The red-and-white merchant ensign hung limply from her stern. The name engraved across her transom read *Larkspur.*

"Help you, my friend?"

The enquiry was voiced in English. A cheroot glowed briefly in the darkness and a tall, bearded figure dressed in a navy blue pea jacket materialized at the ship's rail.

"I'm looking for Captain Larsson," Hawkwood said.

"You've found him."

"I believe you're expecting me, Captain. Permission to come aboard?"

There was a pause.

"You'd be Mr Hooper?"

Hawkwood nodded. "I would."

"We'd almost given you up."

Hawkwood stepped across the gangplank and on to the deck. "I was unavoidably detained."

Larsson took another draw on his cheroot. He eyed Hawkwood up and down. "You won't mind if I ask for your papers. These days, you can't be too careful."

"Not at all," Hawkwood said, handing them across.

Ouvrard had provided the passport; Hawkwood the name.

Matthew Hooper, the alias he'd used to infiltrate the prison ship *Rapacious*. The mythical Hooper was an American officer supposedly attached to a French infantry regiment and captured at the siege of Cuidad Rodrigo. It had seemed an appropriate moment to bring him back to life.

The permit to travel had been provided by Ouvrard's man at Nantes, an apothecary with an acquaintance at the American Consulate, who, for an agreed fee, could provide documentation which allowed the holder the right of passage on any United States merchant vessel departing from the port.

"Everything looks to be in order, Mr Hooper." Larsson returned the papers and eyed the seaman's bag. "That all you've got?"

"It's all I need," Hawkwood said.

Larsson held out his hand. "Welcome aboard."

Larkspur sailed on beneath a starless sky.

Hawkwood, braced against the starboard bulwark, stared off to where the lights of Saint-Nazaire were fading slowly into the darkness astern. Ahead, lay the brooding black waters of the Bay of Biscay.

"Douse all deck lanterns! Lookouts stand by!"

Hawkwood watched as the crew hurried to their stations.

"It's the only protection we have against the British patrols," Larsson said from behind him. "Their ships are copper-hulled. They have the speed. It's hard to outrun them, so we have to rely on stealth. We managed to slip past them coming in. No reason we can't do the same heading out, just so long as we keep our eyes open."

The naval blockade was the reason McPherson had chosen an American merchantman as Hawkwood's means of escape, in the hope that *Larkspur* would be intercepted and boarded by a British vessel. If the strategy worked, he would soon be back in England and free from pursuit.

If not . . .

Hawkwood lifted a hand to his throat, to the ring of bruising hidden beneath his shirt collar. Immediately, the dark shadows of memory began to stir. He lowered his hand quickly.

"We'll make landfall in thirty-one days; weather and our ability to evade the blockade squadrons permitting," Larrson said. He turned. "Do you know Boston at all, Mr Hooper?"

A call came from the deck.

"Stand by braces!"

Blocks squealed. Above them, a sail cracked loudly, sounding like a musket shot.

"It's been a while," Hawkwood said.

Almost as long as he could remember. As spray splattered across his face, he wondered if much had changed.

The thought occurred to him that in thirty-one days, if McPherson's plan failed, he'd be making that judgement for himself.

The last of the coastal lights flickered and died. Lured by the promise of a hot coffee, Hawkwood followed *Larkspur's* captain below deck.

In the galley, Larrson added a measure of brandy to each drink before raising his cup in a toast.

"The Stars and Stripes for ever."

Hawkwood tipped his cup in response. "*Slàinte mhath.*"

Larrson frowned.

"Long story," Hawkwood said.

Wondering if he'd live to tell it.

HISTORICAL NOTE

Whether General Claude-François Malet was in full possession of his faculties or severely deluded or acting under the guidance of some shadowy authority when he embarked upon his audacious plan on the night of 22nd / 23rd October 1812 continues to be a subject for debate. What is not beyond dispute is the fact that the general and his companions very nearly got away with it.

A great many of the events depicted in the novel took place as described. Similarly, with the exception of those individuals recognizable from Hawkwood's previous adventures, all the major characters as well as several of the minor ones did exist. Their actions are based on contemporary accounts.

To my knowledge, Colquhoun Grant did not contribute in any way to the coup attempt, though if he was present in the city at the same time, as his biographer Jock Haswell in his book *The First Respectable Spy* asserts, then he must surely have been aware of events, if not while they were unfolding then certainly during the aftermath. That fact alone was sufficient to prompt in this author the beguiling and age-old question that has continued to bedevil those of us who have had the audacity to put pen to paper:

What if . . .?

Grant and his Spanish guide, Leon, were captured in the manner described, though Leon was not killed with Grant's sword. I crave an author's indulgence on that score. Grant's journey from Salamanca, however, his escape from his escort in Bayonne and his subsequent journey to Paris in the company of General Souham is well documented and shows just what a resourceful officer he was and why he was held in such high regard by friend and foe alike.

The Alien Office, which one could loosely describe as the forerunner of today's Secret Intelligence Service, MI6, did indeed operate from Number 20 Crown Street – where the Foreign and Commonwealth Office now stands – under the guidance of Superintendent Henry Brooke and his very efficient First Clerk, Stormont Flint. Further insights into the activities of Brooke and his correspondents can be found in Elizabeth Sparrow's fascinating volume *Secret Service: British Agents in France, 1792–1815*.

Lieutenant Stuart did command the cutter *Griffin* – one of a number of light vessels employed by the Royal Navy to perform clandestine operations along France's northern coast – and the elderly Jacobite, McPherson, was Grant's chief ally during his stay in Paris which, according to Haswell, lasted from June 1812 to the spring of 1813.

Eugène-François Vidocq was very much a real character. The myths that surround him are too many to recount here. A former soldier, gambler, counterfeiter, duellist and thief, he became so unenamoured with life behind bars that he offered his services as an informer to the Paris police in exchange for an amnesty. His success at catching criminals was such that he later changed sides to become the first head of the Brigade de Sûreté, the department which later became the inspiration for Scotland Yard.

A pioneer of modern police investigative techniques including fingerprinting, the science of ballistics, criminal filing systems, forensic pathology and plainclothes surveillance, he is credited by many as being the first modern police detective. He later went on to create the first known private investigative agency and was reputedly the model for Inspector Javert in Victor Hugo's masterpiece *Les Miserables*. For an account of his life,

I can recommend James Morton's immensely readable *The First Detective: The Life and Revolutionary Times of Vidocq*.

Trying to make sense of the various strands of police bureaucracy employed in France and in particular Paris at the time the novel was set was, frankly, like wading through treacle. During the Revolutionary period and in the years immediately following Bonaparte's ascendance, the rivalry and suspicion that existed between the Préfecture and the Police Ministry was positively tortuous, with all departments spying on each other with Machiavellian relish. I have tried to simplify the structure by dividing duties into two halves, with the Ministry, under Savary and his henchmen Desmarest and Paques, being responsible for the national police and state security, and the Préfecture, which encompassed the Deuxième Bureau and the Sûreté, under Pasquier, Henry and Vidocq respectively, being responsible for what we would now term metropolitan crime. Should any reader wish to pursue his or her own investigation, as it were, I would direct them towards *The Police of Paris* by Philip John Stead.

Frank McLynn, in his biography of Napoleon, writes that Joseph Fouché 'would have found a way to intrigue if he was alone on a desert island'. Whether Fouché was one of the men pulling General Malet's strings, history does not record, but given his reputation as a master of subterfuge it is not beyond the bounds of credibility. He certainly plotted against his Emperor, conducting secret negotiations with both republican and royalist agents as well as the British government, from whom he received substantial financial remuneration. He also maintained contact with the exiled Louis XVIII in an attempt to secure a place with the monarchy in the event Napoleon was overthrown. He was reinstated as Police Minister for a second time following Bonaparte's return from Elba and for the third and final time following the Bourbon restoration, when he hunted down Bonapartists with great enthusiasm until royalists, who could not forgive his savagery during the Vendée uprising, forced him out of office. He went on to become the French ambassador to Saxony; before ending his days in self-imposed exile, first in Prague and then, finally, in Trieste.

As for the conspirators, their fate was sealed.

Henri Clarke, the Minister of War, who played no part in the conspiracy, took full advantage of his innocence. It was his chance to demonstrate to the Emperor his efficiency and loyalty and to unmask Savary's incompetence. In his report, Clarke placed the blame squarely on Savary and his Ministry and anyone else he could think of and he tried to persuade Napoleon that the event was part of a widespread conspiracy. Savary's report, on the other hand, stated exactly the opposite: that Malet had acted alone and that he had even fooled La Horie and Guidal. As to the latter accusation, it is still unclear whether they were in on the secret or whether, like the officers and men of the National and Paris Guards, they were simply unfortunate dupes. For the purpose of the narrative, I have intimated that they probably knew and had been in contact with Malet for some time prior to their release from La Force prison.

The final outcome was that Napoleon felt inclined to believe Clarke, only because it seemed unlikely that one man, acting alone, could deceive so many high-ranking officers and entire units with such ease, though he also considered the bickering between Clarke and Savary to be 'ridiculous and dangerous'. In the end, both men were diminished by the affair.

General Malet, Colonel Rabbe, Colonel Soulier, Captain Piquerel, Lieutenants Borderieux and Lefèvre were stripped of the Légion d'Honneur. They, along with La Horie, Guidal, Steenhouwer, Balthus, Rateau and Régnier, were sentenced to death by firing squad. Rabbe and Rateau's sentences were later commuted to life imprisonment. Both were eventually released from gaol upon the restoration of the monarchy. Rabbe returned to the army. Rateau became a shopkeeper.

A report on the executions stated that General Malet refused a blindfold and gave orders to the firing squad himself. He and General La Horie were left standing after the first volley. A second volley finished them. The bodies of the dead were loaded into carts and transported to the Vaugirard Cemetery for burial.

Abbé Lafon was never caught. Helped by friends in the priesthood, he went into hiding, moving from monastery to monastery, eventually ending up in Louhans where he taught Latin at a seminary. He surfaced eighteen months later but fled again, this time to Switzerland, during the ill-fated One Hundred Days. He finally returned to France following Bonaparte's transportation to St Helena and wrote a short account of the conspiracy. He eventually became a Chevalier de la Légion d'Honneur and tutor to the court pages.

Cajamaño was judged to be harmless. He escaped the death penalty but remained in prison until 1815. Following his release, he returned to live in the bell house of Saint-Gervais from where he sank once more into obscurity.

Doucet became a general; Laborde a colonel. General Hulin received no reward and the bullet was never removed from his jaw. As a result, to his chagrin, he was forever known as General Bouffe-la-Balle – Bulletmouth.

Those officers and NCOs of the Paris Guard who were not executed were either imprisoned or reduced to the ranks and transferred to other regiments. The Guard was subsequently abolished.

The men of the 10th Cohort of the National Guard were transferred to Bremen under new officers.

Savary, Desmarest and Pasquier retained their positions. Prefect of the Seine, Frochot, became the nominated scapegoat, for no other reason than he had arranged rooms for the prospective Provisional Government. His plea of ignorance fell on unsympathetic ears and he was removed from office. He retired to the provinces.

Denise Malet was held in Madelonnettes Prison until the autumn of 1813. Released into a state of near poverty, she was forced into hiding during Bonaparte's brief return to power. Following the latter's defeat at Waterloo, she petitioned King Louis XVIII, eventually securing a pension for herself as the widow of a General of Division, curiously not Malet's true rank but the rank he assumed on the night of the attempted coup.

Their son Aristide became a trooper in the King's Guard.

Grant remained in Paris until he was warned by McPherson that the authorities were becoming suspicious of the American officer who was asking too many questions. As a result, using false papers, he escaped and followed Hawkwood's route to the coast. His aim was also to take passage on an American vessel in the hope that it would be intercepted by the British Navy. However, he was able to bribe a local fisherman into ferrying him out to a British warship patrolling offshore, which delivered him back to England unscathed.

He returned to the Peninsula later that year.